Some things are only
brought to light
after dark...

"In a class with lady sleuths
V. I. Warshawski and
Stephanie Plum."
—*Publishers Weekly*

"Always intriguing."
—*Booklist*

Herbalist and ex-lawyer China Bayles has been called "a leader among female sleuths."* Now, Susan Wittig Albert takes China on a trip down memory lane, where one fresh murder and several cold cases force her to face her dark past . . .

China's herb shop and catering business may be thriving, but she's still reeling from the circumstances surrounding her father's death—and isn't remotely interested in her half brother Miles' investigation of it. Although, when fate forces her to get involved, China realizes it's time to bring the past to light—or else it will haunt her the rest of her life.

But China and McQuaid discover that Miles may have been keeping as many secrets as he seemed determined to uncover—for starters, knowledge of the whereabouts of their father's wrecked car, a key piece of evidence. How deep do the layers of secrecy go? And who has a stake in concealing the truth after sixteen years?

Piecing together clues, China and McQuaid embark on what feels like a wild-goose chase, tracking down evidence that might link several cold case murders to her father's death. But the closer they get to untangling the story, the more China longs for answers she may never get . . .

*Publishers Weekly

"Display[s] a deep sense of the Texas hill country and [makes] good use of the strong, likable cast. Details of herbs and herbal remedies continue to flavor the always intriguing plots."                                    —*Booklist*

"Satisfying . . . Snippets of plant lore, mostly to do with the nightshade family, add spice."        —*Publishers Weekly*

"Does a fine job of bringing together all the bits and pieces."
                                                        —*Kirkus Reviews*

## Acclaim for Susan Wittig Albert's
### *Spanish Dagger* . . .

"Razor sharp . . . Albert consistently turns out some of the best-plotted mysteries on the market . . . *Spanish Dagger*, woven with herbal lore and picturesque sketches of life in a small Texas town, is a welcome addition to an already strong series."                          —*Houston Chronicle*

"Combines a fast-moving plot with the botanical lore and recipes that her readers have come to expect. Solid entertainment."                                          —*Booklist*

"One of her best mysteries to date."            —*Kirkus Reviews*

### *Bleeding Hearts* . . .

"Well-written."                                   —*The Capital Times*

"Engrossing . . . Albert's characterization is strong—China delights."                                       —*Publishers Weekly*

### *Dead Man's Bones* . . .

"China's warmth and sensitivity . . . will endear her to readers, while her investigative skills make her a leader among female sleuths."                      —*Publishers Weekly*

"China Bayles is always trying to teach us stuff: it's not annoying at all but somehow soothing and fascinating . . . An enjoyable journey."                                    —*Booklist*

### A Dilly of a Death . . .

"More than just a whodunit . . . readers will relish this more-sweet-than-sour adventure."    —*Booklist*

"Add another fragrant bloom to the dozen already in the bouquet of Albert's herbal cozies."    —*Publishers Weekly*

### Indigo Dying . . .

"Albert's skill in weaving everything together into a multi-layered whole makes the reading smooth, interesting, and enjoyable."    —*San Antonio Express-News*

### Bloodroot . . .

"Albert has created captivating new characters and a setting dripping with atmosphere."    —*Publishers Weekly*

### Mistletoe Man . . .

"Ms. Albert artfully uses Texas language patterns to bring the down-home town of Pecan Springs alive with eccentrics in abundance."    —*The Dallas Morning News*

"Breezy . . . The characters are an appealing bunch."
—*Chicago Tribune*

### Praise for the China Bayles Mysteries . . .

"[China Bayles is] such a joy . . . An instant friend."
—Carolyn G. Hart

"A treat for gardeners who like to relax with an absorbing mystery."    —*North American Gardener*

"One of the best-written and well-plotted mysteries I've read in a long time."    —*Los Angeles Times*

"In a class with lady sleuths V. I. Warshawski and Stephanie Plum."    —*Publishers Weekly*

# SUSAN
# WITTIG ALBERT

## NIGHTSHADE

BERKLEY PRIME CRIME, NEW YORK

THE BERKLEY PUBLISHING GROUP
Published by the Penguin Group
Penguin Group (USA) Inc.
375 Hudson Street, New York, New York 10014, USA
Penguin Group (Canada), 90 Eglinton Avenue East, Suite 700, Toronto, Ontario M4P 2Y3, Canada
(a division of Pearson Penguin Canada Inc.)
Penguin Books Ltd., 80 Strand, London WC2R 0RL, England
Penguin Group Ireland, 25 St. Stephen's Green, Dublin 2, Ireland (a division of Penguin Books Ltd.)
Penguin Group (Australia), 250 Camberwell Road, Camberwell, Victoria 3124, Australia
(a division of Pearson Australia Group Pty. Ltd.)
Penguin Books India Pvt. Ltd., 11 Community Centre, Panchsheel Park, New Delhi—110 017, India
Penguin Group (NZ), 67 Apollo Drive, Rosedale, North Shore 0632, New Zealand
(a division of Pearson New Zealand Ltd.)
Penguin Books (South Africa) (Pty.) Ltd., 24 Sturdee Avenue, Rosebank, Johannesburg 2196,
South Africa

Penguin Books Ltd., Registered Offices: 80 Strand, London WC2R 0RL, England

This is a work of fiction. Names, characters, places, and incidents either are the product of the author's imagination or are used fictitiously, and any resemblance to actual persons, living or dead, business establishments, events, or locales is entirely coincidental. The publisher does not have any control over and does not assume any responsibility for author or third-party websites or their content.

PUBLISHER'S NOTE: The recipes contained in this book are to be followed exactly as written. The publisher is not responsible for your specific health or allergy needs that may require medical supervision. The publisher is not responsible for any adverse reactions to the recipes contained in this book.

NIGHTSHADE

A Berkley Prime Crime Book / published by arrangement with the author

PRINTING HISTORY
Berkley Prime Crime hardcover edition / April 2008
Berkley Prime Crime mass-market edition / April 2009

ISBN: 978-0-425-22703-9

BERKLEY® PRIME CRIME
Berkley Prime Crime Books are published by The Berkley Publishing Group,
a division of Penguin Group (USA) Inc.,
375 Hudson Street, New York, New York 10014.
BERKLEY® PRIME CRIME and the PRIME CRIME logo are trademarks of Penguin Group (USA) Inc.

PRINTED IN THE UNITED STATES OF AMERICA

10   9   8   7   6   5   4   3   2   1

*For Bill, always a partner*

# A Note to the Reader

Many of the books in the China Bayles series are linked to one another through a continuing plot. *Nightshade* concludes the story of the death of China's father that began in *Bleeding Hearts* and was carried on and developed in *Spanish Dagger*, so that these three books form a trilogy within the series. I realize that plots that bridge several books impose unusual demands on readers. Some people may not be able to read the books in order, while others may be frustrated by an interim conclusion that doesn't wrap up the full story. But one of the pleasures I have found in reading series books is that the characters we care so much about carry on from book to book, living their lives, resolving old issues while trying their best to cope (not always entirely successfully) with the new issues that inevitably emerge. I hope you will feel that the longer mystery (in this case, a mystery that spans three novels) is more complex, more interesting, and more problematic than it would be if it were compressed into one book, and that it's worth the extra effort involved in the reading.

One other important thing about *Nightshade*: All of the previous books in this series have been written in China's voice, and you may have come to expect this style of first-person narration. In *Nightshade*, McQuaid carries out parts of the investigation that do not involve China, and of which she can have no firsthand knowledge. He wanted to tell that part of the story himself, and China and I agreed. I enjoyed getting to know more of McQuaid's story, from the inside out. He has become an increasingly important character in the series and deserves more of our attention.

It is also important to remember that *Nightshade* is

fiction. While it is set against the backdrop of real historical events, it is not intended to be a history of its time and
place. It is story, pure and simple.

One last thing, but also important. Throughout this
book, you will find references to the medicinal uses of
herbs. You may be tempted to try them. But please do your
homework before you use any plant medicine. Herbs do
heal, but each person's health situation is unique, and some
therapeutic plants may have unanticipated and unintended
consequences, especially when used in combination with
prescription drug therapies. I am telling you this for your
own good. Be careful. Be *very* careful.

Susan Wittig Albert
Bertram, Texas

*Go, and catch a falling star,*
*Get with child a mandrake root,*
*Tell me, where all past years are,*
*Or who cleft the Devil's foot.*

—JOHN DONNE

# Prologue

For the past few weeks, I've been dreaming about my father.

I am alone in my dream, walking along the Houston freeway where my father died sixteen years ago. It is dark, and drizzly, and a low fog hangs over everything, tendrils curling and twisting like ghostly snakes in the lights along the highway. I look at my watch and see that it is nearly two a.m. I shiver, wondering what the hell I'm doing out here by myself, without a jacket or umbrella, on a chilly, rainy night.

And then a car, my father's blue Cadillac, roars past me loud and fast, so fast the tires are smoking, like the tires on a cartoon car. It seems to lift off the ground—*ZOOM!*— crashing through the guardrail and down the embankment, cartwheeling end over end in a crashing cacophony, until it reaches the bottom and blooms into a savage flower of flame.

I stand at the guardrail, shoulders hunched, hands in the pockets of my jeans. I'm staring down at the wreckage and thinking how sad it is that I can't cry for my dead father, and not just that I can't cry, but that I can't feel anything at all. There's a cold, hard chunk of ice in that place inside me where there ought to be grief and anger and pain. I stand there and watch the fire, watch the cops arrive, and the fire truck, and the ambulance. Stand there until the night shadows fade and the gray dawn breaks over the Gulf of Mexico and a tow truck comes to haul the burned wreckage away. All that while, that long, long while, I never cry, never shed a single tear.

And then I wake, and my pillow is wet.

# Chapter One

Nightshade is one of the many plants that belong to the *Solanaceae*. This plant family includes such edible plants as the tomato, potato, eggplant, and chile pepper; decorative plants such as the petunia; and toxic plants such as datura (Jimson weed), tobacco, henbane, mandrake, and deadly nightshade, also known as belladonna.

At one time, when the entire nightshade family shared the bad reputation of its more toxic members, it was thought that eating an eggplant might drive you insane. This belief is reflected in the name Linnaeus gave to the eggplant, *Solanum melongena*. It is related to the Italian name *melanzana*, or "mad apple."

"What's this?" Brian asked suspiciously, pushing at his food with his fork.

"Creole Aubergine," I said. "Cass gave me the recipe. She said it was really good."

"Eggplant," Brian said, in his voice of doom.

I sighed. The eggplant was disguised in a spicy Creole sauce, and I'd hoped to sneak it past him. "Did you know," I said brightly to McQuaid, "that it was Thomas Jefferson, the third president of the United States, who introduced the eggplant to North America?"

McQuaid frowned. "Isn't he the one who's to blame for Brussels sprouts?"

"Barf," Brian said succinctly.

I put on a stern face. "Eat it anyway. Eggplant has a ton of antioxidants. Helps to lower cholesterol, too."

"That means it's good for you," McQuaid translated, lifting a hefty forkful and smacking his lips to demonstrate how much he liked it. He winked at Jake—Jacqueline Keene, Brian's girlfriend—who was sitting across from Brian.

"Yeah, right," Brian said, with heavy sarcasm.

Jake, who is as smart and cooperative as she is cute, got the hint. "I think it's great, China," she enthused. "My mom never cooks eggplant."

"There's a reason for that," Brian said, sotto voce.

"Thank you, Jake." I ignored my stepson. At nearly sixteen, he is way too old to smack, which is something I've never done and wouldn't do in front of company—although Jake isn't exactly company. She and Brian went through a tough time together earlier in the year, when they saw the Pecan Springs football coach shot to death. She's around so often that she almost qualifies as a member of the family. With a smile for her and a chastising glance at Brian, I added, "I'm glad you like it. It's more fun to cook for people who sincerely enjoy the food."

"What's for dessert?" Brian asked.

"Cheesecake," I said. "Low-calorie." I've been trying to lose weight for the past couple of months—successfully, I might add. I am now down some fifteen pounds, by dint of dieting, jogging, and yoga. You should see me. I'm looking trim.

"Awesome," Jake said. A girl after my own heart.

"I sincerely enjoy cheesecake," Brian said. "Even low-calorie cheesecake." He went back to his eggplant with a virtuous look and managed to get it down.

When dinner was done, the kids got their bikes and fishing rods and rode off into the balmy spring evening, while

I cleared the table and McQuaid began to load the dishwasher. "Was it really that bad?" I asked, putting the leftover casserole into the fridge. There was a lot of it.

"Was what that bad?" McQuaid said absently.

"The eggplant. *I* liked it."

"It was fine." He looked up, the water running over the plate he was rinsing. "No, really, China. It was great. Fantastic. I mean, I could tell, you put a lot of effort into it." He went back to rinsing the plate.

I think I'll take eggplant off the menu.

While McQuaid and I are getting the kitchen cleaned up, I'll give you some background. I'm China Bayles, and Mike McQuaid—dark-haired, blue-eyed, craggily good-looking—is my husband of nearly three years. Brian is his son. I got into the habit of calling McQuaid by his last name when we met some ten or eleven years ago. At the time, I was a defense attorney in a murder trial involving a battered wife whose husband wound up dead at the foot of the stairs. McQuaid was the Houston homicide officer who reluctantly testified against my client. When she was acquitted, he asked me out for a drink to celebrate. I like a good loser.

One thing eventually led to another (life has a way of doing that, doesn't it?) and before long, both McQuaid and I had left our careers and moved to Pecan Springs, a small town halfway between Austin and San Antonio, at the eastern edge of the Texas Hill Country. McQuaid earned his Ph.D. and began teaching in the Criminal Justice Department at Central Texas State University. But after a couple of years, he took a leave to write a book. At the same time, he went on an extended undercover assignment for the Texas Rangers, during which he almost wound up dead. And last year, because the thrill of the chase is much more exhilarating than faculty politics (although it is only slightly more dangerous), he hung out his shingle as a private investigator. So far, his new career has met with only moderate success, but we're hoping.

As for me, when I arrived in Pecan Springs, I bought a small herb shop called Thyme and Seasons, then went into partnership with my friend Ruby Wilcox to start a tearoom called Thyme for Tea. When Cass Wilde came along with the idea for a personal chef service called the Thymely Gourmet, our duo became a trio. Ruby, Cass, and I are—as Texans colorfully put it—as busy as a stump-tailed cow in fly season. There are always too many flies to swat.

McQuaid closed the dishwasher. "Coffee on the porch?"

It was a loaded question. What he really wanted was to tell me what he'd found out on his latest trip to Houston, which I wasn't eager to hear.

"Okay," I said, not trying to cover up my lack of enthusiasm. Anyway, it wouldn't have done any good to pretend. McQuaid and I have been together long enough to know what's really being said, even when it isn't. I poured two cups of coffee and we took them onto the screened porch. I sat in one wicker rocker. He sat in the other, propped his boots on the rail, and leaned back with a long sigh.

McQuaid, Brian, and I live in a large old Victorian house at the end of a lane off Limekiln Road, eleven miles outside of town. When we sit outside on a May evening, we don't hear illegal mufflers or bickering neighbors or the bone-throbbing *thump-THUMP-thump* of the woofers in some jerk's jacked-up pickup. We hear mockingbirds and wrens and cardinals singing their spring love songs, frogs droning with passionate pleasure beside the creek, hummingbirds whirring ecstatically in and out of the honeysuckle, and the breeze kissing the papery leaves of the big sycamore tree beside the stone fence.

Oh, and Howard Cosell, McQuaid's elderly basset, snoring in the porch swing—although if you look closely, you will see that Howard is not quite asleep. One brown basset eye is open. Howard may have the shape of a lumpy couch potato, but he has the heart of a hunter, always on the alert for unwary bunnies. Should one be so rash as to hop up the back steps, Howard would have to wake up and figure out what to do, although that might take so long that the bunny would get bored and go somewhere else for adventure. While he has the heart of a hunter, Howard's arthritis is catching up with him and his metabolism has slowed so that it approximates hibernation.

I sipped my coffee. "So how were things in Houston?" I asked, aiming for a neutral, offhand tone.

"I should think you'd want to hear this," McQuaid said, slightly aggrieved. "After all, he is your father."

"*Was* my father," I said callously. Sixteen years ago, my father was killed in an automobile accident. He'd been driving well over the speed limit and lost control of the car, according to a witness. He'd been drinking, according to the coroner. Drinking, driving, speeding—a lethal combination. My relationship with him had not been a happy one, for reasons I consider good ones. As the kids say, we had "issues."

"And Miles Danforth is your brother," McQuaid continued evenly. "He only wants to know—"

"*Half* brother."

"Okay, half brother," McQuaid conceded. "But he's still your father's son."

I sniffed. "His *illegitimate* son. Whom I didn't know until three months ago."

Three months ago. That was when Laura Danforth died of cancer and her son, Miles, a partner in the Austin law firm of Zwinger, Brady, Brandon, and Danforth, discovered that my father was *his* father, too. And having learned this troublesome, untidy fact, what did Miles Danforth do?

Did he keep the painful knowledge to himself, knowing that it could only hurt any survivors our father had left behind—survivors who never guessed that Robert Bayles had led a secret life, with Laura Danforth and her son?

Did he decide that whatever ugliness had darkened the past had been buried sixteen years ago, and that the kindest, sanest, most prudent thing was *not* to dig it up?

No, of course not. He had hired my husband, who is a damned good P.I., to help him investigate the past.

And he had a reason for pursuing that investigation, a good one—or so it seemed to him. He had the idea that the car wreck that killed our father was not an accident at all. It was murder. In support of this argument, he gave me a collection of letters he had found among his mother's papers when she died. Letters in my father's neat, precise script. Letters Robert Bayles had written before his death to his secretary, Laura Danforth. Love letters.

At first I had refused to read them. When I was a teenager, I'd been aware that my father was having an affair with Mrs. Danforth—in the way that kids have a vague idea of what adults are up to without understanding much about it. I wasn't aware that the affair had begun before I was born and ended only with his death, or that it had produced a child: Miles, whom I knew as Buddy, Mrs. Danforth's sexy son, who had a summer job in the mail room at Stone, Bayles, Peck, and Dixon, my father's law firm. I refused to read the letters because I didn't want to know anything more about the affair than I knew already. I didn't want to read about my father's desire for a woman who wasn't my mother, about his love for a child that wasn't me. I intended to destroy the letters, thinking what a pleasure it would be to toss them, one by one, into the fire, to watch my father's passion turn into dirty smoke and fly up the chimney.

But in the end, Miles' persistence pushed me into reading them—that, and my growing recognition that there were things I needed to know. Who *was* my father, really? Was his relationship with Laura Danforth mostly sexual, or was there a tenderness inside him that I had never glimpsed? If he loved her, why didn't he divorce my mother and marry her? Did he feel any remorse about his betrayal of his wife and daughter? Or did he rationalize his treason by telling himself that we wouldn't be hurt by something we didn't know, that his secret life was nobody's business but his own? I knew what kind of father he was, but what kind of man had he been?

So I didn't put the letters into the fire. One night, when I was all alone in the house, I sat down and read them, and was so moved that I wept. Rich with a long-held, deeply cherished affection, a comfortable warmth, a shared tenderness, they were written in the way a man writes to a woman he has loved for many years. They made me almost unbearably sad, because they were written to Miles' mother, not to mine, and because they showed me a side of my father that I hadn't known existed. They gave me a glimpse of a different man—a caring, thoughtful man I longed to know—who was hidden inside of the chilly, detached man in whose house I had lived until I grew up and went away to college.

But Miles had a different reason for insisting that I read the letters. My father had been working on a case that troubled him deeply, and some of the letters were written with an edgy, wary apprehension. In one, he told Laura to copy certain documents from the case file and put them into a safe deposit box she was to rent personally, under an assumed name. In another, he told her to set up an appointment with a man named Gregory, in Washington, D.C. In a third, he told her to begin planning to leave Stone and Bayles, to look for another job, rent another apartment. She was to say nothing about any of this to their son. And most important—he wrote this with a clear, compelling sense of urgency—should anything happen to him, she was not to undertake an investigation. Since my father was a calm, deliberate man not given to undue alarm, this latter instruction was chilling. And so was the fact that he had purchased a $250,000 insurance policy on his life, in Laura's name.

Miles said he had found a few other things, besides the letters. Notes documenting an investigation his mother had begun after Dad's death, in defiance of his explicit instructions. A few names, some newspaper clippings, the renewal of a safe deposit box, the receipt for the purchase of my father's wrecked car—a blue Cadillac—which she managed to buy before it was sent to the crusher. According to Miles, she had squirreled it away somewhere, which was not a very rational thing to do, on the face of it. Ghoulish, my mother said, when Miles told her about it. Morbid, she said. Obsessive. Yes, Miles had insisted on involving her, and I had agreed. The damage had already been done, long ago. Trying to keep secrets could only prolong the pain.

But that didn't mean I wanted to be personally involved in Miles' quest for truth and justice, whatever that meant. I might be intrigued by the mystery and I might even agree that my father's death was suspicious. But I wasn't inclined to take the matter any further. Did I resent Robert Bayles for failing to remember that he had a wife, even if she was an alcoholic? You bet. Did I hold a grudge against him for being an absentee father? Absolutely. And when he died, I had closed the book on those chapters of my past that involved him. If Miles wanted to open them for himself, that was his business. But he could count me out. I have my hands full with my family and my business. I am busy getting a life. I—

McQuaid dropped his feet onto the floor, hitched his chair around to face me, and leaned forward, elbows on his knees. There was tension in the lines that bisected the jagged scar across his forehead. His slate-blue eyes were troubled and deeply serious, and he spoke with the contained intensity I have always loved.

"Look, China. I understand why you are still angry at your father. The guy was a first-class jerk. He had a wife at home, another at the office, and a child by both. He cheated on your mom for thirty years, and he never took any responsibility for you. You might as well not have had a father, for all the attention he paid you."

"I couldn't have said it better myself," I replied, not even trying to keep the bitterness out of my voice.

McQuaid reached out and took my hand in his. "But none of that is exactly Miles' fault, is it?"

I frowned.

"Well, is it?" He gave me a crooked smile. "Think about it, babe. Whatever your dad did to you, he did it in spades to Miles. Your brother has been hurt as badly as you—worse, in a way."

"Which is all the more reason Miles should let go of this obsession," I said. "He has Caitlin to think about." Caitlin is his ten-year-old daughter. He is raising her by himself, after his wife, Karen, drowned during a family outing on Lake Travis. "He can spend time with her, instead of digging up old dirt."

McQuaid turned my hand up and kissed my palm. "But maybe he has to dig up the old dirt before he can let it go. Maybe he has to understand what happened. Who his father was, what he was really like." He dropped my hand and sat back. "Try to see Miles' side of it, China. Yeah, sure. Your dad made sure the boy had everything he needed, growing up. Paid for his education, even gave his legal career a boost. But he never acknowledged him."

"He didn't acknowledge me, either," I muttered. "He didn't even come to my high school graduation." How many days, weeks, months, years had gone by since that night? And yet thinking of it was like walking barefoot on broken glass. "As for giving my legal career a boost—" I laughed shortly. "A kick in the butt is more like it. He didn't even want me in his firm."

McQuaid wasn't listening. "Do you have any idea what that can *do* to a man, China? Miles thought his father was dead—that's what his mother told him. And here he is, in his midforties. His mother dies, and he finds out that she lied.

Finds out that 'Uncle Bob,' her boss, the guy who was around so much of the time when he was growing up, was really his dad. And yet the man never cared enough to say 'Hey, kid, you're my son. Know what, boy? I'm proud of you. I'm really proud.' "

I pressed my lips together, thinking how important McQuaid's father was to him, how deeply McQuaid cared for Brian. I thought of the patient, enduring love the three of them shared—grandfather, father, son—and the healthy pride they took in one another's accomplishments. And I thought of what Miles had told me when I asked him whether he'd ever wondered why his mother's boss went on camping trips with them, why all three of them went fishing together, why "Uncle Bob" was there on weekends.

He'd never asked, he said, and his mother never offered to tell him. It was something they didn't talk about. It was the elephant in the room.

The elephant in the room. Yeah, well, we had a few of those in my house, too. And it wasn't just my father's frequent absences, his lengthy business trips, or his indifference. It was my mother's boozing, her reckless and embarrassing behavior. There were lots of things we never talked about when I was growing up. Hidden things, dangerous secrets, skeletons in the closets, shadows in the corners.

"And then Miles reads the letters his mother saved," McQuaid went on, "and he begins to figure it out. He knows now who his father was, who *he* is. But there's still too much he doesn't know. He sees how much his mother cared, and how important it was to her to find out what happened to his father. Can you blame him for wanting to continue her effort? To learn as much as he can?"

"Laura Danforth is dead," I said stiffly. "I cannot see why finding out what happened sixteen years ago will help Miles deal with—"

"Hey, China." McQuaid's voice was soft. "Suppose

Bob Bayles was murdered. That's what Laura Danforth thought, that's what his letters suggest. Suppose Miles finds out that his father was killed doing something—well, something noble. Something good. Suppose what he finds out helps to redeem the guy somehow. Isn't that worth the effort?"

I chuckled sarcastically. "Yeah, right. Well, suppose his father was doing something sleazy? That's a lot more likely, if you ask me."

After I grew up and joined the Houston legal fraternity, I began to understand what was common knowledge in that gossip-driven oil company town: Robert Bayles and his partner Ted Stone had built their legal practice on dubious oil and energy deals, questionable land transactions, and political dirty work. Their clients included polluters, looters, and influence peddlers. Both Ted Stone and my father were frequent guests of the Suite 8F crowd, the group of influential conservatives who met on the eighth floor of Houston's Lamar Hotel and collectively decided who was going to run for what political office, at the state level and beyond. To ensure that their picks—LBJ had been one of them—made it to the winners' circle, Suite 8F slipped wads of campaign cash into the necessary pockets. Their contributions decided which politicians moved into positions of power and influence.

And just as important, their money bought them preferential treatment when the bidding opened on lucrative government contracts for dams, ships and shipyards, oil pipelines, military bases at home and abroad, NASA's Johnson Space Center in Houston. The Lamar Hotel was demolished in 1983 to make room for a skyscraper, but the political influence of Suite 8F lingers like a foul odor, a dirty fog. It's the subject of books, of doctoral dissertations, of documentaries. It's common knowledge.

I hadn't known any of this, growing up. But grown up and on my own in the legal jungle, it hadn't taken long to find it out. And when I had, it was one more reason (if I needed one) that I didn't want anything to do with my father. I hated his politics and I despised what he stood for.

"Stone and Bayles never claimed the moral high ground," I went on, with a glance at McQuaid. "In fact, it's very likely that Miles will find out that his father was killed in the process of doing something unethical, illegal, immoral, or just plain rotten."

"Even that," McQuaid said softly, "would be worth something, wouldn't it? Wouldn't it be worth it to you, too, China? Just to *know*?"

There was a space of silence, during which the only sound was Howard's sputtery snoring and the chirpy chatter of a mockingbird on the fence. I thought of the night, just a few weeks ago, that Miles had sat where I was sitting now and persuaded McQuaid to agree to help investigate Dad's death. I had been against it, of course, but my vote hadn't counted. My husband had connected to something within my brother—some urgent need to learn what had happened, to find out who had been involved—and I might as well have been shouting into the wind. It was still true. I could resist all I wanted, but the two of them needed to know whatever there was to know. And they were going to drag me into it, like it or not.

And to tell the truth, there was something in me that wanted to know, too. Was Dad really nothing more than a philandering husband, a lousy father, and a sleazy attorney? Or was there something else, something that might yet redeem him?

"Okay," I said abruptly. "I give up. I concede. I surrender. I'm throwing in the damn towel. You and Miles intend to move heaven and earth to find out what went on sixteen years ago, and you think I ought to be on board. So okay. So I'm on board. What the hell do we do now?"

McQuaid laughed. "I'd rather you didn't come into this kicking and screaming, China."

His laugh was so deep and throaty, so rich with good humor and easy affection, that I couldn't help smiling. It's been like that between us since the beginning. I hold out against him as long as possible, but he can almost always talk me around to his point of view.

"I'm on board," I said gruffly. "You'll have to put up with the kicking and screaming." I stood, frowning. "If you're going to tell me what went on in Houston, I think I need another cup of coffee."

McQuaid began pulling off his boots. "Cheesecake?" He looked up at me with a grin. "I sincerely enjoy cheesecake, babe."

Howard Cosell lifted his head and opened both eyes very wide. He sincerely enjoys cheesecake, too. Even low-calorie cheesecake.

# Chapter Two

## McQuaid: The Investigation

Cheesecake finished, McQuaid props his stocking feet up on the porch rail and settles back with the coffee China has brought him, wondering whether she really wants to know about the investigation or whether she's merely humoring him, the way she sometimes does. It doesn't matter. He's going to tell her anyway.

"Hawk and I dug up some interesting stuff when we finally finished going through the *Houston Chronicle* files yesterday," he says. "Murray pulled everything that had to do with the deaths of Max Vine and Miriam Spurgin, plus their notes on the stories they were working on when they died. There's quite a bit of material. At this point, though, it's hard to know just how much is related to the Bayles case," he adds.

Clyde Murray is one of the managing editors at the *Houston Chronicle*, a good buddy from McQuaid's days in Homicide. Murray likes to chide McQuaid for moving to a hick country town that doesn't have a baseball team or a ballet or even a decent restaurant, for God's sake, but McQuaid suspects that Murray would change places with him if he could. The guy looks like hell, and he's nursing both an ulcer and high blood pressure. McQuaid has the feeling that leaving Houston added years to his own life, although the investigative juice still pulses as rich and hot in his veins as it did in the days when he was on Homicide. Which is the reason he's become a licensed private investigator, even though it means less cash coming in. And it's one of the reasons he's interested in the case Miles Danforth dangled in front of him, like a come-hither lure in front of a largemouth bass.

Only one of the reasons, though. The retainer—a sizable piece of change—is another. The money is good, and comes at a good time. But China is the third reason, and the most important, as far as McQuaid is concerned.

"Vine and Spurgin," China says. "Sounds like a street intersection." She kicks off her Birkenstocks and pulls her legs up into the rocker, tucking her bare feet under her. "They're the reporters who were killed?"

China has slimmed down some in the past few months, and McQuaid likes her sexy new look. She has a good body, and she's generous with it. He also likes the denim smock and yellow T-shirt his wife is wearing tonight. It makes her seem younger, vulnerable, even—although that's not a word she would use to describe herself. China likes to think of herself as tough, even when she's feeling tender. He's glad she's agreed to listen to his report on the investigation. He knows how hard she's tried to put her father out of her life, how resistant she is to allowing him back in.

And he doesn't blame her. As far as McQuaid is concerned, Robert Bayles was a jerk, start to finish, although it seems to have taken China a while to figure this out. As a kid, she idolized him; later, she tried as hard as she could to impress him, graduating at the top of her UT Law class, getting hired at a prestigious firm. But when it finally dawned on her that her father was never going to reward her with a smile or five minutes of his undivided attention, she cut her ties to him, refusing to talk about him or think about him. When he died, that should have been the end of it.

But it wasn't, of course. Nothing is that simple. China pretends he's gone, but McQuaid knows she's fooling herself. Bob Bayles is still there, hiding in the dark corners of her mind, coloring the way she sees the world, making her skeptical about marriage, about intimacy, about fidelity. McQuaid is no psychologist, but he thinks it would be a good thing if his wife dragged her father out of the shadows and made her peace with him. Being involved in the investigation might push her to clean out some of those dark corners, get rid of a few old skeletons.

"Right," he says, getting back on track. "Vine and Spurgin. The reporters. Miriam Spurgin was struck by a hit-and-run driver in the parking garage at her apartment. No witnesses—could've been an accident. Not long after, Max Vine and his ten-year-old daughter were both killed when his car blew up. Murray says that nobody at the paper connected the two events. They thought of them as terribly tragic, of course, happening together the way they did and involving the kid."

China's mouth has tightened at the mention of the girl. "Nothing on the car bombing?"

McQuaid shakes his head. "Hawk went through both of the files. No leads turned up on the initial investigation, and there's still nothing." McQuaid's cop buddy Jim Hawk, now retired, handled that case. Bombings are always bad news, because most of the evidence is blown to bits. Of course, it was a lot worse back then, when the investigations were less sophisticated.

"Nothing on the Spurgin hit-and-run, either," McQuaid adds. "As I say, maybe an accident. Or maybe not."

"Remind me how these two deaths got linked to my father's," China says, frowning. "Is there any concrete connection, or just something that Miles came up with?"

McQuaid has always liked the way China asks questions. She never takes anybody's word for anything. "Miles found the reporters' names in his mother's notes," he says.

"She apparently copied them from your father's office calendar, so we're assuming he talked with one or both of them. That's the connection."

Laura Danforth had begun her own investigation into Robert Bayles' death, in spite of the fact that he had warned her not to. Mrs. Danforth paid no attention, although she doesn't seem to have gotten much further than buying Bayles' wrecked Caddy and stashing it, God only knows why. Or where. Miles, who is looking for the car while McQuaid is looking into the connection to the reporters, hasn't turned it up yet. Assuming, of course, that it's still there to be found, which is not an assumption McQuaid is prepared to make. Sixteen years is a damned long time.

McQuaid pulls himself back. "There's something else interesting about those reporters, China. Vine and Spurgin were working on the same story, from different angles. It had something to do with Sharpstown."

"Sharpstown?" China frowns, and something like surprised recognition flashes across her face. She's interested now, in spite of herself, and McQuaid thinks he knows why.

Sharpstown, which came unraveled just before Watergate, was the Texas political scandal of the seventies. A high-rolling Houston bank owner named Frank Sharp had bribed state officials to pass legislation requiring the state to insure large deposits at the Sharpstown State Bank. The Feds investigated (at the urging of President Nixon, it was said, on the prowl for anything that might discredit the Democrats). The hullabaloo became headline news, and the governor, the lieutenant governor, and nearly half of the Texas state representatives were booted out of office. Over the next couple of years, a repentant legislature hatched a flock of reforms—campaign finance disclosure, open meetings, open records. But nobody went to jail, and Sharp's fine for influence-peddling amounted to all of five thousand dollars. That's the way things happen in Texas, McQuaid knows.

Everywhere else, for that matter. Press conferences on the Capitol steps, promises in the newspapers, pledges of clean living by the politicos, while the co-conspirators slide out the back way, slick as a whistle.

McQuaid is watching China. "Your father was involved in Sharpstown, wasn't he?" He doesn't need to ask. He knows that Stone and Bayles worked on Frank Sharp's legal team.

"But Sharpstown was early seventies," China objected, her frown deepening. "Long before my father died." She eyes him warily. "Are you suggesting—"

McQuaid holds up his hand, stopping her. "I'm not suggesting anything, counselor. I'm saying that Max Vine was scrutinizing the financial doings of Frank Sharp, who in addition to being your father's client was also one of your parents' neighbors there in River Oaks. And Miriam Spurgin was doing a story on the political connections of the Stone Engineering and Construction Group." At China's puzzled glance, he adds, "That's G. W. Stone, brother of your father's partner. Also a client of Stone and Bayles, and not incidentally, a major customer of the Sharpstown Bank. At the time of the Sharpstown scandal, Stone Engineering was joint ventured with Brown and Root on the LBJ Space Center in Houston."

He shakes his head disgustedly. Talk about cronyism. Houston wasn't the place for the Johnson Center—even then, everybody knew the risk of Gulf Coast hurricanes—and Stone Engineering knew squat about science engineering. Brown & Root, too, for that matter. But LBJ pulled the strings, Houston got the Center, and Stone Engineering got the contract they were after, never mind that the project ultimately cost millions over the bid price. But that was the name of the game, then and now. All politics, all the time.

"I've met G.W.," China says thoughtfully. "Ted Stone often invited me and my parents for weekends to Stonebridge Ranch—that's his place on Mustang Creek, near

Sweet Home. His brother was there fairly often. G.W. struck me as one of Houston's slicker sorts." She frowns. "Stone Engineering merged with Calloway in the late eighties, didn't it? And G.W. died last year, didn't he?"

McQuaid nods. G. W. Stone's company started out as an inconsequential Waco-based road-building business— "Two mules and a wagonload of road rock," G.W. had been fond of saying. The company broke into the big time during the thirties, with a little help from a friend. Lyndon Johnson was a brash young congressman who found it useful to do favors for the good ol' Texas boys who had pitched their pesos into his war chest. LBJ's favors for Stone Engineering began with contracts for a couple of sizable Hill Country dams, continued during the Second World War with contracts for an air station and a half dozen ships, and went into the Vietnam era with lucrative cost-plus contracts for airstrips and supplies depots. With Johnson's help at the get-go, there was nothing Stone Engineering couldn't build.

But the contracts petered out after LBJ left the White House, and the company fell on hard times. In the mid-eighties, Stone Engineering pled guilty to some very nasty charges of bribery and rigged bidding with a subsidiary, and then a couple of top executives died. In fact, it looked like the company might be going down for the third time— until it merged with Calloway, a Houston-based multinational corporation with close ties to Reagan's Defense Department. Now, Calloway-Stone had a slew of lucrative government defense contracts, foreign subsidiaries doing a booming business with Middle and Far Eastern countries, and a web of geopolitical connections flung from Texas to Washington and beyond—to Riyadh, Lagos, Caracas. It might not be quite accurate to say that this mighty behemoth began with G. W. Stone's rinky-dink road-building business, but it wouldn't be wrong, either.

China wrinkles her nose distastefully. "I hope to hell

my father wasn't rolling in that political muck," she says. "That was bad stuff. That'd kill you." The words hang in the air. She stops, and he can see her considering what she has said.

"Do you have something specific in mind?" McQuaid asks.

"Well, it killed a Stone Engineering vice president," China replies. "Keith Madison. He shot himself the week before he was to be indicted on bribery charges. He and my father went to school together."

"I see," McQuaid says. "And that was when? When he killed himself, I mean."

"A few months before Dad died, I think. At the time, I was working on a couple of big cases." She chuckles ruefully. "I didn't have enough energy left at the end of the day to read a newspaper."

"What do you know about the Stone brothers?"

"I knew Ted better. He always struck me as more human than G.W. Decent, actually. When Dad was killed, Ted took it to heart. He sold his share of the firm and left the law."

"I didn't know that," McQuaid says. "Is he still living?"

China shrugs. "Ted? Of course. He was the same age as my father, so he must be in his seventies. He's still active in political circles, I understand. Leatha hears from him at Christmas, I think. He calls her every so often, too, keeping in touch." Leatha is China's mother, now remarried and living on an exotic game ranch near Kerrville—a long way from the upscale Houston suburb where she and Bob Bayles had lived, where China had grown up.

"Ted was very kind to her after Dad's death," China goes on. "When he went to live at the ranch, he invited us out every few weeks. His wife was dead by that time, and I think he was lonely."

"Odd that he would leave Houston," McQuaid says.

"Oh, I don't know. Stonebridge is a pretty place, open range with woodlands and oak groves and a creek. And only a couple of hours west of the city." She smiles reminiscently. "There for a while, Ted was inviting us out almost every weekend. If I couldn't go, Leatha went by herself. In fact, I remember thinking that a marriage might be a good thing for both of them. Ted wanted companionship; Leatha needed someone to steady her. But it never happened, and then of course Sam came along."

McQuaid is glad it didn't happen. Sam, Leatha's husband, is an all-right guy. McQuaid enjoys taking Brian to the ranch to go riding, go fishing, watch football together. He thinks for a moment.

"Your brother was working for Stone and Bayles around the time your father died, wasn't he?"

China scowls, and he remembers, too late, that she resents the fact that her father hired Miles and didn't hire her. But her tone is studiedly neutral. "Miles went there right after law school and stayed until a few months before Dad died. The way I heard it, Dad found him a better position." She looks out toward the darkening trees, losing her neutrality. "Nothing like that for me, of course."

McQuaid grins, teasing her. "Well, you didn't need it, did you? You got there on your own."

"Yeah. That's something, isn't it?" She turns her head and smiles crookedly. She's done plenty to brag about, but she's not the kind of person who makes a big deal about her achievements. "Still, it would've been nice if my father had . . . well, you know. Given his daughter a hand up the ladder, or at least a round of applause when she made it. But he didn't." She drains her coffee cup and sets it down. "So what's next with this investigation? Are you going back to Houston?"

"In a couple of days." He senses what he thinks is a genuine interest, and he's pleased. "Jim Hawk is doing more background work on the stories Vine and Spurgin were working on. And he's pulling the police report on your father's accident." He pauses. "Want to go to Houston with me? I

know a nice hotel. We could get a room with a spa and—"
He waggles his eyebrows suggestively. "Get sexy."

China doesn't take the bait. "Is Miles picking up the tab
for Jim Hawk's work? Sounds like this thing is turning into
a full-scale investigation."

"Miles sent me a pretty good retainer," McQuaid says,
trying not to sound defensive. The detective business has
gotten off to a slower start than he expected. Since the first
of the year, he's had a software case in Albuquerque, a
couple of quick and easy missing-person cases, and the
rare-book theft investigation he did for Jeremy Paxton in
San Antonio. Nice recovery, that, and Paxton's insurance
company paid his invoice without a murmur. But other than
Miles' investigation, nothing else has come along.

"Your brother offered to pay Hawk, too," he adds, "but
Jim says it's part of the pro bono cold case investigations
he does for the department now that he's retired. And Miles
is doing some of the work himself. He's—"

The phone rings in the kitchen. "Was that all the cheesecake?" McQuaid asks as China gets up to answer it. At the
word, Howard Cosell, lying nearby, lifts his head attentively.

"There's one more piece."

"Split it with you," he offers.

She grins and picks up his plate. "You eat it. Save me
from myself."

She's gone for a few minutes. He can hear her voice on
the phone, but not her words. When she comes back, she
hands him his plate, with a slice of cheesecake, and sits
down.

"Thank you, sincerely," McQuaid says, and they both
chuckle. He picks up his fork, cuts off a bite of cheesecake,
and offers it to Howard Cosell.

"That was your client on the phone," she says, as
Howard licks his fingers.

"Miles?" That's a dumb question. Miles is his *only*
client, damn it. "Why didn't you call me?"

"Because he was getting ready to leave the office, on his way home. He just wanted to tell you that he's emailing you something."

"Oh, yeah?" He cocks an eyebrow. "Emailing me what?"

She looks out across the darkening landscape. She doesn't speak for a moment. Finally, she says, "He says it's a map to a place down near Shiner." She turns to look at him, her face pale in the growing dusk. "He wants you to meet him there tomorrow. He thinks he's found Dad's car."

# Chapter Three

Belladonna, n.: In Italian, a beautiful lady; in English, a deadly poison. A striking example of the essential identity of the two tongues.

Ambrose Bierce

Belladonna (*Atropa belladonna*). The name of this poisonous member of the nightshade family is said to derive from its ancient use by Italian women, who dropped the plant's juice into their eyes to dilate the pupils and make them more beautiful. Because pale skin was an attribute of beauty, women also used the juice of the plant to lighten the color of their skin.

I usually try to get to the shop an hour early on Tuesday mornings. We're not open on Sunday or Monday, so there's extra watering on Tuesday—especially when I have trays of herb plants for sale. By mid-July, the plants that haven't been sold go into the garden to get on with their natural lives.

I don't know about you, but I find watering to be a quiet, soothing activity, almost as calming as pulling weeds. After the previous night's conversation with McQuaid, I needed to do something quiet and calming. I was irritated at him for dragging me into the investigation that he and

Miles had cooked up—and at myself, for agreeing to get involved. What's more, Miles' phone call had jolted me. I'd figured that Dad's wrecked car was long gone, or that it was rusting away in some dilapidated old barn or garage and would never be found. Hence, there could be no proof that the accident had been anything other than, well, accidental. Hearing that Miles had located the damn thing and wanted McQuaid to take a look at it had been unsettling—so unsettling that I had dreamed about the accident again last night. I'm standing beside the Houston freeway, watching my father's car burn. It's horrible.

But McQuaid had been jubilant. He had muttered, "Hot diggity dawg," and gone to the phone to let Jim Hawk in on the good news. If it was really Dad's car, their investigation had just taken a giant step forward. Maybe.

I arched the stream of water over the red blossoms of monarda at the back of the bed. A hummingbird flew down from the mesquite tree for his morning bath, looping figure-eights through the glittering shower. The sun turned his throat feathers into flaming ruby, his wings into shimmering emeralds, and suddenly the morning seemed a little brighter, a little happier. I stopped thinking about McQuaid and Miles and my father and that rusting Caddy. The garden has a way of doing that for me—and the shop, too.

Thyme and Seasons is situated in a century-old two-story building on Crockett Street, east of the town square. The solid limestone blocks that built it were quarried and shaped by the crafty German stonemasons who constructed most of the early buildings in Pecan Springs, as well as New Braunfels, Fredericksburg, and San Marcos. The towns around here were settled by German immigrants in the middle of the nineteenth century, who came to America because there was no place for them at home. They built themselves a new place, and their buildings have outlived them.

The Crystal Cave—that's Ruby Wilcox's New Age shop, the only one in Pecan Springs—takes up half of the front of the building, which I bought when I cashed in my retirement account. Thyme and Seasons takes up my half, a small space, which is crowded with fragrant herbs and sweet-smelling herbal products. Come inside, and you'll see antique hutches and wooden shelves stocked with herbal vinegars, oils, jellies, and teas. The pine cupboard in the corner displays personal care products: herbal soaps, shampoos, massage oils, bath herbs. In the middle of the room, a wooden rack is filled with gallon jars of dried culinary and medicinal herbs, along with bottles of extracts and tinctures. Of course there are books—including a counter display of my own book, *China Bayles' Book of Days*, of which I am justly proud—as well as stationery and cards and gift baskets. Wreaths hang on every wall, and the corners are full of baskets of yarrow, sweet Annie, larkspur, statice, and tansy, along with buckets of fragrant potpourri.

Outside the door you'll find racks of potted herbs for sale. And if you follow the path around the building, you can wander through the theme gardens—the Zodiac Garden, the Fragrance Garden, the Kitchen Garden, the Apothecary Garden, the Children's Garden—and eventually find your way to Thyme Cottage (formerly a stone stable), which Ruby, Cass, and I use for demonstrations and workshops, and occasionally as a guest house.

But before you reach the cottage, you might want to step into the tearoom behind the shops. Ruby and I started Thyme for Tea about three years ago, in the space that used to be my apartment. (That was before McQuaid and I moved into the house on Limekiln Road.) The large dining room, with its stone walls, green wainscot, and tall, narrow windows, seats about thirty people. Behind that is my old kitchen, completely remodeled to meet the requirements of the state health department, which cost a bundle, believe me. But happily, Thyme for Tea is a collaborative enterprise: Ruby came up with the capital, I provided the space, and both of us contribute ideas and labor.

Ruby, bless her, is never short on ideas. When the tea-room business didn't grow as fast as she'd hoped, she came up with a plan for a catering service called Party Thyme, our "traveling circus," as she calls it. Party Thyme doesn't cost much to operate (compared to the investment we've already made in that kitchen) and brings in not only additional revenue, but new customers, as well. A couple of weeks ago, for instance, Party Thyme catered a wedding reception at the Springs Hotel (the main event had been an herbal wedding, with Thyme and Seasons providing the herbs). One of the bridesmaids has already arranged a party in the shop's garden, and a couple of the guests are making plans for afternoon teas at Thyme for Tea, so Ruby's idea is paying off. "Paying off big t-h-y-m-e," she likes to say, spelling it out. We're also busy big-thyme. And in my opinion, busy is good, since busy pays the bills.

And then, not long after we launched the catering operation, Cassandra Wilde came along with her scheme for a personal chef service called the Thymely Gourmet. It's a perfect fit for Cass, who has spent nearly fifteen years in the food service industry and is certified as a personal chef by the American Culinary Foundation. It's turned out to be a good fit for us, too. Cass is fun and easy to work with, and the Thymely Gourmet is definitely an asset.

I finished watering, coiled up the hose, and went into the shop, where I was greeted by Khat, our shop cat. In anticipation of breakfast, he was purring so loudly you could hear him at the Alamo. His Imperial Majesty is a Siamese of magnificent proportions—some seventeen pounds—who imagines that the world has been created entirely for his benefit: the Glorious Empire of Khat. Every morning when I unlock the door and step inside, he wraps himself around my ankles and reminds me that my first job is *not* to pick up messages from the answering machine, or to put change in the register, or to sweep the floor. My very first, high-priority job is to fill the emperor's kitty food bowl.

Oh, and I might just add an extra spoonful of chopped liver, since he had only three or four mice and an imprudent pocket gopher since dinner the day before. An emperor could starve on such paltry rations.

I was hunting for the cooked liver in the kitchen refrigerator when the tearoom door opened and closed. "Yoohoo!" Cass called. "Anybody here?"

"In the kitchen," I called back, locating the cooked liver. "Catering to a cat."

"Mrowrrr," said Khat, with the impatient rasp in his voice that means *No interruptions, please. We are engaged in important business here.*

Cass appeared in the kitchen doorway, looking cool and summery in lime green floppy pants and top, with a green, yellow, and orange sleeveless tunic, fringed at her knees, and an orange scarf tied around her blond hair. She is a large woman who dresses as adventurously as Ruby. There's more of her—that is, where Ruby is tall, Cass is wide—so there's more adventure. Today, she looked like a frosty limeade, *grande*, blithely garnished with slices of orange and lemon.

"We have to do something about Ruby," Cass said without preamble.

"Ruby?" I asked, concerned. "Is something wrong with Ruby?"

"Mrrorrw!" said Khat emphatically. *Less talk, more action.*

I put the liver into the microwave for exactly twelve seconds, bringing it up to the requisite temperature. "Is something wrong with her?" I asked again. "She's not sick, I hope." I set the dish on the floor in Khat's corner and he addressed himself to it with undisguised enthusiasm.

"She turned down my offer of a vanilla-cream jelly doughnut," Cass said, holding up a white paper bag. "I stopped by her house and offered her one, but she said she wasn't hungry."

"Uh-oh," I said. When Ruby turns down a jelly dough-nut, things are serious. "Is she on a diet? Is she sick?"

"No diet." Cass sighed. "She's not sick, either. Not phys-ically, that is." The automatic coffeepot had done its work automatically, and the coffee was waiting. She poured us a couple of mugs. "She's grieving."

I echoed her sigh. Ruby, who is basically a happy per-son, has been going through some very hard times. Her significant other, Colin Fowler, was killed in late April. She had broken up with him a couple of weeks before, so when he died in the line of duty (unbeknownst to Ruby, he was an undercover narcotics agent), she felt not only the pain of his death but the guilt that came with the breakup. It's Ruby's nature to take responsibility for what goes on around her, and Colin's death is no exception. She doesn't say much about it, but I know that she hasn't stopped thinking about him, about the things he wanted to do and be, about his hopes and dreams. But most of all, about his unfinished life, which seems to pale into insignificance against his ugly death.

And to complicate things, she's also worried about her mother, Doris, who is gradually losing her grip. Ruby and her sister Ramona have moved Doris to a supervised living situation in her senior community in Fredericksburg. They're hoping she can get help in managing her anger and depression and curbing her kleptomaniacal passion for the silk scarves and other expensive booty she likes to pilfer from the local department stores. Hey, please don't smile. It was comic when we first heard about it, but not anymore. Unlike Ruby, Doris is never a happy person, even in the happiest of circumstances. Now, she is just plain tragic.

"You're right," I told Cass. "Between losing Colin and her mother losing her mind, Ruby has plenty to grieve for. But I don't know what we can do to help. Practically speak-ing, that is."

"Practically speaking, she ought to get away for a while."

Cass opened her paper bag and peered inside. "Vanilla-cream, lemon, or strawberry?"

I sighed. "One of them wouldn't be low-calorie, would it?"

Cass snorted a laugh "Not a chance."

"Okay, then, surprise me." I have just enough willpower to keep from stopping at Lila's Nueces Street Diner on my way to work in the morning, but not enough to stop me from grabbing one of her luscious jelly doughnuts when it magically materializes in front of me. This one turned out to be deliciously lemon. I ate it standing in the kitchen, keeping in mind the old rule that there are no calories in food you eat while you are on your feet. Why this is true, I don't know. It has something to do with gravity, maybe, or the electromagnetism of the earth.

Cass does not concern herself with calories and refuses to be defined by her dress size. "I am abundantly ready to enjoy life and all it has to offer," she says with a flourish. "I am a woman of substance, and I refuse to sell my sizable self short." Nobody else can sell Cass short, either. She is out there in her choice of coiffure (blond and curly), costume color (crayon red, splashy sunburst, magnificent magenta), and costume style (loose and comfortable). She turns heads when she struts her stuff, and she makes the most of all the attention she gets.

Beneath Cass' flirty, frolicsome exterior, though, there is something otherwise. I don't know what it is yet, because she makes a persistent effort to cover it up. But every now and then, I catch a glimpse of a deep melancholy in her eyes, or spot a wary expression on her face, as if she's glancing back to see who's shadowing her. Someday, she'll let me in on the secret. In the meantime, I wasn't surprised when she was the one who connected with Ruby's sadness.

"You think she should get away?" I asked, savoring my jelly doughnut. "A condo at the coast, maybe? But that would be pretty hard right now. Party Thyme has three bookings next week. Unless we can get some more help in the tearoom, she'll never leave."

"I wasn't thinking of getting that far away," Cass replied. "I was thinking about a spa party. Five or six of us—enough to have fun and take Ruby's mind off her troubles for a few hours."

"A spa party?" I asked doubtfully. "What exactly is a spa party?"

"You don't know what a spa party is?" Cass hooted. "Where you been, girl?"

Where had I been? "In the garden?" I hazarded. "Behind the counter?" I counted them off on my fingers. "In the office, in the kitchen, doing the laundry, experimenting with low-calorie cooking, balancing the checkbook, cleaning the house, driving Brian to soccer games." That was nine. "Oh, and jogging with Colin's dog."

That would be Rambo the Rottweiler, who had lived with us until last Friday, when Sheila enrolled him in K-9 training school. Ruby had planned to adopt Rambo, but after his stellar performance the night we caught Colin's killer, everybody agreed that he had a rewarding future as a police dog. He doesn't need training, in my opinion, but the credential won't hurt. Jogging with Rambo hasn't hurt me, either. Since he moved in with us, I've lost five more pounds.

"A spa party," Cass said in a superior tone, "is where girls go to get beautiful together. Pamper themselves. Enjoy great food, get a massage, a manicure, a long soak in a hot tub full of close friends." Cass polished off her jelly doughnut and licked her fingers. "Memorial Day is coming up, and Party Thyme doesn't have a booking for that weekend. We could go on Sunday afternoon and stay overnight and all day Monday."

"Getting beautiful, huh?" Now that I have this sleek, rebuilt body—well, rebuilt, anyway—I wouldn't mind making it beautiful. "Where would we go to do this thing?"

"Why, the Canyon Lake Spa Resort, of course!" Cass said triumphantly. "Haven't you seen the ads on television? My friend Linda Davis works there. She says she'll make us a special price on a party package."

That got my attention. "Linda Davis? Wasn't she the manager of the Pack Saddle Inn?"

"That's her." Cass eyed me. "You know Linda?"

"You bet," I said. "Linda saved my wedding. We were going to have it here, in the garden, but Hurricane Josephine rained us out." Did she ever. Josephine blew in from the Gulf and turned our wedding into a hurricane party at the Pack Saddle, marooning McQuaid and me in the waterbed in the honeymoon suite. "So Linda is at the Canyon Lake Resort now?"

"Yep. And she's offering all kinds of wonderful spa services, like the Essential Rosemary Skin Conditioning and the Nantucket Seaweed Soak."

"Seaweed Soak?"

"Linda says it's very relaxing. It has a special kind of mud in it, along with the seaweed. Pulls the toxins right out through your pores and makes you totally beautiful. And then there's the Citrus Splash, with a sea-salt scrub and a massage with tangerine and grapefruit and orange oils. Or you can have the Eucalyptus Body Polish." She grinned. "Of course, some of this stuff is a little pricey, but what's money when it comes to getting beautiful? Or to improving Ruby's outlook on life?"

"I'll buy that." Seaweed Soak sounded pretty good, and rosemary and citrus and eucalyptus are wonderful for your skin. I'd been working hard lately, and I'd lost all that weight—an overnight at a health spa would be a great reward for myself. And of course, it would be perfect for Ruby. After a few hours up to her chin in a Seaweed Soak, all her toxic feelings would vanish.

"Super," Cass said. "So who should we invite? I was

thinking maybe you and me and Amy and her friend Kate. With Ruby, that would be five."

"Let's ask Molly and make it six," I said. Molly McGregor owns the Hobbit House Bookstore, next door on the east. She and Ruby are good friends. "Laurel, too. That's seven." Laurel works part-time in the shop. "And what about Ruth Ann Gilman?" Ruth Ann recently opened a quilt shop called PatchWorks, in the Craft Emporium next door. At this point, she could probably use a weekend getaway.

"Linda says there's room for ten," Cass said, making notes. "If you think of anybody else, feel free." She paused. "So you think it's a good idea?"

"I think it's a perfect idea," I said emphatically. "I'll check with Amy and Kate right away. Would it be okay if they brought Grace?" Amy Roth is Ruby's daughter, Grace is Amy's five-month-old daughter, and Kate is Amy's live-in partner. Ruby adores Grace. She has a playpen and a baby swing set up in the Cave, and there's a crib in the stockroom. That's one of the nice things about being in business for yourself: your employer always says yes when you want to bring the baby to work.

"Sure," Cass said. "Grace is a doll. We can all take turns looking after her. And even babies deserve to get beautiful, although we shouldn't take her into the hot tub. It wouldn't be good for her."

I snapped my fingers. "Hey, wait! We're forgetting Sheila." Sheila Dawson is Pecan Springs' chief of police. She could probably join us if she had time to plan ahead—if there weren't any law-enforcement crises that weekend.

Cass frowned. "Sheila? I'm not sure that's a good idea."

"They've got to make it up sooner or later," I said. Since Colin died, Ruby has been pretty frosty toward Sheila. I wondered whether she'd heard that Sheila and Colin had once been lovers—a long time ago, when they were both on the Dallas police force. "A spa party might be a good place for them to iron out their differences."

Cass looked uncertain, but she only nodded. "Well, if you think so. I'll talk to the others, and tell Linda to make a reservation for us. Maybe Amy and Kate can figure out some sort of pretext for getting Ruby out to the spa—it'll be more fun if we surprise her." Cass enveloped me in an enthusiastic hug. "This is going to be fabulous, China! And it's just what Ruby needs. Twenty-four-plus hours of pure pampering."

It was what I needed, too. "We have to make sure she doesn't schedule a weekend party for Party Thyme," I said. "Let's put a dummy booking on the calendar."

"Great idea," Cass said, going to the scheduling board where we post our bookings. She took a marker and began to write. " 'Linda Davis Pool Party.' How's that? When she asks you about it, tell her to check with me." She capped the marker and grinned. "You're a crummy liar."

Not true. When I was a lawyer, I lied all day and never thought twice about it. The only time I couldn't lie was in court, and even then, if I chose my words carefully—

The cell phone clipped to the belt of my khakis rang. It was McQuaid, calling to tell me that he was getting ready to drive down to Shiner to meet Miles. The map Miles had sent indicated that the car was hidden on a ranch near there. McQuaid was supposed to meet him in the brewery parking lot in Shiner at eleven. They'd drive to the ranch together.

McQuaid cleared his throat hopefully. "Hey, babe. Would you like to come along?"

"Can't. Laurel's supposed to come in this morning, and I haven't seen her yet. There's nobody to stay with the shop."

"Laurel is already here, China," Cass said, rinsing our cups in the sink. "I saw her when I came in."

I shook my head at her, putting a finger to my lips. To

McQuaid, I added, "Gosh, hon, I'm *really* sorry. Today just isn't a good day for me to take off." I had to confess to being interested in his investigation, but I didn't want to see that car. Dreaming about it had been disturbing enough.

"Yeah. I'm sorry, too," McQuaid said. But from the tone of his voice, I didn't think my refusal mattered that much. He was rarin' to go, find that car, unravel that mystery cha-cha-cha. "I'll call you when we've found it," he added. "Or when we haven't." He chuckled wryly. "Or when I have a better idea of what the hell is going on. I've got my camera. I'll take photos."

"Okay," I said, glad that he was happy in his work. I could stand to look at a few photos, probably. "But be careful. If you're poking around an old barn, watch out for snakes and scorpions." I made kissy noises into the phone and switched it off.

Cass looked up at the menu board and reached for her apron. "Time to get cookin'," she said happily. Cass feels about cooking the same way I feel about gardening. "Tomato-basil soup today. And chicken salad on croissants."

"I'll have to eat standing up," I said, and went out to see if Laurel needed any help.

# Chapter Four

## McQuaid: Frustration

McQuaid is on the road by nine thirty, heading southeast on SR 80 in his old blue pickup truck. The small town of Shiner lies in the general direction of Seguin, where his parents still live in the house where he and his sister Jill grew up. He's thinking he'll swing past the home place before he goes back to Pecan Springs, to see how his mom and dad are getting along. It's one of the reasons he's glad that Miles wanted to take separate cars, instead of driving down together.

That, and the fact that he was hoping China would come along. Shiner isn't far, only fifty, fifty-five miles, and it's a pretty day. Rain is forecast for later, but it's no warmer than usual for May and early enough in the season that the roadside grass is still green and liberally decorated with yellow and red flowers. After they'd checked out the car, he and China could've taken Miles to Davila's BBQ in Seguin, picked up ribs and sausage and barbecued turkey and a quart of cole slaw and some beans, and gone over to the folks' house for dinner. Mom and Dad would've enjoyed meeting China's brother, and it would've given everybody a chance to get acquainted. China could have come if she'd really wanted to, McQuaid figures, but he's only mildly disappointed. Memorial Day is just around the corner. He's thinking that he and China will take Brian down to Seguin for the day. The boy likes to play chess with his grandfather and he's crazy about Davilla's turkey legs. It'll make a nice little family trip. Maybe Miles and his daughter could join them.

Anyway, it's entirely possible that today will be a big waste of time. Miles hadn't sounded very positive in his email. In fact, he had been so noncommittal—wasn't really sure the car was there, wasn't even sure where *there* was, exactly, although he had attached a map and directions—that McQuaid, slightly irritated, almost emailed back to say that Miles should check out the location for himself first, instead of the two of them chasing down there together. McQuaid has plenty of other stuff to keep him busy.

But this is not quite true. Jim Hawk is capable of handling things in Houston, and McQuaid—regrettably—doesn't have any other clients to occupy his time. Anyway, a few hours spent with Miles won't be wasted, even if they don't find the car. McQuaid would like to get to know him better. There are some things about China's brother—China's *half* brother, he amends with a wry chuckle—that puzzle him.

Like why Miles seems not to have figured out that Robert Bayles was his father before he learned it from his mother's papers. You'd think he would've been more curious about his paternity. Apparently, he'd never made an effort to confirm his mother's tale that his father died before he was born—like checking on his birth certificate, or doing a records search to turn up family connections, things you'd think a lawyer would do. Even if it was only a matter of learning the family's genetic history in case there was something Miles might pass down to his children—to that pretty little girl of his, to Caitlin—you'd think he'd want to know. If Caitlin were his daughter, McQuaid was sure he would have made the effort.

And what about Laura Danforth? China says she was

one sharp lady, smart enough to run Stone and Bayles with one hand tied behind her back. So how come she didn't know who might have wanted her boyfriend dead? She was clever enough to buy the car and squirrel it away, persistent enough to dig up the connection between Bayles and the two dead reporters.

But from what Miles said (granted, all they had was his word for it) she seems to have gone so far and no further. She'd started an investigation. Why hadn't she stayed with it? Miles says she'd gotten sick, but is that a sufficient explanation? McQuaid thinks maybe it isn't, that maybe there's another reason. Did somebody tell her to lay off, maybe threaten her son? If so, was the threat anonymous, or did she know who was behind it?

And there's something else. McQuaid can't say quite why or how, but his cop's intuition, honed over years of dealing with criminals, victims, and eyewitnesses, tells him that Miles knows more about his father's death than he has been letting on.

What? What does he know? And why is he keeping it to himself? Why doesn't he just lay all his cards on the table so McQuaid can see the hand they're playing? Is he after somebody specific, and doesn't want McQuaid to know who it is? Or maybe the cards fall the other way, and Miles is protecting somebody, somebody who matters to him, for one reason or another.

The morning sun is heating the asphalt so that the road ahead seems to ripple. McQuaid cranks up the AC another notch and moves his shoulders and butt, trying to get comfortable. The pickup truck has a hard bench seat, and since he got shot a couple of years ago, his neck has a tendency to hurt when he drives. But he figures he's lucky to be alive, so he ignores the ache and goes back to sorting through his questions.

There aren't any answers, but that doesn't especially bother him. McQuaid has always been happier with questions than answers. He's even happier if the answers, when they come, are complicated by even more questions.

That's what keeps life from being boring.


SHINER calls itself "The cleanest little city in Texas." It may not be quite a city—the entire population of the town would fit comfortably into the upper deck of the end zone of the Darryl Royal Stadium, with seats left over. But it's certainly clean. Not only that, but it boasts the oldest brewery in the state, the Spoetzl Brewery, established in 1909 by a bunch of German immigrants who had settled near San Antonio and missed their Old Country brew. If you want a tour of a genuine Bavarian brewery and sample slugs of some pretty fine beer, Spoetzl is the place to go. And since it's also a well-known landmark and easy to find (a big square building, painted white, on SR 90-A, which runs between Gonzales and Halletsville) the brewery is a good place to connect. You can park in the lot and wait until the person you're meeting shows up.

McQuaid stops at a convenience store and buys a soda and a Mounds candy bar, then parks under a skimpy mesquite tree on the highway side of the Spoetzl lot, across the road from a big truck-towing operation. He checks his watch. Ten forty-five. The employees' cars (full employment at the brewery runs about fifty) are parked around the side and the back, and a few visitors are showing up for the eleven o'clock tour. McQuaid, who grew up some thirty miles from here, has taken the tour twice—once when he was in high school, when he wrote a report on the brewing process. He had to get his father's permission for that, since his English teacher didn't think beer was a fit subject for a teenager. And once when Jill's in-laws drove through on their way back to Illinois and he and his father took them around, to the Alamo and Six Flags in San Antonio and the Texas History Museum in Austin. And the Shiner brewery. It was the brewery they liked best, since that was the weekend of Bocktoberfest. The music was loud, the crowd was colorful (especially to a bunch of Yankees), and the beer and sausage were first-rate.

McQuaid flips the tab on his soda and sniffs the air appreciatively. He can smell the heady aroma of barley malt cooking with hops in the polished copper kettles that are the brewery's pride and joy. He knows if China were here, she'd tell him all about hops, which is an herb, he's pretty sure. He remembers that the brewery survived the long dry spell of Prohibition by brewing birch beer (that's the cover story, at least), which might interest her. So far as he knows, she's never visited here. Maybe they'll come on Memorial Day, on their way to Seguin. Brian could probably get in, even though he's a minor, since he'd be with his parents.

By the time the soda and candy bar are gone, it's fifteen past eleven. McQuaid's neck is really aching now, and he pops a couple of aspirins, wishing Miles would hurry. He was the one who picked the brewery as a meeting place, so he must know where it is. Anyway, Shiner isn't Los Angeles; there's no way a guy could get lost. Maybe he's had car trouble, or has been detained. McQuaid flips open his phone, punches in the number of his office at home, and checks the answering machine. Nothing there except a reminder from the dentist to make an appointment to get his teeth cleaned, an invitation McQuaid intends to ignore as long as possible.

At twenty-five past, he hunts through his notebook for the number of Zwinger, Brady, Brandon, and Danforth, wishing he'd remembered to ask for Miles' cell number. The phone call doesn't get him anywhere, though. The receptionist, sounding harried, says that Miles isn't in. No, she does not know when he's expected or where he can be reached. No, she can't give out his cell, but she'll take McQuaid's name and number. He gives it to her, for what it's worth, and tries the phone at China's shop, to see if Miles has checked in there. Busy. He tries China's cell phone, but it's busy, too. Probably no use, anyway. She would have called him if she'd had a message to relay.

The brewery's noon whistle blows, and McQuaid discovers that his growing frustration is now fueled by a sharply rising hunger. Breakfast was hours ago, and Friday's—a well-known local eatery—is nearby. He'll give it fifteen more minutes before he calls it quits.

Twelve fifteen comes, twelve fifteen goes. Frowning, wondering what the hell is going on, McQuaid makes one more phone call to ZBB and D, and nets another zero. He snaps the phone closed, scowling. Well, hell. That does it. Time to pack it in.

A moment later McQuaid is pulling out of the parking lot, heading for Friday's. He's thinking about the deep-fried onion he had the last time he came through Shiner. No dinky pile of cardboard onion rings coated with gooey breading. This was the entire onion, round, sweet, tender, lightly batter-dipped and sliced open so it looks like a flower. Smothered with ranch dressing, it's the best damn fried onion he's had before or since. He hopes it's still on the menu.

# Chapter Five

It may come as a surprise to some people to learn that a fruit as widely used as the tomato was once regarded with suspicion . . . probably because of the realization that it was a relative of mandrake and other plants known to be poisonous. For a long time it was grown in Europe either as an ornamental or a medicinal plant. Why tomatoes should have been grown as ornamentals puzzled Philip Miller [*Gardeners' Dictionary*, 1768], who wrote, "their leaves emit so strong an offensive odor on being touched . . . [that it] renders them very improper for the pleasure garden."

*The Fascinating World of the Nightshades*
Charles B. Heiser, Jr.

I was ringing up a sale just after noon, when Sheila Dawson came in. She was dressed in her blue police uniform, the cap sitting jauntily on her smooth blond hair. It doesn't matter what she's wearing, whether she's uniformed or is togged out in a tee and jeans or a chic beige suit with pearls and heels, Sheila always looks like she should be on the cover of a fashion magazine. Smart Cookie is what her friends call her. But we could just as easily call her Tough Cookie. You don't want to get in her way when she's serious about something.

"Got time for a quick lunch, China?" she asked. "How about going over to the Casa?"

I was surprised by her invitation. Smart Cookie usually spends her lunch hour lobbying members of the City Council, in an effort to boost the sagging police department budget. But I kept my surprise to myself and tactfully suggested that instead of going across the street to fatten the competition's bottom line, we find a corner table in the tearoom.

"I can heartily recommend the chicken salad on croissant," I added. "And the baby spinach salad with strawberries, mandarin oranges, and a mint vinaigrette. Not to mention the tomato-basil soup."

If I sound smug, please forgive me. The restaurant reviewer for *Texas Tables* recently wrote us up as a great little place to eat. She especially liked the "silky-sweet, ruby-red" tomato-basil soup and the "bright, whimsical" mint vinaigrette. The publicity is nice, although I could get along without the adjectives.

Sheila glanced toward the door that opened into the tearoom, where Ruby and Jenna, our helper, were finding seats for a half-dozen Friends of the Library Fund-raising Committee, who had forgotten (as usual) to make a reservation. Seeing Ruby, Sheila's mouth tightened. "Maybe we can eat outside," she said.

"Nothing easier," I replied promptly. "You find a spot. I'll get our food."

When Sheila had gone outside, I stuck my head into the Crystal Cave, where Laurel was helping somebody choose the rune stones that were just right for her personality, and asked her to keep an eye on both shops while I got a bite of lunch. Tit for tat, since I'd been doing double-duty while Laurel was out. That's the nice thing about having everything together here: Ruby's shop, my shop, the tearoom. A few people can keep it all going.

I went into the kitchen and began making up a large tray with soups, salads, and sandwiches, half-size portions for me. I had the distinct feeling that Sheila didn't want Ruby to know she was there, so I didn't call attention to what I was doing. Cass, however, caught a glimpse of Sheila through the kitchen window.

"What's up with the cops?" she asked, stirring the soup pot. She had covered her lime green outfit with a white chef's coat and topped her blond curls with an official-looking chef's toque, which she wears with pride. She says she's earned it.

"Oh, just a friendly little chat over lunch," I said, filling two glasses with iced hibiscus tea.

"Cooler inside," Cass said, eyeing me in a meaningful way.

"Yeah, but Ruby's on hostess duty."

Cass shook her head. "Please see what you can do to get them to make up," she said. "I'd hate to see them spoil our spa party with a fuss." She tasted the soup, pursed her lips, and rolled her eyes. "Silky-sweet," she murmured. "Ruby-red. Bright and whimsical, too."

"Don't knock it," I said, and took the tray. "We're in the magazine, and that's what counts."

I found Sheila on the Thyme Cottage deck, which is about as far from the tearoom as she could get. Clearly, she didn't want Ruby to see us.

"Very nice," she said approvingly, glancing at the tray. She took off her cop cap and tossed it onto the other chair. "Looks like you've got a full house today. You guys are doing okay, huh?"

"We've been hosting some lunchtime meetings," I said, brushing leaves off the table so I could put the tray down. The deck is shaded by a large live oak and surrounded by rosemary and salvia. It's pleasant, although the alley can sometimes be noisy. "The Garden Club, Friends of the Library, Ruby's quilting group." I pulled out my chair and sat down.

Sheila tasted the tomato soup. "I can't imagine why any-body would eat anywhere else. This is great."

"People used to think tomatoes were poisonous," I said. "They belong to the nightshade family."

"Oh, yeah?" She took another spoonful. "They must have been nuts."

"Potatoes, too," I offered helpfully. "And eggplant. All in the same family."

"Eggplant, I understand," Sheila said, making a face. "My mother made me eat it when I was a kid. I didn't like it then, don't like it now."

She lapsed into a silence that was broken only by the rapid-fire yapping of Miss Lula, the nasty little Pekinese who lives across the alley. Lula isn't much bigger than an armadillo, but her bark can be heard around the block. This was her triumphant "I've-treed-a-squirrel" bark. It would go on as long as the squirrel felt like dancing around in the top of the pecan tree.

"Okay, Chief," I said, when I had finished my soup. "You didn't come to talk tomatoes and eggplant. What's this about?"

Sheila sighed, pushed her bowl away, and reached for her sandwich. "Let me get a start on my croissant first."

"That bad, is it?" I asked. Sheila looked tired, I thought. Pecan Springs isn't exactly the crime center of the universe, but there's always lots of little stuff. Gas station drive-offs, illegal dumping, dog bites, burning garbage, door-to-door scams. And of course, the occasional big one. We're lo-cated on I-35, the north-south drug corridor, which is why Sheila is always asking the City Council for more law-enforcement funding. Somehow, the council seems to find it a novel concept that cop cars and other police equipment require frequent replacement and upgrades.

She spoke past a bite of chicken salad. "Not bad, ex-actly. Just . . . difficult."

"Difficult how? Did you put the D.A.'s daughter in jail

again?" Sheila arrested Howie Masterson's daughter Harriet last week for underage drinking. Howie, who is further to the right than Archie Bunker, put family values front and center in his election campaign. Harriet's arrest did not fill him with joy.

Across the alley, Mr. Cowan, Lula's owner, banged on his garbage can. "Shut up, Miss Lula!" he yelled. "Leave that squirrel and git on home, y'hear?" Miss Lula may have heard, but she didn't git on home. She kept on barking at the squirrel, who by now had set up a dandy racket of his own, chittering and chattering as he did squirrel-acrobatics in the pecan tree.

"It isn't Harriet." Sheila took a bite. "It's difficult as in a quarter of a million dollars."

I gulped. "You're asking the City Council for a quarter of a million dollars?" Granted, the Pecan Springs police budget is never big enough for everything it needs to cover, but a quarter of a million would buy a lot of walkie-talkies, with some left over for forensic equipment and a few bulletproof vests.

"This doesn't have anything to do with the City Council. It's personal."

Across the alley, there was a metallic crash and a yelp, and Miss Lula stopped barking. Mr. Cowan had thrown the garbage can lid at her. The squirrel laughed.

"Personal?" I raised my eyebrows. "Well, I suppose the degree of difficulty depends on whether it's a payable or a receivable. I sure hope you don't owe that kind of money."

"It's not me, China. It's Ruby."

I gulped. "Ruby owes *a quarter of a million dollars*? Ohmigosh! How could that happen? What did she spend it on?" I thought of Doris and her kleptomania. Had Ruby's mother started robbing banks?

Sheila shook her head. "No, no, no. Nothing like that, China. The fact of the matter is that Ruby is going to get a quarter of a million dollars, and somebody needs to tell her. I think you should do it."

"A quarter of a million—" I gulped. "But who is giving her— Why are they giving her—" I didn't seem to be able to finish my sentences. "Why do you want *me* to tell her?" I managed finally.

Sheila put down her croissant and rubbed her hand across her face. "Because the money comes from Dan Reid's estate," she said wearily. "From Colin. I don't want to be involved."

"Oh," I said limply. "I see."

This might be moderately confusing unless you know that Ruby's boyfriend, Colin Fowler, was working narcotics undercover in Pecan Springs when he was killed. His real name was Dan Reid. You'll understand it even better if you're aware that Dan Reid and Sheila Dawson had once been lovers, back when they were both with the Dallas Police Department. Ruby knows—now, after Dan's death—about his work as an undercover officer, which was the reason he assumed the name of Colin Fowler and set up shop (Good Earth Goods) on the Pecan Springs square. If Ruby knows about Dan and Sheila, though, she hasn't learned it from me. I'd promised Sheila I'd keep the story to myself. I hate to be caught in the middle between two friends, but I had kept my word.

"Maybe this isn't any of my business," I said, after I had begun to recover from my surprise. "But how did Colin happen to get his hands on a quarter of a million bucks? Was he taking his own personal cut of the drug busts?"

Sheila's laugh was short and unamused. "He was a Federal employee. He died in the line of duty. There's a wad of insurance, plus back pay multiplied by hazardous-duty pay, and a few other things. The bottom line is two hundred forty-nine thousand dollars, plus a few odd hundred. He named Ruby as beneficiary." She hesitated. "Do you think she knows?"

"I think she doesn't have a clue. If she was due to inherit that kind of money, she would have told me."

Sheila's mouth was set in a hard line. Was she jealous? Was she angry that Colin had named Ruby and not her? Or was it pain, pure and simple? Colin was murdered in Pecan Springs—knifed near the railroad track—and the killer was still in Sheila's jail, awaiting trial. For all I knew, part of her was still in love with Colin, although she claimed that their affair had ended years before.

"He was a good man, in his way," she'd said to me after his memorial service. "When he loved you, you were his and he was yours, totally. For at least, oh, thirty seconds." She grinned sadly. "Maybe even a full minute. After that—" She hadn't finished the sentence, but I understood. I'd known a few guys like that.

I took a sip of tea. "How did you happen to find out about the money?"

She picked up her croissant again. "I know Dan's boss, Chad, in the district office. Chad has the paperwork. He called me to ask whether Ruby was Dan's sister, and whether she knows about the money. If not, he thought maybe I should be the one to tell her." Her eyes darkened. "But I can't. She hates me."

"Ruby doesn't hate you. She's just—She's still grieving."

"She probably knows about Dan and me." Sheila narrowed her eyes. "Did you tell her, China?"

"Of course not!" I was indignant. "But there are . . . well, rumors."

A deafening *va-room va-roooom!* thundered through the alley. It was the neighborhood scourge, Bam-Bam Baxter, who is a wanna-be biker. Bam-Bam has a new motorcycle, a big one. He's riding it in the alley until he gets the nerve to take it onto the street.

"Rumors." Sheila's shoulders slumped. "Yeah, I know.

Hark told me." Hark Hibler is the editor of the Pecan Springs *Enterprise*. He makes it his job to keep up with the local gossip, although he does not, as a matter of principle, print most of it. He doesn't have to. By the time the newspaper comes out, everybody's already heard the news. "He says it's going around town that Dan and I were sleeping together behind Ruby's back—which of course is not true." She shook her head sadly. "But she's bound to have heard it."

"Well," I said, "you'll have to talk to her. Tell her it's not so."

She shuddered. "I'm hoping it will blow over. You'll talk to her about Dan's money?"

"I suppose," I said reluctantly. "What's the distribution? Lump sum? Over time?"

"She can decide." She reached into her uniform pocket and took out a card. "Here's Chad's number. Have her give him a call."

I tucked the card into my khakis pocket. A few years back, Ruby had won the lottery and invested a chunk of her winnings in the tearoom. She'd been thrilled, of course—but this was different. This was Colin's money. How would she feel about it? Would it hurt, or would it heal?

"What should I tell her about your part in this?" I asked.

The Pecan Springs garbage truck was rattling down the alley on its weekly scavenger hunt, and Sheila had to raise her voice over the racket. "Tell her as little as possible. The money's nice, but I'm afraid this is only going to make things harder."

"I agree," I said. "Poor Ruby. She's—"

The cell phone on my belt rang, and I reached for it. "China Bayles," I said crisply.

"Who is this?" a woman asked.

"China Bayles," I growled. We were off to a bad start. "Who is this?"

There was a short pause.

"Are you acquainted with a Miles Danforth?"

I frowned. "Who wants to know?"

"Are you related to Mr. Danforth?"

"He's my brother," I said, and gritted my teeth. "Half brother. Who's asking?"

Across the table, Sheila glanced at me, surprised. I hadn't told her about Miles. In the alley, on the other side of the hedge, the garbage truck jarred to a stop. Doors slammed. The garbage can clattered. The squirrel chattered, Miss Lula barked ecstatically, and Mr. Cowan began yelling. At the end of the alley, in preparation for another daring run, Bam-Bam revved up his motorcycle. The caller's next words were inaudible.

"I missed that," I said, pressing the phone hard against my ear. "Say again."

"My name is Sharon Hughes," the woman said, raising her voice and enunciating carefully. "I'm with the Austin Police Department. I'm sorry to tell you that your brother—"

A garbage can crashed. The truck began cranking up its loader.

"I can't hear!" I yelled into the phone. "What was that? What did you say?"

The can clanged, a guy yelled, and the truck loader stopped. In the sudden silence, one word was suddenly loud.

"—dead," she said.

# Chapter Six

If you will follow my counsell, deal not with Nightshade
in any case, and banish it from your gardens and the use
of it also, being a plant so furious and deadly.

*The Herbal*, 1598
John Gerard

The name *Solanum* was in use in old herbals long predat-
ing Linnaeus. Its derivation is uncertain, but Wendy
Zomlefer offers, "Presumably . . . derived from the Latin
'solamen' meaning 'quieting,' which alludes to the narcotic properties of certain plants; sometimes the quieting
effect is permanent." (*A Guide to Flowering Plant Families*,
The University of North Carolina Press, Chapel Hill,
1994)

Killerplants.com

"Dead!" I repeated, feeling suddenly icy cold.
"Dead?" I thought of McQuaid, who had driven off
to join Miles earlier that morning. "Was it an accident?" I
babbled frantically. "Was anyone with him? Is my husband
all right? Where did it—"

"I have no information about your husband," the woman
interrupted, her voice calm. "But yes, it was an accident,

apparently. Mr. Danforth was alone, as far as is known. Details will not be released until the investigation is completed. I'm sorry. I know this must be a shock."

I sucked in my breath. "Where did it happen? When?" Everything around me, everything *in* me, seemed to have stopped, frozen, every sound, every movement. Across the table, Sheila was watching, her eyes wide and fixed on me, her face suddenly pale in the bright sunshine.

"Mr. Danforth's body was found this morning on one of the lower levels of the parking garage adjacent to his office building in Austin. He appears to have been struck by a vehicle late last night." The woman cleared her throat. "I understand that his injuries were quite severe. It is likely that he died immediately." *If that's any consolation,* her tone said.

In the alley, the garbage truck clanked, shuddered, shifted, and drove on. Overhead, the leaves shivered in the wind. On the table, the sunlight shimmered in my glass of iced tea.

Sheila put out her hand. "McQuaid?" she whispered.

I shook my head and mouthed *no,* almost giddy with relief. It had happened last night. In the parking garage. McQuaid hadn't been with him when it happened. McQuaid was all right. McQuaid was—

I swallowed hard, frowning. "In the parking garage?"

"Yes, ma'am," the woman said. "Mr. Danforth seems to have left the elevator and was on his way to his automobile when the incident occurred. That level of the garage—the B level—is poorly lit. It seems likely that the driver didn't see him until it was too late."

*Incident.* My brother gets killed and it's an *incident.* I took a deep breath. "Witnesses?"

"None—at least, none that have come forward. It's being investigated as a hit-and-run."

A hit-and-run in a parking garage. I sat back in my chair, the name Miriam Spurgin banging around in my mind like a hard ball bouncing around an empty racquet court. Miriam Spurgin, the reporter whose death had been linked to my father's. Who died in a hit-and-run in a parking garage some sixteen years before.

"—body was identified by one of the partners of his firm," the woman was saying. "Your number was supplied by Mr. Danforth's secretary. She says he was a single father with a young daughter. Would you happen to know—"

Caitlin! "Where is she?" I asked sharply. "Have you spoken to her? Has she been told?"

"We haven't located her yet." The woman was only slightly apologetic. "Mr. Danforth's secretary believes that the girl may be visiting her aunt—her mother's sister, we understand, who lives in Austin. However, the aunt has recently moved and the secretary does not have that information. Would you know how to locate her?"

*Caitlin.* I swallowed hard. Dark-haired and pixie-ish, Caitlin was just ten, shy, withdrawn, and heart-wrenchingly vulnerable. Her young life had already been shadowed by tragedy—her mother's drowning, only a couple of years ago. Now she had to cope with the loss of her father.

I took a deep breath. "The aunt's name is Sellers. Marcia. Marcia Sellers. She just bought a house in South Austin. I can't tell you where."

I'd met Marcia once, when Miles and McQuaid and I dropped Caitlin off to spend the evening while we went out to dinner at a Mexican restaurant on South Lamar. She worked as a physical therapist, I understood, and was recently divorced, which was why she had moved. She was a very pretty woman, and from the brief interchange between her and Miles—the look on her face, the quick touch of his hand on hers—I'd gotten the distinct impression that there was something going on between them. If it worked out, I had thought, it would be an ideal situation for Caitlin. It wasn't going to work out now. Now, Miles was dead. Caitlin was an orphan.

"Thank you, Ms. Bayles," the woman said. "I'm sure we'll be able to find her." She became businesslike. "Mr. Danforth's body will be released after autopsy. His personal effects are available now at police headquarters, 715 East Eighth, in Austin. Will a family member be claiming them?"

"I . . . suppose I will," I said numbly. Personal effects. Car keys, house keys, billfold, credit cards. What was left of a life after the life was over.

"Good. Please bring a photo ID. There'll be an autopsy form to sign—just want you to be expecting it." Her voice took on a scripted sound as she moved to conclude the call. "And please accept my condolences for the loss of your brother, Ms. Bayles. I know how hard it is to lose a loved one."

"Thank you," I said. I hit the Off button and stared at the phone.

"Your brother?" Sheila asked, frowning. "I didn't know—"

"Neither did I, until a few months ago. Half brother, actually. My father's son, by a . . ." My voice trailed away.

Sheila regarded me. "A previous marriage?"

"An adulterous relationship," I said flatly. "My father and his secretary. It went on for decades."

"Ah," Sheila said. "I gathered from the little bit I heard that he was killed in an auto accident. Your brother, I mean."

"Hit-and-run. Last night, in his office parking garage. They didn't find him until this morning."

"I'm so sorry," Sheila said sympathetically. "Really sorry, China." She pushed back her empty plate, looking carefully at me. "I have to get back to the office. Will you be okay?"

Was I going to pieces? No. Was I okay? No again.

"Yes," I said, still numb. "I'll be okay. But I guess I need to excuse myself. There are some things I have to do."

"Of course." She got up and came around behind my

chair and hugged me. "This other thing—Ruby's money, I mean. If you want, I'll talk to her, China. You have your hands full."

"No, I'll tell her," I said, putting my cheek against Sheila's hand. It felt smooth and cool and smelled faintly of Jergens. "I'll tell her today. This afternoon. But right now, I need to call McQuaid."

"Yes, I know." She hugged me again, straightened, and reached for her cap. "Thanks for the lunch. Hang in there, China. I'll talk to you later."

When she was gone, I speed-dialed McQuaid's cell phone. "It's me," I said. He was probably still sitting in the parking lot at the brewery, waiting for Miles.

"Hey, you." His words were muffled, but his voice was affectionate. He swallowed and said, more clearly, "Wish you were here. Best damn fried onion in the state of Texas."

Fried onion? "Where are you?"

"In Shiner, at Friday's, sitting over a plate of Cajun wings and fried onion." He sounded satisfied. "Miles never showed. I got tired of waiting and decided to get some lunch. You haven't heard from him, have you?"

"I just got a call from the Austin police." I took a deep breath. "He's dead, McQuaid. Miles is dead."

"*Dead?* Did I hear that right? You said—"

"Hit-and-run, in the office parking garage. Probably last night. He emailed you from the office, didn't he? He must've been killed right afterward."

"Hit-and-run? Like—" He coughed, as if he'd choked on something. I could hear him gulping water.

"Yes," I said grimly. "Like Miriam Spurgin."

There was a moment's silence. When he spoke, his voice was gruff. "I'm sorry, babe. Really sorry. Miles was a good guy. I wish I'd had a chance to know him better."

I was swamped by a scalding wave of guilt and came up gasping. I had tried very hard to push Miles away, to make it plain that I didn't want him intruding, didn't want to be involved with him or with his quest. But maybe I'd been wrong. Maybe I should have been more sympathetic, tried harder to understand him, even encouraged him in his search for what happened to Dad. Surely I could have found a way to have some sort of relationship without getting in over my head. Couldn't I? Shouldn't I?

But it was too late for regretful thoughts like these. It would always be too late for Miles and me. Now, Caitlin was the one I had to think about, and the urgency yanked my stomach into a hard knot. I had to connect with my brother's daughter.

"His keys and billfold are at police headquarters," I said tightly. "I'm going to Austin to claim them. The autopsy will take a couple of days, but I can at least get started on the other stuff."

The other stuff. The things that come next, necessarily, after death. Locating Miles' will and contacting the executor, who was most likely somebody in his firm. Making arrangements for a funeral and burial—beside his wife, probably, wherever that was. Figuring out who needed to be contacted, who needed to know. Busywork, but maybe it would keep my mind busy, keep the guilt at bay. But first there was Caitlin.

"Caitlin is with her aunt," I said. "Her mother's sister. I'll find out where, and go. I need . . . I need to see her."

"Yes, you do," McQuaid said, urgently now. "And get Miles' keys, so we can check out his house. We ought to do that tonight, if at all possible."

I frowned. "We?"

"Yeah, sure. Your brother, my client. I want to see his notes. I want to have a look at that file of his mother's. He kept promising to show me what she'd put together, but he never did. I'm wondering whether there wasn't more there than he let on."

I pulled in my breath. "But you don't have to—" I was

going to say that he couldn't be expected to continue the investigation, when he cut in.

"But nothing, China." McQuaid's voice had taken on a hard, sharp edge. "That hit-and-run may not have been an accident."

I thought again of Miriam Spurgin, and felt suddenly cold. McQuaid was right. It could have been an intentional hit-and-run. Murder. Someone could have murdered my brother. My fingers tightened on the phone. "Right," I said. "You're right."

"That's my girl," McQuaid said, more gently. "Do the cops have a line on the vehicle yet?"

"I don't think so. And there weren't any witnesses." Of course, the police don't always need a witness. If the vehicle was damaged, especially if fragments of glass or paint were left behind—

"They're treating it as an accidental hit-and-run?"

"Yes. At least, according to the person who called me. I'll see what the investigating officer has to say." Accidental or not, hit-and-run is by definition a crime. The hit may be an accident, but fleeing the scene is a criminal act. Miles' death would be investigated as a vehicular homicide.

"Okay. But when you talk to the officer, don't let on that you think it might be more than an accident. If you do, they could seal the house and treat it as a crime scene. They might do that anyway, depending on what else they've got going right now."

Of course. If I—if *we* wanted to have a look at Miles' papers, we'd have to keep the police out of it. Which meant that I needed to get those keys quickly.

"The police report won't be available for a couple of days," McQuaid went on. "Ask them to fax it to us as soon as they have it." He hesitated. "Do you know any of the partners in Miles' firm?"

"Not personally," I said. "You don't think—"

"I don't know what I think, China. Just trying to cover the bases. Are you heading for Austin now?"

"As soon as I talk to Ruby," I said. "Colin left her a quarter of a million dollars, and I've been commissioned to give her the bad news."

"A quarter of a million—" He whistled between his teeth. "Good golly, Miss Molly. Where did Colin Fowler get that kind of money? And why is it bad news?"

"Insurance, hazardous-duty pay. He made her his beneficiary. And it's bad news because it will just make Ruby feel guilty." I paused. "What about you, McQuaid? Are you coming back to Pecan Springs? Shall I wait for you?"

"Hell, no." His voice lightened. I could almost see him grin. "I'm going out to that ranch to look for your dad's car."

"No!" I said. "I don't think you ought to do that by yourself!"

"It's got to be done," he said firmly. "Maybe somebody found out that Miles was looking into your father's death. All of a sudden, he's dangerous, and now he's dead. At this point, the car may be our best lead. Go to Austin, China, but leave your phone on. I'll call you as soon as I've got a fix on the situation."

I sighed. When McQuaid takes that tone, there's no point in trying to change his mind. "Be careful," I said.

"I'm always careful," he said jauntily.

*Yeah, sure,* I gritted, as I clicked off the phone. *That's how come you ended up with a bullet next to your spine.*

But I had to admit that McQuaid was right about the car. Miles had been searching for it, and now Miles was dead. He had been killed in the same way that Miriam Spurgin had been killed, all those years ago. A coincidence? I seriously doubted it.

But there wasn't any doubt about one thing.

I was on board now.
I was definitely on board.

RUBY has worn black every day since Colin died. Not full black, mind you, as in widow's weeds, just something black. Black pants or a black top or a scarf or a belt or shoes. This week it was black jewelry and today it was a half-dozen long strings of exotic black-and-silver beads and dangly earrings to match, with a white tunic that came down to her knees, over skinny white pants. She's gone back to frizzing her red hair, and with her dramatic Queen of the Nile makeup, she looked like Cleopatra, all dolled up for Mark Antony.

I took her elbow. "Can you break away for a minute, Ruby? I need to talk to you."

"Sure," she said, glancing around the nearly empty tearoom. "The lunch rush is finished, anyway. Would you believe? There were thirteen Friends of the Library."

"Enough for a coven," I said. "How about the Consulting Room?" That's our name for the supply closet under the stairs, which is just big enough for two people to have a knee-to-knee heart-to-heart.

She frowned. "Serious, huh?"

"Yeah," I said. "Serious."

She peered anxiously at my face. "Is everything okay?"

"Not exactly." I opened the door to the closet, switched on the light, and pushed a carton of toilet paper out of the way. The air smelled of the patchouli incense Ruby stores there. Patchouli is supposed to be calming, but I didn't feel very calm. Ruby sat down on a box of plastic bags. I sat down on a bin of Christmas decorations.

"Has something happened?" she asked worriedly, pulling her knees to her chin.

"Yes," I said. "Miles was killed last night. A hit-and-run in his office parking garage."

"Your brother?" she whispered. Her eyes opened wide. "Oh, China, no! Oh, I'm so sorry!" Ruby has never met Miles, but she's talked to him on the phone and listened to me bitch about him.

"Thank you," I said somberly. "Caitlin's at her aunt's, and I need to see her as soon as I can. And I have to get Miles' personal effects from the police and make sure that everything is okay at his house. I'd like to leave for Austin right away. Can you handle things here?"

"Of course." Her voice was heavy with sympathy. "Take as much time as you need, China—especially with Caitlin. What will happen with her—long-term, I mean? Have you thought of bringing her here to live with you?"

No, I hadn't. I lucked out with Brian. He's a wonderful kid and I feel blessed to be his mom, but the task of raising a teenage son still bewilders me. A daughter would be totally beyond my comprehension. The one time Caitlin and her father had come to our house together, for a backyard barbecue, she had clung to him as if she was afraid to let him out of her sight, which I could certainly understand. She had lost her mother, and her father was the one solid thing left in her life. Now, he was gone, too, and she was alone. She needed someone who understood children, somebody who could help her solve her problems, give her lots of focused attention. Thankfully, there was such a person in her life.

"I'm sure she'll want to live with her aunt Marcia," I said. "Her mother's sister. I've only met Marcia once, but Miles told me that she and Caitlin are close. She works with children. She's a physical therapist at St. David's."

"That's good," Ruby said, sounding relieved. "Good for Caitlin, I mean. You'd make a good mom, I'm sure, but you're already spread pretty thin."

"A good mom?" I muttered. "You've got to be kidding. I wouldn't know the first thing about mothering a young girl."

Ruby ignored that. "Take whatever time you need, China. We'll cover for you here. I owe you, you know. You helped me out when Colin was killed."

It was the lead-in I was looking for. "There's something else." I leaned forward. "It has to do with Colin."

"Colin?" Ruby asked sadly. Sheila might think of him as a rebel, a Lone Ranger who wasn't cut out for team play or long-term relationships. But for Ruby, he'd always be her Colin, the brave narcotics agent who died a hero, in the line of duty.

"Yes," I said. "Colin." In other circumstances, I might have lingered over this, led into it gradually, softened what was bound to be a shock. But I had Miles on my mind, and Caitlin. I was businesslike. "There's insurance, Ruby. And back pay and hazardous-duty pay. Colin named you his beneficiary."

"Oh, that." She sighed. "Yes, I know about that."

I blinked. "You mean, you knew and you didn't *tell* me?"

"Sure, I knew. But what's to tell?" She made a sad face. "It's nice to know that Colin had my best interests in mind, all the way to the end." Her eyes began to fill with tears. "It's just money, though. It can't bring him back."

*"Just money?"* I exclaimed. "You've got to be kidding!"

She frowned. "I don't see what you're making all the fuss about, China. Colin told me that he'd put my name on a little insurance policy he had. I didn't know about hazardous-duty pay, of course, because I didn't have any idea what he was really doing. But if there's some of that, it's okay, too. It's no big deal."

I reached out and took her hands. "Ruby," I said quietly, "it is a very big deal. You're due to get a quarter of a million dollars."

"A quarter—" Her eyes widened. Her face went so white that the freckles popped out in gingery splotches, as if they'd been dotted on by a freckle-marker. "A quarter of a—" She gulped. "You didn't say—"

I gripped her hands harder. "I did. I'll say it again." I emphasized every syllable. "Colin Fowler left you a quarter of a million dollars."

"But . . . but that's . . . that's impossible!" she cried frantically. "He couldn't have!" She burst into a storm of tears. "Not that much! I can't believe it."

"Believe it," I said. I took the card Sheila had given me out of my pocket. "You need to contact this man. His name is Chad, and he has all the details. Apparently, there are some options on the payout you'll need to consider."

"No! I won't!" she cried stormily. "I can't take the money! It would be like getting paid for Colin's death!"

"That's why people have life insurance, Ruby," I said. "It's so that somebody you love will be taken care of when you die."

"But Colin—"

"Colin knew what he was doing," I said. "He wanted you to have the money or he wouldn't have named you as his beneficiary. Anyway, you don't have to make any decisions right this minute. Call this guy and see what's involved. Then give yourself some time to think about it." I stood and bent to kiss her cheek. "Promise me you'll call him. Right away. Like this afternoon. Okay?"

She looked up at me, dazed. "But I have everything I need, China. What in the world would I do with that kind of money?"

"You could buy a new car so you wouldn't get stranded on the interstate, the way you did last week, when I had to go and pick you up. You could sock it away for Grace's college. You could put it into a trust for out-of-work astrologers and fortune tellers. You'll think of something."

At the mention of her baby granddaughter's name, Ruby's face brightened. "Of course! Colin was crazy about

Grace. He'd love the idea that his . . . his legacy helped her get her education."

"There you go," I said approvingly. "Think of this as something that Colin wanted to do for Grace." I glanced at my watch. "I need to get to Austin, Ruby. You're sure you can handle things without me?"

She jumped up and flung her arms around me. "Oh, yes, of course we can. Gosh, China, I'd forgotten all about your brother. Oh, I'm so sorry! If there's anything I can do, you'll let me know, won't you?"

"I'll let you know," I said.

# Chapter Seven

### McQuaid: The Car

Frowning, McQuaid looks again at the map and directions Miles emailed to him. The car is supposed to be in a barn on the Two-Bar Ranch, off SR 531 between Shiner and Hallettsville. There's a name—Ellie Hanson—but no phone number, just a few sentences: *Don't know if this is what we're after. Could be the wrong place. But she's expecting us. Details when I see you tomorrow.*

There'd be no details now, or ever. Whatever Miles knew had died with him. But even if Miles had sent a phone number, McQuaid wouldn't have called ahead. He'd rather walk in on Ellie Hanson, whoever she is. Catch her by surprise.

At the thought of Miles, McQuaid's stomach muscles tighten. As he pulls out of the parking lot and onto 90A, he picks up his cell phone and hits Jim Hawk's number. When Hawk answers, he said, "McQuaid here, Hawk. China just called to tell me that Miles Danforth was killed last night." Hawk hasn't met Miles, but he knows that he's Bob Bayles' son, and that he's the client who's funding this investigation. "In his office parking garage," McQuaid adds tersely. "Hit-and-run."

Surprised, Hawk grunts. "Hit-and-run. Well, goddamn. Familiar, isn't it?" Hawk's voice is muffled, and McQuaid pictures him, sitting back, chewing on his cigar. He's five foot six, with a pendulous belly, and he's headed to a coronary in the next few years. But he likes his food, his booze, and his cigars, and nobody's going to change him. He's a cop's cop, good to have at your back if there's trouble, which there almost always was, back in the days the two of them had worked together.

"Familiar, yeah," McQuaid says. "I haven't spoken to the police, but it sure sounds like a replay of Spurgin. Must've happened right after he emailed me the map. I'm headed out to the ranch now to check out the car. You turn up anything on the stories Spurgin and Vine were working on when they died?"

"As a matter of fact, I did," Hawk says. McQuaid hears his chair creak, as if he's reaching for a file. "Remember that G. W. Stone Engineering vice president who shot himself back in the mid-eighties? Madison, his name was. Keith Madison."

"Yeah," McQuaid says, remembering that China had mentioned the name the night before. "What about him?"

"He was being investigated by the Feds on bribery and price-fixing. About to be indicted, but his death put the QT to that."

"To the company's relief, I'm sure," McQuaid says. "What's the connection?"

"Both Spurgin and Vine were looking into Madison's death. At the time, there was a question about whether it was suicide or something else. Some funny business about the gun. The shooting was finally ruled a suicide, but that didn't resolve all the questions."

"Stone and Bayles did the legal work for Stone Engineering," McQuaid offers. "Ted Stone was G. W. Stone's brother. The families socialized, according to China. She remembers going with her parents out to Ted Stone's ranch a time or two when G.W. was there. She describes him as one of Houston's slicker sorts."

"That squares with what I know about him," Hawk says. "Didn't he die a year or so ago? Cancer of the stomach, I think. Maybe it was the meanness in him, leaching into his gut."

McQuaid chuckles wryly.

"So there's a link," Hawk muses, sounding interested. "Stone, Bayles, Spurgin, and Vine."

"And Madison," McQuaid adds. *Who may or may not have been a suicide.* He tries to remember the details of the case, but can't pull them up.

"And Madison," Hawk agrees. "Yeah. Madison. Maybe I'll dig in that direction. What'ya think, *hombre*?"

"Sounds good," McQuaid agrees. A highway sign announces SR 531, and he slows and hangs a right onto a narrow two-lane. "China's getting Danforth's keys this afternoon. The police appear to be treating this as an accident, so I'm hoping they haven't sealed the house. I plan to get in there this evening and see if I can find any notes he might have made on this case. His mother's stuff, too. It's occurred to me that he might not have been straight with me on everything." McQuaid remembers something he's been meaning to ask. "I didn't make a copy of the Bayles accident report. Can you do that, and fax it to me?" He rattles off the fax number at his office.

"It'll be tomorrow." Hawk pauses, and McQuaid can hear him chewing on his cigar. "You armed? You don't know what you're getting into at that ranch. Could be rattlesnakes." He chuckles. "Could be anything."

"Could be anything," McQuaid agrees. "I'll be okay. Don't worry."

What Hawk says next might be "Watch your back, buddy," but the signal drops. Reception is spotty in rural areas. There are places in Texas where you can drive for a couple of hundred miles without being able to use your cell phone.

Before long, McQuaid makes a left on 77A, and then a

right on a county road, heading south. A few hundred yards down the road, a dusty sign pops up on the left, the painted words barely legible against weathered boards, Two-Bar Ranch. He swings the pickup off the road across a cattle guard, and onto a narrow caliche lane that cuts through a thicket of mesquite, yucca, and prickly pear. It's open range here, and once clear of the brush, he encounters a pair of longhorns standing smack in the middle of the road, tails swinging to sweep off the flies. He taps his horn lightly to move them along and they sashay off the road and into the mesquite, watching without animosity as he drives on, bouncing from one pothole to another.

The caliche lane, escorted by a parade of leaning utility poles, cuts through a grassy pasture and across a willow-fringed dry stream bed, then slants up the side of a hill and tops it, opening a view of a scrubby flat and a meander of cottonwoods along what is probably a creek. Mc-Quaid follows the road down the rocky hill and across another cattle guard to a cluster of weathered buildings. He can see a low wood-frame ranch house with an apron of straggly grass, a lean-to barn with a rusted metal roof, a couple of corrals, a half-dozen small outbuildings, and a long greenhouse.

The greenhouse looks new. The door is standing open and an old red Ford pickup is parked in front, its bed filled with empty nursery flats and stacks of black plastic five-gallon plant pots. A gray tractor is parked on the other side of the greenhouse, next to a five-acre field, plowed and lined with neat rows of young green plants. McQuaid is no gardening expert—that's China's department—but they look to him like tomatoes. There's a fair amount of truck farming in the area, although irrigation water isn't plentiful. Maybe the grower is utilizing the creek.

McQuaid pulls up beside the Ford. He unlocks the glove compartment, finds his digital camera, and drops it into his shirt pocket. Thinking of Hawk's comment, he takes out the

Smith & Wesson Model 19, slips the gun into his ankle holster, and fastens the Velcro safety strap. It's comfortable, as
these things go, and it's saved his bacon a time or two,
when he was with the Houston P.D. That done, he hits the
horn a couple of times to say howdy. When a figure appears in the greenhouse door, he climbs out of the truck
and steps forward, hands loose at his sides.

It's a woman, wearing a plaid cotton shirt open at the
throat and sleeves rolled to the elbows, and trim jeans
tucked into leather work boots. She's slight but wiry and
her face is lined and deeply tanned. Her hair—graying,
from what little of it he can see—is skinned back under a
blue cotton bandanna tied around her head. She might be
fifty, she might be seventy, McQuaid thinks. There's no
way to tell.

He lifts a hand. "Ellie Hanson?"

As if on command, a small gray and white dog with perky
ears races full tilt around the corner of the greenhouse and
skids to a stop at the woman's feet, putting himself between
his mistress and the strange man. She says "Sit, Happy," and
the dog settles his haunches on the ground. She tilts her
head, regarding McQuaid with a slight frown.

"Miles?" Her voice is low and throaty. "Miles Danforth?" The dog's ears prick forward.

"No, ma'am. My name is Mike McQuaid." He's close
enough to put out his hand and the woman grasps it. Her
grip is firm, cool, and businesslike.

She looks past him at his empty truck. "I was expectin'
two o' you boys," she says, in a soft South Texas drawl.
"Where's Miles?" Not Mr. Danforth, but Miles. And yet
she hadn't known what he looked like.

Until this minute, McQuaid hasn't been sure how he was
going to play this, how much he was going to say about what
had happened. But looking at the woman's open face, her
clear blue eyes, he makes up his mind.

"He asked me to meet him in Shiner," he says. "We

were going to drive here together. But he was late, and after a while, I got a call saying he wouldn't be coming."

She gives a short laugh. "Got himself lost, did he? Well, it figgers." She tosses her head and snorts something that sounds like "city boy."

"No, ma'am," McQuaid says quietly, "he didn't get lost. Somebody killed him."

She stares, arrested by the words. Her eyes go wide. "Killed him?" she repeats in a disbelieving whisper. "*Killed* him? That what you said?"

"Yes, ma'am. Late last night in the parking garage of his office building. Hit-and-run."

"Aw, hell," she says sorrowfully. She lets out her breath in a noisy *whoosh*. The dog looks inquiringly up at her and she drops her hand to finger his ears. "Well, accidents happen."

"It's not clear that this was an accident," McQuaid says. He lets her think about this for a minute. After a silence, he goes on. "Miles was looking for a wrecked car. His father's car. He thought it might be stored in a barn here, and asked me to come along to help him check it out. Did he talk to you about it?"

She slices an unreadable glance at him. "You got any identification? Something that says who you are?"

He takes out his wallet and hands her his driver's license. Taking a chance, he says, "My wife, China Bayles, is Miles Danforth's sister. Half sister, actually. Robert Bayles, the man who was killed in the car, was their father."

"Well, then," she says in a different voice, as if that answers a question. She hands back his license. "Did Miles tell you anything about the car? How it got here, anything like that?"

"No. He said he was going to fill in the details when we met in Shiner."

She sighs. "This'll take a while, Mr. McQuaid. Might go some better over a cup of coffee."

"Mike," he says, and slips into her easy way of talking. "Please call me Mike. Thanks, Miz Hanson. I sure could use some coffee."

"Ellie," she says. "This way. Come on, Happy." She leads, quick-stepping, the dog trotting briskly beside her.

The ranch house kitchen is bright and cheerful but spectacularly untidy, with garden paraphernalia, clothing, tools, books, magazines, papers, and cats—yellow cats, black cats, tabby cats—scattered everywhere. One muddy boot lies in the middle of the floor, a tangle of twine is draped across a chair back, and a plastic tray of young green plants in peat pots sits on the table, with a pair of worn leather gloves, a box of fish emulsion fertilizer, and a plate with the remains of breakfast eggs. A white kitten is asleep beside the plate, egg yolk smeared on one small paw, egg yolk clotted in its whiskers.

Happy follows them into the kitchen, trots to a folded blanket in the corner, and settles himself nose to tail, bright eyes watching McQuaid. Another dog, a Lab mix, large, black, and shaggy, shambles through the door from a hall-way and drops down in the middle of the floor, heaving a huge sigh, closing his eyes.

"That's Peppy," Ellie says, nodding to the Lab. "He's about a hundred and two. Sleeps all the time." She lifts the kitten off the table, puts the plate in the sink, and pours two mugs of coffee out of the coffeemaker. She pours clumsily, slopping it on the counter, and catches him watching. "Bunged up my right wrist a couple of days ago," she says. "I've been using arnica, and it's getting better." She lifts her eyebrow. "How do you like it?"

"Black," McQuaid replies. He sits in a chair that has a flannel shirt draped over the back. "Tomatoes?" he asks, gesturing to the tray of green plants.

"Tomatillos. I grow 'em for market." Left-handed, she puts his mug on the table in front of him.

"No kidding," McQuaid says, interested. "That field out there? It's tomatillos?"

She nods. "I've been growin' 'em for five, six years now. You a tomatillo fan?"

"I use them in my salsa verde, with chiles." He grins. "I make good salsa. Melts teeth."

"The best kind," she says approvingly. She goes to a shelf and picks out a jar filled with something green. "Here. Take this home with you. Put it on your enchiladas, or mix it into guacamole. But watch it. It'll toast your tonsils."

"The hotter the better," McQuaid says. A gray cat of immense proportions comes through the door, skirts the Lab, and jumps in his lap and begins to knead his thigh, purring amiably.

"That's Blitzen," Ellie says. "Push him off if he gets too rowdy with those claws." She looks around, wrinkling her nose at the cats scattered here and there, under the table, on the counter, the windowsill, the top of the fridge. "Too many cats. But they're family. All I've got—now." She pulls off the bandanna around her head, shaking her hair loose. "Hit-and-run," she mutters. "Hell's bells."

McQuaid nudges Blitzen onto the floor, noticing that Ellie's hair is mostly gray and revising his estimate of her age upward. She's closer to seventy than fifty, he guesses, although the flesh on her bare arms is firm and taut and her face, while weathered, is youthful.

"You and Miles Danforth are . . . were family?" he asks.

"My cousin's son." She takes a stack of newspapers off the chair, puts them on top of the microwave, and sits down, pushing the tray of tomatillo plants to one side.

"Laura Danforth was your cousin?" *There,* he thinks. *That's the connection. That's why the car is here—if it is.* "I guess you know she died, earlier this year."

She nods. "That's how come I heard from Miles." She picks up the white kitten and puts it on the floor. "Laura and I were close once, when we were growing up, but after that—" She shrugs. "She went her way, I went mine. We lost touch for a long while. Twenty years, maybe."

"She got in touch again when she needed a place to stash the car," he guesses.

"Right you are." Ellie clears a space and puts her elbows on the table. Her hands, McQuaid notices, are rough and callused, her nails clipped short. Working hands. "Laura's mother was my mother's sister, y'see. Laura spent summers here when she was a kid, back when the place was a real ranch. After high school, I moved to San Antonio and took a job in a bank. Laura hung around here for a year or so. She got married and—"

"Married?" McQuaid interrupts quickly.

"Yeah. One of those young love things. Lasted about as long as it takes to tell it. The guy got in trouble with the law and went to prison. Laura's mother made her divorce him." She sips her coffee, holding her mug with her left hand.

McQuaid is thinking. Ex-husbands sometimes come back and cause trouble. "Do you know the man's name?"

Ellie laughs reminiscently. "Sure. Danforth. Danny Danforth. God, he was a good-lookin' kid. He worked here at the ranch when Laura and I were teenagers. Both of us had a crush on him. Don't know why she kept his name, but she did."

"Is he still in prison?"

"Nah. In fact, he owns a garage over in Shiner. Why?"

"Just curious."

She nods, puts down her cup, and massages her wrist. "Anyway, Laura was living in Houston, had this really good job in a law firm. We didn't hear much from her. Then, years later, she calls, wanting a place to put a car. Daddy was amazed when she showed up with it on a flatbed truck. We could never figure out why she wanted to keep the old wreck."

"She didn't say?"

"Just that she had her reasons. Laura was like that. When she made up her mind to something, there was no arguing with her. Daddy didn't care—said he wasn't using that end of the barn for anything."

"Your father is no longer alive?"

Ellie shakes her head. "He quit ranching after Mama died. Died himself a few years later. I shut this place down and figured I'd eventually sell it. Another cousin, Mack, has a ranch just down the road. He's been hot to get his hands on this land for quite a while. Wants to build a dam downstream and create a fishing lake, so the guys who come to hunt with him will have something to do out of season. But I retired early from the bank and decided to move back. Every now and then, Mack sends his guy Sonny over to muscle me around a little, thinking I'll sell." She cocks her head to one side. "But hey. I'm tough. I don't give in to that kind of pressure."

"It's pretty country," McQuaid says. "I can understand why you'd want to hold on to the place."

"Yeah." She nods at the tray of tomatillo plants. "Thought I'd do a little growing to keep me busy, give me something to do." She chuckles mischievously, her eyes bright. "Considered growin' pot, but reckoned that was too dangerous. Don't aim to spend my golden years in jail. That'd make Mack just too happy, wouldn't it? Thought of tomatoes, too, but tomatillos seemed like a better bet. They don't need as much water as tomatoes, and they're easier to harvest. Keep better, too. These are a purple variety. Some folks string 'em like garlic."

"Handle the growing by yourself, do you?"

"A lot of it. José Ramos lives down the road. He and his brother help out with the planting and harvest. I sell most of the crop to a couple of markets in San Antonio. All organic, of course," she adds. "More work, but I get a better price. Market's good, and I've thought of expanding the operation, but don't hardly see the point. I'm mostly doing it to keep busy." She pokes at the plant tray. "Although I like it. In my book, plants beat people any day of the week."

He drinks his coffee. "The car," he says, bringing them back to the reason he's come. "When did Laura Danforth bring it here?"

Ellie screws up her face, thinking. "It was before Daddy went into the nursing home. Call it, oh, eleven years ago, maybe."

*Eleven. So she'd kept it somewhere else first. Miles had mentioned once that he thought it might be in Victoria.*

As if she had read his mind, Ellie adds, "She said she'd been keeping it in a garage. Somewhere over around Victoria, maybe. There was a problem with the owner—he wanted the space for his boat or something like that—and she asked if she could move it here." She shakes her head as if mystified. "An old wreck like that. Go figure."

"What did she say about it?"

"Not much, at least, not then. Laura was like that, y'see. Closemouthed as they come. Played 'em real close to the vest." She chuckles reminiscently. "Perverse, too—she'd do the opposite of what you expected, every time."

McQuaid thinks of what China has told him about Laura Danforth. "She was a take-charge kind of person, from what I'm told."

"You bet. Always managing this, organizing that, manipulating something else. Daddy used to say she should've been in politics." Ellie chuckles dryly. "But she did all right for herself anyway. She had help landing that job of hers—wouldn't have got it if it wasn't for Mack. But what the hell. Once she had it, she made herself indispensable."

"So it seems," McQuaid says, thinking of what China has said about Laura Danforth. "Did you know Robert Bayles?"

"Never met him. She told me about him, though. Finally." She picks up her coffee mug and her eyes meet his.

"Like what? What did she tell you?"

Ellie studies him as if she is trying to make up her mind how much to say. "That he was dead. That it was his wrecked car out there in the barn." She pauses and seems to make up her mind. "That she had a son by him. Miles. Of course, the boy was already grown by that time."

"When did she tell you this?"

"After Daddy died." She hesitates. "Y'know, I always wondered why Laura didn't get married again, after Danny. She was smart and pretty. Smarter than pretty, maybe, but both. Come to find out, her boy's daddy was already married. I reckon she didn't want anybody else." She shrugs. "Then he got killed, and that was that."

"Did you ever meet Miles?"

She shakes her head. "Laura and I, we weren't much for fam'ly. We were only off and on in touch after Daddy died. She had a couple of bouts with cancer, even a stroke. By the time I moved back here, she was pretty sick." She grins ruefully. "I'm not any great shakes around sick folks. Anyway, we'd never been what you'd call close. In fact, I'm not sure her son even knew I existed until just before Laura died. He was going through some of her papers and found my name and address. He called to tell me she was dying. I saw my chance, and brought up that old car."

*Just before Laura died?* "And when was that?" Mc-Quaid asks in a conversational tone. "When he first got in touch with you, I mean."

"Oh, January, I guess. I was glad to hear from him, because José was buggin' me about that old Caddy. He was hoping to get it for parts. The fire didn't damage the engine too bad." The white kitten is clawing its way up her pant leg. She unlatches it and puts it on the floor. "I figured if Miles didn't want the old thing, he might just give it to José."

*January. That was before Miles got in touch with China, pretending that he had no idea where the car was.*

Somehow, McQuaid is not surprised. For some time, his gut has been telling him that Miles knew more about this situation than he was letting on. But it's a puzzle. Why would he go to the trouble and expense of hiring a private investigator, and yet withhold a piece of vital information, like the location of the car he's asked the investigator to search for? What else had he known? Which led to another, even more important question: Was he killed because of what he knew?

"So what did Miles say when you asked him about getting rid of the car?"

"Said he'd just as soon me hang on to it, if it wasn't in the way. Said he'd come down and have a look some time. So when he called, I was sorta expecting it." She pauses. "I didn't want to push him, you know? I'm sure he had his hands full. I did, after Daddy died. I still don't have Daddy's stuff all sorted out."

"When did Miles call you?"

"Yesterday. Said he wanted to come down and bring a friend." She regards McQuaid thoughtfully, her head on one side. "Guess that's you, huh?"

"That's me." He finishes his coffee. "Okay if we take a look at it now?"

"Sure." She shakes her head. "Hit-and-run," she mutters. "Any idea what'll happen to Miles' girl? He told me her name, but I can't remember. She's an orphan now, I reckon. He told me he lost his wife a while back."

An image of Miles' daughter flashes through Mc-Quaid's mind and he's jolted by a sudden compassion. The young girl he had met was sad and wraithlike, still lost in the fog of her mother's death—how would she handle this?

"Her name is Caitlin," he says. "China's going to see her this afternoon. She's staying with another aunt, I understand—her mother's sister."

"Well, at least she's got somebody." Ellie pushes her chair back. "Two aunts and an uncle. She's not all alone in the world." She reaches for a flashlight on top of a stack of folded brown paper bags, then takes a large plastic bag of something that looks like table scraps, cabbage leaves, and potato peelings out of the refrigerator. "Time for us to git along, Mike. The girls are waitin'."

McQuaid stands up. "The girls?"

She chuckles. "You'll see." To the dogs, she says, "Happy and Peppy, you stay here. The girls don't need you to help 'em clean up the scraps." On the way out the door, she says to McQuaid, "Watch where you put your feet. Cats let out a helluva squall when you step on 'em."

The narrow lean-to pole barn, some forty feet long and roofed with corrugated metal, is built against a windbreak of juniper trees on the north and is open to the weather on the south. There's a pigpen, half sheltered under the roof, half out in the open, home to a pair of substantial pink pigs, lounging contentedly in the mud. When they see Ellie coming toward them, they scramble to their feet and trot to the fence, grunting and chortling.

"Primrose and Parsnip," Ellie says, emptying the bag of scraps into a pan in front of the pigs. The larger one shoulders the smaller aside. "Bought 'em as feeder pigs two years ago and got to likin' 'em. Real personalities, I'll tell you. Primrose here is a porker prima donna, always has to have her feet in the feed trough first, flops herself in the deepest mud puddle. Parsnip, though, you gotta watch her. She's sneaky. She waits until Primrose turns her back, then she makes her move."

McQuaid regards the pigs. The smaller has circled around to the other side of the trough and is helping herself with gusto. "That's a whole lot of bacon on the hoof," he says admiringly.

"No way," Ellie says emphatically. "By the time they were ready to head for the meat locker, I'd changed my mind. Didn't figger I needed hams bad enough to kill for 'em. Anyway, they're great watch pigs. Somebody fools around here after dark, they set up a racket." There's a water hose hanging from a hook on a pole, and she takes it down and squirts the pigs, who grunt ecstatically. "Let that be a lesson to you, Mike. Don't name an animal you expect to see swimming in a plate of grits and red-eye gravy." She turns off the hose.

He laughs and follows her down the length of the barn. Five or six red hens and a black rooster with formidable spurs fly noisily down from the rafters, and Ellie shoos them out of the way. At the far end of the barn, she steps through a narrow door in a wooden partition. It's dusky behind the wall and she switches on the flashlight. Dust motes swim through the shaft of light. Somewhere in the darkness above, there is a startled coo and a rustle of wings.

"There it is," she says, gesturing. "Just the same as when Laura left it here. Like I said, José would be glad to get it for parts. And I'd be glad to get it out of here."

The vehicle is covered with a dusty black tarp, held taut with nylon cord. With some effort, McQuaid unfastens the cord, pulls off the tarp, and steps back.

The car, or what's left of it, is definitely a Cadillac. The wire wheel covers still display the Fleetwood insignia—it's a Brougham, he thinks, a four-door sedan that once sported luxurious leather upholstery and dual front seats. The blue finish is visible in areas untouched by the fire—the trunk, the hood. The darker blue vinyl roof is flattened as well as charred—crunched down to the seat-top in the rear—and McQuaid remembers China telling him that the car flipped a time or two before it got to the bottom of the embankment, where it burst into flames. Most of the interior is burned out, the car's squared-off front end is smashed, the headlights broken, the front bumper twisted up. The windshields, front and rear, are shattered, ditto the windows. The two front doors, driver's side and passenger side, look as if they'd been wrenched open, probably in an effort to extract the driver, McQuaid guesses. He hopes to hell that China's father was killed by the impact. He shudders at the thought of the alternative.

Ellie hands him the flashlight and he walks around the car. Hearing squeaks and scratching, he gets down on his knees and shines the flashlight underneath.

"Rats," Ellie says. "Daddy told Laura he could keep this old wreck out of the rain, but he couldn't guarantee it against the rats and dirt daubers. She said she didn't care about critters, she mostly wanted to be sure it stayed dry and out of sight. That's why she brought the tarp to put over it. We get a good hard rain, roof leaks like a sieve."

"Did she say anything else about the car?" McQuaid asks, getting to his feet. "Mention anything that interested her specifically—or was she just sentimental about it?"

"Laura, sentimental?" Ellie scoffs. "That girl was the least sentimental person on God's green earth. Hell, no, it wasn't sentiment. She said the car had a story to tell, that's why she was keeping it."

"Did she tell you what the story was?"

"Nope."

*No, of course not. That would be too easy.* He shines the flashlight on the left-hand side of the cowl and sees the VIN number, stamped on a metal tag. He rubs off the grime with his finger and studies it for a minute. Then he takes out his notebook and copies the string of numbers, seventeen of them, onto a clean page.

Ellie is frowning. "Although, come to think of it—" She stops.

McQuaid puts his notebook back in his pocket. "Come to think of what?"

She gives him an appraising look. "Now that you mention it, there were some papers somewhere in Daddy's stuff. Laura said if there was ever any question about the car, the papers should take care of it. Maybe the title? Registration?"

Or something else. Something more pertinent to the issue of Robert Bayles' death. McQuaid feels a prickle of hope, which promptly dies. Surely this wouldn't be that easy. Still—

"Suppose you can find the papers?" he asks.

"Suppose I can try," she says doubtfully. "Daddy had a ton of junk. It's all upstairs in his bedroom. Like I said, I haven't been through it all. Never saw the need."

McQuaid prowls around the car again, shining the flashlight over it. "I've kept you from your work long enough," he says at last. He takes the digital camera out of his shirt pocket. "I'd like to get some photos before I head back home. Any objections?"

Ellie shrugs. "Have at it." She looks at him curiously. "Got an idea what you're lookin' for?"

"Not really," McQuaid says. It's the truth. "Maybe I'll know it when I see it." He shakes his head. "And maybe not."

What he's looking for is any clue to what caused China's father to lose control of the car. He's looking for evidence that Robert Bayles' death might not have been an accident.

But when he leaves, he still hasn't found it.

# Chapter Eight

Devil's apple, Angel's Trumpet, thorn apple, and Jimson weed are among the common names given to various species of *Datura*. This is an hallucinogenic, highly toxic, and potentially fatal plant that grows across North America, both in the wild and in gardens. This herb has a long history of medicinal and ritual uses in many cultures around the world, and many genera, including *Brugmansia*, are highly decorative. Most people do not suspect that the beautiful trumpet-flowering plant they have just brought home from the nursery represents a serious threat of poisoning to children who might suck the sweet-smelling nectar from the blossoms, animals that might eat the berries, and teenagers who might be inclined to smoke the leaves.

I used to like driving from Pecan Springs to Austin, but not anymore. There was a time when the trip took thirty-five minutes at the outside, but that was before I-35 became clogged with cars all the way south to Buda. The state is building a toll road that will bypass Austin to the east, from Georgetown south to I-10, near Seguin. That should handle the through traffic, and leave I-35 to the local commuters. But God only knows when it'll be finished. Meanwhile, the drive takes more than an hour, and that's on a good day.

Today was moderately good—only one minor slow-down, near the Ben White exit—and my Toyota and I made decent time. The blue sky was laced with white clouds, graying to the northwest and heralding the spring storm front that was forecast to sweep down from the Panhandle later in the afternoon. There used to be wide green fields on both sides of the highway all the way into Austin, filled with herds of grazing cattle and flocks of sheep and islands of live oak—a pleasant pastoral panorama. Now, there are too many urban tumbleweeds, those plastic bags and newspapers and other human debris that get caught up on the fences, and when I let my attention stray from the road, I see fields filled with flocks of shopping malls and herds of apartment complexes, with exclusive gated communities climbing the hills a safe distance above the commercial clutter. City sprawl, charged with wild enthusiasm and raw energy, lapping across the Hill Country in ugly waves of asphalt and neon and Wal-Marts and Bed, Bath, and Beyonds.

Today, I was trying not to notice anything. I was trying not to think, too, or rather, trying to think about absolutely nothing. But of course that didn't work. I thought about Miles, about what had happened, and why. About McQuaid, and the car. About what lay ahead, and what lay in the past. And about Caitlin. Mostly, I guess, I thought about Caitlin.

There was a slowdown at Riverside Drive and another at First, holding up the traffic on the bridge. I got off the freeway at the next exit, headed west for a couple of blocks, then made a right and doubled back east on Eighth Street to police headquarters, a commanding concrete fortress rising three or four floors above the street. Inside, there was the usual hurly-burly of a large city police station. I explained my errand and was directed down the hall and up the stairs to the Custody Officer, for whom I produced my identification and filled out the form requesting my brother's personal effects. The officer, a slender, attractive black woman, disappeared with the paperwork and reappeared ten minutes later, handing over a manila envelope and a typed list.

"Your brother's clothing is being held pending forensic testing," she said briskly, and I nodded.

In a hit-and-run, there's always the possibility of microscopic paint residue on the victim's clothing. The forensic lab can search its findings against an automotive paint library and the Paint Data Query, a comprehensive database that identifies the chemical makeup of various layers of vehicle paint. With luck, the search might turn up the make and model. If an actual suspect vehicle was identified, the paint would be compared both chemically and microscopically to what was found on Miles' clothing. If the case went to trial, the clothes would be introduced into evidence.

I glanced through the envelope to make sure that everything on the list was indeed inside. Then I signed the form, and signed a request for copies of the death certificate (when it was issued, which could take a while) and the accident report (ditto). I also signed a consent form for the autopsy—a formality, since the Travis County Medical Examiner was going to order an autopsy with or without my consent. I did this with an effort at detachment, as if I were doing it for a client, but awareness hovered like a grim shadow in the back of my mind. Miles Danforth was no client. He was my brother, and he was dead.

When the paperwork was taken care of, I asked to see Charlene Wilkins, the investigating officer—who wasn't available just now. As a defense attorney, I'd had a naturally adversarial relationship with the police. I'd never wasted much time waiting around for them, and I certainly didn't expect them to return my calls. These were not habits I could shake, so I left my name and my cell phone number without any expectation of hearing from Officer Wilkins. I walked out, carrying what had been on my brother's person when his life was ended.

Back in my car, I surveyed the lot. Miles' billfold first: driver's license, Bar Association card, a half-dozen membership cards, a fistful of plastic credit cards, and seventeen dollars—three fives and two ones. A jingly handful of coins. A gold Rolex, very nice. A corner torn from an envelope with four words jotted on it: *bread, milk, lunchmeat,* and *grape Kool-Aid,* the last item written in a child's hand. I held it in my fingers for a moment, thinking that there is nothing like a grocery list to remind us how human we are.

The next three items told me that Officer Wilkins was either sloppy or was treating this as an accident, probably the latter. If there'd been any suspicion that the hit-and-run was intentional, she would have held on to them. Miles' cell phone. A clutch of keys, among which was a car key, reminding me that his car—a black BMW, if I remembered correctly—was presumably waiting in the parking garage. A thin black book full of telephone numbers, including mine, with a few business cards stuck in the back—Miles apparently belonged to the pre-PDA generation, maybe because he had a secretary to keep track of clients and calendars. I should probably go to the office and see her. That could wait, though. Before I did another thing, wasted another moment, I needed to see Caitlin, although what I was going to say to her, I hadn't a clue.

What under the sun can you say to a child who is both motherless and fatherless? What possible comfort could there be?


IF I'd been able to talk to Officer Wilkins, I might have gotten Marcia Sellers' address from her. As it was, I located Caitlin's aunt by the simple expedient of calling Information and learning that there was only one listing for an M. Sellers on the south side of the river. I punched in the number and heard a woman's husky voice, low and full of tears. Yes, she was Miles Danforth's sister-in-law. Yes, Caitlin

was there. Yes, the police had been there already, and
Caitlin knew what had happened. Her voice was urgent
when she said, "Caitlin and I want to see you, China. Come
right away, please."

The address was on Mission Ridge Trail, a short street
of smaller, older homes in shady yards on the south side of
the Colorado River. Travis Heights, an older neighborhood
that lies west of I-35, between the river on the north and
Oltorf Street on the south. Most of the homes were built
just before the First World War, after the Congress Avenue
Bridge and the streetcar line spanned the river and opened
up the rolling countryside for development. One of my favorite herb shops, the Herb Bar, is located just off South
Congress, and the surrounding area is a hip community of
boutiques and cafes. Travis Heights is the address of choice
for young professionals who want a quiet neighborhood
without a long commute.

At the number Marcia Sellers gave me, I found a
comfortable-looking two-story white frame house with
huge live oak trees in the front and a large backyard visible
from the street. The yard next door was full of kiddie toys,
and down the street I saw a boy on a bike. It looked like the
kind of neighborhood in which a shy young girl could find
herself at home, perhaps more easily than in the affluent Cat
Mountain neighborhood where she lived with her father—
a social pressure cooker where kids are pushed into growing up too fast.

As I stepped up onto the porch, I noticed a large plant pot
sitting in a shady corner. It held a flowering shrub decorated
with dramatic trumpet-shaped orange flowers, heavy and
pendulous. I breathed in the light, lemony scent, thinking
that plants don't come any more beautiful than this Angel's
Trumpet. But the plant itself is hardly angelic. This is *Brugmansia,* formerly called *Datura,* a member of the Deadly
Nightshade family that contains hallucinogenic and potentially fatal tropane alkaloids. Devil's apple, its relative is

sometimes called, and with good reason. I frowned, wondering if the owner of this plant—presumably Marcia Sellers—knew about its toxicity. The neighborhood was full of kids.

Marcia answered my knock so fast that I knew she must've been waiting at the door. She was a woman of striking beauty, her fair hair swept back from a strong face with a broad forehead and high cheekbones. She was slender, with a trim figure, but she had lost weight since I had seen her a few months before. Her designer jeans were no longer such a neat fit and her T-shirt hung loosely on her. There were dark circles under her eyes, her face was swollen from crying, and her nose was running.

"I'm so glad you've come, China," she said in a low voice. "I called Miles' office for your number, but his secretary was so upset that she had to go home for the day, and nobody else could find it." She blew her nose into a tissue. "It's awful for Caitlin. Awful for both of us. Right now, I don't know how we'll make it—this, on top of everything else."

On top of everything else. Her divorce, probably. I remembered my impression that Marcia and Miles were involved. Clearly, there were losses on all sides. I put my arm around her shoulders. "Yes, it's awful for us all. I'm so sorry, Marcia."

She took a deep breath and straightened under my touch, as though she did not want to show me the depth of her grief. "Caitlin is in her bedroom upstairs." She blew her nose again. "I finally got her to lie down. She's taking a nap."

"No, I'm not," said a childish voice from the top of the stairs. "Aunt China? Aunt China, is that you?"

"It's me, Caitlin," I said, and went up the stairs to gather her into my arms.

What did I say as I held her, shaking, against me? I don't remember. At least, I don't remember the words, just the sounds. Caitlin's fierce, inconsolable weeping as she buried her face against my shoulder, my own voice, as soothing as I could make it as I smoothed the child's hair. I was weeping, too, for Caitlin, for Miles, for myself, perhaps even for my father. For what I had lost, what *we* had lost, what we had never been able to share. For the wrenching fact that I hadn't wanted a brother, hadn't wanted Miles as a brother, hadn't wanted to summon up the ghost of my father—our father. And now it was too late for any of that. Miles was dead, and all the regrets in the world wouldn't bring him back.

After a few minutes, the turbulence passed. Caitlin quieted and I let her go, swiping my eyes on my sleeve. We went downstairs. Marcia had gone to the kitchen at the back of the house, and we followed.

The kitchen was large and pleasant but chaotic, the way it is when you're moving in—cookware stacked on the counters, dishes piled here and there, groceries not put away, boxes on the floor, no curtains at the windows. Caitlin took a soft drink out of the fridge, and Marcia poured two mugs of tea from a pot that was brewing on the counter. The three of us took our drinks to the breakfast nook with a window overlooking a green backyard. And then, as the afternoon sunlight filtered through the green leaves of the pecan tree outside the window, I had a good look at my niece.

I had seen Caitlin twice in the past few months, both times with her father. My impression then had been of a shy, painfully awkward girl, small, with skinny wrists and no hips and large brown eyes in a pale, freckled face. Nothing was changed. Her dark hair was pulled back into a ponytail and secured with a plastic band, and she was wearing a mouthful of silver braces. Her delicate face would be pretty when it filled out, but now her skin was splotchy, her eyes were red, her lips were pinched with pain. Her hands trembled so much when she tried to pick up her glass that the ice cubes in it rattled, and I saw that her nails were bitten down to the quick. Two deaths—her mother's and her father's—in just a few years. It was a tough hit for a young girl to take.

It was obviously a tough hit for Marcia, too. In the brighter light of the kitchen, I could see that her face had an unhealthy ashen color. She was struggling for composure, not wanting Caitlin to see how completely undone she was. And not just by Miles' death, either, I supposed. I was sure that it had awakened memories of her sister's drowning, which must have been as big a blow to her as it had to been to Miles and Caitlin. I hadn't heard any details, just that Karen had fallen off a friend's houseboat into Lake Travis three years before. Caitlin, who was only seven, had witnessed it. There's no good age at which to lose your mother, but when you're seven and you've watched your mother drown, the loss must be unspeakable.

I cleared my throat and glanced around the room. "You've just moved here, Marcia?" I was searching for something to talk about, other than death.

"About two weeks ago." She waved her hand at the chaos. "I've been too busy with appointments at the—" She hesitated, biting her lip and frowning. "I guess you know that my husband and I divorced."

"Miles mentioned it."

"That's why I moved. I haven't finished unpacking yet. There's a lot left to do." She looked around the room with dismay. "Sometimes I think it would be easier if I left everything as it is, and just lived out of the boxes." She closed her eyes. "I don't know how it will all get done."

"I'll help, Aunt Marcia," Caitlin said.

Marcia opened her eyes and smiled. "You've already helped a great deal, dear." To me, she added, with an artificial cheeriness in her voice, "Caitlin's a whiz at unpacking boxes."

There was a silence. Still casting around for something

to talk about, I said. "That Angel's Trumpet on the porch— have you had it long?"

"It just came," Marcia said. She shook her head sadly. "It was a housewarming gift. From Caitlin's father." She put her hand over Caitlin's and managed a smile. "Honey, I'll bet that crazy squirrel is hanging around, just waiting for you. There's a loaf of bread on the counter. Why don't you take a couple of slices out to the picnic table and see if he'd like to have some?"

Without a word, Caitlin got the bread, took her soft drink, and went out the back door, closing the screen silently behind her.

"She's in shock," Marcia said, rubbing her hand over her eyes. "She's hardly said a word since the police left. I've tried to comfort her, but I'm not doing too well myself."

That was clear from the lines of pain around her mouth and the darkness in her eyes. I didn't know what to say. Finally, I settled for: "It's too soon, Marcia. Something like this takes time. Caitlin is safe and she has you to take care of her. That will make all the difference." Maybe, eventually. But who would take care of Marcia?

Marcia pounded a helpless fist on the table. "It's not fair, damn it! She's at the age when life ought to be simple and good, when she can still believe she can have everything she wants." There was pain and despair in her voice, and longing. She looked away, then looked back. "Have you talked to the police?"

"Just the custody officer, to get Miles' personal effects. The investigating officer was out. Did they give you any of the details?"

She shook her head. "Only that they think he was hit some time after nine thirty last night. That was when he sent an email from his office computer to his secretary's about a case he was working on." She swallowed. "The car must have hit him pretty hard. They found him off to the side, between two parked vehicles. I guess he was thrown there."

"Thrown?" I frowned. "Or dragged?"

"Dragged?" She shuddered. "I didn't think of that." Her glance went to the window, where we could see Caitlin, forlorn, sitting on the picnic bench. She had torn a slice of bread into pieces and scattered them out on the table, but so far, the squirrel hadn't shown up. "Dragged," she repeated, in a whisper. "Oh, god."

"I was just wondering," I said lamely. "Since he wasn't found early this morning. When people first came in to work, I mean."

She thought about that for a minute, frowning, turning the mug in her fingers. "I don't know if I ought to say this—I mean, it's just a . . ." She pulled in a deep breath. "Miles was . . . He mentioned once that he thought he was in danger." Another breath, a head shake, then: "I might not have thought about it at all, if you hadn't said that about being dragged. Like maybe somebody didn't want him found right away."

I waited, thinking there might be more, but there wasn't. I leaned forward, feeling urgent. "When did he say that—about being in danger?" I prompted.

"Two or three weeks ago, maybe." She slanted me a look. "Did he tell you that we were . . . seeing each other?"

"No," I said, "but I guessed, sort of. When I saw you together."

She smiled sadly. "Obvious, huh?"

"I'm a good guesser." I returned the smile, but I wondered whether she and Miles had been involved before her divorce, and if so, whether that was a factor. Was Miles the cause of the breakup?

"Miles and I knew each other before he met my sister," she said, as if she felt the need to explain, or maybe to justify. "We weren't dating or anything—mostly, we used to go jogging together at Town Lake. One morning, Karen went with me. When she and Miles got together, it was sort of like—well, fireworks, I guess you'd say. Love at first sight. They got married a couple of months later." She passed her hand over her face. "Her death was so hard, I think it might have drawn us together. I'm not sure either of us could have made it by ourselves. We leaned on one another. Then Zeke and I—well, our marriage was breaking up, so there wasn't any reason not to . . . get together. I was hoping it would work. Especially because of Caitlin."

"Actually, I thought it was a fine idea," I said. "You and Miles, I mean. As you say, it would be good for Caitlin." I paused. They'd been close. Miles might have confided in her. "What kind of danger did he think he was in? Did he mention specifics?"

She shook her head. "I think he was afraid it might worry me."

"Did he tell you he'd hired a private detective to look into his father's death?"

She set her cup down, frowning a little. "Your husband, he said. I wondered about that. His father—that was a long time ago, wasn't it?"

"Sixteen years." Sixteen years. Yes, a long time ago. But unfinished business, all the same.

She sighed. "I remember wondering why he wanted to dig up that old stuff again. But I don't know whether that had anything to do with the way he was feeling." She laced her fingers together. "Did you know that he was thinking of leaving the firm?"

"Really?" No, I hadn't known, and I was surprised. Miles had been at Zwinger, Brady, Brandon, and Danforth long enough to make partner, and from what I knew, his future there was assured. "Why?"

She shrugged. "Maybe he just wanted a change. He didn't always see eye to eye with the other partners. You used to be a lawyer, didn't you? I guess you know how it is."

"I do. I was glad to get out." That was the understate-
ment of the year. When I left, I'd felt like I was walking out
of prison.

She seemed calmer now, as if talking had eased her. "I
think he envied you. He said he wished he could come up
with something else he'd rather do with his life, the way
you did." She chewed on her lower lip for a minute, then
came back to the subject, seeming a little calmer now. "Did
they say when they're going to release the body? There'll
have to be some sort of service."

I hadn't gotten to that point in my thinking, but I had
an answer. "The autopsy will probably take a while, a
week, maybe more—longer than you'd think. If you'd
like to have a memorial service instead, that's certainly
okay with me. We ought to do whatever you and Caitlin
want."

She nodded and picked up her cup again. "Miles and
Karen had a cemetery lot. It would be best for Caitlin if her
mother and father are together. And I have the guest book
from Karen's service. I'll go through it and get the names
of people that Miles would want notified. I'll check with
his secretary, too. She's sure to have other names." She
sighed heavily. "It'll give me something to do while I—"
She stopped very quickly. "Is there anybody on your side
of the family? Anybody to contact, I mean."

I shook my head. "We weren't exactly a family," I said
with some irony. "I didn't even know Miles—as my brother,
I mean—until last February."

"Sorry, I forgot." She paused. "Can you handle the legal
stuff? The will and all that?"

"Of course," I said. "Are you his executor?"

"His executor?" Her eyes widened. "Oh, lord, I hope
not. I just couldn't cope with that, in addition to . . . to all
the other stuff."

"If he didn't discuss it with you, I'm sure he's appointed
someone else," I said, in a comforting tone. "Probably one

of the partners at his firm." I took a deep breath and asked the question that was at the front of my mind. "Caitlin— she needs a legal guardian. That's probably in the will, too."

She closed her eyes, sighed, and opened them again. "I think it might be. Miles and I talked about it. Of course, we didn't imagine—" She broke off.

"She'll be staying with you?" I persisted.

Marcia looked out the window again, turning so that I couldn't read her expression. "For the time being, I hope, although—" She turned back to me. "Would you and your husband—"

"I'm sure that's in Caitlin's best interests," I said quickly, not wanting her to worry that McQuaid and I might contest the girl's custody. "She's known you for as long as she can remember. You're her mother's sister. The continuity will be important to her."

"Of course. Yes, I know, China." Her eyes filled with tears and her chin trembled. "But I'm worried about her. I don't know what will happen to her if I— That is, if I can't—" She stopped, as if she had gone inside herself to search for words and hadn't found them.

Something was going on here that I didn't quite understand. Something was troubling Marcia deeply—and it wasn't just Miles' death. But whatever it was, she wasn't going to tell me.

"Please don't give it another thought," I said soothingly. "I'll take care of that end of things. Of course, my husband and I want to see Caitlin often. And if you need any help, all you have to do is call me. Pecan Springs is only a half hour away. Maybe an hour," I amended with a small smile, "depending on the traffic." I reached out and took her hands. Her fingers felt as cold and brittle as thin sticks. "I'll be in touch often. And you will call me, won't you, Marcia? Any time?"

She nodded wordlessly.

I squeezed her hands and let go. "Is there something I can do now? Errands? Calls that ought to be made?"

Marcia looked out the window. She seemed to be struggling to focus on my question, or maybe she was just mentally scanning a long list of things that had to be done, trying to think of something I could help with.

"Have you been to the house yet?" she asked finally. "Caitlin needs some clothes—undies and socks and things. I could take her, but I'm not sure she should . . ." Her voice trembled, and she managed a laugh. "I guess it's me, actually. I'm not sure I can go there. Not today, anyway, or tomorrow. Maybe not ever. The four of us had some good times in that house, when Karen was alive. After that, too, just Miles and Caitlin and me. And now—"

*And now it was just Caitlin and her. How sad, how very sad.*

I cleared my throat. "I need to go to the house anyway. I'll be glad to get whatever Caitlin needs." I drank the last of my tea, wrote down my phone numbers and email address on a paper napkin, and handed it to Marcia. "I'll stop by with the things later this evening."

"If we're not here, just leave them on the porch," Marcia said. "We might go out for pizza." Her smile was thin and tremulous. "I'd like to make things seem normal for her, if that's possible. For me, too," she added in a lower voice. "I'm on leave from work just now, so I'll have some time to spend with her."

I nodded. "Listen, I hope you don't mind my saying this, but that plant on the porch. It's called Angel's Trumpet, but it has other names—Devil's apple, for instance. It's highly toxic. It might be a good idea to mention that to Caitlin. And to put it in the backyard, where the neighborhood kids aren't so likely to notice it." I smiled a little. "Sometimes teens are inclined to smoke the leaves, which is definitely not a good idea."

She was frowning. "You're sure about this? Wouldn't the nursery put some sort of tag on it?"

I shook my head. "Sometimes nurseries don't like to discourage potential buyers. Sometimes tags get lost. And lots of times, employees of the big chains have no idea what's in the pot they're selling. Trust me, Marcia. The plant is beautiful, and it has its medicinal uses. Ritual, too. But it's a hallucinogen. And deadly."

"I'll move it around back," she said decidedly. "And I'll tell Caitlin not to touch it." A brief smile ghosted across her face. "Caitlin is never a problem, you know. She's the most obedient child you can possibly imagine."

I wanted to say that sometimes obedience wasn't the very best trait for a young girl, unless she was surrounded only by grown-ups who could be trusted to give her good direction. But now wasn't the right moment for child-rearing philosophy. Anyway, who was I to act like an expert? My only claim to mom-fame is Brian, who seems to have come with a built-in roadmap for good growing up. And he has McQuaid, who is a very good father. I certainly can't take any of the credit for the way Brian is turning out.

So I said good-bye to Marcia, promised to be in touch, and went out to the backyard. Caitlin was hunched over the table, her chin on her hands, her eyes on a squirrel warily poised on a branch some five or six yards away, watching her, deciding whether to come closer. She sat still as a stone, waiting. Waiting.

"I have to go now, Caitlin," I said, dropping onto the bench and putting my arm around her. "I'll see you soon. Aunt Marcia knows how to reach me. And if I write you an email, will you answer me?"

She nodded mutely, her eyes still on the squirrel. I wanted to say that everything would be okay, in time, but I knew it wouldn't. It wouldn't be okay today, or tomorrow, or next year. I knew, because when I was a child, I had waited, too, waited for a father who was never really at home, even when he was in the house, even when I could hear his voice. Waited for him to hold me, love me, like me. Waited and waited. In a way, I was still waiting.

I dropped a kiss on the top of Caitlin's head and left without saying anything else. It was hard enough for her to cope with her loss without coping with an intrusive aunt whom she barely knew.

# Chapter Nine

The mandrake (*Mandragora officinarum*) has perhaps had more superstitions connected with it than any of the other members of the *Solanaceae* family. The parsniplike root of the plant is frequently branched, so that those with a vivid imagination might think it looked like a pair of human legs. In fact, the Greek mathematician Pythagorus described the plant as an anthromorph, or tiny human being, which was said to utter a piercing scream if it was dragged from the earth. Thomas Newton, in his *Herball to the Bible* (1587) says of the mandrake, "It is supposed to be a creature having life, engendered under the earth of the seed [sperm] of some dead person put to death for murder." The mandrake's supposed resemblance to the human figure gave it a magical significance. It became highly valued as (among other things) a love philter so powerful that even an unwilling partner could be led into dalliance.

Out in the car, I turned on my cell phone and checked for messages, thinking that Officer Wilkins might have called, or perhaps McQuaid. There was nothing from either of them, but there was a call from Laurel about an important order that had been delayed.

"We solved it," she reported when I reached her. "Sorry

to have bothered you. Have you seen Caitlin? Is everything okay there?"

"Yes, I've seen her," I said. "And everything is as okay as it's going to get. McQuaid hasn't called the shop, has he?"

"Not as far as I know. Somebody else called, though. Martha Edmond. She wondered if you'd remember her."

Of course I remembered her. Martha is a native-plant expert and local historian in Mississippi, where my mother was raised by her aunt Tullie Coldwell, on a plantation called Jordan's Crossing, on the Bloodroot River. Aunt Tullie was in a nursing home now, and the plantation had been sold. "Did Martha say what she wanted?"

"It's about a workshop she's doing in Kentucky, at one of the Shaker villages. She wants you to go with her and give a talk on herbs."

"When is it?"

"Sometime in June."

Normally, I'd jump at the chance to visit a Shaker village to talk about herbs, but not now. "That's only a month away," I said. "I don't see how I can do it, after what's just happened. Maybe you should call Martha back and tell her to look for someone else. I'd be glad to suggest some names."

"Don't say no right away," Laurel urged. "I told her you had your hands full just now, but she sounded pretty urgent about it. Said she'd try calling you at home."

We said good-bye. I was still holding the phone when it rang in my hand. It was McQuaid.

"Where are you?" I asked, glancing at my watch. Nearly four. Stopping to see Caitlin had taken longer than I thought.

"Heading in your direction," he replied. "I'm just about to hit I-35. Hey, I found the car, China! It's your father's Cadillac, no doubt about it."

"No kidding," I said, not sure whether I should be glad or sad. "Where is it?"

"In a barn, on a ranch that belongs to Laura Danforth's cousin. Ellie Hanson. A nice lady. She raises tomatillos and pigs. And cats."

Tomatillos? That was interesting. Ordinarily, I would have asked him to tell me more. But at the moment, I was focused on the car. "What kind of shape is it in? Could you tell anything about it?"

"The same shape it was in right after the wreck, as far as I can make out," he said. "It's pretty well scorched, not to mentioned pancaked. But I don't think there's been any substantial deterioration. Whatever Laura Danforth's reason for keeping the car, she kept it pretty well. But if you're asking about evidence, I'd have to say that nothing jumped out at me." He paused. "There is one odd thing, though. Ellie says that Miles had known about the car for some time. He contacted her about it in January, *before* his mother died."

"Before?" I frowned. "Hey, wait. That's not what he said. He told us he didn't have any idea where—"

"Yeah, I know. It doesn't fit. I had the feeling he was holding something back, and now I know what it was. Some of it, anyway." A horn honked, and McQuaid muttered an evil word. "Same to you, jerk," he said, then: "Did you get the stuff from the police?" His voice dropped. "Have you seen Caitlin?"

"Yes and yes," I said. "Caitlin is with Marcia. They're both very upset, of course, although Marcia is calm enough to start thinking about the funeral service and where Miles will be buried." There was more to tell him, but it could wait. "Are you coming to Austin?"

"You've got the keys to the house?"

"Yes. I'm going there now."

"I was supposed to go to the baseball game with Brian

this evening," McQuaid said. "I'll call and let him know I can't make it. How about if I meet you at Miles' place in . . ." He paused, and I pictured him checking his location, assessing the traffic, and consulting his watch. "Maybe an hour? Ninety minutes, outside."

"Okay. I'm going there now, though. I need to look for his will. I'm hoping he's settled the issue of guardianship, although I tried to let Marcia know that's not in question, as far as you and I are concerned. Caitlin should be with *her.*"

When he spoke again, his voice had hardened. I could almost see him frowning. "Listen, China. I don't think it's a good idea to go to that house by yourself. Why don't we meet somewhere and get something to eat first? That Mexican restaurant on South Lamar, maybe? We could leave one of the vehicles there and drive out to Miles' place together."

I was tempted, but I knew where my duty lay. "Don't be silly. The house is in a very safe neighborhood. I'll be fine."

"I'm not talking about the neighborhood, and you know it," McQuaid said darkly. "That hit-and-run—it wasn't an accident."

"I'll be fine," I repeated firmly, glad that I hadn't mentioned Miles' feeling that he might be in danger. "I have my cell phone. And I'll lock the front door if that'll make you feel better. Ring the doorbell three times—two longs and a short—and I'll let you in."

McQuaid sighed. "Why do you always have to do the opposite of what I ask?"

"Because I'm contrary," I said. "Can you find the house?"

"On Riverview Heights Drive, isn't it? At the end, on the cul-de-sac?"

"That's it. See you there."

"I still don't think—" he began.

"Two longs and a short." I clicked off the phone.

MILES and Caitlin lived on Cat Mountain, one of Austin's most prestigious residential neighborhoods, valued for its pricey exclusivity and its panoramic views of the Hill Country to the west of the city. From Travis Heights, I took Barton Springs Drive past Zilker Park to MoPac Expressway, which is named for the Missouri Pacific Railroad tracks that run along the highway median between West Eighth and Northland Drive. MoPac is the main north-south highway on the west side of town, with three and four lanes funneling the rush-hour traffic in and out of downtown Austin, the state capital complex, and the university area. It was definitely rush hour now, and the bumper-to-bumper traffic was slow and go all the way to FM 2222, where I got off with a sigh of relief and headed west to Mount Bonnell Road.

As the afternoon went on, the temperature and humidity had climbed, and I was glad for the car's air-conditioning. The spring cold front the weather forecasters had promised was blowing down from the north, which might cool things off, at least temporarily, although it looked as if we were in for a storm. The buildup of purplish thunderheads over western Travis County darkened the sky and the breeze was getting frisky, whipping the trees and tumbling leaves along the streets. Off to the northwest, an occasional flash of lightning split the towering clouds like a silver knife. May is a prime tornado month, and although Austin isn't in as much danger as, say, Dallas or Lubbock or Abilene, every now and then one of those whirling dervishes roars across the Hill Country, tearing up houses and trees and tossing cars around like toys. It pays to be on the lookout.

I switched on the radio to check for storm warnings, but

if there were any, they weren't urgent enough to break into the music. The rain began to come down hard, gusting across the road, and I switched on the windshield wipers. One of Dolly Parton's oldies was playing: "Here You Come Again." I hummed along, remembering that Dolly had once joked that she had agreed to bare those famous boobs for *Playboy*—on her hundredth birthday. I smiled. Yeah. My kind of woman.

But my smile faded as I turned off onto Mount Bonnell Road and was reminded that I wasn't here to listen to Dolly or admire the million-dollar homes that lined the street. I had come to look for my brother's will, because my brother was dead and his death had left a ten-year-old orphan and a woman who loved him. Somehow, my habitual correction— Miles wasn't my brother, he was my *half* brother—no longer seemed important. In fact, it now struck me as mean-spirited and churlish. I had blamed Miles for something that was entirely my father's fault. I was ashamed of myself and wished I could make it up to him. But the dead are immune to efforts of that sort. The living are left to feel guilty.

I had been to Miles' house before, and had no trouble finding it again. A handsome house, built to impress, it stood well back from the street, on the brink of a cliff that fell off sharply down to the river. The surrounding yard, lush with perfectly clipped green grass, was meticulously landscaped with native grasses and carefully pruned small trees. At the front corners of the property, massive chunks of limestone were strategically arranged in aesthetically balanced group-ings to symbolize the unruly wilderness of cedar and scrub oak and mustang grape out of which this cul-de-sac had been carved. But the symbolism didn't work, for there was a sterility to the plant groupings that undercut any reference to nature. The rocks were "natural," yes, and the trees moved with a certain grace in the gusting winds. But they might have been sculptures for all the real life they held.

I pulled into the long driveway and parked on the apron in front of the garage. In this neighborhood, my small white Toyota looked plebeian and humble, of a kind with the yard maintenance truck down the street. What's more, there were no kiddie toys in the yards, no boys riding bikes on the street, no girls walking arm-in-arm on their way home from school. It wasn't a neighborhood that welcomed kids, I thought, or invited them out to play. If there were kids here, they were probably sprawled in front of the sixty-four-inch television in their parents' media room.

Privacy is one of the perks you pay for when you buy into an exclusive neighborhood. The lots were large and the houses on either side and across the cul-de-sac were screened by shrubbery and set well back behind manicured lawns and formal flower beds. I doubted that anybody could see me running from my car to the secluded entryway—it was raining hard and I didn't have an umbrella. The second key I tried opened the heavy front door, which swung open soundlessly. I held my breath, expecting to hear the braying of the burglar alarm, then let it out again with a whoosh of relief when I remembered Miles saying that he'd stopped using the alarm system because Caitlin kept tripping it when she came home from school.

Once inside, I closed the door, flicked the lock, and stood for a moment, looking around, feeling like an uninvited guest. The house was deathly still and the air already smelled flat and stale, like a model home that's open only on weekends. This wasn't a large house, as Cat Mountain houses go. In fact, it might have been among the smaller houses in the neighborhood, with only four bedrooms, three and a half baths, and no media room, which Miles had explained by saying that both he and Karen had preferred reading to television and movies.

But the ceiling in the entryway was two full stories high, with a round skylight and narrow windows following the line of the staircase to the second floor. The floor was of

handmade Mexican Saltillo tile polished to the luster of
dark leather and spread here and there with Persian car-
pets. In the living room, the massive stone fireplace was
open on two sides and large enough to barbecue a good-
size pig. The French doors that opened onto a deck—there
were several decks, one built below the other, down the
cliff—offered a breathtaking view: a dramatic panorama
of Lake Austin, the Loop 360 arch suspension bridge in the
distance, and the storm-darkened hills beyond. A million-
dollar view.

Or two million, I thought, walking across a pale ivory
carpet so thick that I sank in it nearly up to my ankles and
so plush that it muffled every sound. I don't keep up on
Austin real estate values, but a view like this would sell the
house in a hurry. The furnishings—enormous leather sofas, velvet chairs, richly veneered tables, a well-stocked
liquor cabinet—matched the carpet for opulence, and the
artwork on the walls and the accessories on the tables and
shelves were all equally splendid, a fine testimony to career achievement and social success. He'd come a long way,
my brother had. And I couldn't begrudge him a single square
inch of it.

I turned to the window again, admiring the view that
encompassed the best of everything Austin and the Hill
Country had to offer. It was too bad—really too bad—that
Miles wouldn't be able to enjoy it. Which brought me back
to the will. It was probably in his desk, I thought. If I lived
in this house, I would have wanted to put my desk where I
could enjoy the scenery, so I was betting that his study was
at the back of the house.

Never mind that I was here on family business. I
couldn't help feeling like an intruder as I went through a
large dining room with a polished walnut table that could
easily seat twelve, past a stainless-steel kitchen with a
work island that a gourmet restaurant chef would have envied and a side-by-side that could refrigerate enough food

for a small army. Miles' study was the room at the end of the hall. Its main feature was a massive masculine desk, facing more French doors and a deck looking out on the river from a slightly different angle. The walls were lined with books—law books, some of them, but also books on history, politics, and economics—and with pictures, the sort of photos I had seen when I visited Miles' law office in downtown Austin. Miles shaking hands with the current governor. Miles cutting a ribbon with a previous governor who had raised his sights from Texas to the world. Miles sharing a hot dog with another, earlier governor, better loved than all the rest, with her wide eyes, bouffant white hair—Big Hair, we call it in Texas—and engaging grin.

But then I saw something unexpected. On the wall beside Miles' chair, where he could look directly at it if he turned his head, there were five or six framed photographs of Dad. I had never seen any of them, but I recognized them all immediately. One was a childhood photo, a small boy in short pants and knee socks, wearing a solemn look, standing beside my grandmother in the living room of their uptown New Orleans house. In another, Dad was older, wearing a cap and gown, striding across a stage at Tulane University to receive his diploma. The rest were outdoor photos. My father, Miles' mother, and Miles, as a boy, at a fishing camp. Father and son—Miles must have been in his early twenties—seated beside a campfire, mountains behind them looming against the evening sky. Companionable photos, family photos.

And there was a group shot, taken at Ted Stone's ranch. Dad, handsomely rugged in a shooting vest, with Miles and three other men. One of the men was Ted, my father's law partner, hunting cap pulled over his eyes. The other was Ted's brother, G.W., tricked out in camouflage gear, the kind of thing hunters wear when they want the deer to think they're a hackberry tree or a cedar bush. The third man, thick and muscular, was Sonny Bryce, whom I recognized from the old days at Stone and Bayles. Sonny, who seemed to come and go whenever he felt like it, was known around the office as the "Engineer." When I asked my father what he did and why he didn't keep office hours like everybody else, Dad said that his specialty was removing obstructions, and that he mostly worked after dark. "Sonny does his best work at night," he said, and laughed, not in a nice way. As a kid, I was a little frightened of the Engineer. I imagined him lurking ominously in the shadows, doing whatever he did after dark. But all this mystery held a certain shivery attraction, and he was really a nice man, after all. When he came to talk to Dad, the Engineer would give me a handful of dimes and send me downstairs to the vending machine to get Mars bars.

In this photo, Miles was the star of the show. He was kneeling, supporting the head and heavy rack of an impressive trophy whitetail buck. Dad wore a proud, proprietary smile, although I wasn't sure whether he was smiling about Miles, the buck, or both. This jaunty quintet was posed in front of the Stonebridge casita—the adobe guest house that was part of the ranch compound. The place looked pretty much as it had the last time I'd stayed there, a courtyard in front, paved with limestone rock and centered by a Spanish-style fountain landscaped with native plants. Ted Stone had spent quite a lot of money to make his place look as if it belonged to the land.

I swallowed and looked away, trying to ignore the sudden, painful stab of jealousy. Not that I would have wanted to go hunting with my father and brother—blood sport is not my idea of fun. It was their closeness, their easy camaraderie, that I envied. My father and I had never shared anything remotely like it.

There were probably other photographs like these—I didn't need to see them. I sat down in the desk chair and tried the right-hand drawer, which is where I keep my important papers at home. I figured Miles might think the same way. He did. The drawer was locked, but the key was in the same place I keep mine, in the left-hand desk drawer. Mine is among the paperclips. His was with the rubber bands.

My brother had been organized. The first file was neatly labeled MORTGAGE, the second AUTOS. The third was marked WILL, INSURANCE, ESTATE. I took out the will, unfolded it, and skimmed the fine print. Miles had rewritten it since Karen's death, for she was not mentioned in it—in fact, when I checked the date, I saw that it had been executed only a couple of weeks ago, signed and notarized at his law office and witnessed by Beverly Bolton, his secretary, and someone named Rachel Burke. There was the usual preamble, the appropriate whereases and wherefores, and the expected disposition of property. Everything went to Caitlin, in trust until her majority with Marcia as the trustee. Marcia was also named as Caitlin's legal guardian, and I breathed a sigh of relief. I was glad to see the designation settled and in print—it would mean an important peace of mind to Marcia.

I flipped down to the executor clause, expecting to see the name of one of Miles' legal partners, and was astonished to see my name. My first response was a flash of anger. How dare he saddle me with a huge job like this, without even asking? And then a flash of memory: Miles saying on the phone several weeks ago that he wanted to talk to me about some family business, which I had dismissed because I thought it had to do with his obsession over what had happened to Dad. But he must have been talking about the executorship. I had brushed him off, and he had been killed before he had a chance to explain.

I put the will on the desk in front of me, frowning. I was perfectly within my rights to ask the probate judge to appoint another executor. But that didn't feel right. I would be letting my brother down, shifting my—face it—familial responsibilities to a nonfamily member. It's likely that I would manage her resources with greater attention and concern than would a stranger. Marcia was doing her part, serving as trustee and Caitlin's guardian. I should do mine.

And there was something else. A few moments ago, I had felt like an intruder here, an uninvited guest, the sort of feeling I've had on the occasions—admittedly rare, but there have been a few—when I've found myself snooping in someone's house without permission. While I admit to being as curious as the next person, I am also a nut about the right to privacy, my own and other people's. I could never in the world engage in the sort of property searches that Kinsey Millhone and V. I. Warshawski conduct without blinking an eyelash. If I've got to do something that involves any sort of trespass, emotional, physical, or otherwise, I always end up in an extended debate with myself. The sort of thing I was doing right now—going through Miles' desk, reading his papers, uncovering his private affairs—makes me nervous, even apprehensive.

But Miles' will gave me a reason for being here. If a cop suddenly materialized at the door and demanded to know who I was and what I was doing, I could not only say that I was the deceased's sister, but his executor, as well. It was my right *and* my fiduciary duty to be here. It was my responsibility to probate the will, inventory the property, deal with the life insurance company, manage the estate, pay the creditors, and take care of the taxes.

A big job, yes. But Miles had been a well-organized man, the will was recent, and—when I flipped to the last page, I saw that he had appended a dated and detailed inventory of assets. It was unlikely that there would be any major messes to mop up. What's more, he had trusted me to do this. You might say that I owed it to him as a final act of friendship, of . . . well, family affection, although I hadn't felt very affectionate toward him while he was alive. You might even say that I owed it to him in partial reparation for my efforts to brush him off.

I sat back in his chair, and another thought came into my mind. Marcia had said that Miles was afraid. Afraid of what? Of whom? Why? And why was he thinking of leaving his law firm? Was it just the usual burnout that most lawyers feel at various times in their careers, perhaps exacerbated by a particularly unpleasant client? Or was it something else? I reached for the Rolodex and flipped it open to the Bs, thanking my lucky stars that my brother had not belonged to the digital generation. Beverly Bolton's card was at the front, and I made a note of her home phone and address. She had worked with him for a long while. She might be able to give me some insight into his thinking about leaving the firm.

Next to the Rolodex was the answering machine, and I saw that the light was blinking. I pulled out a piece of paper to take notes and hit the Play button. Three calls, and all three had come in today. The first caller identified himself as Jake and wanted to know when someone would be at home so he could come and repair the broken glass. Broken glass? I'd have to call him back and find out what was involved before I scheduled anything.

The second was from Estelle Jenner, president of the Homeowners' Association, wanting to talk to Miles about serving as secretary. "I'm asking you," she said, "because I know how well organized you are, and because you share my concern about property values in this area."

The third was from a woman with a rich Gawgia peaches-'n'-cream drawl. She sounded nervous and harassed, but was trying to make light of it.

"Call when you get a chance, dahlin'. I'm in deep, serious trouble here. James found somethin' I wrote to you." She managed a deep-throated chuckle. "An indiscreet little somethin' meant for your eyes alone, I'm afraid. He's in a humongous snit about it, roarin' and stompin' around. I jes' have to see you, sweetie." There was no call-back number. Whoever she was, the Gawgia Peach would have to deal with her deep, serious trouble—and James, her husband, I guessed—all by herself.

I considered the situation for a moment. I should put a message on the machine to notify callers of Miles' death. I'd leave his office number, where somebody was around to answer the phone. I needed to check this out with Beverly Bolton—Mrs. B, as Miles called her. If she was willing to help, she could give out the funeral information, once it was available, and make a list of the names and numbers of anybody I needed to get back to.

What else? I looked around, taking note of where things were. A desktop computer, with a stack of backup floppies beside it. Checkbooks and bank statements in the desk drawer. A triple-decker file tray on the desk, filled with legal-size file folders that contained documents that might be pertinent to his current cases. They should probably go to Mrs. Bolton. A classy-looking wooden file cabinet next to the multipaned French doors that opened onto the deck. A smaller wooden cabinet, on the other side of the doors. A—

I stopped. The pane of glass next to the handle in the French door had been broken. The missing pane was covered with a taped-on rectangle of heavy, nearly transparent plastic that looked like it might have been cut from a plastic file folder. A temporary fix until it could be professionally repaired—by Jake, no doubt. I went to the door and knelt down, noticing that a few glittering shards of glass still lay on the carpet, missed in the cleanup. I unlocked the door, pushed it open, and stepped outside, into the rain-cooled air left behind by the fast-moving storm, already well to the south. The deck turned the corner, and I saw a path leading to the front of the house and the street. You wouldn't have to be a cat burglar to break in here.

I was wondering when the glass had been broken and whether the intruder had actually managed to steal anything when the doorbell rang, long, repeated, urgent peals.

I went back inside and hurried down the hall, thinking that McQuaid had made better time than he expected. When I opened the door, I was primed to tease him about forgetting our prearranged signal: two longs and a short.

But the person urgently thumbing the doorbell was not McQuaid. She was dressed in a chic, form-fitting jogging outfit constructed of a silky silver material, the shoulders freshly spotted with raindrops. Her auburn hair was highlighted with gold streaks and sleeked back from her tanned face with a band that matched her jogging suit. A thin gold chain hung around her neck. She was lean but generously endowed, and so drop-dead gorgeous that her age—the tiny lines around her eyes suggested the high end of forty—scarcely mattered (though I'd bet it mattered to her). She registered surprise and annoyance when she saw me, and a flicker of something else. Jealousy?

"Yes?" I asked, drawing it out. Something in me was not feeling kindly toward this person.

She erased as much of the annoyance as possible from her face, although the jealousy (if that's what it was) showed in her voice. "Miles Danforth, please," she drawled, in a rich Southern accent. "Tell him it's Belinda. If he's got a minute, I'd appreciate it."

Belinda was the Gawgia Peach, sure as shootin', the one whose husband was in a humongous snit. She had not waited for Miles to call her.

"Belinda who?" I asked evenly, not giving anything away.

She paused, and then, in a grudging tone, said, "Belinda Harcher. I'm a neighbor." She jerked her head toward the house next door, which was the size of a medieval castle. "Miles will want to see me." There was just the tiniest threat in the assertion.

I cleared my throat. "I'm sorry to have to tell you this, Ms. Harcher. Miles was killed last night."

"Killed!" she gasped. Her face went dead white.

"You'd better come in and sit down," I said, opening the door. There was a chair in the entrance hall. I made her sit and pushed her head between her legs. I went to the living room liquor cabinet, took out a bottle of Scotch, and poured a hefty slug. She had straightened up by the time I returned and was sucking in air in deep, shuddery gulps, but the color had not yet come back to her face. She downed the Scotch in a few quick swallows and set the glass back on the table beside her.

"How did it . . . happen?" she asked. And then, with a return of the jealousy, she added sharply, "Who are you?"

"My name is China Bayles," I said, although that wasn't exactly what she wanted to know. "Miles was struck by a vehicle in the parking garage at his office last night. It was a hit-and-run. The driver fled the scene."

"Hit-and-run?" She closed her eyes. "Oh, my god." Her eyes opened again, wide, frantic. "What time?"

It struck me as an odd question. Miles was dead. That was the important thing. What did it matter what time he had been killed? Unless, of course, she suspected somebody. James, for instance. The husband who had been rompin' and stompin' over his wife's real or imagined indiscretions.

"The police aren't sure," I said. "Yet."

"The . . . police?" she asked faintly. "Were there any witnesses? Do they think it was . . . Do they know what kind of a car it was?"

More odd questions. "I haven't spoken to the investigating officer yet," I said truthfully. I paused and added, in a helpful tone, "I believe you left a message for Miles on the answering machine. Is there anything I can do to help?" Sometimes something smarmy in me just has to push its way out. This was one of those times.

She colored, and I saw her trying to recall what she had said, and when she remembered it, wishing she hadn't. I waited.

She settled for what was obviously a lie, not well told.

"I was calling about . . . It was about a neighborhood get-together. James—he's my husband—asked me to check and see if Miles could help us with the planning. So no, I don't think there's anything you can do." She clasped her hands between her knees and shot me an edgy look. "You're a friend of Miles'?"

I wasn't inclined to satisfy her need to know, so I gave her a short nod. "Nothing's been settled yet about the arrangements. If you'll leave your phone number, I'll make sure you get the details." There was an embossed leather note-and-pencil holder on the table beside Belinda's chair, and she jotted down a number.

Shakily, she stood up to leave. "I . . . I . . ." She swallowed and tried again, not quite looking me in the eye. "I think Miles might have some papers of mine. I wonder if I might look for them. It won't take but a minute."

I didn't have to be Sherlock Holmes to understand that the Gawgia Peach had sent my brother more than one message, in addition to the "indiscreet somethin' " that had sent James into a humongous snit.

"I'm so sorry," I said regretfully. "Nothing can be removed until the executor can go through Miles' papers, looking for documents pertaining to his estate. But I have your phone number, Ms. Harcher. I'll be sure to let you know when your papers—"

"Who's the executor?" She was shrill. "I want to talk to him. I—"

"That would be me," I replied, in a pleasant tone.

What Belinda might have replied was lost in the peal of the doorbell. Two longs and a short. McQuaid hadn't forgotten. She took it as a signal to leave. Expeditiously.

# Chapter Ten

In Texas, the best-beloved member of the nightshade family is not the potato or even the tomato, and certainly not the eggplant. It is the chile pepper. I have never seen a Texan rude enough to test a hot-pepper sauce by pouring it on the tablecloth to find out if it was hot enough to scorch. And I've never seen a pot of chile so hot that it came to a boil on a cold stove.

But it is undoubtedly true that Texas towns are judged, as Will Rogers once said, by the chili they serve. It is also true that some macho Texans regularly chow down on jalapeño peppers (2,500–8,000 on the Scoville heat scale) for breakfast, serrano peppers (10,000–23,000) for lunch, and habanero peppers (100,000–350,000) for supper, by which time they are all fired up and feeling ornery enough to shove all the other good ol' boys into the nearest prickly pear patch.

China Bayles
"Hot Pods and Fiery Fare"
Pecan Springs *Enterprise*

I gave McQuaid the most important bit of news—
that Miles had named me as his executor—and
showed him the damage to the French door. I left him listening to the message from the Gawgia Peach on the answering machine and went upstairs to have a look at the
bedrooms.

The master bedroom was large and beautifully furnished,
with a wall of windows and a deck that offered a wide view
of river, hills, and rain clouds rapidly retreating toward the
southern horizon. But there was no sign of the love letters
Belinda had been so anxious to get her hands on, or anything
else that might suggest a romantic involvement.

There were plenty of Miles' personal effects scattered
around, however—a jacket, running shoes, toilet articles in
the bathroom. Seeing them was a painful wrench. At some
point, I would have to box up and dispose of all these
things, take them to the local Goodwill or Salvation Army,
probably. But by then, maybe some of the shock would
have worn off, and I'd be better able to deal with the task.

I did find an address book in the top drawer of the bed-
side table and took it with the idea of checking it against
Marcia's list of people who should be notified about the
services. In Miles' closet, I found a classy red cocktail
dress that I took to be Karen's—or maybe Marcia's. And in
the back of the second bureau drawer, I discovered a box
of condoms, three-quarters empty, which suggested that
Miles had been practicing safe sex—although whether sex
with the Gawgia Peach was truly safe was a matter of some
conjecture, given James' predilection for reading his wife's
letters. Marcia seemed to me like a better bet for a personal
companion. But what did I know? Maybe the Peach had a
few tricks Marcia hadn't even thought of.

Caitlin's room was done in pretty-girl pink and frosted
with ruffles and ribbons. The neatly made bed was heaped
with stuffed animals, the shelves were full of collectible

dolls, and the bulletin board was filled with family photos, mostly of her and her father. Sadly, I retrieved a pink duffle bag from the closet, filled it with things I thought Caitlin would need, and went downstairs to see how McQuaid was coming along.

He looked up from the bottom drawer of the file cabinet. "I hope, Madame Executrix, you won't have any problem with my continuing the investigation."

"Executor," I replied. " 'Executrix' has gone the way of 'waitress' and 'actress.' But no, I think you ought to go on with it."

"Really?" he asked, raising an eyebrow. "So you're on board?"

I made an impatient noise. "I told you I was, didn't I? And even if I wasn't, Miles would've wanted you to go on. I'm carrying out his wishes." I frowned. "You have a signed contract, I suppose?"

"Of course I have a signed contract. And a retainer." He eyed me. "I just want to be sure that when I submit the bills, they'll be paid."

"Get in line," I said with a sigh. "There are probably plenty of other creditors."

He got to his feet and gave me a quick, appreciative hug. "Okay, Madame Executor, since you're going to pony up, let me show you what I've found. I'll need your permission to remove it from the premises for further investigation."

McQuaid had hit pay dirt. In the bottom drawer of the larger file cabinet, he had discovered a cardboard shoebox (Sturdi-Step Ladies' Lace-up Oxfords, medium heel, brown, size 8½) containing what looked like the notes Laura Danforth compiled after the accident. He'd take it home with him and inventory the documents, hoping that it might contain some leads that Miles hadn't noticed or had kept to himself.

While McQuaid was finishing his search, I gave him a brief update on my conversation with the Peach, including my suspicion that she and Miles had been involved. He wasn't impressed with my idea that the Peach might be afraid that her husband was the killer, but he did agree that the missing door pane looked like a break-in attempt. I called Jake the glass repairman and left my cell and home numbers on his answering machine. I wanted to get the door fixed as soon as possible—which probably meant that I'd need to come back here tomorrow.

But first there was tonight.

"I need to drop off Caitlin's clothes," I said. I gestured at the file folders stacked on the desk. "And those go to Mrs. Bolton, Miles' secretary. They seem to pertain to cases he was working on."

"Can we fit dinner into that scheme?" McQuaid asked.

"Sounds like a winner to me," I said. "I'm starving. Let's go."


McQUAID was in the mood for something hot, so we agreed to meet at Threadgill's No. 2 on West Riverside Drive, not far from Marcia's. I made a quick detour to drop off the duffle bag of Caitlin's clothes and the teddy bear I had found on her bed, well-worn and obviously well-loved. The look on the little girl's face when she saw the teddy bear told me she needed its comfort.

And at the risk of upsetting her, I asked (as gently as I could) if she knew when and how the pane in the French door got broken. It had happened a few nights before, she said. Her father had heard the noise and gone to investigate, before the intruder was able to get into the house. He hadn't called the police. I had a moment alone with Marcia, and told her that the custody situation was settled: Miles' will named her Caitlin's guardian and trustee. She seemed relieved, although there was a look on her face I couldn't read. Once more, I had the feeling that there was something going on with her that I didn't understand.

Threadgill's is a place you'll want to go when you come to Austin. Kenneth Threadgill got the first beer license in Travis County in 1933, right after Prohibition, when he converted an old Gulf filling station into a beer joint on North Lamar Boulevard. Threadgill played guitar and yo-deled with his band, the Hootenanny Hoots, and by the sixties, the beer hall was home to every country musician who came to town—including Janis Joplin, a lost young girl who poured some of her first public songs into the Thread-gill mike. Kenneth Threadgill died in 1987, but his legacy lives on, and in 1996, Threadgill's No. 2 opened up next door to the National Guard Armory that was once home to the Armadillo World Headquarters. Look up when you go inside. The piano hanging from the ceiling was memorably played by the likes of Jerry Lee Lewis, Ray Charles, and Fats Domino.

McQuaid indulged his chile passion by ordering a buffalo chicken sandwich and a plate of cheese-stuffed jalapeños. Not having an asbestos-lined gut, I took some time to consider the issue, pondering the bronzed catfish (with Cajun spices) and the grilled pork chops and apple-sauce and finally going for a Rio Grande veggie burger and a plate of fried green tomatoes. While we waited for our food, McQuaid filled me in on the details of his discovery of Dad's car, hidden under a tarp in a barn on the Two-Bar Ranch, next to a tomatillo field. He turned on his digital camera and showed me the pictures he'd taken.

A chill went through me and I shivered. I hadn't seen that car since the day after the crash, in the police impound yard. But it certainly looked like the car my father had died in. The burned, flattened wreckage was mute testimony to the blazing horror of his death. I had to turn away.

"This is the VIN number," McQuaid said, showing me the photo he'd taken of it. "I'll check it against the police report, but unless there was a substitution somewhere along the line that Laura Danforth didn't know about, this is the car. She thought so, anyway." He shook his head and clicked to another photo. "If there's any clue to the cause of the wreck, it isn't immediately obvious. But of course, I haven't had time to go over it carefully."

I frowned, thinking of what had happened to Miles. "Do you think the car is safe there, McQuaid? We don't know why Laura Danforth felt she had to keep it. Now Miles is dead, and we don't know the full story there, either. What if somebody else figures out where that car is hidden and decides it's time to get rid of it?"

"Good point," he said thoughtfully, dropping his camera into his pocket. "It might be smart to get it moved somewhere else. I'll talk to Ellie about that first thing tomorrow. Hey, look!" As our waitperson set a plate in front of him, he reached for the bottle of hot sauce in the middle of the table.

I shuddered at his plateful of fire power. I enjoy a mild jalapeño, as long as I don't crunch down on a seed, and enchiladas without chopped green chilies are like a dog without a bark. But I'll take a fried green tomato any day of the week. Tomatoes don't fire back.

McQuaid finished dosing his chicken sandwich and picked it up. "So tell me about Caitlin," he said.


MRS. BOLTON lived near St. Edward's University, a small Catholic institution built in the 1880s when everything south of the river was open farm country and the students and faculty were still safely isolated on their remote campus. I had phoned before I left the restaurant and got her after five rings, just as her answering machine kicked in. She sounded breathless and out of it, but she'd said it would be okay if I dropped off the files I had found on Miles' desk.

McQuaid headed back to Pecan Springs to pick up Brian after his baseball game. I drove down Riverside and made a right onto South Congress. Twilight was falling by the time I reached the neighborhood of modest single-story bungalows that had sprouted like mushrooms in the forties and fifties. The western sky was washed with the sun's last light, while to the east and south, fingers of lightning still flickered through the lavender and mauve storm clouds that were moving south and east, toward the coast.

I made another right off Congress, checked the street numbers as I drove a couple of blocks west, and parked in front of a green-shingled house set well back from the quiet street. My Toyota felt much more at home here than it had on Cat Mountain. In this neighborhood, there was a pickup truck in every driveway, Harleys and Hondas were parked on front porches, and pot-bellied guys in Houston Astros caps, beer cans in their hands, stood around watching the kids kick soccer balls in the street while the kids' dogs ran circles around them, barking gleefully.

There was a red older-model Ford in Mrs. Bolton's driveway, so I knew she was at home. The front of the house was screened by forsythia bushes—in the Far East, where the plant originated, the roots are boiled to treat bacterial and fungal infections—and the sweet scent of honeysuckle drifted from the vine that climbed across the porch, host to a hummingbird who had dropped in for a late-evening sip. Roses bloomed under a window, and the front walk was bordered by johnny-jump-ups, their cream-and-violet faces turned up. As I knocked at the door, I felt more cheerful than I had for most of the day. A world where kids kick soccer balls, dogs bark, and flowers bloom overhead and around my feet is the kind of world I'm glad to live in.

The heavyset woman who peered through the crack in the door was anything but cheerful, and she certainly didn't look like the same well-groomed, competent woman I had met in Miles' office. Her short, gray-brown hair was mussed, her white blouse and dark skirt were rumpled, as if she had worn them while she napped, and her nose was red. She held a pair of gold-rimmed glasses in one hand, and she was pressing a tissue to her eyes.

"Thank you for coming, Ms. Bayles," she said through the door. She spoke in a dry, precise voice, although the words seemed slightly slurred. "You can just put the files beside the door. I'll get them later."

I felt a stirring of sympathy. She was probably undone by Miles' death. If I hadn't had to come to Austin to deal with the aftermath, I might have been tempted to put down a few myself. "Please call me China," I said, holding on to the files. "Would you mind if we talked for few minutes? Marcia—Miles' sister-in-law—and I have some funeral arrangements to work out. We were hoping you'd be able to help."

Her face crumpled. "Funeral? Oh. Oh, yes, of course. What am I thinking? I'll be glad to help." She put her glasses back on and slid the chain off the door. "Please accept my . . . my deepest condolences," she added. The formality of her words was slightly marred by a hiccup that she tried to cover with a cough.

"Thank you," I said, stepping inside, near enough to her to smell the liquor on her breath. "I know it must have been a shock for you, too."

She shook her head despairingly. "I haven't been able to stop thinking about it. Your brother was always so kind to me, especially when I had to take time off to—" She swallowed, her eyes tearing up again behind her glasses. "Would you like a drink? Or coffee? I've made a pot."

*Especially when I had to take time off for alcohol re-hab?* Everybody seemed to be doing it these days. "Coffee would be great," I said. I set the files on the hall table and followed her.

The kitchen was neat and orderly to a fault, the counters sparkling, the white tile floor glistening, a red-and-white checked cloth on the white table and matching red-checked curtains tied back with jaunty red bows at windows that looked into a backyard bordered by blooming roses. The windowsill displayed a collection of forties' ceramic salt-and-pepper shakers made in the shapes and colors of yellow ears of corn, round green cabbages, and ruby red tomatoes. On the gleaming white gas range, a red ceramic rooster kept watch over his ceramic red hen, and a large bowl in the shape of a cauliflower sat on top of the microwave. But there were two tell-tale signs of Mrs. B's emotional disorder: the overflowing ashtray on the kitchen table and the nearly empty bottle of Jack Daniel's on the counter, a highball glass with a couple of ice trays beside it. I guessed that Mrs. Bolton was a carefully controlled person, and when life smacked her in the face with something unpredictable and uncontrollable, she drank.

With a quick glance to see if I had noticed, she emptied the ashtray and wiped it out. Then she poured a cup of coffee from the pot in the coffeemaker and set it in front of me, with a neat little tray of sugar, sweetener, and those plastic tubs of creamer that you get in a restaurant. She hesitated for a moment, a cup in her hand, then set it down and, almost defiantly, added ice to the glass and slopped it half full of whiskey. If she wasn't sloshed already, she soon would be.

We sat down at the table. "Your roses are lovely, Mrs. Bolton," I said, glancing out the window. A black cat was stretched out on the outer sill, having a nap in the sun.

Mrs. B reached into the pocket of her wrinkled skirt and took out a package of cigarettes and a lighter. "They're prettier this year than they've been for a long time. The rain this afternoon kind of beat them down, though." She lit the cigarette and inhaled deeply, turning to look out the window. "I cut a big bunch of the white roses this morning, and put them on Mr. Danforth's desk. He liked me to bring flowers. Said it made things feel homey. Karen—his wife, so sweet, such a lady—always brought flowers to the office." Her voice trembled, and she pulled on the cigarette again, as if for strength.

I sipped my coffee. "You've worked for Miles a long time?"

"Since he came to the firm, eleven years ago." She took a hefty swallow of whiskey, and a note of something like pride came into her voice. "I was Mr. Brandon's secretary for a year before that, so I already knew the ropes, you might say. I like to think I was a lot of help to Mr. Danforth." The cat jumped down from the windowsill and came around to the kitchen door, meowing to be let in. "This is Merlin," she said, getting up to open the door. "He's my baby."

"I'm sure Miles valued what you did," I said, as she scooped the cat into her arms and sat back down at the table. "I know what a challenge legal work can be. Having somebody you can count on makes all the difference." Eleven years is longer than many marriages, and a good secretary not only knows where the bodies are buried, but which closets conceal the skeletons. If Mrs. Bolton wanted to tell tales, she undoubtedly knew a great many.

She buried her face in the cat's fur and the tears started again. "Mr. Danforth was a real gentleman. So easy to work for, not like some." She looked up with a blurry glance. "I'm not saying anything against any of the partners in the firm, mind you. They're all gentlemen, except for—" She bit back whatever she had been going to say. "But Mr. Danforth, he was special. We never had a cross word in all our eleven years together. He was the soul of kindness. The very soul."

"I'm sure that Miles wouldn't have known what to do without you," I said. I wondered what would happen to her now that Miles was dead, what other niche in the firm she would be able to fill.

My remark prompted a fresh flurry of tears, too much for Merlin, who jumped off her lap and headed purposefully toward the living room. There was a napkin holder on the table—two bright yellow ceramic ducks propping up a sheaf of green paper napkins between their upraised bills. She pulled out a napkin and blew her nose.

"I knew something was wrong when he didn't come in this morning," she said disconsolately. "He always called when he was going to be late, even if it was only a few minutes. He sent an email to my computer before he left last night, giving me a list of papers he needed for a case he was working on. He wanted me to get them for him first thing, so he could do some personal business later in the day. So that's what I did. I got everything together—" She hiccupped delicately. "And I put it on his desk. But he never . . . He never came."

Personal business. That would be his meeting with Mc-Quaid, no doubt, to look for the car.

"I haven't been able to talk to the investigating officer yet," I said. "Who found him?"

Mrs. B stubbed out her cigarette, then picked up the ashtray and carried it to the sink, where she dropped the butt in the garbage and wiped out the ashtray. "Jeannie. One of the interns. About nine thirty, I happened to mention to Mr. Brady that Mr. Danforth hadn't come in yet, which was odd because he'd been very definite about wanting the papers early, and Mr. Brady said it *really* was odd, because he'd seen Mr. Danforth's car in the garage, in the regular parking place, and where was he? So he sent Jeannie down to have a look. She came back white as a sheet and hysterical, and we called the police. Mr. Brady and Mr. Brandon went down and waited until they arrived." She came back to the table and sat down. Her eyes were silvered with tears. "He was . . . They said Mr. Danforth was lying between his car and Mr. Zwinger's—actually, it's Mrs. Zwinger's car. It's parked there while she's in Miami. He was probably thrown there by the impact. Or maybe he . . . crawled."

I shivered. "How awful," I whispered. It was. It was horrible.

There was a silence. After a moment, I said, "Did the police come up to the office? Did they talk to anyone?"

"They talked to me," she replied. "They wanted to know what time I thought he had left the night before, what time he was expected in. That sort of thing. I don't think they talked to anybody else, though." She reached for another napkin and blew her nose again. "Is Caitlin—is she with her aunt?"

I closed my mind to the image of Miles, lying dead in the parking garage, and took a deep breath. "Yes. She's at Marcia's. I went out to the house and got Caitlin some clothes. That's when I found the files."

Mrs. Bolton's hand trembled as she picked up her glass and emptied it with a swallow. "Poor little girl," she whispered. "First her mother, now this. I don't know how she'll bear it." She closed her eyes. "How any of us will bear it."

"It's tough," I said, thinking that getting seriously sloshed was probably a good thing for this woman. She would be so hung over in the morning that the pain—and whatever she took to ease it—would dull her grief. "I saw several photographs of the two of them when I went to pick up her things. She and her father must have been very close."

"Oh, very," she said earnestly. "Mr. Danforth thought the sun rose and set in that little girl. Personally, I was hoping that he and Marcia—" She broke off with a sniff. "Of course, it was none of my business and I would never have said a word to him about it. I'm not the type to meddle in anyone's private affairs, especially when we worked so closely together. But I could see how much Karen's sister loved Caitlin, and I knew that she and her husband weren't getting along. Mr. Sellers was terribly jealous. That was before the divorce, of course."

"He was?" Marcia's husband had been jealous? That was news. And for someone who wasn't the type to meddle in her boss' private affairs, Mrs. Bolton certainly had a great deal of private information about him.

"Oh, yes," she said firmly. "He called Mr. Danforth

once and—" She broke off, coloring slightly, but I got the message. She had listened in on the conversation and had overheard whatever jealous anger Zeke Sellers had unloaded on Miles.

"In that case," I said, "it's probably a good thing that Marcia got a divorce." Although maybe the divorce had not put an end to Sellers' jealousy.

"Oh, absolutely." Mrs. Bolton lit another cigarette. "She was a whole lot better for Mr. Danforth than that other one. I don't mind telling you, I was relieved when he broke off *that* relationship. The complications made me very uneasy. I kept wondering what Mr. Zwinger would say if he found out—and he was bound to find out. In fact, I wouldn't be surprised if the whole office knows by now. It's a terrible place for gossip."

I'd bet. But this game was becoming more than a little confusing, and I wasn't sure I had the players straight. "You're talking about Belinda?" I hazarded. There would certainly be plenty of complications surrounding the Peach, and none of them pleasant.

She stopped just short of rolling her eyes at my ignorance. "No, of course not. Not *her*. There was never anything serious between Mr. Danforth and Mrs. Harcher, I'm sure, although she certainly flung herself at him. Calling him at the office, emailing him about her 'secret longings,' coming by to see if he wanted to go out to lunch." She sniffed distastefully. "But Mrs. Harcher is married, and she means to stay married. She has to. There's a lot of money involved—and all of it belongs to Mr. Harcher. She signed a prenup. If they divorce, she doesn't get a dime."

Trust a secretary to know what's going on in her boss' life, including a neighbor's domestic arrangements and the content of the emails on his computer. I thought fleetingly of my father and Miles' mother. Like father, like son. Miles had fostered the same kind of deep loyalty in his secretary that his father had fostered in Laura Danforth, although it probably wasn't good for either woman. That kind of loyalty, and love, can be inextricably involved with dependence. However, I wanted to know what Mrs. Bolton knew.

"Yes, of course," I murmured. "If you're not talking about Mrs. Harcher, then you must mean—" I paused suggestively.

"Yes, Rachel. Rachel Burke. That's exactly who I mean." Her voice took on a bitter twist and she blew out a stream of smoke. I wanted to get up and open the window, but I wasn't about to break her train of thought. "Unfortunately, Rachel is not the sort of person to take no for an answer," she added. "She's dangerous. In fact, now that I think about it, I wouldn't trust her not to tell her mother."

Rachel, the other witness to the will. Why was Rachel dangerous? And what under the sun did her mother have to do with anything?

But Mrs. Bolton was playing with her cigarette, looking away, as if she were afraid she had said too much. I guessed that she herself had her own secret longings where Miles was concerned, although she might not be fully aware of them—or aware at all. I was sure about one thing, though. This woman knew a great deal, but she was used to keeping her mouth shut and her feelings under wraps. She wouldn't be talking this way if she hadn't had several whiskeys.

But she must have thought she'd gone too far. She stubbed out her cigarette and laced her fingers together, knuckle to knuckle. "You said you wanted to talk about the arrangements."

Drat. What I really wanted to talk about was Rachel Burke, for it sounded as if she and Miles might have had some sort of relationship, which Miles ended. But I only said, "Yes. Yes, of course. Marcia and I were wondering if you could make a list of the people who ought to be personally notified about the funeral services. Marcia has the guest book from Karen's service. Maybe the two of you could compare notes and make sure that no one is left out."

She was nodding, so I went on. "And I was thinking of leaving your office phone number on Miles' answering machine, so that anybody who calls the house can phone you for information." I paused. "His will names me as his executor, so I may be asking you for some additional help."

"Of course," she said, trying not to slur the syllables. "I witnessed his will, you know, just recently. Anything I can do, I'd be more than glad. Mr. Brandon suggested that I take some time off, but I told him I didn't think it was a good idea. I'll feel happier if I'm at my desk."

I was sure that was true. Mrs. Bolton was the kind of woman for whom work was the most significant thing in her life, the way she defined her reality, the cable that connected her to a world beyond herself. Cut it, and the spirit would go out of her. She would be all she had left, and it wouldn't be enough.

"One more thing," I said, leaning forward and lowering my voice. "There's nobody else I can ask about this, Mrs. Bolton. You were so close to my brother, I'm sure you know the answer."

"Yes, we were close," she said, and shut her eyes. "We were very close. Very, very—"

I put my hand on hers, and her eyes came open. "Marcia mentioned that Miles was unhappy at the firm," I said. "He had even talked about leaving. He didn't tell her why, but I'll bet you know."

She focused, with some difficulty, on my face. "Oh, I do," she said. "Yes, I do indeed. There were lots of things, really. But it was mostly because of Mr.—" She seemed to lose track of her thought.

"Yes?" I prompted.

"Mr. Brandon. Christopher Brandon."

Ah. The Brandon of Zwinger, Brady, Brandon, and Danforth. *Christopher* Brandon? The name sounded vaguely familiar. But perhaps Miles had mentioned him in conversation.

She was hesitating, and I could see her wondering whether she could trust me. I said, "It's okay. I won't say anything about this, I promise. But if something was troubling my brother before he died, I'd like to know what it was. I'm sure he wouldn't mind if you told me."

That decided her. "Mr. Brandon and Mr. Danforth weren't— Well, they didn't get along."

"Was there a special problem?"

She clasped her fingers. "Well, I don't know exactly. At first, I thought it was just sort of . . ." She twisted her fingers together. "The same as it was with the others, I mean. The whole firm is like that, you know? There's a lot of infighting and tittle-tattling. I've gotten used to it over the years, as much as you can get used to something like that. But it's not a very harmonious place to work."

I almost smiled. If you're looking for harmony in your work environment, a law firm isn't the place to find it. I'd been there, done that, and still had the scars to show for it. Law firms do their level best to present themselves to the outside world as calm, controlled, and cooperative, but the inside story is something else again—and sometimes it isn't very pretty. Litigation is a combative, contentious business that keeps you constantly on edge, and even when you aren't litigating, you're always under pressure, always dealing with conflict. You sharpen your sword for court, for the client, and you carry that sword back to the firm itself, where everybody else has his or her own personal arsenal. The partners are at one another's throats. The associates, disillusioned and bitter, try to stay out of the fray, but often fall victim to it. And the support staff—the administrative personnel, the paralegals, the interns—are usually the first to feel the heat, because they're not lawyers. They're not swaddled in a lawyer's asbestos ego.

Was this what was going on at Zwinger, Brady, Brandon, and Danforth? Did it have anything to do with Miles' death?

I leaned forward. "These problems between Miles and Christopher Brandon. Did they arise from anything specific, do you think?"

Her face had taken on a greenish tint. "It's been going on for a while, a year or more, maybe. But things really came to a head a couple of weeks ago. It was about . . . something personal Mr. Danforth was working on."

I took a chance. "Something personal? I know he was concerned about a matter that grew out of his mother's estate. He spoke about it to me."

"Yes. His mother." She seemed relieved that I knew what she was talking about. It somehow made it okay for her to tell me the rest of it. "He caught Mr. Brandon in his office, going through one of her files. They had quite an argument about it." She closed her eyes and pressed her lips together. Her face had gone from green to pasty white.

"An argument?" I prodded.

Her eyes came open. "Yes. In fact, it was rather loud. They— Excuse me." She put her hand over her mouth and pushed back her chair.

She didn't quite make it to the sink. I held her head, and by the time she was finished, she was limp and incoherent. I wanted to know what happened when Miles caught Brandon going through his mother's files, but I wasn't going to get the story out of her, not in this condition. I walked her down the hall to her bedroom, stripped off her blouse and skirt, and put her to bed. She was sound asleep before I finished cleaning up the mess on the kitchen floor. I stuck a business card into the frame of her bathroom mirror, with a note on the back. *Let's talk again when you're feeling better.*

I left her sleeping, but the recollection of her quiet desperation haunted me as I drove home to Pecan Springs.


BEFORE we called it a night, McQuaid uploaded his digital photos to his computer and we spent some time looking at them and talking about what he had learned from Ellie Hanson: the story behind the car, what had happened to it, where it had been, when it was moved to the ranch, and why.

The big question, of course, was *why*? Why in the world had Laura Danforth insisted on preserving that wrecked car? What shadowy secrets did she imagine it held? Was she on to something real, or driven by a romantic obsession? It was too bad that car couldn't talk, but maybe that shoebox of notes McQuaid had found in Miles' filing cabinet would answer a few questions. He planned to spend the morning sifting through it, to see if there were any leads worth following up. He was also going to check out somebody named Danny Danforth, to whom Miles' mother had once been married.

And for my part, I was now deeply curious about Christopher Brandon. What possible reason could he have had for rummaging around in Laura Danforth's files? What did he know about any of this? How was he involved?

With all these questions echoing around in my head, I guess it's no surprise that I dreamed about my father. Again, I am walking along the Houston freeway, in the dark, in a nightmarish fog and misty rain, no umbrella, no jacket, not even a sweater. I look at my watch and see that it is, yes, a few minutes before two, and I shiver, asking myself once again what I'm doing here—the same question I always ask in this dream. Why am I always brought here, to this shadowy place? What is it I'm supposed to do, to see, to learn?

And as always in this dream, I don't know the answer until it roars out of the night shadows, my father's blue Cadillac, loud as crashing thunder, faster than a lightning bolt. As I stand watching, the car swerves to the right, its wheels seeming to lift from the pavement, and crashes through the metal guardrail and down the steep embankment, flipping and bouncing end over end, each bounce a bone-shuddering metallic crash. It reaches the bottom and—*KAROOM!*— bursts into lavish, astonishingly beautiful flame.

It's raining harder now. I stand at the guardrail, shoulders hunched against the wet and cold. That's my father down there in that flaming wreckage, that funeral pyre, but there's nothing I can do to save him. And what's worse, much, much worse, I can't cry, not only can't cry, but can't feel. There's no emotion at all, not terror, not grief, not anger, not pain. There's a lump of diamond-hard, brutally cold ice inside me, and it's never going to thaw.

To this point, the dream is the same as always. I stand at the guardrail, at the top of the embankment, and watch the fire, watch the cops pile out of their cars and run toward the wreckage, watch the fire truck arrive and the firemen foam the blaze with their powerful extinguishers, watch the ambulance come, watch cops and firemen and med tech guys standing around, talking in muted tones until the flames are gone and the wreckage is cool enough to retrieve my father's corpse. Stand there until the dawn turns the night shadows to gray, until the wrecker comes to haul the burned car away, until all that's left is a seared black scar in the weeds at the foot of the embankment.

But tonight, something new has entered my dream, someone new, rather. As my father's car goes over the guardrail, Miles steps out of the night shadows and stands beside me. He doesn't say anything, only puts his arm around my shoulders and holds on to me, tight, as though he'll never let me go. I still can't cry, but he is crying, crying for both of us, wracking, wrenching sobs that shudder up from his gut and tear the night open. We stand there, watching, until the dawn lifts the night shadows and there is nothing more to see.

When I wake, my face is wet with Miles' tears.

# Chapter Eleven

Tobacco (*Nicotiana tabacum*) is arguably the most widely used and problematic member of the nightshade family. The plant offers neither food nor drink and has for centuries been considered harmful, but its commercial production continues to increase. In 2010, consumption of this dangerous nightshade, worldwide, is expected to be about three pounds per person. Tobacco use is the leading preventable cause of death in the United States, resulting in an estimated 440,000 deaths each year, while some eight million people suffer from at least one serious smoking-related illness.

Sometimes things just don't work out the way you plan.

I intended to go back to Austin first thing the next morning to see the investigating officer, collect my brother's personal things from his office, pick up his car from the garage, and drive it to the Cat Mountain house, where McQuaid was supposed to pick me up late in the afternoon.

But first there was the little matter of costume. It might not be a good idea to visit Zwinger, Brady, and Brandon (would somebody be promoted to fill the Danforth slot?) togged out in my usual casual jeans and T-shirt. So I got up early, shampooed my hair, and dug out the only outfit I own that approximates power dressing—charcoal skirt, silky black blouse, red blazer, and black pumps with inch-and-a-half heels. I even put on hose. And a bra that wasn't stretched out. And makeup, for pity's sake. As I got suited up, I reminded myself that I used to do this every day. It wouldn't kill me to play the game again, just once.

I needed a bag, though. My favorite denim fanny pack wouldn't do. I hunted all over the house for the spiffy black leather portfolio bag that Leatha gave me for Christmas a couple of years ago, and finally found it hanging on Brian's doorknob, full of his CDs. I had to clean it up first, but when I slung it over my shoulder and studied myself in the mirror, I decided I still looked enough like a lawyer to fool anybody who didn't sneak a peek at my fingernails, which might be mistaken for gardening tools.

Ruby had volunteered to drive me into Austin so I wouldn't have to juggle two cars. But around breakfast time, she got a call from Cedar Summit, her mother's retirement community in Fredericksburg, about an hour's drive from Pecan Springs. Doris was in the third day of a hunger strike, and the woman who looks after her was desperate enough to call her daughters. Ramona couldn't come (Ruby's sister always seems to have something on her calendar that's more important than her mother), so the task unfortunately fell to Ruby.

"I'm really sorry, China," she said, as she came into my shop. She was dressed in black again this morning, enlivened by touches of purple. Black pants, purple top, purple scarf and thong sandals, a half-dozen strings of purple and black beads. She was carrying a canvas tote bag full of snacks—Cass' lemon cake, some coconut cookies, a box of chocolate truffles—that might tempt her mother. "Maybe Cass can drive you to Austin," she added. "Want me to ask her?"

"It's okay," I said. "I'll manage. You tell Doris to stop acting like a two-year-old and eat what's on her plate." I went to a shelf and took down a package of herbs. "And slip her some of this."

"What is it?"

"An appetite stimulant tea. Ginger root, anise seed, cinnamon, and alfalfa. If that doesn't work, try this." I gave her another box. "Angelica root, peppermint, and celery seed, along with cinnamon."

"I'll make some for her," Ruby said, stowing the packages in her tote bag, "but I can't guarantee she'll drink it. Mother never listened to me before she began losing her mind, so why would she start now?"

I smiled, although I probably shouldn't have. Senile dementia is not funny. I put my arm around her and squeezed. "Can you think of anything else I can do to help?"

She frowned into her purse. "You wouldn't happen to have a spare twenty, would you, China? I'll pay you back as soon as—"

I went to the cash register and took out a pair of twenties. "As soon as they've sent you Colin's insurance, for which you applied yesterday." I eyed her. "You did, didn't you?"

She took the twenties, not looking at me. "Actually, I—"

I sighed. "Ruby, what am I going to do with you? If you don't want it for yourself, think of your children. Think of Grace. If you invested that money now, you could give her four years at Harvard and follow up with a Princeton Ph.D."

"Invested what money?" asked a sprightly voice. "Mom, Kate sent some goodies to take to Grandma."

It was Amy, Ruby's wild child, who is perhaps a little less wild now that she has Grace to look after. Of course, Amy still wears gold rings in unexpected parts of her anatomy, her makeup looks like she's trying out for a part in *Dracula*, and her outfit—skin-tight black jeans with astrological designs stitched across the rear, black-leather rhinestone-studded belt, and neon-painted black tee— might lead you to mistake her for a punk rocker. But Amy's kinky style is part of her charm, as far as I'm concerned. And she's a good mom. This morning, her baby was peering cheerily out of a pack on Amy's back. Grace, who is breast-fed, is an apple-cheeked and healthy five months.

"Good morning, my precious papoose!" Ruby cooed, and planted a smacky kiss on Grace's strawberry curls. "And thank you, Amy," Ruby added, taking the plastic bag her daughter gave her. "I'm sure your grandmother will appreciate this."

"Not if you tell her it came from Kate and me, she won't." Amy tossed her red curls. Doris may be going off the rails about some things, but she knows what she likes. And she does not like the relationship between Kate and Amy. Whenever their names are mentioned, she gives a pious, moralistic sniff and growls, "Lesbians."

But Amy is not deterred by her grandmother's disapproval. "You were talking about Grace going to Harvard when I came in," she went on. "So who's picking up the tab?"

"Never mind," Ruby said briskly, with a warning glance that forbade me to tell her daughter about Colin's legacy. "Amy, dear heart, would it be asking too much for you to give China a ride into Austin? She needs to pick up her brother's car and take it to his house. McQuaid's going to pick her up this afternoon."

"Is that why you're all dressed up?" Amy asked, giving me a raised-eyebrow inspection. "You look wicked, China. Have you lost weight?"

"Where the heck have you been?" I replied. "I've been losing weight for months. Twenty pounds since the first of the year."

"You look great. And I don't think I've ever seen you in heels before. Makeup even." Amy grinned. "I'll bet you're even wearing a bra."

"I am not dressed up," I retorted. "Dressed up is suited up, all one color, with pearls. This is corporate casual. And you'd better look twice, kid, because you won't see me in heels again for a long time." I paused, getting serious. "Listen, Amy, if this is inconvenient for you, I can take my Toyota. Really. It's no big deal." Amy drives an old green Dodge Neon that has definitely seen better days. I wasn't sure that the Gracemobile, as Ruby calls it, would make it all the way to Austin. But Amy was undaunted.

"I can take you," she said confidently. "Grace and I are on our way to Austin, anyway. We have to pick up some medications for Jon." Jon is Jon Green, the veterinarian at the Hill Country Animal Clinic for whom she works parttime. She gave me a sober look. "Kate and I were so sorry to hear about your brother, China. It must be just awful for you."

"Yes," I said. "But lots more awful for his daughter. Caitlin is just ten. She lost her mother three years ago. She's an orphan."

"Horrible for her," Amy murmured, and reached back to tug at Grace's pudgy foot. "It was an auto accident, Mom said."

"A hit-and-run," I replied grimly. "As to whether it was an accident, the jury's still out."

Ruby frowned at me. "Really? You mean, it might be—" She stopped, her eyes widening.

I gave a noncommittal shrug. "It's still under investigation, as the cops say." I knew that Ruby, aka Nancy Drew, Girl Sleuth, would have liked to hear more, but she was in a hurry.

"I'd better get going before Mom starves herself to death." She gave Amy a hug. "'Bye, dumpling," she whispered to Grace, who laughed and patted her grandmother's face. "Take care of my girls," she said to me. "Don't let them get into trouble." And with that admonition, she was gone, in a swirl of purple and black.

"Poor Mom," Amy said sadly. "If it's not one thing, it's another. Her mother, Colin—" She shook her head. "It's a lot to handle all at one time."

*And on top of that, there's Colin's money,* I thought to myself, but I kept my mouth shut. What Ruby did about the insurance was her business, not mine, although I considered it my duty to make sure she did *something*.

"I'll be ready to go as soon as Laurel comes in," I said. "In the meantime, I think I just heard Cass going into the kitchen. She usually stops at Lila's diner on the way in, to pick up some jelly doughnuts. Why don't you go and see if she's got any?"

Amy gave me a disapproving look. "I'll see if she's got a banana," she said. "Grace and I don't need all that sugar."

AMY let me out in front of police headquarters, and I went inside to see what I could find out. But I had no better luck today than I'd had yesterday. Officer Wilkins was working a messy vehicular homicide on Airport Boulevard, involving a drunk driver, an eighteen-wheeler, and three people waiting for a bus. She was obviously going to be busy for a while, so I left my cell phone number, then walked to the offices of Zwinger, Brady, Brandon, and Danforth on Lavaca Street—not an easy thing, I'll tell you, in my pumps. By the time I got there, I knew I should have stuck a pair of tennies into my spiffy leather bag.

I'd been to Miles' office a couple of times before, so I knew my way around, sort of. I went first to the B level of the parking garage. Miles' black BMW—a nearly new four-door sedan—was still there, parked in the farthest corner, where the ramp made a left turn down to the A level, the lowest level. I saw no sign of skid marks. If there had been any vehicular debris, the police had removed it, but the yellow chalk $X$ that designated the presumed point of impact was visible on the concrete, some five yards from Miles' car.

I spotted the chalked outline of the body where it had been found sprawled between the BMW and a silver gray Lexus, which presumably belonged to the absent Mrs. Zwinger. The Lexus was covered with a film of gritty dust. There was a pool of dried blood on the cement between the cars.

Staring at the outline, I was almost swamped by a wave of anger and sadness. A man's life had been taken. A daughter had lost her father. Accident or something worse, this was an unspeakable tragedy, and it made me feel empty and raw. But I pushed the feeling away and tried to picture what had been going on in those last fatal seconds before my brother was killed.

I turned to look up the ramp in the direction of the elevator. Miles must have come out of the elevator and headed down the ramp in the direction of his car, walking fast, probably, maybe thinking of what he was going to do the next day, the trip he was going to take with McQuaid. I could see for myself that this underground level of the garage was badly lit. There was one parking level below this, so the vehicle that hit him might have been coming up from Level A or down from Level C—or from somewhere higher, from the street, even. These three lowest levels of the garage were reserved for office parking only, not public parking. Had the police interviewed the holders of the parking spaces? Had they checked any of the parked vehicles for damage? Were there any vehicles that should have been in the garage, and now were not? These were questions I'd have to ask Officer Wilkins, when I finally managed to catch up with her.

And what about the entry to the parking garage? Had there been an attendant on duty the night before? I wouldn't have to wait for Officer Wilkins to turn up to get an answer to that question, though. I asked the man stationed in the booth at the Lavaca Street entry.

"Ain't got no night attendant," he told me, in what sounded like a New Joisey accent. He was a short, white male in his late fifties, balding, with a paunch that strained the buttons of his gray uniform shirt. "I close up and go home at eight, so there ain't no nighttime public parking, neither. But if youse work here and youse wanna park at night, youse can buy a card that'll let youse punch in and out."

What youse punched into and out of was a card reader stationed on a metal pole beside the gate, which recorded the after-hours entrances and exits. Except that this gizmo was out of commission.

He jerked a grimy thumb at the wrecked card reader, which looked like it had been hit by a fair-sized truck—or whacked with a sledgehammer. "See that thing there? Found it all bent over like that when I came in one morning last week. Sure would like to see the damage that did to somebody's vehicle." He chuckled cheerily.

I looked at the card reader, thinking that if I intended to run somebody down and wanted to come and go without leaving a record, I'd disable it, too. But that line of inquiry was better left to the cops. I could only hope that Officer Wilkins had the inclination—and the investigators—to pursue it.

I took the elevator upstairs to the twenty-second floor. When I got off, the first thing I saw was a large black wreath on the door to the offices of Zwinger, Brady, Brandon, and, yes, Danforth. A tasteful, black-bordered sign announced, with regret, the accidental death of Mr. Danforth. The receptionist at the front desk—a slender, well-groomed young woman in her middle twenties, with smoky lavender eyes and champagne-colored hair snugged back into a chignon at the nape of her neck—was dressed in a classy black suit that could only have come from Saks or Neiman Marcus, a heart-shaped diamond pendant sparkling at her throat. She was the picture of restrained and tasteful grief. Seeing her, I instantly regretted my red blazer, but was glad for my black blouse and heels, small tokens of mourning.

I asked for Mrs. Bolton, and wasn't surprised to learn that she wasn't in this morning. After last night, it was no wonder. "I'm China Bayles," I said. I was about to add that I was Mr. Danforth's sister, when I found myself hesitating, remembering what Mrs. Bolton had said about the currents of animosity that swirled through the firm. It might not be a good idea to identify myself too specifically. I settled for, "I'm a member of the family and the executor of Mr. Danforth's estate. I came to pick up his car." I paused. "I thought I might get the personal things from his office, while I'm here. Is this a convenient time?"

Elaine Sanders—the receptionist's name, according to the gold plaque on her polished mahogany desk—smiled, showing impossibly white teeth. "Oh, yes, of course," she said, and pressed a button on the phone with a beautifully manicured nail, gleaming and frosty. "Mr. Brandon asked me to let him know if any of the family came in. Please take a seat in the waiting area. He'll be right with you."

"Thank you," I said, and went where I was directed. The waiting area, like that in most law firms, was designed to impress the high-end clients and let the low-end potential wanna-be clients know they couldn't afford the firm's services. There was a carpet that muffled voices and footsteps; garnet velvet sofas and chairs that suggested comfort and stability; *Wall Street Journal* and the *National Review* on the tables; and original oil paintings of Texas ranch life on the walls and lush potted plants in the corners—touches of the "natural" in an entirely artificial environment. For years, I had moved easily through offices like this one, felt comfortable in them, even imagined, from time to time, that I belonged. It wasn't true any longer. This was not my world. I felt uneasy, out of place.

I was pretending to admire a painting when a man came toward me, his hand outstretched. "Christopher Brandon, Ms. Bailey. I'm very glad to meet you."

He had my name wrong, but I didn't bother to correct

him. So this was Christopher Brandon, the man Miles had caught going through his papers. He was tall, perhaps six-one, and about thirty pounds over his ideal weight. Early fifties, with square jaw and heavy jowls. Brown hair combed artfully over a large frontal bald spot, watchful blue eyes that gave nothing away. Well-tailored dark gray suit, black silk tie with a handsome gold tie clip, black leather shoes, highly polished, heavy Rolex. His grip was firm and his hand was as smooth as his face. I was uneasily aware that mine was rough from garden work. I repossessed it as soon as I could.

"I am so sorry," he said. His voice was deep and firm and resonant. This man would be impressive as hell in front of a jury. He'd have them eating out of his well-manicured hand. "*We* are so sorry—the whole firm, that is. In fact, we're all in a state of shock, just in shock." He shook his head, pressing his lips together. "What can I say? It was a horrible, horrible accident. Please convey the firm's deepest condolences to the family, Ms. Bailey. Miles was a fine lawyer, and a gracious and generous human being. We shall all miss him."

"Thank you," I said, feeling inadequate to his eloquence. But there was more: I had the strong feeling that I had seen this man before, or at least heard him speak. He had a memorable voice. But I couldn't for the life of me remember where. In court, maybe?

Mr. Brandon put his head to one side and studied me as if he were calculating my potential as a paying client. Then he smiled slightly, a dismissive smile that made me feel as if I had been measured against a secret standard and rejected. "You're the executor of Miles' estate, I'm told." He made it a statement, and I nodded. "I understand that you'd like to pick up his personal things this morning. Let me show you to his office. You've been here before?"

"Yes," I said, as we walked along a hallway.

"Then I'm sure Miles showed you around," he replied.

Without waiting for an answer, he stopped at an open door and gestured. "Our library." It was a large room, the walls filled floor-to-ceiling with leather-bound reference books, rows of bookshelves at one end, a polished wooden conference table in the center. "We're proud of our substantial resources for legal research," he added. "We're passionate about research. We do quite a bit of it, as you might guess."

What I guessed was that the paralegals and associates did 99 percent of the research and document review, each of them working some seventy hours a week, billable hours, of course.

He picked up the pace again, stopping at another open door. "This is where our paralegals and interns work." A bullpen with a dozen cubicles, several of them occupied by young women and men staring at computer terminals, with copy machines, fax machines, and file cabinets lined up along the wall. All of them kept their eyes studiously glued to their work. It was another glimpse—a revealing one—into the culture of the firm.

Brandon indicated a closed door. "Mrs. Bolton's office," he said. "I'm sorry she isn't here to help you today. She worked for Miles for a very long time, as perhaps you know. She's feeling the loss, as we all are." She was also feeling the consequences of last night's injudicious drinking, I suspected. I'd give her a call later in the day. I wanted to continue the conversation that had ended when she threw up and had to be put to bed.

He opened another door and stood back. His voice—where *had* I heard it before?—deepened and slowed respectfully. "And this is Miles' office, of course. I'm sure you'll want to spend some time here, so I'll leave you. If there's anything you need, anything at all, just buzz Rachel at the front desk. She'll be glad to get it for you."

I lifted my head. *Rachel, not Elaine.* I hazarded a guess. "That would be Rachel Burke, would it?"

"Yes. Mrs. Zwinger's daughter. She's in for Elaine

today." He smiled. "Shall I ask her to bring you some coffee?"

"Coffee would be nice." He had just answered one of my unasked questions. Rachel Burke was the other witness to Miles' will, the woman whose relationship with Miles had recently ended, according to Mrs. Bolton. The one who was "dangerous."

And it answered another question, too. I remembered Mrs. Bolton saying that she didn't trust Rachel "not to tell her mother"—who, it turns out, was the wife of the senior partner, and everything suddenly became clear. Relationships in law firms can be as convoluted and stormy as any long-running soap opera, with alliances established and broken, angers awakened and assuaged, antagonisms aroused and soothed. But whatever else goes on, one thing is a given. It is a very, very, *very* bad idea to sleep with a senior partner's wife's daughter. Unless you're serious about her, that is. Unless you're willing to make her an honest woman, if that's what she wants you to do. Unless the senior partner's wife is happy to welcome you into the family. And even then, it is not recommended.

I shook my head. I could personally testify that my brother, as a teenager, had been a very sexy guy. As a grown man, he had been equally sexy, and there were several grown women who obviously found him disturbingly, perhaps irresistibly attractive. I knew about his sister-in-law Marcia, whose recently divorced husband, Zeke, was in the habit of making harassing phone calls; his neighbor Belinda, whose husband was in a humongous snit; and the boss' wife's daughter Rachel, who was "dangerous." Not to mention his secretary, who clearly had her own secret longings. Were there others I did not yet know about? It was a disturbing thought.

And then an even more disturbing thought crawled out of a dark corner of my mind, where unpleasant things like this go to hide from the bright light of day. McQuaid was certain that Miles' death was connected to their investigation into Dad's death. But maybe the investigation was totally beside the point. Maybe Miles had been killed because of his relationship with one of these women. Maybe one of *them* had killed him!

I shuddered. It was a possibility, certainly. An automobile is a weapon that can be wielded in passion—on the irrational impulse of the moment—or with deliberate, cold-blooded malice aforethought. It's an equal-opportunity weapon, a killing tool that a woman might feel much more comfortable using than, say, a gun. I remembered a case not too long ago, where a jury found a woman guilty of murder after she slammed her SUV into her philandering husband in a parking lot outside the hotel where she'd found him with his lover. Witnesses had watched, horrified, as the killer backed up and ran over her victim several times, laughing merrily like Kathy Bates in *Fried Green Tomatoes*.

Could that have happened to Miles? Were the police investigating his death from this angle? I doubted it. I would be very surprised if any of these women had surfaced in their investigation.

I had enough on my plate at the moment, though, and this was not something I wanted to think about. I pushed the questions out of my mind and focused on the task at hand. The shelves were full of books, but I had no way of knowing which of them belonged to Miles and which to the firm. I gathered up the photographs of Caitlin that stood on the credenza, the usual framed diplomas and board certificates on the wall, and more of the same political photos I'd seen in his office at home. I found three handball trophies and a ceramic cup that said "World's Greatest Boss," as well as a heavy onyx ashtray that bore his initials in gold, with the matching set of gold pens and a letter opener in an onyx holder.

I stacked everything on the table, then sat down in the leather chair behind the desk—an imposing executive model that looked like it belonged in the Oval Office—and pulled out the drawers, one at a time. They were full of the usual stuff, paper clips and rubber bands, but there were no personal files. Miles must have taken everything home after he found Brandon going through them. What was Brandon after? And why? I frowned. And who the devil *was* he, anyway? Why did I keep remembering that voice?

I was pondering this when I heard a light tap on the door. "I've brought your coffee, Ms. Bayles," Rachel Burke said, coming into the room and putting a small tray on the desk. In addition to the coffee, served in a gilt-edged porcelain cup, there were two biscottis, individually wrapped in foil. Not a doughnut, or peanut butter and crackers, but biscottis. This was definitely a high-class law firm.

"Thank you," I said, and smiled. "I was wondering—could you leave a note for Mrs. Bolton? I'd appreciate it if she would go through the shelves and separate Miles' books from those that belong to the firm."

She frowned. "Didn't Mr. Brandon tell you? Mrs. Bolton has decided to leave the firm."

I stared at her, an alarm bell clanging in my head. No, Brandon hadn't told me, even though he had had a very good opportunity to do so. The decision must have been very abrupt. Mrs. B certainly hadn't given any indication of it the night before. And why hadn't Brandon mentioned it?

"I'm sorry to hear that," I said slowly. "I know how much Miles valued her work."

"Yes." Rachel's face was tight, her mouth pinched. "Well, she and Mr. Danforth worked together for a very long time. I think she just couldn't bear to come back and find him . . . gone." She paused, glancing around. "I'll be glad to sort the books, if you would like."

"Thanks," I said. "That would be great." Now that I knew who Rachel Burke was, I couldn't help wondering why she was working here. Her stepfather was the senior partner. She surely didn't need the money, unless her parents made her pay her own Neiman Marcus bill. It actually gave me some pleasure to give her a job. "Do you suppose you could find a box for me? There are a few personal things here that I need to take."

"Yes, of course." She went to the door, put her hand on the knob, hesitated, and turned to face me, leaning against the closed door as if for support. She spoke with obvious reluctance, fingering the heart-shaped diamond pendant at her throat. "I . . . I was wondering if it's okay if I stopped at Miles'—Mr. Danforth's—house today or tomorrow, whenever you're going to be there. I left . . ." She frowned and bit her lip, distracted and uneasy. "This is really awkward, I'm afraid. I hope I can trust you to keep it confidential."

"Of course," I said. Now, really. Whatever it was, who would I tell? Her mother?

She shifted uncomfortably. "Well, to be perfectly honest, I left a dress in Mr. Danforth's closet. I know how this sounds, and I suppose I really shouldn't ask. But it's my favorite dress, and I'd really like to have it back."

Ah, yes. The classy red cocktail dress, which I thought might have belonged to Karen or even to Marcia. Silly me.

"Sure," I said, and smiled, in a kindly way, I thought. "That won't be a problem, Rachel. I'm going to the house after I leave here, and I'll probably be there for a couple of hours. Perhaps you'd like to stop by this afternoon?"

She gave what can only be described as a sigh of profound relief. "Yes, I would, thank you," she said gratefully "About three o'clock?"

I nodded, and she went to get the box.

# Chapter Twelve

**McQuaid: The Missing Piece**

McQuaid has a long list of things to do this morning, but first things first.

China left early, and McQuaid gets Brian off to school. He helps hunt for the kid's math homework, finds his lunch (how the lunch sack got into the bathroom is a mystery that neither he nor Brian wants to tackle at this hour of the morning), and shoves him out the door about two minutes ahead of the school bus.

There's something about giving your son a good-bye hug and watching him go off to school that puts the rest of the world in perspective, McQuaid thinks as he closes the front door and goes back upstairs. It's hard to believe, but Brian will be a sophomore in high school next year, and after that, college is just a few homework assignments away. The house is going to seem pretty empty without the boy and his collections of spiders, snakes, and lizards.

McQuaid wishes, just a little, that he and China could've had kids. But she was nearly forty when she ditched her high-octane career and a few years past by the time they got married. And while she loves Brian dearly, she always claims to be glad that she was not part of the team during the Diaper Days. McQuaid knew when he married her that kids weren't an option. It's never been an issue, and it's only occasionally that he wonders how their lives would be different if she'd gotten pregnant.

Upstairs, he dumps a load of sheets and towels into the washer, adds soap and turns it on, then retrieves Brian's lizard from the bathtub and puts it back in the terrarium with the others, making a mental note to remind the kid that he's going to lose his lizard privileges if he can't control their wanderlust. Then it's back downstairs to the kitchen, where he puts in a quick call to Blackie Blackwell—Adams County sheriff and longtime personal friend—to find out where their traveling poker game will be that night. Turns out to have been cancelled, which is okay with McQuaid. He's already got enough to do today.

The kitchen seems too quiet, with everybody out of the house. McQuaid and China usually have breakfast together there, or they go out on the porch for orange juice and coffee and a few quiet moments to get in gear for the day. But China had to leave early for Austin, where she's picking up Miles' car from the garage and taking it to his house. McQuaid will pick her up around three thirty or four. She's got a big job ahead of her just getting a handle on what's involved with the estate, for which she is now the executrix. *Executor*, he reminds himself. He shakes his head ruefully, wondering if she knows what a helluva job she's getting into.

In the kitchen, McQuaid makes a pot of coffee and pulls a couple of breakfast burritos—China's handwritten label says these are beef and chipotle burritos—out of the freezer. Howard Cosell comes in off the porch where he's been lying with his chin on his paws, hoping that Brian might miss the bus and come back home but knowing gloomily that he won't. He looks up at McQuaid, wondering if he can have some burrito, too. A little bit of burrito would go a long way toward easing the pangs of loneliness.

"Not a chance, Howard, old boy," McQuaid says cheerfully, as the burritos go into the microwave. "Chiles are on your no-no list, remember?" Howard ate a jalapeño pepper once, and suffered mightily from the experience. You'd think he'd have the sense to stay away from them. But you can't teach an old dog new tricks, and Howard definitely has a few years on him.

Seeing Howard's downcast expression, McQuaid goes to the cookie jar and gets a dog biscuit. He has the feeling that Howard misses Rambo, the Rottweiler that belonged to Colin Fowler and was recently recruited to the PSPD's new K-9 Corps. The two dogs didn't see eye to eye on most things, especially when it came to who owned which territory, but they were company for each other. Rambo has now gone on to greater glories as a cop dog, and Howard's been moping around, a gloomier-than-usual look on his gloomy face. Bassets are extremely intelligent dogs, and McQuaid suspects that Howard (who is already inclined to take a dismal view of the world) feels that his true potential has never been fully realized. He, too, would love to join the K-9 Corps, but he's a realist. He knows this isn't in the cards.

McQuaid takes the burritos out of the microwave, opens the jar of Ellie Hanson's tomatilla salsa, and doses them liberally. Plate in hand and Howard at his heels, he walks to work down the hall. His office is a large room that used to be a bedroom, high-ceilinged, like the rest of the old house, with a polished wood floor that reflects the morning sunshine. His desk and computer workstation are arranged against a wall, which makes it harder for him to kill time by staring out the window. There are three chairs (in case there are two clients) in the corner, in front of the bookshelves, which McQuaid built himself of dark oak.

The shelves are full of the cop books—texts on forensics, methods of detection, legal issues, and so on—he used when he was doing his graduate work in criminology. There are also shelves of research materials for his book about the Texas Rangers, which he hopes to finish before too long. The only other important history of the Rangers is a 1935 book by a Texas historian named Walter Prescott Webb, which has been called "The beginning, middle, and end of the subject." Except that Webb was a dyed-in-the-wool Ranger fan who made them look like a gang of good guys, conveniently overlooking the unarmed men they shot and the citizens they assaulted. McQuaid's revisionist history—if it ever gets finished—isn't likely to earn him any praise from the Rangers.

The rest of the office is pretty standard. Fax, copier, printer, filing cabinets, more shelves. Beside the desk, there's a Howard-sized basset bed that smells just like Howard. The room has its own outside door, which bears the legend: Michael McQuaid and Associates, Private Investigator. McQuaid has explained to Howard that "Associates" does not refer to him, but to the consultants—professionals in specialized areas such as forensic computing, forensic photography, forensic accounting, insurance fraud, and so on—with whom he plans to associate when the need arises. It hasn't yet, but it will, he hopes.

In fact, on McQuaid's list of things to do today is to get in touch with the person who designed China's website, which looks really great. He needs a website, and he's been thinking about some things that ought to go into it—like his bio (emphasizing his police work and teaching) and the fields the firm specializes in (right now, that's just about everything, from background checks to bug sweeps). He's also going to let Charlie Lipman know that he's available for divorce work. McQuaid doesn't like divorce, but somebody's got to pay the bills. He doesn't like marketing much, either, but he's beginning to realize that clients are not going to just leap eagerly into his boat, gasping for help. As Charlie says, he's got to fish for them, and hook them, and haul them in.

Either that, or go back to teaching, part-time, anyway. McQuaid is not crazy about the idea. This has nothing to do with the students, whom he likes, but with faculty politics in the Criminal Justice Department at CTSU, which is pretty nearly as bad as the politics at Houston PD, where he put in more years than he likes to remember. And he'd a helluva lot rather work here at the house in his sweats than get dressed, drive to campus, and hunt for a parking space. But he will, if push comes to shove. And from the looks of the checkbook, shove isn't far away. As soon as he wraps up the Danforth case (actually, he is now working for his wife, in her new role as the estate executor), he has to focus on bringing in new work.

But thinking of the case brings him back to this morning's tasks: asking Hawk to check up on Danny Danforth, doing some online research on the Bayles' Cadillac, and sorting through the shoebox of stuff he retrieved from Miles' filing cabinet. And McQuaid is still puzzling over the questions that came up yesterday. Why the hell didn't Miles just come out and tell him where the car was? What else had he known? Did what he know have anything to do with his death?

The desk is a mess, as usual, and McQuaid has to clear a place to set the plate of burritos down. He boots up the computer and eats one burrito while he's waiting for it to come up (which gives him time to appreciate Ellie's salsa, which is indeed hot enough to toast tonsils) and the other while he's waiting for the dial-up so he can go online. The wait is frustrating, but this far out in the country, there's no way they'll ever do better than dial-up. So it goes. You learn to live with what you've got.

He shuffles things around on the desk until he finds the notebook he was carrying yesterday, then flips to the page where he copied the vehicle identification number for the Caddy. Without the VIN, it would be tough to make a positive ID on the car. It's like human DNA—a full description of a car's pedigree and an invaluable resource for car collectors, as well as cops, private investigators, and insurance companies. If you've got the VIN, you can pretty much tell what kind of car you're dealing with, even if there's nothing left of it but a bucket of bits and bolts.

The computer is up and online. He checks the email for anything interesting, maybe from a potential client, but there's nothing worth spending time on. He opens his browser and logs on to a website that gives him a chart to decode the VIN number for 1980s Cadillacs. The chart comes up and he studies it, making notes. The first number, 1, identifies the country of manufacture. The second, 6, identifies the manufacturer, General Motors; the next, the division: Cadillac. And so on. From the VIN, McQuaid can tell that this car is a Brougham, a Fleetwood rear-wheel drive four-door sedan with a V8-350 diesel, a 1985 model, off the Detroit assembly line.

There's some fine print at the bottom of the chart, historical notes and stuff, and he reads with a mild interest. The Fleetwood was introduced in April 1984. The model-year production was close to 395,000, which included only 1100 V-8 diesels—not a popular option, apparently. Robert Bayles' car was a tank, weighing in at nearly four thousand pounds. Diesel-powered and carrying all that armor, it must have been a real slug. A noisy slug, too, McQuaid thinks with a grin, remembering how those early diesels clattered. But the Fleetwood was certainly a luxury car, no doubt about it. Twenty-five thousand dollars back in 1985, which calculates out to around forty-four thousand of today's dollars. No wonder that the market share was less than 4 percent.

McQuaid sits back, marveling once again at the stuff you can find on the Internet, but frowning a little as he studies the chart. There's lots of information, maybe too much information. Something here is nagging at him, some anomaly is rattling around at the back of his brain, but he can't quite pin it down.

*Coffee,* he thinks. *Coffee is what I need. Must be ready*

*by now.* He gets out of the chair. Howard comes to full alert and lurches out of his bed. The two of them go back to the kitchen, where McQuaid pours a mug of coffee and snags another burrito while he's at it, plus a biscuit for Howard, his faithful associate, who will give him no peace unless he has something to chew on, too. Then back to the office, where Howard takes his biscuit to his bed and munches contemplatively. McQuaid eats his burrito and stares at the chart, trying to put his finger on whatever it is that's bothering him about this car.

After a few fruitless minutes, he figures it's time to go on to a more productive task, such as sorting through the materials in the shoebox he found in Miles' file cabinet. He starts clearing a place on his desk to lay things out so he can inventory them. Handwritten notes, scraps of paper, receipts, a couple of dated newspaper clippings, nothing that seems very informative on the face of it. But the more McQuaid thinks about the holes in his brother-in-law's story, the more curious he is about what might be hiding in this unpromising pile. The identity of Robert Bayles' killer, maybe? Or—

The fax machine goes into action, interrupting his thoughts. After the first page is printed, he reaches over and pulls it out, noting with satisfaction the Bayles' accident report that Hawk promised to fax him. He sits down in his chair to read it and is halfway through the page when the phone rings. It's Martha Edmond, calling from Mississippi to say that she would really, really appreciate it if China could get back to her about a workshop next month someplace in Kentucky.

"Actually," she adds, "it's not just the workshop. There's . . . well, actually there's a problem. And a mystery. I think China would be intrigued, and I could really use her help."

McQuaid has met Martha, who has been working with China's cousin Amanda to help their aunt Tullie through some health-related difficulties. He takes Martha's number and promises that China will call her as soon as she can.

"This is a bad time, though," he adds. "She's just lost her brother." At Martha's voiced surprise, he adds, "Yeah, well, she didn't know she had a brother, either. Half brother, actually. Killed night before last. And yesterday, she found out that she's the executor of his estate. She's going to have her hands full for a while."

"Tell her I'm very sorry about her brother," she says soberly. "But I hope his death won't keep her from taking a little time for herself."

The fax has delivered the rest of the police report by the time McQuaid hangs up the phone and settles back to reading. This isn't new information—he read it carefully a couple of weeks ago when Miles first asked him to look into the matter. But now he reads the whole thing over again from start to finish, trying to put himself into the event, to see the wreckage the way the cops on the ground had seen it that night. Trying to make sense of the cryptic report, which isn't as detailed as he would like.

The name of the witness, for example—the guy who stopped at the scene and reported that Bayles had been speeding and lost control. The last name isn't legible— Powell? Burrell? Burrett?—and the first name is given simply as Ed, which might be short for Edward or Edgar or even Edwin. There's a street address but no city. There's a driver's license number, but the last two digits might be either a nine or a seven or a four, and the state is missing. Maybe the cop's writing can be deciphered on the original, but McQuaid doubts it. He hopes the guy was a rookie and got better at writing reports as the years went along. If this case had gone to court, either civil or criminal, the witness would have been crucial, and without his full and correct name and address and driver's license number, he might be hard to find.

McQuaid is reading the report for the second time when

he spots it: the weird thing, the anomaly that's been nagging at the corner of his mind ever since he pulled up that VIN chart. He stops, frowns, and reads the scrawled phrase again. Well, heck. Maybe he made a mistake. He goes back to the number he copied from the burned-out hulk in the barn on the Two-Bar Ranch and checks it against the number in the accident report. Nope, they're the same. He checks the VIN once more against the online chart to make sure of his facts. That's correct, as well.

Which means that he's right, by damn. He's found it. Against all the odds, after all the years, he's *found* it.

He sits back in his chair, feeling the thrill of excitement and pleasure—yes, pleasure, intense, focused pleasure—that always comes when a missing piece of a puzzle falls into place. And this is an important piece, a critical piece. It makes sense of what happened on that night in Houston sixteen years ago. Well, a certain sense, anyway. All the answers aren't there yet, but McQuaid now knows why Robert Bayles lost control of his Cadillac, went through the guardrail and plummeted down the embankment to die in a fiery crash at the bottom. And while Bayles might have been drinking and driving too fast, the wreck was no accident. It was murder.

McQuaid reaches for the phone. The other stuff he was planning to do this morning will just have to wait. He needs to call Jim Hawk to let him know about this and get him started on the next phase of the investigation—oh, and have him check out that guy, that Danny Danforth. Then he'll call Ellie Hanson at the Two-Bar Ranch. He has to get that car out of there and put it somewhere safer. The sooner he gets that process started, the better he'll feel.

But first he'll phone China. She'll want to know what he's found, and he's itching to tell her.

# Chapter Thirteen

The fruit of the silver-leaf nightshade (*Solanum elaeagnifolium*) is a berry that is yellow or blackish when ripe. It was used by Southwestern Indians in making cheese. The berries were also used to treat sore throat and toothache. Nightshade berries mixed with cream have reportedly been used as a cure for poison ivy.

*Wildflowers of Texas*
Geyata Ajilvsgi

In addition to furnishing man with important food plants, condiments, narcotics, and drugs, the nightshade family has also supplied several fine ornamentals. . . . Petunia without doubt is the most important, particularly in the United States. *Petunia*, which is the common name as well as the scientific name, comes from a Brazilian Indian name for tobacco, *petum*, and the plant does bear a slight resemblance to the tobacco plant. . . .

*The Fascinating World of the Nightshades*
Charles B. Heiser, Jr.

I had never driven a BMW before, and it was definitely different from my Toyota. Intimidating, too, to tell the truth, and not as much fun as you'd think it might be. I am not accustomed to driving automobiles that cost more than I make in a year. More than I make in two years, maybe.

And then there was Miles. I thought of him as I got into the car and turned the key, remembering that he had been the last person to sit in this seat, and now he was dead. The thought knotted my gut, but I had a job to do, and I couldn't let grief get in the way. After a few anxious moments figuring out how the buttons and widgets worked and a couple of close calls as I tried to maneuver the big sedan around the tight turns in the parking garage without scraping the paint, I made it onto the street.

I checked my watch. It was getting close to noon. Maybe I should get something to eat before I drove out to the west side of town, where there are fewer restaurants. Anyway, I was in luck. Katz's New York–style delicatessen was only a few blocks away on Sixth Street, directly in my line of travel, and it just so happens that Katz's is one of my favorite places. So while the lunch crowd around me—the usual assortment of Austin's legal eagles, capital cronies, and lounge lizards, dressed in everything from power suits to sixties vintage togs—sipped margaritas and Mexican martinis and debated whether it was going to be knockwurst with sauerkraut or turkey pastrami on challah, I was decisively (and happily) ordering lox on a tomato-basil bagel, with sliced fresh tomato, red onions, and cream cheese, and a lemonade.

While I was waiting for this very healthy lunch, I caught up on my telephoning. I had turned my cell phone off to conserve the battery—the damn thing needed charging again—and the voice mail had picked up a message from McQuaid, who sounded as if he had just won the lottery.

"I know how it happened, China," he said jubilantly. "How your father died, I mean." His voice was threaded through with excitement. "It was no accident. It was murder. I'm sure of it. Call me when you can, and I'll explain."

I felt suddenly cold. Murder? How could McQuaid be so positive, so long after the fact? I closed my eyes and took a deep breath. And what had happened to change his mind? Last night, after we got back from Austin, we had looked over all his digital photos, studying each one. I had asked him specifically about bullet holes in the car, and signs of impact by another auto—any indication that someone else had been involved in the car crash. There was nothing, *nada*, zilch. So what had he found this morning that we hadn't seen last night?

But we were playing phone tag. The answering machine in McQuaid's office kicked in after the fourth ring, and when I tried his cell phone, I got his voice mail. I left messages, then punched in Mrs. Bolton's number. I wanted to know more about the disagreement between Miles and Christopher Brandon, he of the mysteriously familiar voice. And I also wanted to hear why Mrs. B had decided to leave the firm—an abrupt decision, or so it seemed to me. The night before, she had promised to help Marcia and me by fielding phone calls. She had certainly given every indication that she planned to go on working for Zwinger, Brady, and Brandon, even though Miles was no longer there. So why had she left? But I struck out with her, as well. There wasn't even an answering machine to pick up calls. I let the phone ring a dozen times and finally gave it up as a lost cause.

I had better luck reaching Officer Wilkins. She had nothing significant to tell me, although she did it in a very professional manner.

No, the autopsy report wasn't back yet, and probably wouldn't be available for another day or two, after which time the victim's body would be released to his family for burial.

Yes, they had found some debris at the scene—glass from a broken-out headlight and a piece of a chrome headlight rim—although whether it came from the hit-and-run vehicle, she was not prepared to say at this time. However, they were checking the victim's clothing for any trace evidence—including glass—that might enable them to make that determination.

Yes, she was aware that the card reader in the garage had been disabled, but there was no way to say whether the vandalism was or was not related to Mr. Danforth's death.

Yes, they had checked out the vehicles that regularly parked in the levels immediately above and below, but had learned nothing of interest. She would get in touch with me if something turned up. In the meantime, please accept her deepest etcetera etcetera.

Lunch arrived at that moment, but the conversation with Officer Wilkins had been depressing, and I was no longer in the mood to enjoy it. Anyway, the lunch-hour revelers at the next table, a group of young lawyers who worked for one of the state offices, were having a very rowdy time of it. I'm afraid my lox and bagel didn't get the appreciative attention it deserved. I hurried through lunch, paid my tab, and left.


THE drive to Cat Mountain was much more pleasant today, with fewer cars sharing the road and the sun shining cheerfully in a perfectly blue, perfectly cloudless sky that would have made a great background on a postcard. The chaste trees (the South's answer to the North's springtime lilacs) were covered with sprays of lavender-colored blooms and decorated with ruby-throated hummingbirds, arcing like neon sparks through the branches. Beneath the trees, among the grasses, grew spreading colonies of silver-leafed nightshade, generously tossed together with winecups, brown-eyed Susans, purple prairie clover, and the rambunctious yellow blossoms of Navajo tea. In Texas, bluebonnets and Indian paintbrush attract most of the attention and all of the photographers, but there are plenty of other beauties to admire, if you'll take the time to look for them. For me, those gentle flowers were a soothing balm to the spirit, and by the time I got to Miles' house, I was feeling better.

But the feeling was short-lived. It lasted only until I pulled onto Miles' street and saw the three police cars and two EMS ambulances parked in front of the residence next door—the house that belonged to Belinda Harcher and her husband James. *Two* ambulances? It was an uh-oh moment, and I could feel goose bumps rising on my arms. I parked in the drive and walked out to the curb, where I accosted the first uniform I saw, a young woman officer wearing a pair of mirrored sunglasses—the kind that don't allow you to see the eyes.

"What's going on?" I asked, trying to sound casual. "Somebody sick?" Two somebodies sick?

"Sorry. I don't have that information, ma'am," the officer said, courteous but uncommunicative. "Please stand out of the way."

At that moment, the front door swung open and a couple of EMS guys trundled a gurney down the sidewalk to the waiting ambulance. They were moving deliberately, without haste, and the still form on the gurney was covered head-to-toe with a white sheet, which they don't do unless the passenger on board has cashed it in. I sucked in my breath. Who was it? James? Belinda? How had he, or she, died?

A small knot of spectators stood huddled in the middle of the cul-de-sac, exchanging apprehensive whispers as they watched the gurney being loaded into the ambulance. I went up to a heavyset woman in a peach-colored suit and matching pumps, a large leather purse slung over her shoulder and a real estate sales brochure in her hand. Her lips were pressed together and she was shaking her head, in obvious distress. Whatever had happened here, it wasn't the sort of thing that was allowed to go on in this exclusive neighborhood.

I touched the woman's arm and she turned. "Do you know what happened?" I asked urgently. "Somebody have a heart attack?"

The woman cast a questioning glance at the BMW I had just parked in Miles' drive, then at me. "You're a friend of Mr. Danforth?" she asked warily.

"I'm his sister," I said. "My name is China Bayles."

Instantly, her face softened and her manner changed. "Oh, my dear," she exclaimed sympathetically, and grasped my arm with a well-manicured hand. "My husband and I read about the accident in the *Statesman* just this morning. We couldn't believe it! Miles was a fine man, a wonderful father, and a generous neighbor. To die in such a horrible, senseless accident—" She shook her head. "Well, it just seems impossible, that's all. You have our sympathy, Ms. Bayles."

I was touched by her genuineness. "Thank you, Mrs.—"

"Estelle," she said. "Estelle Jenner. My husband and I live on the other side of the Harchers." She gestured in the direction of their house, a stately three-story house with a long, narrow reflecting pool in front, reminiscent of the Taj Mahal. "If there's anything we can do, anything at all, please don't hesitate to ask."

Ah, yes. Estelle Jenner. The president of the Homeowners' Association, who had left the phone message asking Miles to serve as secretary. From the look of her house, I wasn't surprised that she was concerned about property values.

"I'm very grateful," I said. "Perhaps you wouldn't mind letting other neighbors know about Miles' death. Not everybody will read about it in the newspaper."

"Of course," she replied warmly. "As soon as you have information about the funeral arrangements, I'll pass that along, too. Our neighborhood association is very active. We're close, and we all stay in touch. I know everyone will be just devastated when they learn of it." Her eyes darkened. "And what about Miles' little girl? I've been thinking about that lovely child ever since I found out, and feeling so very, very sad. First her mother, now her father—what in the world will become of her?"

"Caitlin will go to live with her aunt, her mother's sister," I replied. "It's the best thing, I think. They're very close."

"Oh, yes," she said earnestly. "Marcia has been such a blessing to Caitlin. I was even hoping that Miles and Marcia might—" She broke off. "Oh, gracious," she said distractedly, and put a hand to her mouth in horror. "Oh, dear god, *look*! I don't believe this! I just don't believe it!"

The door of the Harchers' house had opened and another team of EMS people were pushing a second gurney down the walk. On it lay a still, sheet-covered figure. I stared. Two dead? This wasn't any heart attack.

I repeated my question, now more urgently. "Do you know what happened, Mrs. Jenner? Was there a shooting?"

"I'm afraid so," Estelle Jenner said. Her voice was thin and brittle. "At least, I think that's what happened. I was on my way to a real estate sales meeting this morning—I have some new neighborhood listings." She paused, and a different expression crossed her face. "Will Miles' house be on the market, do you think?"

"I think it might," I said. "Do you have a card?" She scrabbled in her purse, found one, and handed it to me. "About the shooting," I prompted, putting the card into the pocket of my blazer.

"Oh, yes, of course," she said. "Well, I backed my car out of the garage, and then remembered the dry cleaning I meant to drop off. I was going back into the house when I heard two shots, close together. A few seconds later—maybe five seconds—there was another shot." She stopped, as if she had suddenly run out of breath or energy or both.

"I heard it, too," someone else said, at my elbow. "Two shots. I was working in my garden and I heard them as clear as day. I may be in the market for a hip replacement, but there's nothing wrong with my hearing."

I turned. The speaker was a tiny woman in her seventies, her hair silvery white, her face wrinkled from a lifetime in the sun and wind. A trowel in one hand, she was wearing a green jumpsuit with sprays of flowers embroidered on the front and dirt on the knees and a smear of dirt on her leathery cheek. But the dirt could not detract from her air of grande dame authority. I glanced past her and saw that she had been working in a yard that was bordered by beds of blooming petunias, ruffled, doubled, variegated, striped, starred, and all in luscious colors: pink, red, burgundy, peach, salmon, blue, lilac, purple, white, and silver. Several flats of petunias, also in bloom, were waiting to be settled into the ground. It was one of the most colorful demonstrations of petunia power that I had ever seen.

"Oh, Mrs. Mason," Mrs. Jenner gasped. "Can you believe it? Isn't it just *awful*?" From her deferential tone, I understood that Mrs. Mason was not just a petunia fancier, but a force to be reckoned with, outranking the president of the Homeowners' Association.

"Of course I can believe it," Mrs. Mason snapped. "It's a wonder they didn't murder one another sooner."

Before I could ask her what she meant, a police photographer, loaded with camera gear, came out of the house and went toward her car. As she was leaving, a white van rolled up. It had a satellite dish on top and *KVUE-TV* in big blue letters painted on the sides. A pretty young blonde in a neat khaki jacket got out of the van, took out a mirror and some lipstick, and did a quick job on her mouth. A man got out on the other side, opened the back, and began fiddling with the transmission equipment.

I turned back to Mrs. Mason. "Murder one another?" I prompted.

Evidently feeling the need to soften Mrs. Mason's remark, Mrs. Jenner turned to me. "Mr. and Mrs. Harcher sometimes had . . . disagreements," she said. She turned her hand over. "Not often, of course. Just occasionally."

"Don't be a fool, Estelle," Mrs. Mason snapped. "James and Belinda were at it hammer and tongs all the time. They hated one another and they didn't make any secret of it." She looked at me over the tops of her bifocals. "Who are you?" she asked suspiciously.

I explained, and got a short nod in return. "My condolences," she said. "Your brother was a nice man. He came over last week to tell me how much he liked my petunias." She cast a glance at Mrs. Jenner. "No one else has seemed to notice."

"I noticed, Mrs. Mason," Mrs. Jenner said quickly. "They're beautiful, really, they are." She gulped a breath and went on with the story she had begun telling me. "Anyway, after I heard the shots, I ran into the house and called nine-one-one. The police got here right away, and the ambulances soon after, but I guess . . ." She shuddered and her voice dropped to a shaken whisper. "It looks like they were too late."

I thought of the broken pane in the French door that opened from the balcony into Miles' study. "Could it have been an intruder?" I hazarded. "A break-in?"

"I don't think so." Mrs. Jenner frowned. "Nothing like that ever happens in this neighborhood. We pride ourselves on our low crime rate here—it's one of the sales points for homes in this area. We all have security systems, and the Homeowners' Association sponsors a Neighborhood Watch program. And at this time of day—" She broke off, shaking her head. "The police were everywhere, all around the house. But they couldn't seem to find anybody to chase."

"Of course they couldn't," Mrs. Mason said authoritatively. "There wasn't anybody. I heard one policeman telling another that they've found the gun."

"The . . . the gun?" Mrs. Jenner turned to stare at her, openmouthed.

"It's usually a gun that fires a shot, isn't it?" Mrs. Mason said, with some sarcasm. She lowered her voice. "I heard the policeman say that the gun was in James' hand, under his body. Belinda was in the bathtub. You don't have to be Sherlock Holmes to figure it out, Estelle—it's the kind of thing you read in the newspapers all the time. He shot her, then turned the gun on himself."

"Oh, no!" Mrs. Jenner protested, horror-struck. "No!"

"Yes," Mrs. Mason said, as if that settled it.

"Ah," I said regretfully. "What a pity." Murder-suicide. This wasn't going to do anything for Estelle's low-crime selling point, but it ought to simplify the police investigation. No wonder the photographer had wrapped things up so quickly. Snap photos of the bodies, photos of the gun, and you're done.

"Yes. Yes, a pity," Mrs. Mason replied archly.

"Murder-suicide," Mrs. Jenner whispered. "How awful! Something like that—nobody will ever want to buy that house."

"A pity indeed," Mrs. Mason repeated, as if Mrs. Jenner had not spoken, "but as I said, it's a wonder they hadn't done it sooner. It was one of those May-December marriages. James was my age," she added to me. "Belinda was in her forties. She was *hot*."

I hid a smile. Mrs. Mason might have problems with her hip, but there was nothing wrong with her eyes. Or her tongue.

Mrs. Jenner cleared her throat, casting an anxious glance at me. "*Dear* Mrs. Mason. I really wish you wouldn't—"

"You know I always call a spade a spade, Estelle," Mrs. Mason said, flourishing her trowel. "Perhaps you weren't fully aware of what was going on between Belinda Harcher and—"

"Oh, Mrs. Mason, *please!*" Mrs. Jenner cried, with all the flurried consternation of someone who finds it distressing to see the neighborhood's dirty laundry flapping in the breeze. She was probably afraid it would lower the property values.

"—between Belinda Harcher and Miles Danforth," Mrs. Mason went on, unperturbed. "And of course, he wasn't the first. Not by a long shot."

"Mrs. Mason!" Mrs. Jenner implored. "There's no need to speak ill of the dead. We should let bygones be bygones."

"Was something really going on between Belinda and Miles?" I asked, thinking of what Beverly Bolton had said. "I had the impression that any relationship was mostly in her imagination."

Mrs. Mason arched a significant eyebrow. "Does it matter whether Belinda was really having an affair with Miles, as long as James *thought* she was?"

Mrs. Mason certainly had a point. "So you believe that James Harcher shot his wife because he thought—"

Mrs. Jenner made an inarticulate noise, which was overridden by Mrs. Mason's snorted, "Huh! How should I know why he shot her? Maybe the poor fellow just reached his limit. There's only so much a man can take, after all. That's what I told that nice detective, too, when he asked me just a moment ago."

"Oh, Mrs. Mason, you *didn't!*" Mrs. Jenner moaned, distraught.

"Of course I did," Mrs. Mason said practically, lifting her chin. "I couldn't conceal information like that from the authorities, not when it might help them solve their case. It explains the motive, you see," she added in a Miss Marpleish tone.

"But you're just guessing!" Mrs. Jenner exclaimed, putting her hand on Mrs. Mason's arm. "Dear, *dear* Mrs. Mason, I really don't think it is wise to speculate about—"

"Yes?" I prompted. "How does it explain the motive, exactly?"

Mrs. Mason shook off Mrs. Jenner's hand. "James had an abominable temper," she replied. "And everyone in the neighborhood knows that he was simply in despair over the way Belinda behaved around men. Before she threw herself at your brother, it was that good-looking young stockbroker, David Kemmis. And at last year's Christmas party, she even caught old Mr. Williams under the mistletoe. She made a fool of him, in a quite disgraceful way."

"She was just having a little fun," Mrs. Jenner said helplessly. "Really, Mrs. Mason. Belinda wasn't a bad sort, perhaps just a little . . . unfocused. Undisciplined, maybe. She—"

"Belinda Harcher was a common trollop," Mrs. Mason said sternly, drawing herself up and wielding her trowel as Elizabeth the First might have wielded her scepter. "And James Harcher had a hair-trigger temper." She turned to me. "In fact, I think the police should look into the possibility that James ran down your brother and killed him. Then killed his wife when she confronted him about what he had done. And then killed himself, because he knew he was going to be charged with both of their murders." And having solved three killings in less time than it takes to deadhead a rose, she folded her arms.

"But James wouldn't do a thing like that!" Mrs. Jenner cried desperately. "Yes, of course, he had a temper, especially when he'd had a little too much to drink. But he wouldn't— He couldn't—" She broke down in tears.

"My dear Estelle," Mrs. Mason said, in a kindly tone. "I'm surprised that you didn't make the connection for yourself. Especially with this—" She waved inclusively toward the ambulances, whose exit from the scene was being filmed by the TV crew. "With this happening so soon after what happened to Miles." She shook her head with a what's-this-world-coming-to look. "One tragedy right after another. They have to be related. There's no other explanation."

It wasn't hard to buy Mrs. Mason's theory. I remembered the odd question that Belinda (to think of her now as the Gawgia Peach seemed tasteless and irreverent) had asked. "What time did it happen?" she had demanded, when I told her how Miles had died. Why would you ask that question unless you had a suspect in mind and needed to know whether that person had an alibi? It might seem a bit too pat, but—

I turned to Estelle Jenner. "What kind of vehicles do the Harchers drive?"

She took out a lace-edged handkerchief and blew her nose. "Well, James bought a new Mercedes sedan a few months ago—silver, and very nice. And he gave Belinda a silver Mercedes roadster with a convertible top for Christmas last year. He was very generous."

"Generous, hell," Mrs. Mason retorted. "She nagged him until he did it."

Mrs. Jenner sighed. "He loved to joke about their his-and-hers matching cars." She tucked her hanky away, frowning. "Why do you ask?"

Mrs. Mason gave me an approving look. "Because she has reason to think I might be right. Don't you, Ms. Bayles?"

"Perhaps," I said slowly. The symmetry of it was appealing, I had to admit. But now that I knew what kind of cars the Harchers drove, the next question was "Is one of them damaged?" And since the house and the garage were sealed off with crime-scene tape, that was a question that only the cops could answer.

"Good morning, ladies," said a pleasant voice. "I know you must be stunned by what's gone on here this morning, but I wonder if you'd be willing to say a few words for our camera?" It was the TV reporter, microphone in hand, cameraman behind her, and it gave me my exit cue.

"Sorry," I said. "I'll have to pass. There's something I need to do."

Leaving Mrs. Mason and Mrs. Jenner to the reporter's tender mercies, I went to the uniformed officer at the door. I gave my name and asked to see the detective in charge of the investigation. "The house next door belongs to my brother," I added. "I may have some information about what happened here today."

Ten minutes later, I had finished telling my story, in my most concise and lawyerly manner, to a tall, gangly detective not much over thirty, who was obviously grateful for anything that might move his investigation along. When I finished, he asked if I would make a formal statement and let him have the answering machine tape on which Belinda Harcher had left her message about her husband's "humongous snit" over her "indiscreet somethin'."

I agreed, but asked if he'd reciprocate with a couple of answers. "Was it really murder-suicide?" I asked.

"We're still in the preliminary stages here," he says cautiously. "The coroner will release his ruling later. But if you ask me, that's the only explanation that makes sense of the scene." He eyed me. "And the other question?"

"Okay if I tag along when you check the cars in the garage?"

"Nobody's stopping you," he said, and started down the hall. I fell in behind. When he stopped at the door and turned on the light, I stood on my tiptoes to look over his shoulder. There was only one car in the garage, Belinda's sporty Mercedes convertible, sleek and silvery. The other Mercedes—James' car—was gone.

Mrs. Mason would no doubt have said that you didn't need to be Sherlock Holmes to suspect that the Mercedes was in a local body shop, waiting for repair. That's what the detective suspected, too, and while I had to admit to just the tiniest bit of skepticism at the neatness of this solution, I couldn't see any reason to nay-say. When I left, he was keying his radio, barking instructions for a search of local automobile repair shops.

I could relax and get on with my day. The cops were on the case. And if James Harcher's missing Mercedes was in a body shop getting its front end fixed, no doubt they would find it.

# Chapter Fourteen

## McQuaid: The Back Story

McQuaid hangs up after leaving the message on China's voice mail and calls Hawk next. Hawk answers on the second ring and is as excited as McQuaid when he hears the news, although, as usual, he doesn't show it.

"Diesel," he grunts. "Shit. How the devil could the cops on the scene overlook something as simple as that?"

"Easy," McQuaid says. He's in the kitchen now, pouring himself another cup of coffee. "How many Caddy diesels you think were on the road back in 1985?" He answers his own question. "Eleven hundred. Just eleven hundred, nationwide, Hawk. Anyway, you couldn't tell just by looking." He grins. "You'd only know it was a diesel when you heard it coming down the highway, or when you looked under the hood."

For that's the final piece that has fallen into place for McQuaid. The VIN number on the wrecked Cadillac tells him that China's father was driving a V8-350 diesel. The officer at the scene, however, had clearly noted that the car had been engulfed by a *gasoline* fire. He had even jotted the conjecture, "Possible fuel tank puncture??"

But if the fuel tank on Bayles' Cadillac had been punctured, the officer wouldn't have smelled gasoline. He would have smelled diesel, an odor that is hard to mistake. He would have seen less flame and plenty of smoke, too—diesel smoke is black and characteristically sooty. What's more, McQuaid is pretty sure that there wouldn't have been a fire at all, even if the fuel tank had ruptured. Diesel fuel is much harder to ignite than gasoline. In the tank, its flash point is 140 degrees Fahrenheit, compared to -35 degrees for gasoline. The most likely ignition source for a diesel fuel fire in a rollover or collision is the vehicle's battery, and from what McQuaid saw of the car the day before, the engine compartment hadn't been involved in the fire.

So McQuaid is betting that the gasoline noted by the officer came from a different source. From a Molotov cocktail, say, tossed into the car and exploding in a searing flash of flame and flying shards that caused Robert Bayles to lose control of the vehicle. Which is something that the witness, if he'd been on the up-and-up, would certainly have seen and reported. So McQuaid is also betting that the witness is their perp. It's too damn bad that the witness information is so sketchy.

Hawk, who has come to a similar conclusion, gives a derisive snort. "Hell. You know as well as I do that those uniforms weren't halfway doin' their jobs, or else they took a payoff. You get a look at that report I faxed you? Can't read the witness' name for shit. No driver's license number, neither."

"Yeah," McQuaid says. "I don't suppose it'll do any good, but if those two officers are still around, wouldn't hurt for you to have a chat with them." Howard is nudging him with his nose, so he goes to the door and lets him outside to do his business.

"Glad to, buddy," Hawk growls, in a let-me-at-'em tone. "You're thinkin' what I'm thinkin'? Guy drives up alongside, motions the window to come down, and lobs a molo in Bayles' lap. Bayles loses it, goes over the rail, and that's all she wrote."

"It's possible," McQuaid says, taking his coffee onto the back porch and sitting down in one of the wicker rockers. "It fits."

"Hell, yes, it fits," Hawk retorts. "Ask me, it's what happened."

"Could be," McQuaid says. "Hey, I've got a name for you, Hawk. Danny Danforth. Could you look him up? All I know about him is that he did some prison time in the sixties, seventies."

"Danforth," Hawk says. "Any relation to your brother-in-law?"

"His mother's ex," McQuaid says. "Maybe."

"I'll check him out." Hawk pauses. "Any developments on the hit-and-run?"

"Not so far as I know," McQuaid says, watching Howard hike up his leg, a little creakily, because of his arthritis. "China was going to try to see the investigating officer this morning, and have a look at the garage, then go to the house to get the estate work set up. Haven't heard anything from her yet." He pauses. The dog has finished and is sniffing around the mesquite tree. He puts his forelegs on the trunk and peers up into the branches, looking for squirrels. "What're you up to, buddy?"

"Following up on that business I mentioned to you yesterday. The back story."

"Back story?"

"That Stone Engineering VP who shot himself before he could be indicted."

"Oh, yeah, Madison." McQuaid gulps his coffee. "Some funny business about the gun, you said."

"Maybe there was, maybe there wasn't," Hawk replies. "But there was certainly some funny business about the autopsy report. The second page is missing."

"What do you mean, missing?"

"As in gone. Vanished without a trace. Would you believe it?"

"I'd believe almost anything you tell me about that outfit," McQuaid says grimly. Over the years, the coroner's office has been the source of more stupid mistakes than anybody can count.

Hawk chuckles dryly. "Yeah, well. The report was available to the investigating officer, and the D.A. saw it when the case was ruled a suicide. But it's not available now. It's not in the coroner's files, it's not in the newspaper morgue. What's more, Mrs. Madison—the dead man's widow—tried her level best to contest the ruling. She maintained that her husband was murdered. She even said he'd been threatened. It was an issue, see, because of the insurance. Half a mil, which was a fair amount at the time."

"A new policy?" McQuaid guesses, putting his coffee down. Most insurance policies won't pay off if you commit suicide within two years of taking out the policy. He looks out across the yard. Howard has spotted a squirrel in the elm tree and is barking now, rumbling, thundering basset barks designed to strike fear into the heart of the squirrel and frighten it into falling out of the tree at his feet. The squirrel does not seem impressed.

"Right," Hawk says. "Mrs. Madison dropped the matter when Stone Engineering gave her the equivalent of her husband's policy, plus an extra hundred grand." He snorts. "The old payoff trick."

The squirrel has now jumped from the elm tree to a hackberry on the other side of the rock wall that skirts the eastern side of the property. Howard is too short to scramble over the wall, so he's digging frantically, trying to tunnel under it, his powerful forepaws scrabbling in the hard soil.

"Hang on a sec," McQuaid says. "Got a little problem here." He puts down the phone and whistles shrilly. Howard keeps on digging and doesn't stop until McQuaid goes out and hauls him away, protesting, by his collar.

"Sorry about that," McQuaid says, picking up the phone

again as Howard sulks, panting, beside his feet. "What happened to Madison's indictment?"

"It was dropped when he died. The Feds apparently hadn't targeted anybody but him, which seems a little odd to me. Usually, a case of corporate collusion and price-fixing, the Feds have their eye on more than one person." He chuckles in an ugly way. "Of course, there might have been a political angle."

"So where's all this going, Hawk?"

"Where?" Hawk barks a laugh. "I'll tell you where. It just so happens that Madison had a pretty strong connection with our man Bayles."

McQuaid sits forward, and Howard looks up at him accusingly, still bearing a grudge over the squirrel. Howard is not a dog who forgets easily. "Oh, yeah? What kind of connection?"

"Bayles was Madison's personal attorney. Not Stone and Bayles, just Bayles. He represented Madison in several actions in the previous couple of years. Small stuff, the kind of thing a friend would do. Turns out that they played Tulane football together, Bayles on offense, Madison on defense. Frat brothers, too. Kappa Sig." A raspy laugh. "And in case you're thinking I dug this up myself, I didn't. The connection was there, in both Spurgin's and Vine's notes. Looks to me like the reporters got on to the relationship, and were following it up. Hell, it was probably the reason they had that appointment to see Bayles. The one that was in his calendar."

"Interesting," McQuaid says slowly, remembering now that China had said that her father had gone to school with Madison. "Very interesting. So bottom line, you're thinking that Bayles knew something he wasn't supposed to know about how Keith Madison died. And that Vine and Spurgin figured out what it was."

"Yeah," Hawk says. "And pretty soon they were all dead. Madison, Spurgin, Vine, and Bayles. And whoever did it is home free. It's too freakin' bad this was all so long ago. There'll never be enough to build a case on." Hawk heaves a heavy sigh. "So what's on your plate for the rest of the day?"

"I found Mrs. Danforth's materials in a filing cabinet at her son's place yesterday evening. I want to give them a quick look." McQuaid stands up and stretches, and Howard scrambles to his feet. "Plus, I'm thinking it might be a good idea to make arrangements for securing that Caddy. I'd feel better if I could lock it up someplace and keep the key."

"Bet that thing weighs a ton," Hawk tells him. "You'll have to get yourself a tilt-bed wrecker."

McQuaid chuckles as he goes into the kitchen, Howard at his heels. "Yeah. It'll be a bitch to move." He's already thinking about that truck-towing operation across from the brewery on 90A, in Shiner. They've probably got a tilt-bed he can use to pick up the car. But once he has the damn thing, what's he going to do with it? He frowns. This requires thought. Meanwhile—

"Well, watch yourself, you hear?" Hawk says. "Remember that the last guy who drove it is dead. And so is the guy who was looking for it. You don't want to be *número tres.*"

"I hear you," McQuaid says grimly. "Have a good one. And let me know what you find out about Danny Danforth."

Back in his office, he finds the phone number that Ellie Hanson gave him and punches it into his phone. Her recorded voice on the answering machine is cheerful, sprightly. "Hey, thanks for callin', whoever you are. I'm either out sloppin' the pigs or pullin' weeds in the tomatillo patch or engaged in some other gainful employment. You can try again when you get a chance, or leave me a message at the beep, whichever suits. You have a good day now, okay?"

At the beep, McQuaid identifies himself and says, "Hey,

Ellie, I'm thinking that it's time to make other arrangements for that hunk of junk you've got out there in your barn. Let me know what day it would be convenient for me to come and pick it up—tomorrow, the next day, next week. Whatever works for you, works for me. Thanks."

As he puts the phone down, something occurs to him. There's an empty garage behind his folks' place in Seguin, with access to the alley. The tilt-bed could back right up to the garage and slide the Caddy off. Once the door is closed and locked, the car will be safe as a bug in a rug. And since it's at his folks' place, he can get to it anytime he wants. No storage fees, either.

He congratulates himself on having solved the problem and goes back to sorting through Laura Danforth's notes, a couple of receipts (one for a safety deposit box at a Houston bank—but there's no key), paper scraps, newspaper clippings. He arranges the items in what he figures is chronological order, just to get a handle on what's here, while half of his mind is still playing with the back story Hawk related to him. And as if his thoughts had conjured it up, he picks up one of the newspaper clippings and sees that it's Keith Madison's obituary. There's a phone number written in ink in what he has come to recognize as Laura Danforth's script, and the notation, "talk to Mrs. Madison."

He clenches his fist in silent exultation. Here it is, just what Hawk was looking for, something to build a case on. There was a connection, and Laura Danforth knew what it was. Maybe she followed up with a phone call to the grieving widow, who was so certain that her husband hadn't killed himself. Now what he needs is something that tells him exactly how Madison's suicide (if that's what it was) is related to Bob Bayles' murder (he *knows* that's what it was).

He goes back to his sorting with a renewed interest, and is still at it when the phone rings again. He lets the answering machine take it on the fourth ring, but when he hears the caller's voice, he picks up.

What he learns throws a major monkey wrench into his plans for the day.

# Chapter Fifteen

## McQuaid: A Change of Plans

The caller is Ellie Hanson. Her voice is flat and bleak.

"I got your message about the car, Mike," she says. "I was going to phone you. There was trouble here at the ranch last night."

McQuaid puts down his handful of papers and straightens, feeling the hair rise on the back of his neck. "What kind of trouble?"

"The bad kind. The barn burned. About three a.m. The Sweet Home VFD guys got here right away, but all they could do was keep it from spreading to the other buildings."

*VFD. The volunteer fire department.* He lets out his breath. "Hell," he says. "The house okay?"

"Yeah. But the barn is pretty much a total loss. I got the girls out before their bacon got fried. The rooster got out, too, but most of his hens didn't make it." She clears her throat, and he thinks she might be crying. "I'm gonna miss those eggs."

"I'm sorry, Ellie," he says inadequately, but with genuine sympathy. "It's good you got the girls out, though. The dogs and cats are okay? The greenhouse?"

"The greenhouse is fine, the tractor is okay, and so are

the dogs and cats. The animals are what counts. Life without them would be pretty damn dull." She sniffles, and he pictures her wiping her nose on her sleeve.

"So what do you think?" he asks. "Any idea what caused it?"

"Hell, yes," she snorts. "It was torched. Fire chief says so. He's not finished his investigation, but he thinks he's found the accelerant."

"Why would somebody do that?" McQuaid has an idea, but he wants to hear her take on it.

She laughs harshly. "Why? Well, hell, Mike. It's gotta be that damn car. Daddy should've had better sense than to let Laura park it here. I'm to blame, too. If I'da junked that wreck when I took over the place, I'd still have a barn."

"Why?" he parries. "I mean, what makes you think so?"

"Come on, you're smarter than that." Ellie sounds disgusted. "Day before yesterday, Laura's son says he's gonna come down here and take a look at it. That night, somebody mows him down in the parking lot. You show up yesterday and poke around and take pictures. Last night, the barn goes up. That's too much coincidence for me. There's gotta be a connection."

"I take your point," he says quietly, although he was hoping for something beyond the circumstantial. "You're okay, Ellie?"

She laughs grittily. "No, I'm not okay, damn it. I'm a mess. The girls are in the garage, what's left of the chickens are in the garden, the barn is a pile of ashes and hot tin. My wrist is killin' me. And I could sure as hell use some sleep. I was making coffee and helping tote fire hose until after seven this morning. I'm too old for this shit."

He clears his throat, hating to ask. "What about the car?"

"What about it?" Her tone is sarcastic. "It was pretty much burned up already, wasn't it? Couldn't be much worse, could it?"

Well, yes. It was already pretty much of a loss. Still. "Is there *anything* left of it?"

"As a matter of fact, there is," she says, surprising him. "Happens that there was a pretty good east wind last night. The fire was started at the east end of the barn, where the car was parked, and the wind blew the flames from east to west. Burned the tarp off the car, but that's about it. A helluva lot more damage to the barn than the car. Mack didn't take the wind into consideration."

He frowns. "Mack?"

"Yep," she says with satisfaction. "Although I'm sure he sent Sonny to do it. Mack hates like hell to get his own hands dirty. And I don't give a damn whether he's kin or not, I'm pressing charges. That's what I told the fire chief this morning. You get the evidence. I'll get the bastard."

"Wait a minute," McQuaid says. "How do you know it was your cousin?"

Ellie chuckles dryly. " 'Cause Sonny hit a deer a day or two ago, and the right headlight is out on that old ranch truck of Mack's. Happy woke me up, barkin', and the girls were makin' a ruckus out in the barn. So I got up and looked outta my bedroom window and saw this one-eyed truck, heading off down the road like a singed bat outta hell. Saw the flames a minute later."

*A one-eyed truck?* McQuaid frowns.

Ellie has paused and now adds bitterly, "Trouble is, the county sheriff is Mack's good buddy. They go hunting and fishing together all the time. So I'm not expecting any help from the local law. I tell you, McQuaid, this is one time I'd like to own a gun. I'd take care of this business myself."

McQuaid is glad to hear that she doesn't have a gun, although he seriously doubts she has it in her to use it on somebody. But she's mixing up two possible motives for the torching. Somebody could've been out to finish off the car, which was his first thought. But if her cousin was the torch—"Why would your cousin have any interest in that car?" he says. "It doesn't add up."

"Don't have a clue," she snaps. "But you can bet your sweet ass I'm going to find out. And before I'm a day older. I'm headed over there right now."

"No way," McQuaid says, quickly and firmly. "You're not going to do that, Ellie. You have to turn this over to the cops."

"Didn't you just hear what I said, McQuaid? The county sheriff is in Mack's back pocket, and for good reason. Mack holds all the political cards in the county. Every time there's an election, he turns out his base and Sheriff Grady wins another term in office. He'll never lift a hand. Fact is, he'll do everything he can to get in the way of any serious investigation. There's a deputy who would help, but I don't want to put her on Grady's shit list. Anything gets done about this, it's gonna be me that does it."

"That could be dangerous."

"Damn right it's dangerous," she growls. "Dangerous for Mack. That bastard's played enough dirty tricks on me over the years, trying to get this land. I'm sick of it. Time he had his hand called, and I aim to do it. Period. Paragraph. End of story."

*Dirty tricks. Trying to get the land.* McQuaid thinks that this is a more likely motive than the destruction of the car. Ellie's cousin probably has the idea that if he burns the barn, she'll give up and sell him the ranch. But it's still a bad idea for her to confront a possible arsonist on her own.

"Okay," McQuaid says in a conciliatory tone. "Okay, Ellie. But I want you to stay right there. Don't go anywhere. I'm on my way. If you don't think the sheriff will deal with it, we'll go see Mack together. How's that?"

Her tone is suspicious, and he can imagine the frown creasing her forehead. "Why? What's any of this to you?"

*Because I like you,* McQuaid wants to say. *Because you're a scrappy old gal, tough as longhorn cowhide, but you don't know what you're getting into*. Because he wants to get a look at this cousin, and see for himself whether there's any connection to the car—unlikely, but he ought to check it out.

Aloud, he says, "Because I think it's high time I got that car out of your way, what's left of it. But first I need to see the car and figure out what kind of a tow vehicle I can use to pick it up. And while I'm there, I can go with you to see your cousin." He grins, and puts the grin into his voice. "Won't hurt for you to take some muscle with you."

"Muscle," she says wryly. "Yeah, well, he's used plenty of that on me. Don't reckon it'll hurt to use a little on him. Might surprise him some."

He glances at the clock. "Look. It's after one. I can be there by three, three thirty. How does that sound?"

A silence. McQuaid wants to urge her, but she's stubborn. If he pushes too hard, she'll push back. She might even run off and confront that cousin of hers just to show him she can do it.

Finally, she says, in a grudging tone, "I've got some work to do in the greenhouse this afternoon. Guess it won't hurt me to wait for you. Mack's not going anywhere, the jerk." She pauses. "Oh, by the way. I spent an hour last night going through Daddy's papers. I found the stuff Laura gave him. Looks to me like the registration papers are there. You can pick the stuff up when you come."

*Hey. A break.* "That's good news," McQuaid says emphatically. "Thanks, Ellie. I'll see you in a couple of hours."

He's already hung up the phone when he remembers that he was supposed to pick up China at three thirty or four, in Austin, which is the opposite direction. But she won't mind, when she hears the situation. Anyway, she's not stranded. She can drive Miles' BMW back to Pecan Springs. He'll call and tell her.

# Chapter Sixteen

Ashwagandha (*Withania somnifera*) is an evergreen shrub in the *Solanaceae* family. It grows up to six feet in height in the Mediterranean region, as well as the Middle East, Africa, India, and Pakistan. Its fruits, like the berries of other nightshades, have been used to coagulate milk in cheese-making.

Ashwagandha is widely used in Ayurvedic, Unani, and Middle Eastern traditional medicines, where it is regarded as an aphrodisiac, a rejuvenative, and a panacea. Large doses of ashwagandha should not be used during pregnancy due to its actions as an abortifacient.

The detective assigned an officer to follow me to Miles' house, where I gave her my statement regarding Belinda's remarks and surrendered the tape from Miles' answering machine. When she had gone, I settled myself at my brother's desk. My task for today was to make a list of all the documents and materials I would need to carry out my job as the executor of his estate and assemble everything in one place. I hadn't done work like this for a while, and I found it engrossing.

An hour later, I came up for air and a cup of coffee. It was nearly two, and I reached for my cell phone to try McQuaid and Mrs. Bolton. But when I flipped it open, I saw that it was out of juice. And when I reached into my bag to get the charger, it wasn't there. Drat. I'm not a great fan of cell phones and I put off getting one as long as I could. But I'll have to admit that I've learned to live with the idea of being plugged in, to the point where I feel naked and vulnerable when I don't have the cell, or when it isn't working, or when I've lost it. That happened once. It was almost as bad as losing my credit card.

However, there was hope. I used the phone on the desk in front of me—for all the good it did. There was still no answer at Mrs. B's house, and I got no further with McQuaid than the answering machine in his office and his cell phone's voice mail. I was beginning to get irritated. His habit of taking off without telling anybody where he was going was sometimes annoying, but when he was working on a case, it was downright dangerous. The last I had heard from him was his urgent message that my father had been murdered. What had he discovered that brought him to this conclusion? Where was he now? Would I have to wait until three thirty or four, when he came to pick me up, to learn what he had found out?

But I pushed those questions to the back of my mind and got on with the job at hand. I was so wrapped up in it that I was startled when the doorbell pealed. I glanced at my watch, seeing with some surprise that it was three o'clock. And that had to be Rachel Burke, here to pick up her dress.

I was right. She had shed her chic suit and was wearing white shorts, a brief white top that revealed a gold ring in her navel, and strappy white sandals. Her champagne-colored hair was drawn back into a loose ponytail, her legs were long and tanned, her skin glowing with a youthful health that made me envious. Out of the adulthood of the office, she seemed much younger—fifteen, maybe, seventeen, tops—and innocently, touchingly vulnerable.

"I hope I haven't interrupted you, Ms. Bayles," she said, with an apologetic smile.

"Call me China, please," I said. "I've been doing paper-work, and I'm ready for a break. Would you like something to drink? I made a pot of coffee a little while ago, or there's probably something cold in the fridge."

But Rachel knew her way around Miles' kitchen better than I did, and in a jiffy, she had supplied us with glasses of white wine and a tray of cheese and crackers. A few minutes after that, we were sitting on the deck, gazing out over the river. Rachel, looking perfectly at home and per-fectly beautiful, the afternoon sunshine kissing her sun-shiny skin, was telling me her story, not because I primed her with questions, but because she was still unnerved by the suddenness and sadness of Miles' death—maybe the first death she'd had to cope with in her life. She had to talk with somebody, and I must have seemed like a safe audience.

As a lawyer, I learned a long time ago that sympathetic listening is just as important as smart talking. You learn more about your clients when you listen to them. In fact, you learn things about them that they don't know they're telling you. So I listened to Rachel, and encouraged, she told me more than she might have intended.

She'd had a major crush on Miles since she was seven-teen and first began to work in her stepfather's law office. But nothing had . . . well, happened (as she put it) until a couple of years after Karen drowned, which of course was such a horrible shock that it took poor Miles a long time to get over it. By that time, Rachel was finishing her market-ing degree at UT and was working twenty hours a week at Zwinger, Brady, et al., as a gofer and backup receptionist. She dropped in at the office one evening to pick up some files for her stepfather. Miles was there, working late. He asked her out for a drink, and a couple of nights later, they went out to dinner. One thing led to another, and pretty soon they were going steady (her phrase). But not publicly.

"We kept it very quiet." She munched on a cracker,

looking reflectively out across the river. "We didn't want to advertise."

Why not?

"Like, well, the obvious," she answered, with a lift of her pretty eyebrows. "My mother wouldn't have approved at *all*. Not that she didn't like Miles. Of course she did." She laughed self-consciously. "Maybe even a little too much."

A little too much? I tried not to react. Did I need to add Mrs. Zwinger to the list of adult females who had lost their hearts to my brother? Was there *anybody* who'd been immune to his attractions?

Rachel was going on. "But Miles was . . . well, you know." She gave a little shrug. "He was twenty years older, which is old enough to be my father, biologically speaking."

Yes. Biologically speaking, this was indisputably true. And I was old enough to be her mother, which made me infinitely sad.

"Miles had been married," she continued. "He had a child. And Mother has always been like absolutely determined that I'm going to New York to have this big, high-powered career in my uncle's advertising firm." She looked down and her smile, softly sly, made me think that perhaps her secret affair with Miles might have been one way to defy her mother. "Miles didn't think it was a good idea, either," she added quickly. "To advertise, I mean. He always said it would mean more if it was just our own private secret."

The smile, sad now, played around her mouth and her hand, unconsciously, went to her breast. "We came here a lot, to this house. We used to sit here at this very table and look out across the river and tell ourselves that what we had was just *ours*. Something we shared that nobody else knew. Of course, we knew it couldn't last. But we were living for the moment."

Cliché or not, I was moved. And I thought I understood the attraction. A good-looking, sophisticated older man, previously married, with a child. The boss's beautiful daughter, delightfully alluring, sexually mature, but young enough to be his daughter. Forbidden fruit, eaten secretly, always tastes sweeter—and *much* sweeter when there's a deadline. Didn't I know that from my own experience? Sure, I did.

But it wasn't true that nobody else knew. Mrs. Bolton had known, and thought that Rachel was "dangerous." Who else had been in on their secret? Rachel's mother? The Gawgia Peach?

Aloud, I said, "And then?"

She shrugged. She looked away. "And then I got pregnant," she said, in the same neutral tone she might have used to say, "And then I got chickenpox," or "And then I got a C in Public Relations."

"Ah," I said, genuinely surprised. If Mrs. Bolton had known that Rachel Burke was pregnant, she would surely have told me. But that didn't mean that the pregnancy was entirely a secret. "Did you and Miles think of getting married?"

"Married?" Rachel's lavender eyes opened wide in innocent surprise. "Are you kidding? I mean, of course not. We knew—*both* of us knew—that marriage was never a possibility. Miles understood that there are other things I want to do with my life, and being a wife isn't one of them—at least for now." She tossed her head. "Anyway, my uncle had already offered me that job in New York. I'm starting the first of September, as soon as Mother and I get back from the Caribbean."

So she'd had an abortion.

"When?"

"Oh, a couple of months ago." She frowned, counting on her fingers. "No, I guess it was three months ago. Around Valentine's Day." She looked down at her flat stomach and shook her head in profound amazement. "Gosh. I'd be out to here by now, wouldn't I?" She held out her hand, measuring the possible dimensions.

Three months ago. My brother was a man of secrets. Many secrets.

"How did Miles feel about it?" I asked. "About the abortion, I mean."

"Oh, he agreed," she said, without hesitation. A bee buzzed her wineglass and she waved it off. "There was never any question. He knew it was the right thing to do, and so did I. Don't you?"

I cleared my throat. "Does your mother know?"

"My mother?" Rachel was shocked. "Oh, definitely not." She rolled her eyes. "She would *kill* me if she knew."

Not a happy choice of words. I thought of Miles' death, of the way he had died. I might understand a crime of passion, a fit of sudden rage, an uncontrollable urge to kill. But it hardly seemed likely that either Rachel's mother or stepfather would be motivated to run down a daughter's lover a whole three months *after* she'd had an abortion— although I didn't know Mrs. Zwinger, and anything is possible.

"I spoke to Caitlin's aunt yesterday," I said. "Miles' sister-in-law. She said that Miles mentioned once that he might be in danger. Did he ever talk to you about this?"

"Danger?" A frown furrowed her forehead, and she looked truly puzzled. "What sort of danger could he be in?"

"No idea. He didn't say anything about it?"

She shook her head, her frown deepening. "Wait a minute. You're not suggesting that he . . . that it was *deliberate*!" She looked up, startled, eyes wide.

"The police are treating it as an accident," I said. "Do you have any reason to think it's anything else?"

"No, no!" She shook her head again, violently. "No, of course not! Nobody would do such a horrible thing! It's got to have been an accident." Her protest sounded convincing enough, and I have a pretty good ear for a lie.

"Mrs. Bolton told me that Miles and Mr. Brandon didn't exactly see eye to eye. Do you know what that was about?"

"Oh, Mrs. Bolton," she said, rolling her eyes with half-pitying scorn. "Gosh. That woman is a mess. *Such* a mess." She lowered her voice confidentially. "She drinks, you know."

"So I understand," I said. "Does she drink a lot?"

She considered. "Well, sometimes. She went away for a couple of weeks last winter to dry out. Really, if it had been anybody but Miles—" She shook her head in exasperation, as if she hadn't quite approved of his leniency. "He paid for it, you know. For her rehab, I mean. He located a place where she could go, and he picked up the entire tab. He was always kinder to her than anybody else at the office. He tried really hard with her."

"I spoke to her last night," I said slowly. "She'd been drinking again."

"I guess I'm not surprised." A lock of hair had come loose and she brushed it back. "The poor old thing must be just devastated. She probably can't cope."

"Still, I was surprised to hear that she'd left the firm," I went on. "When I left her last night, she was definitely planning to come in this morning. She was eager to help with the arrangements for Miles' service."

Rachel gave a little shrug. "You'll have to ask Mr. Brandon. He's the one who handled the details."

"Details? The details of what?"

"How should I know?" Another shrug. "That was between the two of them. I don't have a clue." She waved her hand. "Anyway, there's no point in her coming back. What would she do? None of the partners would have her—they don't have Miles' patience. They might put her in charge of the interns, I suppose. Or the library."

I went back to my earlier question. "Is it true what Mrs.

Bolton said, Rachel? About the conflict between Miles and Mr. Brandon?"

"Well . . ." She looked into her wineglass, as if trying to find the answer there. "Well, Miles didn't like to talk about it, you know, maybe because my stepfather is the senior partner. I picked it up from being around the office." She smiled a little. "Mom thought it would be a good idea if I put in some 'desk time,' as she calls it. Before I go to New York, I mean." She made a face. "As if I don't already know what office life is like. All those bad vibes and negative energy. All that cutthroat competition, and for what? A few square inches of turf. I'd rather be a model. Or an actress."

Gosh. If she thought office life was competitive, wait until she got into modeling. "What about Miles and Mr. Brandon?" I persisted.

"Well, they've never been what you might call close friends. I guess it goes back quite a ways, nearly twenty years, maybe." From her tone, it might have been the Dark Ages—and probably was, as far as she was concerned. Twenty years ago, she was still playing with Silly Putty and taking afternoon naps. "They worked together at a law firm in Houston," she added. "It probably started back then."

*A law firm in Houston.* Oh, for pity's sake. Brandon. Chris Brandon. No wonder that voice had seemed familiar. Twenty years ago, he'd been an associate at Stone and Bayles. A very young associate, right out of law school, forty pounds thinner, with a full head of hair. Come to think of it, I hadn't much liked him then, either.

"I think I know the firm," I said thoughtfully.

"Really?" She said it with a slight surprise, and I realized that it hadn't occurred to her that I might have some background in the business, or that my connection with Miles might go back into ancient history. "Anyway, Miles and Mr. Brandon were always competitive, much more so than the other partners. But things got a lot more . . . well, tense between them about the time Miles' mother died. He was pretty stressed out, going back and forth to the hospital and all that stuff. Then he came into the office late one night and caught Mr. Brandon going through some of his files. He blew up." She chuckled. "He was massively torqued, believe me."

"Mrs. Bolton said that the current state of bad feeling had to do with an old case Miles was working on. Do you happen to know what it was?"

"I'm not sure, exactly. As I said, he really never told me anything. But it had something to do with his mother. And a car."

I stared at her, the hair prickling on the back of my neck. Here it was. The connection. "A car?"

"Yeah. His mom was a legal secretary or something like that. Apparently, she had been researching something that happened light-years ago. Miles had her stuff at the office. He was going through it in his spare time. Checking on stuff."

"It was about a car?" I repeated urgently. *And why would Chris Brandon have any interest in my father's car, unless—*

"I guess." She shrugged, puzzled by my persistence. "Like, it was an old family mystery, or something like that." She eyed me defensively, feeling the need to explain why she hadn't taken a greater interest. "It wasn't like it had anything to do with *me*. All I know is that Miles was upset. At first, he said he thought that Mr. Brandon had actually taken some stuff out of his files."

"I see," I said, although I didn't, at all. Below us, on the river, someone pushed a sailboat out of a slip and it hesitated, caught the breeze, and moved silently away across the water's green, placid surface. Along the far bank, a pair of Jet Skis chased each other in widening loops, churning up turbulent wakes. Above, a red-tailed hawk wheeled, silent and wary, through the clear afternoon air.

"But then later," she went on, "Miles said he thought he was wrong. Mr. Brandon hadn't taken anything after all. He'd looked at it, or maybe copied it, and put it back in the wrong place. But Miles took the stuff home with him anyway. He said he didn't trust Mr. Brandon." She smiled reminiscently. "He said Mr. Brandon was a real sleazebag."

She had to be talking about the box that McQuaid had found in the filing cabinet—and it didn't matter, in the long run, whether the material had been actually taken or merely copied. I thought of the attempted break-in. Had Christopher Brandon found part of what he'd been looking for in Miles' office, and then come here to get the rest? But that was nonsense. He couldn't have had anything to do with what had happened sixteen years ago.

Still, Brandon had worked at Stone and Bayles before my father's death. He knew my father. What's more, he knew Miles' mother, too. I frowned. Did he know that Miles was Robert Bayles' son? But what if he did? Why should the relationship be of any interest to him? Why should he go to the trouble—and the risk—of rifling through a file in Miles' office?

She drank the last of her wine and pushed her glass away. "Did you know that Mr. Brandon is planning to run for the legislature?" she asked idly. "My stepfather says he's sure to be elected, since his family will be behind them. His uncle used to carry a lot of weight, I understand, which is what it takes if you want to get anywhere in Texas politics. I've noticed that everybody who gets voted into office seems to be related to somebody important."

Out of the mouths of babes, I thought. "Who is this heavyweight uncle?"

She looked at me as if to say *What's with all these questions?* "Somebody named Strawn. Or Stone. Or maybe Strand. Something like that."

I frowned. "Stone?" *No, it couldn't be. Not—*

At that moment, Rachel's cell phone sang a jazzy tune,

and she fished it out of her bag. After a murmured conversation, she pushed back her chair and stood. "Listen, I'd better get that dress and get out of your hair," she said. "I'm sure you have things to do."

"That uncle," I said. "Chris Brandon's uncle. What did you say his name was?"

"Storm?" she guessed. "Hey. I'm not very good with names. Even when I write them down, I get them wrong. Like yours, this morning. Sorry about that."

I wasn't. If Chris Brandon had heard the name Bayles, he might have put two and two together. I stood. "I'll get the dress." I had wrapped it in tissue paper, folded it into a box, and stashed the box in the hallway. "It's a great dress," I added, when I handed it to her. "Sexy. I'm sure it looks nice on you."

"Miles liked it," she said. She looked down, and when she raised her eyes again, they glistened with tears. "I really did care for him, you know," she said in a low voice. "He was a good guy. If he just hadn't been so . . . well, old—"

I gave her a little hug, resisting the temptation to tell her that the problem was that she was just so . . . well, young. We said our good-byes at the front door. As she went out, she glanced curiously at the house next door, which was still quarantined with crime-scene tape and guarded by a policewoman stationed out front.

"Hey," she said. "What's going on at the Harchers' house? Looks like it's seriously off limits."

"There was a shooting this morning."

"Wow." She turned, startled. "Not Belinda, I hope."

"Do you know Belinda?" Of course she did, if she'd been here at the house very often. Belinda had probably made it a point to know *her*, sensing that there was a rivalry.

She slid me a glance that made me realize, young as she was, she was already wise in the ways of women and men. "Sure. Honestly, that woman was crazy for Miles—she made no secret of it, even when her husband was around. Miles swore he'd never encouraged her, and I believed him. He'd laugh and say she was just making a fool of herself, but I thought she was . . . well, dangerous. She considered herself a femme fatale. And Mr. Harcher was awfully jealous. He's older than Belinda, by quite a bit." She frowned. "The shooting. An accident, was it? Was anybody hurt?"

"The police haven't said yet officially," I replied quietly. "But I understand that Mr. Harcher shot his wife, then killed himself."

The words hung between us, raw and ugly. Rachel looked as if I had just slapped her. She stood there for a minute, then took a deep, shaky breath. "Miles always said the Harchers were a disaster waiting to happen."

"I guess he was right," I replied.

I went back to Miles' study after Rachel left. I was finished with my work for the day and ready to head for Pecan Springs, as soon as McQuaid came to pick me up. I'd gathered Miles' papers, checkbooks, and so on into one large box, ready to take home with me. I'd have to check his safe deposit box for the insurance papers, and make an appointment with his banker and his lawyer—who was not, it turned out, someone in his firm, but a guy I knew from law school. I hadn't yet found all the income tax records from previous years, however. So I made another tour through the upstairs, looking for them.

That's when I opened the closet at the end of the upstairs hallway, which I had missed on my earlier tour. I found a box labeled TAX RECORDS—exactly what I was looking for—and something else, too. A Sturdi-Step Ladies' Lace-up Oxfords shoebox containing a jumble of odds and ends: thimbles and sewing scissors, a cough drop box filled with pearl shirt buttons, a spool of red thread with a needle stuck into it, a chain of safety pins. And an unlabeled audio cassette. I stared at it for a moment, wondering what was on it, then dropped it into the TAX RECORDS box. It might be worth a listen.

I stopped in Caitlin's room to pick up a few more things for her, and went downstairs. Three thirty. McQuaid would be here any minute. I put the boxes beside the door and waited.

I poured myself a cup of coffee and waited. And waited. And waited some more.

At four, I tried McQuaid's cell phone, and got his voice mail again. "Where the heck are you?" I asked plaintively. "Are you *coming*?"

At four ten, I tried his office at the house, and got the always-on-duty answering machine. I tried Thyme and Seasons and found out that he hadn't called there, but Brian had. He was having dinner at Jake's, and after dinner, he was going to watch Jake's softball team play the New Braunfels girls—Jake was pitching. Well, that took some of the pressure off, anyway. I didn't have to be home to cook dinner for Brian.

By four twenty, I was pretty well convinced that McQuaid wasn't coming, and pretty well steamed about it. Honestly. A promise is a promise is a promise. What was I supposed to do if he didn't show up? Drive that damn BMW back to Pecan Springs? Through the rush-hour traffic, with cars zipping at sixty-five-plus on MoPac southbound? Just the idea of it made me queasy.

By four thirty, I *knew* he wasn't coming. It was up to me to get myself home, and the BMW was my only option. I put a note in the mailbox (just in case), picked up my boxes, and headed for the car. But just as I was backing out, a silver Mercedes stopped at the curb in front of the Harchers'. A skinny young man with jug ears and Howdy Doody freckles got out. He was wearing a gray uniform shirt with *Carl* on the pocket and the Mercedes logo patch on the sleeves. He stood at the curb, staring at the crime-scene tape with a puzzled expression.

I stopped the car and got out. "Can I help you?" As I spoke, I took a good look at the front end, and my pulse quickened. No sign of damage. Even if there had been, there wouldn't be—*now*. It had already been repaired. But the Mercedes dealer would have a record of the work that had been done and the parts—the fender, the headlamp, the grill—that had been replaced. And with a little encouragement from the police, the dealer might even be able to locate the damaged body parts. Hope rose inside me, warm and fervent. It was entirely likely that, by tomorrow, we would know who had killed Miles.

Carl shoved his hands in his pockets, looking from me to the crime-scene tape. "Mrs. Harcher's supposed to give me a lift back to the shop," he said. He nodded toward the cop standing guard at the entrance. "Think it's okay if I go to the door and knock?"

I walked around the Mercedes. "Pretty car." Pretty expensive, too. Way out of my league. "In for some body work, was it?"

"Body work?" Carl shook his head. "No, ma'am." He stroked the shiny top of the car with a loving hand. "Just a good wash and wax. Did it myself, y'know."

I frowned. "No front-end damage?" I persisted, trying to keep the hope alive. "No scratches, broken headlamp, nothing like that?"

Carl looked horrified at the thought that such an incomparable work of automotive art might have been damaged. "Nah, nothin' like that," he said definitively. "Just the wash and wax. Mr. Harcher gets it once a week. He's particular about this car."

The hope shriveled and died.

Carl cast a critical eye at Miles' BMW. "You got a nice car, too. But it could sure do with a wash and wax."

"I'm sure it could," I said, "but it's not mine. It belongs to my brother."

"It's still dirty." He looked apprehensively toward the Harchers' house. "Problem, is there?"

"Not for you," I said with a sigh. I should have known it wasn't going to be this easy. "Just tell that cop at the door what you told me. I'm sure that somebody will be glad to give you a lift back to the shop."

He brightened. "Yeah. Thanks. Hey, you have a good day now, y'hear?"

"You, too," I said, and went back to Miles' dirty car.

# Chapter Seventeen

## McQuaid: At the Two-Bar

The drive down to the Two-Bar Ranch takes longer than it did the other day, because McQuaid stops at DD's Towing operation in Shiner, across from the brewery on 90A. He goes into a grimy office that smells of degreaser and stale cigarette smoke and sports an old *Playboy* calendar on one wall. A kid with a buzz cut and a blue snake tattooed on his forearm tells him, yeah, sure, he can rent the tilt-bed, but he's gotta rent the operator, too. The whole deal goes for seventy-five bucks an hour, which is cheap, dirt cheap, ask anybody in town, they'll tell you. Torres Wrecker, over in San Antonio, is getting one-twenty-five for the same deal.

McQuaid looks out the window at the tilt-bed and thinks it will do the job. He calculates that it'll take an hour to drive to the Two-Bar and load up the car, two hours to his folks' garage in Seguin, an hour back. Call it four hours, five at the outside. Three hundred, three-seventy-five. He figures that Miles' estate is good for that much, especially since there won't be any rental on his folks' garage.

"I'll call you tomorrow and we can set up a time," McQuaid tells the kid. As he turns to go, he catches something out of the corner of his eye. A plaque on the wall, one of those gold things on fake walnut, with an enameled football and curlicued engraving. *Danny Danforth, Shiner Co-manche Boosters, 1992–93.*

Danny Danforth. DD's Towing. McQuaid turns. "The boss around?"

"Somewhere, I guess. You want to see him?"

"Yeah. Right."

The kid sighs as if this presents a special challenge, hoists himself out of the chair, and goes to the door. "Dad!" he bellows. "Some guy here wants to see you!"

A moment later a man steps into the office, wiping his hands on an oily shop rag. He's about McQuaid's age, a little younger, maybe. Muscular build in blue twill coveralls, dark hair under a red and blue Houston Texans gimme cap, which he wears with the bill turned back. "Yeah?" he asks pleasantly.

"Danny Danforth?"

"Nah. That's my pa. My name's Rick. Rick Danforth." He squints. "You lookin' for Pa?"

"Right," McQuaid says. "He around?"

"Nope. He's dead. Five years ago."

McQuaid considers. "Maybe I've got the wrong Danforth. Was your dad married once, to a woman named Laura?"

"That's him," Rick says. "Jeez, that's ancient history. How come you're asking?"

"Just thought we might have a mutual acquaintance," McQuaid says. "Sorry I bothered you." To the boy, he says, "I'll give you a call tomorrow about that tilt-bed." If Laura Danforth's first husband had anything to do with Bob Bayles' murder—a remote possibility at best—it's pretty much too late to do anything about it.

McQuaid gets back in the car and heads south, on his way to the Two-Bar. Off the county road and onto the lane, he meets the same pair of longhorns, standing in the same spot where he met them the day before, tails swinging at flies. He stops and waits until they amble sedately into the mesquite and prickly pear, then drives on down the caliche lane, escorted by the same parade of leaning utility poles, across the dry stream bed and the scrubby flat to the gate in a barbwire fence and Two-Bar's ranch buildings.

The old red Ford truck is parked in front of the ranch house, and he can see the gray tractor sitting alongside the undamaged greenhouse, next to the field of sturdy green tomatillo plants, still lined up in orderly, weed-free rows. But the barn that used to stand between the house and the greenhouse has been reduced to charred timbers and twisted ribbons of corrugated tin roofing. McQuaid can't see the car from where he parks his truck, but he knows that it must be at the far end, under the rubble.

McQuaid pauses a moment, considering the situation that he and Ellie might be heading into, and gets his gun and ankle holster out of the glove box. Armed, he hits the horn with the heel of his hand, then hits it again. There's no sign of Ellie. Maybe she's in the kitchen.

But she isn't. The untidy kitchen is full of cats and Peppy is there, serenely asleep on the floor. The old dog raises his head and opens one lazy eye before he goes back to sleep. But Ellie is nowhere in sight.

"Ellie," McQuaid calls. "Hey, Ellie, it's me. Mike."

But there's no answer. The house is quiet enough to hear Peppy's wheezing and the *tick-tick* of the clock over the re-frigerator. McQuaid frowns, feeling a twist of foreboding in his gut, and casts a glance around, taking in the details of the room—empty plant trays on the table, stacks of news-papers, dirty dishes in the sink, half-finished sandwich on the counter, glass of milk, three-quarters full. The kitchen is pretty much the way it was the day before, but his cop's instinct tells him that something isn't right. His gut tight-ens. Ellie was expecting him—where is she?

As if in answer, he hears a sharp one-two bark, from somewhere outside. He goes back onto the porch and hears it again. *Happy*, he thinks. The barking is coming from the direction of the greenhouse, now a flurry of frantic, painful yelps, as if the border collie is tied up, or maybe stuck in a barbwire fence. McQuaid lengthens his stride, casting around for the dog, then sees him, tied by a length of clothesline to the trunk of a scrappy desert willow beside the greenhouse.

"Hey, Happy," McQuaid says, bending over. The dog is wearing a collar, but the oily rope isn't fastened to that. Instead, it's looped twice around his neck and tied with a slip knot that has tightened, nooselike, as the dog has lunged against it, to the point where it's choking him.

McQuaid frowns as he unties him. "What's going on, boy? How come you're roped up like this?"

Released, the little dog doesn't hang around to say thanks. He's off like a shot, like greased lightning, streaking to the greenhouse door. It's shut, but he shoulders it open and scoots through.

McQuaid follows. Inside the greenhouse, it's warm and bright, the afternoon sun shining through the translucent poly fastened to the aluminum frame. It's humid, too, so humid that he feels suddenly smothered, as though somebody's slapped a hot, wet towel over his face. The greenhouse isn't large, no more than thirty feet from end to end, maybe fifteen feet wide. Wooden plant benches hung with shade-cloth awnings are lined up on both sides. The plants are in the field now and the benches are mostly empty, except for stacks of plastic trays and plant pots. The center aisle is neatly mulched with pea gravel, hoses are coiled, tools and equipment stacked. Beside the door, wooden pegs hold a jacket, rain gear, a hank of nylon line. At the far end, a ventilation fan is set head-high into the wall, and McQuaid can hear the *thwack-thwack-thwack* of its slowly rotating blades. He can also hear Happy, frantically whining, the whines punctuated by sharp, anguished yelps.

McQuaid, moving fast, follows the sound to the far end of the greenhouse. That's where he finds Ellie. She's sitting with her back against a plant bench, behind a head-high stack of plastic trays, out of sight of the door. Her knees are pulled up, feet flat on the gravel. Her head is slumped forward, forehead resting on her knees. Her arms are loose at either side. There's a revolver in her open right hand, a Smith & Wesson Model 657. Happy is frantically licking her cheek, pawing at her shoulder.

McQuaid's first reaction is a cop's reaction. The feelings—the pity, the horror, the anger—will come later, they always do, he can't keep them back. But there's work to be done now, quickly, and feelings get in the way. He pushes the dog aside, kneels, and lifts Ellie's head. The front of her plaid shirt is soaked with blood. Her jeans are bloody, too, where her upper body has rested against her thighs. There's an exit wound in her lower back, below her ribs.

At first he's sure she's dead. She doesn't seem to be breathing, and he can't find a pulse in her neck or her wrist. But Happy, refusing to be pushed away, has darted around to her right side and is licking her arm and neck and cheek furiously, shoving roughly against her, butting her with his head, yelping, pawing, imperative, urgent. And then, to McQuaid's amazement, Ellie's pulse flutters. She gulps air, then begins breathing, fast and shallow, ragged. She's not conscious, but she is amazingly, miraculously alive.

"Hang in there, Ellie," McQuaid mutters. He gropes for his cell, then remembers that there's no signal out here. "Stay with her," he commands the dog—hardly necessary, surely—and sprints for the house, for the phone in the kitchen, to call for help.

IT comes in stages.

A sheriff's deputy, a brown-haired, stocky Hispanic woman in her mid-thirties, gets there a few minutes before the ambulance and paramedic team arrives. She knows El-

lie Hanson. From the look of painful distress that crosses
her face when she sees the victim, McQuaid guesses that
she and Ellie might even be friends. He wonders whether
she's the deputy Ellie mentioned on the phone, the one who
might be willing to help with an investigation into the barn
burning. He notes with approval, though, that she doesn't
let her feelings get in the way of what has to be done. She
gets on with the grim business of processing the crime
scene in a quiet and competent way, while the paramedics
do what they can.

The Starflite helicopter is the next to arrive, after the
paramedics determine that this is a case for a San Antonio
hospital, rather than one of the smaller local hospitals or
clinics where most of their patients are taken. The county
sheriff, a big beer gut of a guy in mirrored sunglasses with
a white hat and a silver belt-buckle the size of a hubcap,
shows up twenty minutes after that, with another deputy.
Sheriff Grady. McQuaid remembers Ellie's remark about
him, that he owes his job to Mack.

That's not the reason McQuaid dislikes him, though.
Grady is obviously a rural politician, an elected official,
not a professional lawman. Worse, he is brusque, impatient, and self-important, barking out unnecessary orders
to both the deputies and the paramedics, even though Mc-
Quaid can see that they're doing a competent job. The
sheriff is especially generous with his muttered curses
when it comes to the Hispanic woman deputy—*Isabelle
Ramos* is the name stamped on her black plastic pocket tag.
He peers over her shoulder, crowding her aggressively, as
if he's hoping to push her into making a mistake. McQuaid
wonders how long this situation has been going on, and
how Deputy Ramos, who impresses him as an effective,
meticulous investigator, can tolerate it.

Less than thirty minutes from the time McQuaid found
Ellie's body, the helicopter is airborne. The paramedics have
stabilized Ellie, stopped the bleeding, inserted an airway,

installed a drip. One of them, noting where the bullet has entered and exited, remarks that there's a lot of internal damage and that her chances aren't very good. "Lucky to be alive," he says, as they strap her to the stretcher.

"Doesn't deserve to be," Grady growls, glancing at the gun, which has been bagged as evidence and lies on the plant bench. "Jeez, I hate these would-be suicides. Waste of resources. Waste of time."

"This isn't an attempted suicide, Sheriff," McQuaid says quietly. He's already identified himself, handed over his private investigator's license, and mentioned his law enforcement credentials, ten years in Houston Homicide. But Grady isn't impressed. Suspicious, mistrustful, dismissive. McQuaid can see it written on his heavy-jowled face.

*Houston dick. City cop. Figures he's smarter'n us backwoods hicks. Well, I'll show the sumbitch.*

McQuaid repeats himself, emphasizing the words. "It's not suicide."

"Oh, yeah?" Grady growls, hitching up his pants. "How you figger that? Had the gun in her hand, didn't she? Sure looks like a suicide to me."

McQuaid regards him. The gun will be printed back at the lab, and Deputy Ramos has already taken Ellie's prints. While she was working, McQuaid quietly suggested that she swab Ellie's hands for gunpowder residue, as well. Ramos nodded, agreeing. She didn't have a test kit with her, but she's bagged Ellie's hands so they can be tested later. Grady rolled his eyes at that, making it clear that as far as he was concerned, it's a waste of time.

"Well, there's a couple of things, Sheriff," McQuaid says pleasantly, folding his arms across his chest. "One, Ellie Hanson doesn't own a gun. That's what she told me, and I don't have any reason to disbelieve her." He pauses. "Two, she's right-handed, but—"

"Yeah," the sheriff grunts sarcastically. "You know, I did just happen to notice that. She was holdin' the gun in her right hand. Wound's in the left chest. The usual place people try to shoot themselves. Aimin' for where she thinks the heart is." He chuckles. "Most folks don't have a clue."

McQuaid shakes his head. "Ellie was right-handed," he repeats, "but when I was here yesterday, her right wrist was giving her so much trouble she couldn't pick up a half-empty coffeepot. She'd never manage to hold that heavy Magnum in one hand, which she'd have to do to get that shot. Plus, I'm surprised that the recoil didn't send it flying. I'd sure expect that, wouldn't you?"

The sheriff frowns but doesn't answer.

"Anyway, the trajectory is wrong." McQuaid knows he's pressing Grady too hard but he's not willing to give it up.

"Huh." The sheriff grunts again, and McQuaid wonders if it's possible that he hasn't noticed this. By the time Grady arrived on the scene, the medics had already gone to work on Ellie. She was flat on her back on the stretcher on which she'd take her helicopter ride. So maybe he didn't get a good look.

"The exit wound is just above the belt in the back," McQuaid says. "The docs will say for sure—or the coroner. But it seems to me that it'd be pretty tough to shoot yourself so that the bullet enters just above the collarbone and exits a foot lower down without leaving powder residue on the fabric. And if it's there, it's not visible to the naked eye."

Not saying a word, not giving anything away, the sheriff takes out a bag of tobacco and a packet of papers and rolls a cigarette. This takes a while. When he's finished, he flicks a lighter to the tip and pulls, then breathes out heavily.

"So," he says, narrowing his eyes against the curling smoke. "So if this isn't attempted suicide, it's something else. You got an idea, Mister McQuaid?" *Mister* is said with exaggerated courtesy.

"Yeah," McQuaid says dryly. "Attempted murder."

"Uh-huh. You got a suspect in mind, have you?"

"Sorry, Sheriff." McQuaid shakes his head. "Wish I did."

"You'd tell me, would you?" This is said with a dry chuckle. "You'd give me the benefit of your wisdom?" Grady pauses and adds, "Or maybe you'd rather tell that pretty little deputy, huh?" He winks suggestively.

The hair prickles on the back of McQuaid's neck. He hates it when authority is misused, abused. Guys like this give law enforcement a bad name. But at the moment, the sheriff holds the cards. McQuaid knows he won't get anywhere by challenging him.

"Sure," he says mildly. "I'd tell you if I could." *Or maybe I wouldn't, you prick.*

"Well, then." The sheriff takes another long drag on his cigarette. "Suppose you tell me what you were doin' here when you happened to find her, Mr. McQuaid. You're a long way from home, ain't you? Just ridin' around? Havin' a nice afternoon, lookin' at the scenery?"

McQuaid has had a while to think about this question, which he knows is legitimate. He has decided on the truth— or a reasonable facsimile thereof. His account might be notable for what it omits, but he knows that everything he says will check out.

"I'm doing some investigative work for an Austin attorney, Miles Danforth. Ellie Hanson had been storing an old wrecked Cadillac in her barn for Danforth's mother. Earlier today, she phoned to tell me that the barn burned during the night. I drove down to see if the Caddy was salvageable. On the way, I stopped at DD's Towing in Shiner to see about getting a tilt-bed truck out here to load up the wreck, if it turned out there was anything left to load. Talked to a kid with a buzz cut and a snake tattoo, and to his dad, who owns the place. It was close to two when I was there. You can confirm that with them."

"You bet I will." The sheriff blows a cloud of acrid smoke in McQuaid's face. "And when you get here to the Two-Bar, you find the dog tied to the tree out there and Miz Hanson shot. That your story, is it?"

"That's what happened," McQuaid says, without emphasis.

"You touch that gun?"

McQuaid shakes his head. "No, Sheriff."

"You carryin'?"

"There's a Smith and Wesson 19 in the glove compartment of my truck." Not eager to explain why he was armed, McQuaid put the gun and holster back while he was waiting for help to arrive. "I've got a concealed carry permit."

The sheriff gives him a steely-eyed look that tempts McQuaid to laugh, except that this is no laughing matter. "So it's your considered opinion as an invest-i-ga-tor that somebody shot this lady, is it?" The question is loaded with sarcasm.

"That's how I see it," McQuaid says, not rising to the bait. "He grabbed the dog and tied him up. Ellie was out here, working. He overpowered her and forced her to sit where we found her. Then he stood over her and shot her, intending to make it look like suicide. He might have realized that the shot was off—that the trajectory was wrong. He also knew he hadn't killed her outright. But he probably figured she would bleed to death before she was found. And suicides don't usually shoot themselves twice. He couldn't risk a second shot to finish her off. So he put the gun in her right hand and got the hell out of Dodge."

"Clever." This is said with enough irony to stop a train, although it's not clear whether the sheriff is speaking about McQuaid's cleverness or the shooter's.

"Oh, I don't know." McQuaid shrugs. "Maybe not. Depends on whether the serial number on the gun is traceable." *It isn't, or it wouldn't have been left behind. Whoever shot her is smarter than that.* "Also depends on whether she survives and can identify the bastard." He looks directly at the sheriff. "Might be a good idea to put a deputy in front of Miz Hanson's door at the hospital. If the shooter hears she's still alive to finger him, he might decide to give it another try."

Grady makes a noise that might express either disdain or disbelief. He takes one last, long pull on his cigarette and crushes it under his boot. "Well, now, Mr. McQuaid. Maybe while you've been concocting all these smart hypo-the-ses"—he drawls out the word contemptuously—"you've had a little time to figger out why somebody would want to go to all this trouble. 'Course, we're just country folk down here. We're not used to comin' up with fancy theories. So maybe you'll see fit to tell me what you think is the motive for this here complicated crime scheme?"

McQuaid feels the hot anger rise up in him, along with the strong desire to punch this fat guy's lights out. But that'll only get him charged with assault. He pushes the anger back down and replies with a rueful shrug and a head shake. "I don't know any more than you do, Sheriff. I'm just hoping that the gun can be traced, or that Ellie will be able to say who shot her."

The sheriff narrows his eyes. "I don't expect you'll have any reason to talk to her, though."

McQuaid straightens. "Are you telling me I can't?"

The sheriff pushes his mouth in and out. "Haven't made up my mind yet," he says finally. "Better check with me before you make a trip to the hospital, though. Might be off limits. To you." He raises his voice. "Hey, Ramos," he barks. "I'm gonna leave now. You get over here and take *Meester* McQuaid's statement. Pronto."

McQuaid suppresses the urge to tell this two-bit tinbadge jackass where he can get off, and watches him leave. Deputy Ramos, armed with a clipboard and ballpoint, quietly and competently takes his statement, and gets his signature, address, and phone number. McQuaid knows that she's already run the registration on his truck and driver's and P.I.'s licenses and found him clean.

Finally, she clicks the pen closed and tucks her clipboard under her arm. "Well, that about wraps it up, sir." Her voice has the soft lilt of a native Spanish speaker. "Thank you for your help. You're free to leave now."

"I need to check out a vehicle that was stored in the barn," he says. He nods toward the pile of burned rubble.

"The fire was a bad thing," the deputy says soberly, following his glance. "The scanner woke me up, and I came over to help. I live just a little way up the road."

McQuaid glances again at her name tag. *Ramos.* "Are you related to José Ramos? Ellie told me he helps her out in the field sometimes."

She nods. "My husband. José got up and came over to help fight the fire, too. We've known Ellie Hanson since we were kids. Her father, too. They've been good friends." She looks away, past the barn, to the fields and woods, lying peaceful in the spring sunshine. McQuaid can hear the regret in her voice. "First the fire, now this shooting. It's hard to understand why somebody would do such horrible things to such a nice lady. Everybody knows how willing she is to give a helping hand."

McQuaid feels some relief. At least somebody in the sheriff's office is on the mark. "So you don't think she tried to kill herself?"

"No way," Isabelle Ramos says firmly, shaking her head. "She didn't do this, sir. She couldn't." The smile that ghosts across her mouth does not reach her eyes. "I think Sheriff Grady will agree, once he has all the facts in front of him."

*And he will, if you've got anything to say about it,* McQuaid thinks approvingly. Aloud, he says, "Do you have any idea who might have set the fire, or why, Deputy Ramos? Do you think it's the same person who shot her?"

Her face slips into that neutral, bland expression habitually worn by good law enforcement officers, but he knows what she's thinking. She's wary. She's reminding herself that he may have been a cop once, but now he's a civilian, a private investigator. She's wondering just how far she can trust him. He'll give her some help.

"When I talked with Ellie on the phone earlier today, she told me she thought her cousin was behind the fire," he says quietly. "In the night, just before the blaze got going, the dog woke her. She got up and looked out the window. She recognized his truck, even in the dark, because the right headlight is out." He pauses, watching her. "Does that surprise you, Deputy?"

Her mouth tightens. "I'm afraid not. There've been several other incidents over the past few years. 'Dirty tricks,' Ellie called them."

"Dirty tricks are one thing, attempted murder is something else," McQuaid says wryly. By this time, of course, it might be murder. For all they knew, Ellie Hanson might have died on the way to the hospital. "What's the story on this cousin?"

"The way Ellie tells it, it's one of those family things. At one time, the two ranches were both part of the same big spread, which belonged to Ellie's grandfather. Ellie's father inherited this piece, with the old ranch house. He kept the original name—Two-Bar—and ranched it some, not in a big way, just running enough cows to keep the place going. Mack—that's short for MacKenzie, his middle name—inherited the other piece. It's to the east of here, on the other side of Mustang Creek. He built a big house there, but lived in Houston and mostly used the land for hunting and fishing. He moved out here permanently some twelve, fourteen years ago. Ellie told me that he's had his eye on the Two-Bar for a long time. Apparently figured to buy it when Ellie's dad was gone. He's been pushing her."

McQuaid frowns. Pushing her is one thing. Shooting

her is another. "Do you really think he'd do something like this?"

"Somebody did it," she says factually. "I can't think of anybody else who would want Ellie gone." She frowns, and her voice drops. "The barn-burning I can understand. The shooting—" She shakes her head. "Must be more. Something I don't know."

McQuaid agrees. "Do you know this guy? Her cousin, I mean. Mack, his name is."

"Yes, I know him, Mr. McQuaid." The deputy's voice is quiet, even. She gives him a direct look, a measuring look, and he can almost see the calculations going through her mind. "Are you thinking of having a little talk with him?"

"Yes, I am." He pauses, returning her look. He's not sure whether this is a good idea, but it's the best he's got. "Would you be interested in going with me?" He frowns. "Or maybe you're thinking of having an official conversation with him. If so, can I tag along?"

There's no hesitation. She has already made up her mind how she wants to do this. "I'll be glad to go with you, Mr. McQuaid. It'll have to wait until I go off duty, though." She gives him a straight look. "I don't think Sheriff Grady would be too enthusiastic about the idea. He and Ellie's cousin are pretty good friends—hunting, fishing, politicking. If there's any official contact, the sheriff will want to be the one to make it." She pauses. "So it's good to keep this unofficial."

"Gotcha," McQuaid says.

Actually, he's glad that Deputy Ramos wants to do it this way—just two friends of Ellie Hanson, dropping in on a neighbor to find out whether he can shed any light on what's happened at Ellie's place. McQuaid also understands the substantial and unenviable risk that Deputy Ramos is taking, going outside of channels. Mack has political clout in the county, according to Ellie. And the sheriff is going to be very unhappy if he finds out that his buddy has any responsibility for what's happened at the Two-Bar. If that's the case, the law will have to come into it, and Grady may turn up the heat on Isabelle Ramos. There's no way around that one, unfortunately. But it looks like Ramos is willing to risk her boss' anger to get the job done. It's an attitude he admires.

"What time is good for you, Deputy?" he asks. He looks at his watch and is astonished to see that it's nearly five.

"I go off-shift at seven thirty, and I have to stop at home and check on the kids. Eight thirty is probably the earliest I can make it. Where do you want to meet?"

"How about right here? There are a few chores that need doing." At her quizzical look, he explains. "Have to feed the girls."

"Oh, yes, the girls," she says, and laughs lightly. "Primrose and Parsnip. God forbid that those pigs should miss a meal. They eat better than lots of people—on both sides of the border."

He chuckles. "The dogs and cats have to be fed, too. And I need to check out that vehicle in the barn."

These aren't the only things he wants to do, of course. There are the papers Ellie mentioned over the phone. He hopes he won't have to hunt too hard to find them. But before he does anything else, he's got to reach China. He's left messages on her cell phone, but since she hasn't answered, he's thinking that maybe her phone isn't working, or that she's lost it again. He'll leave a message at home, too. She should be back in Pecan Springs in the next hour or so. He doesn't want her to worry.

"It's not a problem if I hang around the place, is it?" he adds.

"It's fine as far I'm concerned, Mr. McQuaid." Deputy Ramos extends her hand. Her grip is cool and firm. "Thanks for your help," she adds, and McQuaid knows that she means it. "If you hadn't found Ellie when you did, she'd be dead by now. Whoever did this—I want to get him."

As Isabelle Ramos speaks, a sudden, fierce anger shows on her face, in her eyes, in her voice. Her mouth firms into a hard line. McQuaid knows that he has glimpsed something steely in her, something tough and determined. It's the kind of controlled passion for justice that a good cop needs. It'll keep her going when the other deputies—the ones who are in it for the money or the ego-satisfaction—have long since folded.

Her mouth softens. "Oh, and I'll be glad to take responsibility for the animals after today," she adds. "Until Ellie comes home, that is."

*Until Ellie comes home.* "That'll be good," he says, nodding. They're speaking as though Ellie has gone on a quick trip to Austin, or overnight to Dallas. But that's not the way it is. Coming home is a long shot, and they both know it. A very long shot.

"I'll see you later this evening, then," she says, turning to go. "I don't know what we'll find at Stonebridge, but we should probably be prepared—"

"Hang on," he says urgently, stopping her. "Did you say *Stonebridge*?"

"Yes. That's the name of Mack's ranch."

He shakes his head, frowns. "This cousin of Ellie's. What's his name? His full name?"

"Stone," she says. "Theodore MacKenzie Stone. His mother was a MacKenzie. They're an important family in this county. I guess that's why he likes to be called Mack." She smiles slightly. "Brand identification."

*Jeez.* McQuaid exhales, a hard, long breath, and feels his heart banging at his ribs, feels the apprehensive shiver at the base of his neck. *Stonebridge. Theodore Stone.*

*Ted Stone.*

He has to reach China. He's got to stop her from doing

any more poking around in Miles Danforth's business. He's got to keep her from finding out what he knows now, for if she does, that knowledge will place her in the same danger as her brother.

And her brother is dead.

# Chapter Eighteen

Black nightshade (*Solanum nigrum*) is named for the color of the poisonous berries, which are at their deadliest when green and immature. In the Victorian language of flowers, the plant signified "Your thoughts are dark." It is symbolic of sorcery, witchcraft, and death.

Driving south, I saw that the sunshiny day was looking stormy. The sky was darkening, with thunderheads piling up to the west, and when I turned on the radio to one of the local stations, I heard that a severe thunderstorm watch had been issued for the counties up and down I-35, from San Antonio to Waco. No surprise, from the look of those clouds, I thought. The situation wasn't helped by the fact that the temperature was climbing. It was at least hot enough to sear steaks. But with luck, the storm would hold off until I had done my errands—stopped at Marcia's and Mrs. Bolton's—and made it home.

It was still early and the rush-hour traffic had not yet gathered full steam. I zipped down MoPac, exited on the south side of the river, and drove east past Zilker Park to Travis Heights to deliver Caitlin's clothes—a bundle of clean jeans, shirts, socks, and undies, to supplement what I had dropped off the night before. I was hoping to have a minute to chat with Marcia about the current status of the police investigation into Miles' death. There would be some decisions and some choices to be made, and it would be good if we were on the same page when it came time to make them.

But Caitlin met me at the door, looking sad and forlorn, and told me that Marcia had just got back from the doctor's and was lying down.

"She isn't feeling well?" I asked, remembering how pale and shaky Marcia had seemed. I'd thought it was due to the shock of Miles' death, but maybe there was something else.

"She's okay," Caitlin said defensively. "She's just tired."

"I'm sure she's had a lot on her mind lately," I said, and made a quick decision. "Tell you what, Caitlin. Why don't you slip into her room and tell her that you and I are going out for a fast burger." I looked at my watch. "Tell her we'll be back in thirty or forty minutes. Ask her if she'd like us to pick up some takeout for her supper."

Caitlin brightened. "Cool," she said, and skipped up the stairs to Marcia's room.

The air was warm and heavy, smothery, almost, and I had long since shed my red blazer. I judged that the rain would hold off for another hour, though, so we passed up the fast-food places in favor of a small sidewalk cafe on South Congress. Caitlin ordered a cheeseburger, I got an avocado burger with crunchy sprouts and a slice of tomato and red onion, and we shared a large plate of hot, crispy French fries as we watched the South Austin yippies walk and bicycle and skateboard past us. The conversation began slowly but went faster as Caitlin lost some of her shyness and I lost a little of the stiffness I usually have around kids.

I learned that her favorite subject was art and her least favorite was arithmetic, and that the prospect of going to middle school in the fall was really, really, *really* scary. Her best friend was a girl named Anya who had moved away a couple of months before, but they wrote letters and emailed back and forth, and were planning to go to camp together in the summer, which was going to be very *cool*. She liked playing soccer (except for getting hit in the nose by the soccer ball) and taking pictures and hiking, although the thought of not doing these things with her dad brought tears to her eyes, and she looked away fast, so I wouldn't see them. When she grew up, she wanted to be a photographer and take pictures of animals. I told her that we had a basset and several lizards who might be coerced into posing for pictures, and when she came to see us, she should bring her camera. By that time, we had finished our food, so we picked up Marcia's order—a salad and potato soup— and I took her home.

"Will you come again, Aunt China?" Caitlin asked, when we got out of the car in front of Marcia's house.

I was surprised by the question. "Sure," I replied, and was even more surprised when she asked, eagerly, "Like, soon?"

I fumbled a little in my astonishment. Did she *really* want to see me? I was just a boring old aunt. I settled for the nonspecific phrase, "In a few days, honey." I didn't want to name an earlier time and have to disappoint her. I'm not sure I understand kids, but I had the feeling that this one would cling to any promise I made her. Any promise *anyone* made her, for that matter. It would be too easy to hurt her. The girl was so vulnerable that she made my heart ache.

But "a few days" seemed to be enough. "Thank you," she said, and threw her arms around me to give me a hug.

"Tell Aunt Marcia she's under orders to eat this and feel better," I said as I handed her the takeout. "You take good care of her, will you?"

"I will," she promised, and went up the walk. She turned at the door and gave me the first real smile I had seen. A pretty smile, too. I drove away, feeling warmed by the glow of that sunny surprise.

THERE was another surprise waiting for me at Mrs. Bolton's house, a much less comforting one. I was glad to see her car in the drive, which meant that she was at home. I was knocking at the front door when a woman with frizzy blond hair came around the house, a key in one hand and a cigarette in the other. She was wearing a red halter top and a pair of very red, very short shorts. I eyed her enviously. My black blouse was stuck to my back, my gray skirt felt clingy, and I would've liked nothing better than to strip off my panty hose.

"You looking for Bev Bolton?" she asked. "She ain't here. Won't be back for a while." She looked over my shoulder at the BMW parked at the curb. "Fancy car you got there, hon. Set you back a bundle, huh?"

"It's my brother's," I said. "I was here last night, and Mrs. Bolton didn't mention going away." I paused. "I have something for her," I said, holding out what I had brought. It was the cup I had found in Miles' office, the one that said "World's Greatest Boss." "She worked for my brother for more than a decade. He died a few days ago. I found this in his office and thought she might like to have it. I think she must have given it to him."

"Bet she'd like that," the woman said, tossing her cigarette on the ground and placing a thong sandal firmly on it. "Bev was real broke up over that guy dyin'. Sorta the last straw for her, y'know? Sorry to hear he was your brother. It's hard when somebody goes like that—accident, I mean. Cops find out who hit him?"

"Not yet," I said. "They're still investigating. I guess these things take a while."

She eyed the heavy gray clouds. "Looks like we got a storm coming, don't it? Listen, hon, I gotta feed Bev's cat and pick up some mail that needs stamps." She nodded at the cup in my hand. "Wanna come in and leave that for her?"

"Oh, could I?" I said, with enthusiasm. "I'll leave her a note, too. When will she be back?"

"Dunno." She unlocked the door. "She was pretty upset when she called me this morning. Said it'd be a while. Couple weeks, maybe. Hey, I'm Tammy, by the way."

"I'm China. China Bayles." I frowned. "A couple of weeks? But isn't that her car in the drive?"

"Sure is." Tammy was looking around. "Listen, hon, I gotta do this cat. You wanna leave a note, there's some paper by the phone. Have at it." She raised her voice. "Merlin, kitty-kitty-kitty? Time for your dinner. Merlin, get your ass out here."

Tammy went down the hall, calling the cat. I put the cup on the desk and was looking for something to write on when I heard a loud exclamation. I dropped the pen and went to see what was wrong.

"Wouldja look at this?" Tammy said, hands on her hips, standing in a bedroom door, surveying the scene. She made a *tsk-tsk* sound with her tongue. "What a helluva mess!"

The bedroom where I had left Mrs. Bolton asleep the night before was a shambles. Clothing was strewn over the unmade bed, the chair, the dresser, even the floor. Drawers were open, things had been pulled out of the closet, toiletries were spilled. The door to the bathroom was open, and I could see towels on the floor. It looked as though someone had left in an enormous hurry—or had been forced to leave.

"What did Mrs. Bolton say when she called you this morning?" I asked urgently. "What time did she call? How did she sound?"

"Time?" Tammy frowned. "Musta been about five thirty, maybe five forty-five. Billy—he's my husband—drives an eighteen-wheeler, and he's out the door by six. I was makin' his lunch when she phoned. Bev said she hadda leave for a while and would I feed the cat while she was gone, and buy stamps for some envelopes she was going to leave on the counter—bills and stuff she needed mailed, but she didn't have any stamps. So I said sure, I'd do it. Merlin's a great cat, and I gotta go to the post office anyway." She shook her head, mystified, picking up a pair of panties from the floor. "She sounded sorta rushed, frantic, even. But the thing is, Bev is such a neatnik, always has things arranged just so, down to the quarter-inch. I mean, compulsive, really compulsive." She shook her head again, puzzled. "Beats me how she could bring herself to leave her place like this when she's going off on a trip."

I took a tour of the room, looking for anything that might indicate foul play. "Did you hear anything unusual?" I asked. "Did you see her leave?"

"Nah, nothin' outta the ordinary. But I didn't see her leave. After Billy left, I got in the shower. The hot water kinda wakes me up, you know? I was sorta surprised when I looked out and saw her car still sittin' in the drive, but I figured, hey, somebody musta picked her up and took her where she was going. To the airport, maybe."

Somebody must have picked her up. Somebody from the office? I thought of how Brandon had pretended to me that Mrs. Bolton would be coming in later, when—according to Rachel, anyway—he knew she wouldn't be coming in at all. Did he have something to do with Mrs. Bolton's abrupt departure? Had she been coerced to leave? Forced to leave? Why?

For a moment, I considered calling the police. But there was no evidence of foul play, and the lady had arranged with her neighbor for the care of her cat. The cops would not be inclined to treat this as a disappearance and even if they were, missing person cases have very low priority.

I turned back to Tammy. "Does she have any relatives? Any children?"

"A niece, maybe?" Tammy hazarded, casting her eyes toward the ceiling, as if to find the answer there. "Really, I dunno. Bev keeps pretty much to herself. Not much of a one for neighboring." She pulled herself together. "Well, I ain't gonna worry about her, you know? There's nothin' I can do, one way or another. I hate to rush you, sweetie, but I gotta feed the cat and pick up that mail and get outta here. It's nearly six, and Billy and me, we're goin' bowling to-night. He has a hissy if I'm late."

I left the cup with a note for Mrs. Bolton, explaining that I thought she might like to keep it in Miles' memory. I also left my phone number with the request that she call me as soon as she got home. I left a card with Tammy, too, with the same request, and collected her phone number. Something unusual had happened in this house. I intended to keep in touch.

I was on my way out to the car when I heard Tammy yelling. "Hey!" she cried. "Hey, wait!"

I turned. She was running down the walk after me, waving an envelope over her head. "Hey, didn't you say your name was Bayles?"

"Yes," I said. "China Bayles."

"Well, ain't that a kick?" Tammy handed the envelope to me, beaming. "You've just saved Bev a first-class stamp, by golly. She was sendin' you this."

The envelope was addressed to me at the shop—the address on the card I had left on the kitchen table the night before.

"Thank you," I said, surprised. "Thanks very much."

"Don't mention it," she said cheerfully and went off, whistling.

I sure as heck wasn't going to wait until I got home to read what Mrs. Bolton had written. I got into the car and used a nail file to slit the envelope. Inside was a single folded sheet of paper with the intertwined initials BB printed at the top. The message was written in a neat but hasty hand, on both sides of the paper. The style was formal and stilted, as you might expect from a woman who has spent her entire working life in a law firm. I could almost hear the whisper of her dry, papery voice.

> *Dear Ms. Bayles,*
> *As I'm sure you have guessed by now, I am a recovering alcoholic. Mr. Danforth understood my struggles and was always sympathetic. But even he would have been horrified by the spectacle I made of myself when you were here last night. I apologize. But that isn't why I'm writing. I was about to tell you something last night when I became ill. Since I didn't finish it, I am taking the liberty of writing to you.*
> *Mr. Danforth was very angry at Mr. Brandon for entering his office without his permission and going through his mother's files. But what troubled him most was Mr. Brandon's discovery of the name of Mr. Danforth's father. I don't know who that person is—I didn't hear that part of their discussion.*

Didn't hear it? More likely, she *couldn't* hear it. Maybe the door was shut or their voices were too low. It was certainly something she'd have loved to learn, if she could. I went on reading.

> *But I do know that Mr. Danforth felt that Mr. Brandon had invaded his privacy, and was even more upset when he found out that Mr. Brandon had told his uncle, Mr. Stone. I am unclear as to your relationship to Mr. Danforth, whether on his mother's side or his father's, and have no idea whether this information is important to you. Still, I thought it was something you might want to know.*
> *I do not wish to speak ill of Mr. Brandon, for I am very grateful to him. He came over to check on me*

*early this morning, and when he saw that I had been drinking, offered to pay for a few weeks at the rehabilitation center where I stayed before. I have accepted his offer. I am very sorry that I won't be able to help with the arrangements for dear Mr. Danforth's funeral service. Perhaps Miss Burke might be of service. I suppose she ought to be good for something.*

> *Sincerely yours,*
> *Beverly Bolton*

*P.S. I will be at the Pinnacle Recovery Center in Houston, should you need to contact me.*

The letter was food for some very serious thought as I started the car and began the drive back to Pecan Springs. The sky had grown even darker and the piles of thunderheads were more threatening, with occasional streaks of lightning. But that was nothing, compared to the whirlwind of information I was trying to sort through. The rehab center, for instance. It was much too convenient an exit, and Chris Brandon was too eager to get Mrs. Bolton out of the way. He must have been hoping to hide his difficulties with Miles, in case the police came around, asking questions about people in the office. He didn't want Mrs. Bolton to tell what she knew. Was she at the Pinnacle Recovery Center? I'd check that out.

But just as important, Rachel Burke had gotten the name right, after all. When I asked her who Chris Brandon's politically heavyweight uncle was, she had replied, in her careless way, "Somebody named Strawn. Or Stone. Or maybe Strand. Something like that."

But of course it wasn't Strawn or Strand, it was *Stone*.

Theodore MacKenzie Stone. Ted Stone, my father's partner.

I narrowed my eyes. So Chris Brandon was Ted Stone's

nephew—which was no doubt why he'd been invited to become an associate at Stone and Bayles, some seventeen or eighteen years ago and fresh out of law school. And earlier this year, Chris Brandon had found out that Miles was the son of Bob Bayles and Laura Danforth. He had gone through Laura's files and discovered the existence of the car, and maybe even its whereabouts. And he had doubtless told all of this to his uncle.

Well, he would, wouldn't he? Wasn't that a natural thing to do? *Hey, Uncle Ted, you'll never guess what I've just found out about your old partner and that woman who used to run your office. Remember Laura Danforth? Well, she and Bayles had been getting it on for years and nobody had a clue. They had a son, too. And get this, will you? That crazy Danforth woman kept that car, that burned-up old Caddy. Would you believe?*

I frowned as I negotiated the entrance ramp onto I-35 and joined the steady stream of rush-hour traffic heading south from Austin to Buda and Kyle and San Marcos and Pecan Springs. Well, if that's how it had happened, so what? Surely there wasn't anything very earth-shattering about any of this, was there? Of course, it might be embarrassing for Miles if his colleagues knew that he was the illegitimate son of a now-deceased Houston lawyer, but seriously—how bad was that? Ninety percent of the lawyers in town had closets full of family skeletons of one description or another. Beyond embarrassing, what?

*Except.*

Except that Miles had been killed on the eve of a planned trip to check out that burned-up Caddy in which Bob Bayles had died.

Except that this morning, my husband had phoned me in great excitement to tell me that he knew—how, I couldn't begin to guess—that Bob Bayles' death wasn't an accident, it was murder.

Except that there were too many coincidences, too

many crossed paths, too many intersecting, interwoven lives, some in the present, some in the past. Ted Stone and Bob Bayles, Bob Bayles and Miles Danforth, Chris Brandon and Ted Stone. *Except, except, except.* Where to start unraveling the threads of the past? How to make sense of all these crossed connections?

Then, as I slowed to pass an eighteen-wheeler loaded with cattle, I remembered the audio cassette tape I had found in the Sturdi-Step shoebox in the closet at Miles' house. It was probably music, or maybe even blank, but I could at least check it out. I fumbled through the TAX RECORDS box on the front seat, found it, and popped it into the car's tape deck.

But the tape wasn't blank, and what was on it wasn't music, either. I recognized the precise, dispassionate narrator as Laura Danforth, and the tape as a compilation of her research notes, arranged and recorded in a logical and orderly way. The tape had been made some years ago, around the time she dropped her investigation. I listened to this voice from the dead, at first with an intense interest and then in mounting horror and anger, as she laid out the pieces of information she had assembled, pieces that told the story—most of it, anyway—of what had happened to my father, and why. There were a few holes, a few questions unanswered. But by the end, I knew most of what had happened in the year my father died. I also knew why Laura Danforth had abruptly abandoned her investigation, and who had been responsible. I could only guess why she had kept her silence for the rest of her life. I had no idea why she hadn't been killed for what she knew.

I knew, and I was entirely overwhelmed. There was too much detail here to take in all at once, too much story awakening too many feelings, too much pain, too much regret. So my father knew that Keith Madison had been murdered. He could not stomach the killing and was planning to take what he knew to the Feds. *Keith Madison.* Now, prompted, I remembered him more clearly. He and my father had both been Kappa Sig at Tulane, and both played football. Dad had handled some minor legal business for him from time to time.

But Dad was planning to do more than just reveal who had killed Keith Madison. According to Laura Danforth, he knew a great deal about the inner legal (and illegal) workings of G. W. Stone Engineering, which at the time was the top engineering and construction firm in the nation, with strong ties both to Austin and to Washington. He was planning to testify to the federal grand jury that had been investigating Madison. If he told a fraction of what he knew, he could put some very powerful men—not just G. W. Stone, but some high-level movers and shakers—in jail for a very long time. His testimony would open the door to a string of devastating criminal charges and civil suits over price-fixing. The fines and penalties and damages would cost Stone and its subsidiaries millions of dollars. The bad publicity would sink them.

So Bob Bayles had been killed because he was doing something right, something necessary, something you might even call noble—Miles might call it that, anyway. Did this redeem him, in my eyes? Not yet, maybe, but someday, when I had worked it all through, understood what it all meant, yes, I thought it would. And in the meantime, I felt humbled by all that I hadn't known about the man who, even in death, had dominated so much of my life.

I felt more. I felt anger, too, and the longer I listened to Laura Danforth's dry, almost clinical recital of the facts she had compiled, the more anger I felt. Red-hot lavalike anger, seething, boiling up, spilling over. I could feel it pounding in my veins, taste it on my tongue, hear it ringing in my ears. The briberies and betrayals, the collusions, deceptions, duplicities, sellouts. All that and, murder, murders, plural—it was all there, a long litany of crimes, dirty, ugly, unjustifiable, indefensible crimes. I sucked in my breath, feeling the air in my lungs fueling the anger pulsing through me.

How dare they? How *dare* they do such things! How could they live with what they had done? How did they rationalize it, reconcile it, justify it, explain it to themselves? Didn't they worry about getting caught, being called to account? But they had gotten away with it for so long, for years, for decades, that they must have felt they were bulletproof, immune from prosecution. They must have felt they could escape justice forever.

I have no recollection of anything that happened on that drive. I don't know how I managed to pilot the unfamiliar car through the interstate traffic, how many stoplights held me up as I made my way across Pecan Springs, how I got home at all. It was not a long tape, only about twenty minutes, but there were quite a few passages that were compressed or obtuse or just plain hard to hear, and I had to push the Rewind button again and again. By the time I pulled into our driveway, I had listened to the whole tape twice, and some parts of it three or four or five times. I knew the whole sordid, ugly, bloody story—or rather, as much of it as Laura Danforth knew when she made this recording.

I sat in the car for a moment, hanging on to the steering wheel as if it were a life preserver, trying to catch my breath, trying to come to terms with what I had just heard. Given what she knew and what she guessed, how had Laura Danforth survived? What—or who—had kept her alive to die a natural death? Had Miles listened to this tape? I didn't think so, for surely he would have put it with the rest of his mother's material in the file cabinet. If he had heard this story, he would have behaved differently, wouldn't he? The tape answered all the questions he'd been trying to answer, or almost all. Surely, if he'd been aware of these facts, he would have gone to the police or . . .

I closed my eyes. No. Even if Miles had listened to this

tape, even if he had known as much of the story as I now knew, he wouldn't have taken the case to the cops, and for a very good reason. When he gave this material to the police, they would take over. They would shut him out of the investigation, and from that moment on, he'd be entirely in the dark. They might decide to investigate further or they might not, depending on how promising the evidence looked, depending on their caseload, available manpower, budget, depending, depending, depending. Whether the case went to the D.A. or got dropped, Miles would be out of the decision chain, and he couldn't stand the thought of that.

And there was more, too. The tape, as it stood, was inadmissible. It could not be authenticated, or even dated. It was only a statement of Laura Danforth's theory of a crime, of a series of crimes, rather, a theory that was mostly based on hearsay and undocumented allegations. As far as I was concerned, it was all pretty convincing. From the smallest detail to the biggest bombshell—what Laura Danforth had learned when she talked to Keith Madison's widow, for instance—it had the ring of solid truth.

But no matter how solid and truthful and convincing Laura's story sounded, Miles would have known, as I knew, that no judge would ever let a jury listen to it. He knew the standards for the admission of evidence. He knew the tape couldn't pass the test.

I rested my forehead against the cool steering wheel. That's why he had come to me, wasn't it? He had his mother's notes and other background material. He had a fairly clear idea of who killed his father and why. He must have felt the same anger I was feeling now, the same fierce desire for justice. But what he needed was evidence, and somebody to help him get it. I was Bob Bayles' daughter. I had practiced criminal law, and this was a criminal case. Of all the people in the world, he must have thought, I was the one most likely to share his passion for building the case that his father—*our* father—had been murdered, a case so solid that no D.A. could turn it down, or, however stupid or careless, lose it.

But Miles had been wrong. I might have seemed like the right woman for the job, but I hadn't shared his passion. My father had died and was buried sixteen years before, and as far as I was concerned, that was the end of it. I had put Bob Bayles and everything connected with him out of my life. I wasn't going to get involved.

But as things turned out, Miles didn't need me, did he? Through me, he met my husband, a former homicide cop, an experienced, competent, and tenacious investigator, and McQuaid was an even better choice. From the day they first talked, it must have been evident to Miles that what McQuaid loves, almost as much as he loves Brian and me, is a complex investigation. If there is any proof to be found, any place, any time, he wouldn't stop until he found it. He would dig up the facts *and* the evidence, no matter how deep it was buried. He would construct the case and take it to Miles, and Miles—having been in control, having been in on the whole thing from the get-go—would take it to the D.A.

I frowned. But McQuaid had barely gotten started. Miles had his mother's suspicions but few facts and no evidence—not yet. He wasn't a danger to anybody. So why had he been killed? But of course, it didn't matter whether Miles actually had enough evidence to build a case. What mattered was whether the killer or killers *thought* he did, or thought he might be able to come up with what he needed, if he happened to look in the right places. In fact, the moment it was known that Miles Danforth was Bob Bayles' son, and that Laura Danforth had been collecting evidence of what she believed was a murder—the moment those things were known, my brother was a marked man. It was only a matter of time before an attempt was made on his life, and Miles understood it. That's why he had told Marcia that he was in danger. That's why—

I sucked in my breath and opened the car door. And now my *husband* was involved in this damned affair! I had to find McQuaid and get him to back off the investigation, at least until we could figure out what to do.

My father had been murdered for what he knew. My brother had been murdered for what he might have found out.

And if I didn't do something, my husband would be next.

# Chapter Nineteen

Harebell shall haunt the banks,
And thro' the hedgerows peer
With wind and snapdragon
And Nightshade's flower of fear.

Robert Bridges
(1844–1930)

I hurried toward the house, making a sketchy mental list of things that had to be done right away. I hadn't heard from McQuaid since this morning and couldn't even guess where he might be, but I had to get in touch with him and tell him what I had learned. He might have called my cell phone and left a message, so I'd plug in the cell phone and check. I'd also listen to all the messages on both our answering machines, the one in his office and the one in the kitchen. I'd start making phone calls to people, asking if they had seen him.

But as I unlocked the kitchen door and stepped inside, I was met by Howard Cosell, wearing the accusatory expression he likes to use when he wants us to feel guilty about leaving him alone all day, not to mention being late with dinner. I've never quite figured out how he does it—something with his eyebrows, maybe, or the droop of his lower lip. I bent over to pat his head and stroke his floppy basset ears, adding *Feed Howard* to my to-do list, right under plugging in the cell phone.

*Now,* Howard said, adding *Right this minute, please,* with the urgent whine, barely audible, that always goes straight to my heart. "Okay, Howard," I conceded. "You're here, so you're first."

I got out the dry food and a can and reached out to punch the Play button on the answering machine. But at that moment, the phone rang. It was McQuaid.

"Thank God, China." His voice was urgent. "You're finally home! I've been trying to reach you all day. Did you lose your cell again?"

I tucked the phone against my shoulder and ran a can opener around the rim of the dog food can. "I just got here," I said. "My cell's out of juice, and I left the charger at home. Where are *you*? I've been calling and calling and you didn't answer."

Howard, who is an impatient dog where his dinner is concerned, put his paw on my foot and stood on it, reminding me that he was first, wasn't he? and I'd better hurry, by golly, or he'd pee on my leg.

"I've been at the Two-Bar Ranch all afternoon. No cell signal." McQuaid's voice dropped. "There's bad news here."

I removed my foot from under Howard's paw. I didn't want to hear this. "Why are you at the Two-Bar, McQuaid?" I said, more shrilly than I intended. I swallowed and lowered my voice. "Come home. Right now, *please.*"

Losing patience, Howard growled, low and threatening. Hurriedly, I filled his bowl with dry dog food and added a spoonful of alfalfa powder and another of flaxseed oil—herbs that help him cope with arthritis and other ailments experienced by elderly bassets. I stirred in a generous spoonful of canned dog food and set it on the floor in front of him. He looked at it.

"I came down to the ranch because somebody burned

the barn last night," McQuaid was saying. "When I got here, I found Ellie Hanson, shot. In the greenhouse."

"Shot!" I gasped, a half-dozen frightening scenarios skittering crazily through my mind. "Is she— Are you— You didn't—"

"I haven't heard how she is." McQuaid's voice was taut. "It didn't look too good when Starflite lifted her out. I got here a few minutes after it happened, and the bastard had already gone. He tried to make it look like suicide. The sheriff is a politician, not a lawman. If Ellie doesn't make it, he might sign off on suicide as a cheap, no-fault way to mark the case closed. But there's a sharp-eyed deputy— she's a friend of Ellie's, and a neighbor—who isn't about to let that happen."

Howard was staring disconsolately at his bowl. Then he looked up at me and whimpered. Good grief. I'd forgotten his gravy.

"But why in God's name would anybody shoot Ellie Hanson?" I picked up Howard's bowl, ran it under the hot water tap, and stirred again, producing something that Howard imagines as gravy. "And the barn? Why burn the *barn*, for pete's sake?" As I put Howard's bowl on the floor, I thought of something else. "Omigod. The car. Somebody was after the car, weren't they? Was it destroyed?"

With a sigh of contentment, Howard began to lap up his gravy.

"It's pretty hard to burn up a burned-out car," McQuaid said in a practical tone. "There's still plenty left."

I leaned against the counter, thinking of Ellie Hanson, shot. Thinking of my father, my brother. Like a black flower, fear blossomed inside me. "Come home," I said urgently. "Come home *now*, McQuaid. There are some things you need to know. We have to talk about this. We—"

"Wait, China," he cut in roughly. "There's something else. When Ellie called this morning to tell me about the barn, she said that the guy who torched it was driving a truck with one headlight out. She recognized the truck as belonging to her cousin. It hit a deer a couple of days ago, she said."

I frowned. *One headlight out. A deer?* Well, what of it? People hit deer all the time. It was one of the hazards of driving across open rangeland. And then I thought of something, and my breath came faster. The cops had found headlight debris in the parking garage—glass and a piece of chrome ring. But that was too much of a coincidence, surely. I was grasping at straws. There could be no connection between—

"Listen, China," McQuaid said. "The truck belongs to Ellie's cousin. He lives on the adjacent ranch, which once used to be a part of the Two-Bar. All in the family, I guess." He paused. "You know this guy, China. His name is Ted Stone. The ranch is Stonebridge."

I sagged against the counter, dumbstruck. "My God," I whispered.

"Amen," McQuaid said grimly. "It's all connected. Your father, your brother, Laura Danforth, the car, and now Ellie—they're all pieces of one big puzzle. I'm not coming home until I've put it all together."

I knew it was connected, and now I knew how. But I also knew that tone. McQuaid's bulldog tone. His I'm-not-quitting-until-it's-done tone.

"I'm seeing Stone tonight," he went on. "The deputy, Isabelle Ramos, knows him, and she knows her way around his ranch. She's meeting me here at the Two-Bar at eight thirty. By the time the evening is over, that old bastard is going to come clean about what happened. He's going to tell the truth—about Ellie, about your father, your brother. The whole nine yards."

"No!" I cried. "No, you can't go! It's too dangerous!" I was babbling now. I knew it, but I couldn't stop. "Listen, McQuaid. Listen to me! If you want to know the truth, we've got it. It's all on tape. I found it in Miles' closet, in a shoebox, and I listened to it on the way back from Austin. Laura Danforth knew everything, or most of it. She spells it all out, the whole ugly story. Come home and listen to the tape, and we can figure out what to do."

"I'll come home as soon as I can, China," McQuaid said, with a quiet finality. "But I have to finish this first. Don't worry. I'm armed, and so is Deputy Ramos. She's a smart, competent officer—she'll be good backup. It'll be okay, babe. Trust me."

*It'll be okay. Trust me.* The last time McQuaid had said that, he'd been shot and nearly killed. I chewed on my lip, trying to figure out how to get him to listen to me, to do what I wanted him to do.

But before my brain could come up with something so logical, so persuasive that he couldn't refuse, my heart had it all figured out. I heard myself saying, "I'm coming down there, McQuaid."

"No!" he exploded. "Absolutely not, China! Forget it. There is no way that I will allow you to get mixed up in this mess. It's not safe."

"It's not your call." This was the right thing to do, no matter how stupid it might seem. "This is about my father and my brother, and now it's about me, so you can't shut me out." I took a deep breath. "What's more, you need me. I know Stonebridge—I've been there more times than I can count. I know Ted Stone. And Ted Stone knows *me*. He was a good friend of my father. Hell, he even wanted to marry my mother! He probably remembers when I was still wearing Mary Janes." I managed a chuckle, having by this time almost convinced myself. "You need me, McQuaid. I'm crucial to the success of this mission."

There was a silence. "You may be right on a point or two," McQuaid replied slowly, "but that doesn't change anything. This isn't old home week, China. This is dangerous business. And anyway, somebody needs to be home with Brian."

"Brian is at Jake's tonight. I'll call and ask if he can stay over. Jake's mom won't mind."

"Nothing doing," he growled. "Didn't you hear me, babe? This is dangerous. I don't want you here."

I lightened my voice. "Hey. Didn't you just tell me it'll be okay? You and the deputy will be armed, and Ted Stone is a friend of my family." I chuckled again. "For God's sake, McQuaid, Ted is an old man. He's past seventy. What do you think he's going to do? Threaten me with a gun? Shoot me?" I was leaving something out—no, I was leaving *someone* out. I knew it, and the thought of it scared me silly. Did McQuaid know it, too? I looked up at the old Seth Thomas clock on the wall over the refrigerator. It was seven o'clock. "I can be there by eight fifteen."

He countered with a sarcastic laugh. "Oh, yeah? Not so fast, babe. You don't know where to come. And I'm not telling you."

That stopped me, but only for a second. "You forget, dear heart," I said sweetly. "I know where Stonebridge is. Since the two ranches are adjacent, I'm betting that the turnoff to the Two-Bar is just to the north of Stonebridge, on the county road that runs off 77A. I'll find it."

There was a silence. I knew I must be right.

"Damn," he muttered. "I hate strong-minded women."

"No, you don't," I said, more gently now that I could see that I was winning. "You love a strong woman. And I love a strong man. That's why we've stayed together all these years." I paused, picturing his face, the firm jaw, the quirk of his mouth, the tender eagerness in his dark eyes. "You wanted me on board, didn't you? Well, now I'm on board. I'm *really* on board. And I'm coming down there."

"Shut up and let me think," he said.

There was a silence. Howard finished eating his dinner and pushed the empty bowl around with his nose to make sure he hadn't missed any small bits lurking underneath.

Then he padded to the kitchen door, where he stood, wagging his tail with a meaningful look.

When McQuaid spoke, his voice was slow, reluctant. I pictured him scowling. "You're right. Ted Stone knows you. He would probably listen to you before he'd listen to me or Deputy Ramos." There was another silence. "So I'll let you talk to him—under one condition."

He'll *let* me? But I kept my tone neutral. "What's that?"

"That you follow my orders precisely." McQuaid was using his don't-mess-with-me cop voice: deep, stern, unyielding. "No sass, no backtalk, no questions. Just. Follow. My. Orders. If you can't do that, don't bother to come. You got that, China?"

"I got it," I said meekly. "Sir." I didn't ask if he would send me back home if I *didn't* follow his orders.

"Good. Now, listen up. We can talk about what we're going to do when you get here. But since you're coming, you can bring me some stuff." He rattled off a short list of items. "Figure you can handle that?"

"Yes, sir. You bet, sir. I'll be there at eight thirty, sir."

"Don't be a smartass," he said darkly. "You promised to love and obey. Remember?"

"That was a mistake," I said. Really, it was, although McQuaid likes to pretend that it is now cast in concrete. We were married by our friend Maude Porterfield, the oldest Justice of the Peace in the state of Texas. Maude remembered to turn up her hearing aid for the ceremony, but she forgot to omit the word *obey*.

"Mistake or not," McQuaid growled, "you promised."

"I had my fingers crossed. And don't you and that deputy leave without me," I added in a warning tone. "Remember that I'm crucial to the success of this mission."

McQuaid sighed. I could picture him rolling his eyes.

"Gotta go," I added. "Howard needs to pee."

# Chapter Twenty

### McQuaid: A Plan, More or Less

McQuaid hangs up the phone in Ellie Hanson's kitchen, muttering. He's kicking himself for calling China, but he didn't want her to worry about him. He just wanted her to know where he was, and that he would be home very late, after he'd taken care of this business.

He goes to the coffeepot and pours himself a cup of coffee, scowling. *Damn.* He should have expected her to insist on coming down here. That's China, always able to offer four or five very sound, very logical reasons for doing whatever it is she wants to do, always ready to argue the case. Once she gets started, there's no stopping her.

McQuaid puts the coffee on the table. He doesn't want her here, but he has to concede that he needs her. She knows the layout at Stonebridge. She can make some suggestions about how they go in there, how they deploy their limited forces. And like it or not, Ted Stone is a helluva lot more likely to listen to China Bayles, whose family he has known for years, than he is to listen to either Mike McQuaid—whom he's never met—or the female Hispanic deputy, whom he is likely to dismiss. And the stubborn tenacity in argument that sometimes makes China hard to live with is exactly the skill McQuaid needs right now. His wife is smart, fast, and tough. She knows how to bully a hostile witness. If anybody can push Stone to tell what he knows, she's the one.

McQuaid shoves one of Ellie's cats away from his coffee cup. What's more, it's good that China is coming from home. She can bring him the weapons he needs. He wasn't expecting a situation like this when he suited up this morning. The game has changed, big-time, and all he has with him is his backup gun. He's sure that Deputy Ramos will be armed, but he'll definitely be happier with a more substantial arsenal at his disposal.

He goes to the refrigerator and opens the door. While he's got a few minutes, he'd better get something to eat. He's already fed the dogs and the cats and the livestock, and he's had a look at the car. Ellie was right, there's not much additional damage, how could there be? While he was poking around the wreck, he'd also checked out the front-seat floor and damned if he didn't find a few pieces of broken bottle glass, brown, like a beer bottle, which supports his theory that the weapon that killed Bob Bayles was a Molotov cocktail tossed through the window—not that this is admissible evidence, of course. Even if there is fuel residue on the fragments, which is pretty unlikely after all this time, there's no way to establish when the glass got into the car.

He's also located those papers Ellie mentioned, on the kitchen table. There's the car's registration, made out to Robert Bayles, with a VIN that matches the one McQuaid recorded from the auto itself. Ellie also located a handful of receipts for a garage rental in Victoria, covering the period between the time Laura Danforth acquired the car and the time it showed up here. And a brief, handwritten note signed by Laura Danforth and addressed to Ellie's father— Uncle Jack, she called him—thanking him for storing the car and mentioning that she was enclosing a check for six hundred dollars for the first year. McQuaid is glad to have this backup material. It will help to establish the car's whereabouts over the years, if it ever becomes a legal issue. And he's curious about the relationships here— especially that between Uncle Jack and Ted Stone. Cousins, are they? And exactly how were Laura Danforth and Ted Stone related? He'll have to ask Ellie.

But that thought stops him cold, because he's not sure that Ellie has made it. He has called the sheriff's office to find out which of the San Antonio hospitals she was taken to, but if the dispatcher knows, he isn't telling. He refuses to say anything about her condition, either. Not that Mc-Quaid faults him. Ellie must have known her assailant, and until he's caught and jailed, she's potentially in danger. The fewer people who know about her situation, the better.

McQuaid moves things around in the refrigerator and finally locates a quart jar half-filled with something that looks like leftover soup. There's chicken in it, and onions. He sniffs. Tomatillos, too, he bets. Smells pretty good, so he pours it into a dish and sticks it in the microwave. While he waits for it to heat, he thinks about what's ahead that evening, how he's going to put China—his wife, the person he loves most in the world, next to his son, of course—into the same room with Ted Stone, who has been part of this whole bloody affair since the beginning. Hell, for all he knows, Stone might have burned the barn and shot Ellie, although McQuaid thinks it's more likely that he assigned the dirty work to one of his hired hands. It'll be up to China to get the information they need out of Stone, but it's up to McQuaid to get her out of there when it's done. How is he going to put her in there and keep her safe? How is he going to get her out without running unnecessary risks?

These are important questions, urgent questions, and he's got to think of some answers. He takes his soup to the table, shoves a cat off the chair, and settles down to eat. It's good, very good. And by the time he's finished, he's come up with a plan, more or less. On the surface of things, it seems workable.

At least, he hopes it'll work. He rubs his hand across his forehead, thinking of China, thinking of the way she frowns when she's serious, the way she laughs when he tickles her, the way she gives herself to him, with passionate abandon.

A cold shadow of fear falls over him. Oh, God, he hopes it'll work.

# Chapter Twenty-one

But still in that valley . . . there is a certain place called Baaras, which produces a root of the same name [mandrake, *Mandragora officinarum*, a member of the nightshade family]. Its color is like to that of flame, and towards the evenings it sends out a certain ray like lightning. It is not easily taken by such as would do it, but recedes from their hands, nor will yield itself to be taken quietly, until either the urine of a woman, or her menstrual blood, be poured upon it; nay, even then it is certain death to those that touch it. . . .

*Wars of the Jews*, Book 7, Chapter 6, 75 C.E.
Flavius Josephus

By the time I collected the things I'd been instructed to bring plus a couple of items of my own, and changed into jeans, a shirt, khaki vest, and sneakers, the sky was almost as dark as night, thunder was rumbling in the distance, and ominous flickers of lightning lanced the cloud tops. The cold front that was causing all this ruckus was sliding from northwest to southeast across Burnet and Blanco and Williamson counties, causing thunderstorms and severe weather—gully-washers, frog-chokers, roof-rippers, hail—all along its leading edge. Austin was probably already getting walloped—maybe even a repeat of the famous Memorial Day Flood of 1981. That storm stalled out over the city, dumping something like ten inches of rain in four hours and killing thirteen people in the subsequent urban flooding. But the front hadn't reached Pecan Springs yet, and I'd be heading south faster, I hoped, than the line of storms. I planned to drive my own comfortable white Toyota, rather than Miles' bigger and faster BMW, but maybe I could still outrun it.

I did. At this time of year, sunset is around eight twenty and dark doesn't fall until nine. But a curtain of purple-black storm clouds already blotted the evening light out of the sky to the west and north, and by the time I got to the Two-Bar Ranch, I was driving with my lights on, through a tunnel of night shadows across a landscape of darkly blurred shape-shifters. My headlights caught a whitetail buck flashing like a comet across the road in front of me, an armadillo blindly following his nose, and a pair of young raccoons sitting on their haunches like eager puppies, their paws folded across their chests, their masked eyes gleaming. I drove through somber legions of mesquite thickets, platoons of prickly pear, and brigades of bunch grass. Back from the road, glowing like pale ivory in the darkness, stood the branching, white-flowered candelabras of Our Lord's candles—also known by a more ominous name, Spanish dagger. I was glad there was no moon. The landscape, occasionally lit by the jagged flicker of lightning, was menacing enough as it was.

The Two-Bar yard light—one of those "dusk-to-dawn" security lights that makes people look like corpses—shone across the ranch yard. In its bluish light I saw McQuaid's pickup truck parked in front of the ranch house, a black Bronco beside it. Beyond lay the shadowy outlines of the greenhouse where Ellie Hanson had been shot and the pile of burned timbers and pieces of metal roof that had been the barn. I shivered. Somewhere in all that black rubble my father's car, twice-burned, was buried.

As I got out of the car, McQuaid came out onto the porch and down the steps. With him was a stocky Hispanic woman in her mid-thirties: brown eyes, high cheekbones, and brown hair cut short, boy-style. She was dressed in neat chinos, a striped shirt with the sleeves rolled up to her elbows, and a loose denim vest. She had a competent, no-nonsense look about her that I liked immediately. She wasn't wearing her service belt, but looking closely, I could make out the outline of the underarm holster under her vest. It made me feel better—that, and the 9 mm Beretta tucked snugly into the back waist of my jeans, over my left kidney.

The gun was a gift from my father the year before he died. Then, I had wondered why in the world he would give me such a thing, and take the time to make sure I could use it. Now, I thought I knew. He had wanted to protect me against whatever—or whoever—he feared. I don't like the Beretta. I'd been forced to fire it in self-defense once, a long time ago, and a man was dead. This is something I try not to think about, but I had to admit that there was a certain comfort in the feel of it against my back.

McQuaid didn't say he was glad to see me. Instead, he said, "Hey, thanks, China!" and reached for the weapon he'd asked me to bring him, a Remington Model 870 police shotgun. I had also brought (at his request) a bandolier that held double-ought shells and a black long-sleeved shirt, plus the miniature tape recorder that fit conveniently and invisibly into the pocket of my vest. I didn't think I'd mention the Beretta. If he knew I had it, he might try to take it away from me.

"Deputy Isabelle Ramos, my wife, China Bayles," McQuaid said, managing introductions while he slipped the bandolier over his head and one shoulder and buttoned the black shirt over it. In the dark, he'd be nearly invisible.

"Good to meet you, ma'am." The deputy's contralto voice was husky and softly accented. But there was nothing soft about the unflinching sharpness of her glance or the hard strength of her grip as we shook hands. This was not a woman to be messed with.

"Good to meet you, too," I said, meaning it. "Any word about Ellie Hanson?"

"The doctor says she's going to make it," the deputy replied, and I breathed a relieved sigh. There had been too much blood already.

McQuaid finished buttoning his shirt, picked up his shotgun, and took command. "We need to go over the play-book. Deputy Ramos and I have the game plan pretty well laid out. We can't afford any mixed signals."

Spoken like the ex-quarterback he is. "Before we do that," I said, "there's something you need to know." I had listened to Laura Danforth's tape again on the drive from Pecan Springs, and it had reminded me of what was going to be the real danger here. "It will definitely enter into the equation."

McQuaid gave me a narrow-eyed look. "Something you haven't told me?"

"There wasn't time," I said. "I'm telling you now."

McQuaid listened in growing disbelief as I sketched out what I had learned on the tape. When I was finished, he shook his head. "Shoots the hell out of the game plan," he said darkly. He looked at the deputy. "Maybe we'd better call in a few reinforcements."

Deputy Ramos frowned. "I don't think so. I've been to Stonebridge. It won't be a piece of cake, but the three of us can pull this off." Her brief smile did not reach her eyes. "Might be a good idea, though, if I asked Jake Pollock— he's on duty tonight—to hang out on this side of the county and stay in radio contact. Just until this is over with."

McQuaid nodded. "Yeah." He looked at me. "Wish I'd thought to ask you to bring that mini tape recorder. It might've come in handy."

I reached into the pocket of my vest and took it out. "This what you're looking for?"

He grinned. "I knew there was a reason I kept you around," he said.

# Chapter Twenty-two

> You must gather mandrake in this manner: when you approach the plant, you will recognize it because it shines at night like a lantern. When you first see its head, mark around it quickly with an iron tool lest it flee from you. . . . And then you must dig around it, being careful not to touch it with the iron. . . . When you see its hands and feet, fasten them. Take the other end and fasten it around a dog's neck (make sure the dog is hungry). Throw some meat in front of him so that he cannot reach it unless he snatches the plant up with him. As soon as you see that it has been pulled up, and you have power over it, immediately seize it, twist it, and wring the juice from its leaves into a glass bottle.
>
> *The Old English Herbarium*, circa 1000 C.E.
> translated by Anne Van Arsdall

It was hard to tell in the darkness, but it didn't look like Stonebridge Ranch had changed much in the five or six years since I had last been there. The house that Ted Stone and his wife had built in River Oaks had been an elaborate, expensive French Colonial mansion in a sweep of carefully kept green lawn. For their rural retreat overlooking Mustang Creek, they built an elaborate, expensive Spanish Colonial adobe hacienda, with foot-thick, ocher-colored walls and deeply recessed multipaned windows. The house had five or six bedroom-bath suites, a dining room big enough to seat the governor and his entire staff, and a living room big enough to entertain the entire legislature. The guest casita could sleep another half-dozen people, so there was plenty of room for the huge hunting parties Ted had always liked to host. Nearby, there was a four-car adobe garage, a barn where the ranch vehicles were parked, a couple of corrals, and a half-dozen outbuildings. The entire compound was surrounded by a fence, adobe around the front and sides, wooden fencing in the rear.

The inside of the main house, as I remembered, was elegant. Mrs. Stone had collected Spanish and Indian pottery and art, and the walls were hung with tapestries, paintings, and carvings. There were enough stuffed heads of native and exotic game animals to keep a taxidermist busy for a couple of years: whitetail bucks with record racks, glass-eyed antelope, javelinas with ferocious tusks, bass fighting to get free of the hook. The Saltillo tile floors, like polished mahogany, were covered with rugs. The furnishings were Spanish Colonial, those massive pieces of carved oak and hobnailed leather that look as if they are constructed for a family of giants. In the living room, a huge fireplace was topped with a longhorn skull wearing an eight-foot pair of horns. It faced a wall of windows that looked out onto an irregularly shaped swimming pool surrounded with native plants and made to appear that if it had been carved out of the local limestone.

Ted Stone had always had plenty of hired help around the place to run the cows—he had a herd of longhorns, bred for show, plus a half-dozen horses—and keep things looking good outside. Inside, a cook managed the kitchen, with extra help for parties, and a housekeeper and a couple of maids kept the rest of the place looking good. But the help wasn't live-in, or it hadn't been, when I'd been there. There was a small *colonia* farther on down Mustang Creek, where the ranch hands and house servants lived. At this time of night, and unless Ted had several guests, he would be alone in the house. I hoped.

The storm seemed much closer as I drove my Toyota down the narrow caliche lane, over the creek's low-water crossing, up to the automatic gate that blocked the road. A movement-activated halogen light came on, illuminating a narrow circle around the car. I pushed the button on the box on the metal pole and waited. After a moment, I pushed it again.

"Yes?" asked a man's wary voice. Ted Stone's voice, although it wasn't nearly as strong and robust as it had been the last time I heard it. "Who's there?"

I leaned out of the window and spoke into the intercom grill. "It's China Bayles, Mr. Stone. Bob and Leatha Bayles' daughter. I know it's late, but I was out this way and thought I'd drop in. Do you have a few moments to visit?"

"China!" This was said heartily, without hesitation. "Well, for pete's sake, girl. I haven't seen you in a coon's age. Come on in!"

A buzzer sounded loudly and the gate swung open on its electronic hinges. I drove through to the parking area outside the adobe fence. I parked at the edge of the lighted area and got out. McQuaid opened the door on the far side of my car, away from the light, and he and Deputy Ramos got out. They slipped silently into the darkness as I walked to the wrought-iron gate in the center of the adobe fence. Puffs of wind lifted the lacy leaves on the mesquite trees, carrying with it the smell of wet dust. In the distance, thunder rumbled ominously.

I crossed the courtyard and headed for the entrance. The oak double doors at the front of the house were several hundred years old—hijacked, as Ted liked to say, from a seventeenth-century church in Mexico. By the time I reached them, they'd been flung open wide and Ted was waiting for me.

The years had not been kind to him. The last time I'd seen the man, he'd been tall and ramrod straight, with a thick build and sturdy shoulders. Now, frail and stooped, he leaned on a carved walking stick. He couldn't be more than seventy-five, but he looked ten years older. His once-gingery hair was white, his cheeks sunken, his face chalky gray. But he held himself with dignity, as far as he was able, and he seemed genuinely pleased, if surprised, to see me.

"China Bayles, I can't believe it," he said, shaking his head. "You picked a helluva night to drive out this far." He peered over my shoulder. "Is it raining out there yet?"

"Not yet," I said, stepping hurriedly inside. "But it's threatening." As if to punctuate my words, the sky was lit by a flash of incandescent lightning, followed by a bone-shuddering clap of thunder.

"That was close," he said. "They've posted flash flood warnings for all the counties south of I-10—just heard it on television. Why didn't you phone and let me know you were coming? Here I am, all by myself—I would have had you to dinner, you know." He laughed. "You remember Maria? She still cooks for me. Grills a mean steak, from our own Stonebridge beef."

"I remember Maria." I smiled. "Gosh, she must be a hundred years old by now."

"A hundred and twenty. None of us are spring chickens anymore." He gave a rueful laugh. "Present company excepted, of course. You're lookin' fine, my dear." His voice softened. "You look like your mother, y'know? Same good bones." He seemed to recollect himself. "Come in and let me fix you a drink."

He led me down several steps and into the living room, which was as warm and elegantly welcoming as I remembered, the dark adobe walls brightened by colorful hangings and lighted niches holding pieces of Spanish sculpture. One wall displayed an exhibit of antique silver spurs, another Ted's collection of lariats. As I had recalled, the far wall was a wide expanse of glass, with patio doors opening to the flagstone terrace and swimming pool directly behind the house. From the window, I could see the guest casita off to the left, like the short side of an L, at right angles to the terrace. The casita's living room window was lit, and I could see a figure moving around inside. Ted might be alone in the house, but he wasn't alone in the compound.

Ted was headed for the bar in one corner of the room. "What'll it be, my dear?" He was leaning heavily on his cane, shuffling and unsteady on his feet.

"White wine, if you have it handy," I said, and watched as he opened the refrigerator hidden behind antique copper panels. With difficulty, he poured the wine and handed the glass over the bar. His hand was trembling.

"I'd love to join you, but I'm off the sauce," he said, making a regretful face. "Doctor's orders."

I took my wine to a large brown leather chair that faced the bank of windows. The swimming pool was lit by underwater lights, and the wind-rippled water sent formless, flickering reflections dancing over the rocks and plants. At the end nearest the casita, water cascaded down a limestone waterfall and into the pool. In the darkness, the tall cacti and other native plants that surrounded it assumed an almost human bulk. Through my shirt, I felt for the switch on the minirecorder and turned it on.

"You've been well, I hope," I remarked, as Ted crossed in front of me to take the matching leather chair.

"About as well as anybody can be, at my age." He lowered himself gingerly into the chair and leaned his walking stick against his knee. "Too many headaches lately. Bad headaches, terrible headaches. The scourge of creeping decrepitude." He sighed and rubbed his temple, as if his head might be hurting at the moment. "How's your mother? Enjoying married life, is she?" He sounded regretful. "I hope she's happy, although I'm selfish enough to wish she'd taken me up on my offer. We would've been good together."

"She seems very happy. She and Sam—the man she married—have started a B and B on Sam's ranch, near Kerrville." I chuckled. "She got about as far from River Oaks as she could get."

"That's good," he said emphatically. "Good for her to get out from under all that society bullshit. And you're married now, too, she tells me. You have a boy?"

I nodded. "Brian. He's fifteen."

"And your husband? What does he do?"

"He teaches at the university," I said briefly, not wanting to mention that McQuaid was an investigator.

But Leatha must have told him. "A policeman, wasn't he?" he asked casually, but his glance had suddenly sharpened.

"In a former life," I said, and chuckled.

He paused, eyeing me, smiling, and I saw that one side of his mouth was slightly drawn down. I wondered if he'd had a stroke and felt a shadow of pity, remembering the hearty, handsome man I had known when I was younger. But he hadn't been just hearty and handsome, I reminded myself. He had done bad things—or if he hadn't done them himself, he had been an accessory, before and after the fact.

As if he'd read my mind, his mouth tightened. "Well, well. What brings you here, China?"

Outside, a streak of lightning sliced the black sky like a hot knife. The wind was blowing harder now, whipping the plants into a maelstrom of moving lights and shadows.

"I'm sure you know," I said quietly.

He smiled wearily, and I thought he was making an extra effort to focus his eyes on my face. "Do I?"

"The barn at the Two-Bar Ranch burned to the ground last night. My father's car was there."

His smile went away. "Yes, I heard about the barn. Too bad. I've told Ellie she ought to sell that place and—" He leaned forward, frowning. "Did you say your father's *car*?"

"The burned-out wreck of my father's Cadillac. Laura Danforth persuaded her uncle Jack to store it for her in the Two-Bar barn. Ellie left it there after her dad died. Not the smartest move, I suppose, but she had no idea that the car had any importance."

He was shaking his head, frowning, as if he were confused. "Laura? Laura Danforth? But how did *she* get the car? And why in the hell would she want to keep it? She wasn't the sentimental sort. Not the Laura I knew."

If this had been the old Ted, healthy and slick as a greased rattler, I would have said that he was lying through his teeth. Now, I wasn't so sure. He was old. He was sick. He could be confused. He could have forgotten—or he could be lying.

I gave him a long, steady look. "She kept it because it was the proof she needed that my father was murdered."

"Murdered? You can't be serious, China." If his face had any color, it was gone now. His skin was ashen, his eyes wide, the pupils dilating. "I don't believe—" He choked on the sentence, then went into a spasm of coughing that wracked him so hard he almost couldn't catch his breath. When it subsided, he wiped his mouth on the back of his hand, leaving traces of spittle. He made an effort to assume something like a comforting, avuncular tone, although it missed by a mile.

"Bob wasn't *murdered*, China. You know that. *I* know that. He and G.W.—my brother—and I, we'd been out to dinner. It was late. We'd been drinking. I wanted Bob to take a taxi, but he insisted on driving. He lost control of the car and went over the embankment. Read the police report. It's all there."

It was his tone that decided me. When you're interviewing a witness, you watch for shifty eyes, sliding glances, down-turned mouth, wrinkled nose—the subtle body language that tells you that the words coming out of the witness's mouth are not truthful words. But for me, the dead giveaway has always been the tone of voice. I wasn't sure exactly what Ted Stone was lying about, but he was lying, and I knew it.

"Come off it, Ted," I said flatly. I set my wineglass on the table beside me and pushed myself out of my chair. I stood looking down at him, arms crossed over my chest, face stern. Classic cross-examination posture. "We both know that somebody tossed a Molotov cocktail into Dad's car to keep him from telling the Feds that your brother had Keith Madison murdered."

When Ted was at the top of his form, he would have shrugged that accusation off with a laugh, jumped out of his chair, and ushered me to the door. Or he would have fixed me with a piercing glance, snarled something like "Don't be a goddamned fool, girl," and threatened to sue me for slander.

But Ted had lost his old moxie. He sagged back into the chair as if his bones had turned to rubber.

"How did you—" He stopped and swallowed. His gaze slid to one side. "It's not true, China. Keith Madison killed himself."

"Of course it's true." I turned and took two steps toward the window, looking out. The pool reflections flickered, the plants tossed wildly. The light still burned in the casita window. If there was anything else moving around out there in the dark, I couldn't see it.

I turned back to him. "Well, hell, Ted," I said, in a practical tone. "Anybody with half a brain can see why it had to be done. Stone Engineering couldn't afford to have all those questionable business practices laid out in front of God and the *Houston Chronicle*." I shook my head. "Bribery, fraud, collusion, cooking the books—an investigation would be like opening the lid on Pandora's box. And the company was in serious trouble anyway, wasn't it?"

"I don't know where you're getting all this," he protested weakly. "I don't—"

"Of course you do." I began reciting the story I had heard in Laura's tape. "By the early seventies, Lyndon Johnson was gone and Stone Engineering had run out of pet politicians in Washington. G.W. put all his money on John Connally, thinking he'd be Nixon's pick for vice president when Agnew was forced out of office. But that political horse turned out to be a big-time loser, didn't he? Connally was sunk, and by the early eighties, the government contracts were drying up like puddles on a July sidewalk, and everybody in the company was working every possible angle to get whatever contract they could. Keith Madison knew what was going on, and where all the bodies were buried. If he turned state's evidence, it would be the end of everything. Which is why Madison had to go."

"Not Keith." Ted tried to make his voice sound reasonable. "Keith Madison shot himself, China. You're right. The times were terrible. The company was in trouble. And Keith couldn't take the heat. So he—"

"And then there were the other murders," I said, as if he had not spoken. "*Murders*," I repeated emphatically. "That's plural, Ted. Keith Madison was shot in a way that made it look like suicide. There were those two *Chronicle* reporters, Miriam Spurgin and Max Vine, who were getting too close to the story. Spurgin was run down in her parking garage and Vine died when his auto blew up. Oh, and Max's ten-year-old daughter—we have to count her, although I'm sure she was a mistake."

Ted made a noise deep in his throat. "You can't possibly think that I had anything to do with—"

"And Dad, too," I said. "Your partner. He was killed because he no longer had the stomach for all this rotten meat. He knew what was going down, and after Madison, he was cutting a deal with the Feds." I held up my hand in front of his face, fingers spread out. "Madison, Spurgin, two Vines, and a Bayles. I make that five, don't you? Five murders, Ted."

He was gasping now, his mouth opening and closing like the mouth of a fish drowning in air. "How do you . . . What makes you think . . ."

I have seen a great many guilty people try to pass themselves off as innocent, and Ted's act didn't impress me. It was true that these killings had been orchestrated by his brother—at least, that's what Laura Danforth had said on the tape.

But Laura had also said that Ted knew everything that had happened. If true, that made him an accessory to murder—to five murders. No, six.

I shook my head. "Don't try to bluff your way out of this, Ted. Not now. Not after what happened to my brother."

He blinked. "Your . . . brother?"

"Miles Danforth. Laura's son."

"Laura's son, yes," he managed weakly. "I knew Miles— Buddy, we called him, when he was young. He was often at the office. He came into the firm, too, later. But . . . your brother?"

Now I was on firmer ground. "Come off it, Ted. I know that your nephew Chris, Chris Brandon, went through Miles' papers and learned that he was Bob Bayles' son. Miles thought he must have told you. But that's a moot issue now, isn't it?" I didn't give him time to answer. "Miles is dead. Hit-and-run, like Miriam Spurgin."

Outside, there was a blue flash of sudden lightning and a host of moving shadows seemed to spring into electric life. Ted pressed his hand to his head and closed his eyes against the glare. Or perhaps he was trying to shut himself away from what I was saying, from the truth of what had been done.

I went on, brutally. "You must have thought it was all over and done with. Keith Madison, the reporters, Dad— all behind you, years ago. Behind you, and behind your brother, too. He was the evil genius, after all. You were only the accessory. And then your brother died, and you must have felt free. With G.W. gone, you were safe. Is that right?"

"Not quite," he said, so low that I could barely hear him.

"Yes, not quite. Miles was getting too close, wasn't he? Learning too much, pushing too hard. And he had his mother's help, of course. When she died, he began looking through the records of Laura's investigation into Dad's death."

"Laura," he said, and repeated her name as if he couldn't help himself. His voice had dropped to the barest whisper. "Laura. Dear Laura."

I stared at him, suddenly glimpsing something I hadn't known, something that hadn't been on the tape. "You, too, Ted? My father loved her—did you?"

He seemed suddenly weary, old, defeated. "Yes, I loved her."

"Speak up, please," I said, as I would say it to a witness. "I can't hear you, Ted."

He raised his voice, defiantly, now. "Yes, I loved her. Of course I loved her. I began loving her before I began shaving, before I got my first car. Laura was still a scrawny kid then, legs like broomsticks, hair like corn silk, a grin a mile wide. And she loved me, too. She said we should run off to Mexico and get married." His mouth turned down. "But she was a MacKenzie, my mother's sister's daughter, and cousins don't get married. That's what I told her. So to spite me, she married that kid who worked at Jack's ranch. Danforth. Danny Danforth." He winced. "Poor guy. He didn't know what hit him."

I was facing the window now. Off to the left, I saw the casita door open, and light fall out. A figure stood briefly in the door, then disappeared back into the house.

Ted sighed heavily. "Things might've been different if we'd done what she wanted—if we'd gone to Mexico and got married. But I didn't dare cross the MacKenzies, you see. They were my bread and butter, especially back then, when I was just getting started. And Laura, she was wild to come to Houston. The marriage to Danforth didn't work out—he got drunk and killed somebody and she divorced him when he went to prison. So when I opened the firm, I gave her a job and a desk, right up front. She liked that. She was smart and pretty, and she liked being important."

"I see," I said, watching the casita. Yes, Laura Danforth liked being important.

"And then she met your father." His voice cracked, and he cleared his throat. "I hadn't counted on that, you know. I warned her to be careful. Bob was married, and what she was doing could only hurt your mother. But she wouldn't listen. Laura never listened to anybody." He shook his head helplessly, as if what had happened next had been entirely beyond his control.

And perhaps it had. Perhaps my father and Laura Danforth had fallen so passionately in love that no force on earth could have kept them apart, certainly not her cousin or his wife. Or perhaps it was nothing like that at all. Perhaps it was my father who had fallen in love with Laura, and she had recognized the opportunity he presented. Perhaps she had used their relationship to take revenge on Ted Stone for rejecting her, or to maintain a position of power in the firm. Perhaps she had even allowed herself to conceive his child in order to strengthen her hold.

But I was only guessing. The truth of their relationship, whatever it was, had died with them. One of my questions had now been answered, however. I had wondered how Laura Danforth had survived, knowing what she had known about all those murders and guessing so much more. It hadn't been simply that she didn't yet have the proof she needed—that wasn't enough to save her. It was Ted who had protected her after my father was gone. It was Ted who had stood between her and his brother, keeping her alive.

The door of the casita opened again. The figure reappeared, stood for a moment framed in light, then stepped out and began to cross the terrace. I pulled in my breath with a little shiver and turned back to Ted, deliberately putting my back to the window.

"But it wasn't true that Laura Danforth never listened, was it?" I demanded. "She listened when G.W. threatened to kill her son, didn't she?"

Ted sighed. "Yes, you're right. G.W. never trusted Laura. He told her to stop digging around in the past and get in line. If she didn't, her son would pay the price. She heard that, and she dropped what she was doing." He looked up at me and his old blue eyes suddenly brimmed with tears. "But you're wrong about one thing, China. I had nothing to do with Miles' death. I didn't intend for that to happen." His voice became urgent. "Honest to God, it wasn't my idea. I swear it."

"And Ellie?" I countered. "What about Ellie?"

He stared at me. "Ellie?"

"Was it your idea to kill her?"

"Kill her? Kill Ellie? *Ellie?*" He pushed himself out of his chair, gasping for breath. "You're telling me that . . . that goddamned brute *killed Ellie?*" He stood for a moment, trembling, gasping for breath, all the color gone from his face.

My eyes met his. "Was it?" I asked again. "Did you give that order, too?"

And then, all at once, there was a blinding flash of electric blue lightning and an almost instantaneous explosion of thunder, so loud that it seemed that a bomb had gone off.

A heartbeat later, the window shattered. Ted Stone pitched forward at my feet, and I went down on top of him.

# Chapter Twenty-three

### McQuaid: The Last Act

As China steps through the double doors and disappears into the main house, McQuaid begins working his way around the perimeter of the compound inside the fence, Deputy Ramos five paces behind. Shotgun in hand, he stays close to the adobe wall to his left, the open compound to his right. Before they left the Two-Bar, China and the deputy collaborated on a sketch of the Stonebridge layout, putting in all the details they can remember, and McQuaid carries the outlines in his mind. The casita stands at the rear of the main house, at a right angle to it at one end of the terrace and the swimming pool. If their quarry is at Stonebridge, the man who's doing Mack's dirty work, that's most likely where he's staying.

McQuaid crouches low as he and the deputy circle around the back of the casita, listening hard for the sound of barking. Surely there's a ranch watchdog, isn't there? But all he can hear is the crackle of lightning, the almost continuous rumble of thunder, and the rustling of cottonwood and sycamore trees along the creek. They come around the far side of the building, and Deputy Ramos closes up behind him, puts a hand on his shoulder. He turns, and she motions him to stop and stay where he is. She's going to take a look. McQuaid knows this makes sense. She's had dealings with the guy they're after, Mack's right-hand man, Sonny Bryce. Ramos will recognize him. If that's not Bryce in there— McQuaid hasn't figured out what they'll do then. Watch and see what happens, he guesses.

While Ramos is scouting their quarry, McQuaid steps just beyond the corner of the building, behind a bush. Through the foliage, he can see across the terrace and the swimming pool to the brightly lit living room of the main house. His heart knocks against his ribs. There she is, there's China! She's with an old man—yes, he really is old, white-haired, leaning on a cane. McQuaid's concern eases a bit. The old man, surely he's not much of a threat. He's handed her a glass of something, wine, it looks like, white wine. She takes it to a large leather chair facing the window, like a character in a play. Yes, that's good. She's in the right place. But she's too damned exposed, an easy target, sitting there in the bright light. And here comes the old man, hobbling. He eases himself down into the chair at right angles to hers, and they begin to carry on a conversation. Two characters in a play. And it's the last act.

Crouched under the window at the front of the casita, Deputy Ramos cautiously raises her head and peers inside. She holds herself there for a moment, then lowers her head and turns to look at McQuaid. She nods, and McQuaid purses his lips and blows out in silent exultation. The man inside is the one they're looking for. Bryce. Sonny Bryce. The man China calls the Engineer, who did his work after dark.

Ramos straightens and in two steps she's at the front door. She twists the knob sharply and shoves it open, hard, as if the wind has caught it and slammed it against the wall. Four more steps, in a crouching run, and she's joined Mc-Quaid in the shadows behind the bush. They position themselves where they can see the front door, open now, the light flooding out, without being seen.

And it happens just as they had hoped, as if it were

scripted. Bryce leaves whatever he has been doing—watching television? reading?—and comes to the door to shut it. As he does, he looks across the pool into the lighted living room of the main house and sees that Ted Stone has an unexpected guest, a woman. He stands for a moment, leaning forward as if puzzled, peering intently across the terrace. McQuaid can tell what he's thinking from the sudden tenseness of his posture. He's wondering if the woman is who he thinks she is, if she's really Bob Bayles' daughter, sister to the man he ran down in the parking garage. Bryce pauses, assessing the threat, figuring the odds, reviewing his options. Then he turns and goes back into the casita.

"Went for his weapon," Deputy Ramos whispers, and McQuaid nods shortly. They wait. A couple of endless minutes later, the light goes off in the living room of the casita. Carrying a rifle, Bryce steps through the front door and closes it behind him. He starts across the terrace, and McQuaid and Ramos split up and move silently after him, Ramos going to the right and McQuaid to the left, the Remington in his hands.

But Bryce, picking his way easily behind the waterfall and through the large rocks and clumps of native plants, has a definite advantage. He knows where he's going, and McQuaid silently curses that fact when he trips over a jagged hunk of limestone and barely saves himself from lunging into the pool. McQuaid and the deputy have a different advantage, though, because Bryce believes that Ted Stone's guest has come by herself. He has no idea that he's not all alone out here in the dark. Still, McQuaid is grateful that the rush of the wind and the low, almost constant rumble of thunder masks whatever sounds they might make. The glimmering reflections of the underwater lights and the play of lightning in the sky give the whole scene an almost surreal feeling, as if the three of them are moving through an impressionistic painting, or across a stage in the glare of footlights. Even if Bryce hears a sound and turns around, he probably won't see them in the confusion of lights and shadows.

Their quarry stops behind a man-sized barrel cactus and fixes his attention on the lighted living room. Raising his rifle, sighting it, confidently intent on his target, he has no idea that Ramos has a gun trained on him from behind and to his right and that McQuaid is fifteen paces behind him on his left, shotgun raised. McQuaid's heart is rattling inside his rib cage, his breath is coming short. It's Ramos' turf. It's her call. Shit. What the hell is she waiting for? Lightning glares, and he sees her step forward.

"Police!" Ramos shouts. "Freeze!"

That should have stopped him. But the shout is lost in an exploding clap of thunder, loud as a roar of applause. At the same instant, Bryce squeezes off a shot, shattering the window. McQuaid doesn't wait for the second shot, or for Ramos to use her gun. He fires. The blast catches Bryce's legs, sending him crashing, thrashing, screaming, to the ground. Ramos is astride him fast, jerking his arms behind his back, cuffing his hands, but McQuaid is rushing for the patio door.

He slides it open, hard, and barges through. China is getting to her feet, slowly, but she looks to be unharmed. Stone is facedown on the floor, motionless.

"You okay, China?"

"I'm okay," she says testily. "No thanks to you. What the hell kept you guys? Why'd you let Bryce get that shot off?"

He grins, almost dizzy with relief. That's his China, all right. He looks down at the still figure on the floor. "Did Stone get the bullet?"

"I don't think so. He went down a split second before that. A stroke, maybe." She kneels and feels for a pulse. "He's still alive."

McQuaid looks through the window at the deputy. She's

on her radio. "Ramos is calling in her backup and the medics," he says. "The other deputy will be here in a few minutes." He takes a breath. "It's the last act. It's over, China. It's all over."

"I hope so," she says, getting to her feet. "Oh, god, Mc-Quaid, I *hope* so." Her face crumples and she begins to cry, huge, wrenching sobs.

And then, in one step, McQuaid has her in his arms. He holds her close against him as she cries—cries for her father, for her brother, for all the others. He knows he'll never let her go.

Outside, the heavens open and it begins to pour down rain.

# Chapter Twenty-four

*Nightshade Spa Secrets*

For a skin-softening facial that will remove dead cells and restore the acid balance of your skin, try this tomato astringent scrub. Mix up to 3 tablespoons tomato juice with ⅛ cup of granulated sugar until it has the consistency of frosting. Pat the mixture onto your face and rub with gentle, circular motions. Rinse and pat dry.

Potatoes can make you beautiful, too. Puffy skin under your eyes? Cut six thin slices of potatoes. With a washcloth and cool water, moisten the skin around the eyes. Lie down, place three slices of potatoes over each eye, and fold the damp washcloth over them to hold them in place. Rest for ten minutes—when you get up, the skin will be tighter and feel much cooler.

Or try this old recipe for potato elbow-and-heel cream. Peel, cook, and mash one medium potato. Mix with 1 teaspoon honey, 1 teaspoon olive oil, and enough potato water to make a smooth, thick paste. Massage into rough elbows and heels; after ten minutes, rinse off. For rough skin on the feet, apply potato cream before going to bed, and put on a pair of cotton socks.

Ruby Wilcox's Spa Secrets

"Wow, China," Ruby said breathlessly, when I had finished my tale. "What a story! I can't believe that all that has happened to you since the last time I saw you!" She lifted her arms over her head and stretched out in the hot, bubbling water of the spa. "Oh, girls, this is blissful. I can't think of a better getaway present. Whose idea was it?"

"Mine!" said a chorus of laughing voices: Cass, Sheila, Molly, Kate, and Amy. Laurel and Ruth Ann would be along tomorrow, Memorial Day, just about the time I'd be leaving. I had decided to split the Memorial Day weekend: Sunday afternoon and night at the spa, with Ruby and my friends; all day Monday with McQuaid and Brian, at Mom and Dad McQuaid's, in Seguin.

"It was Cass' idea," I said, setting the record straight. "She figured you needed some downtime. We *all* needed some downtime." Me especially. I'd been a basket case for the past week, trying to deal with Miles' estate and Caitlin's needs and the fallout from what happened at Stonebridge. I was looking forward to the Nantucket Seaweed Soak, which was going to happen in another hour. All that seaweed and the mud—guaranteed to pull all the poisons out of my system. Right?

Amy popped up out of the water like a red-headed seal. She was wearing a bikini that was nothing more than some strings with a few purple patches attached in strategic places. All her piercings glittered. "Yeah, Mom, you can thank Cass for everything. She connected with Linda here at the spa and made all the arrangements."

"Well, it's wonderful," Ruby said, rolling her eyes. "Totally, indescribably wonderful. And that lunch we just had? It was perfect."

"Actually," Cass said critically, "Seemed to me that the presentation was a little sloppy. I'll ask Linda to mention it to their chef."

Molly did a flutter kick with her feet, admiring her bright red toenails. After lunch, we had had a toenail-painting session, and Molly's had been judged the sexiest. "Cass, you're incorrigible," she said. "This is a *party*, not a culinary critique session."

"I know, I know." Cass sighed. "But I can't help it. I'm a chef—right? And it's the spa's reputation we're talking about here. I mean, what if I happened to be a restaurant critic? I'm sure Linda will want to hear my opinion."

A plastic cup of iced hibiscus tea in her hand, Sheila came down the steps into the spa pool. She settled into the water, a high-fashion nymph in her sleek white swimsuit. "So what happened to Ted Stone, China? He had a stroke, you said? It didn't kill him, did it? He's going to be charged with accessory to murder—I hope."

"Stone is paralyzed," I said. "He can communicate, in a minimal way, and he's been cooperating with the police. His attorney has already pled him out, though. Nobody had much of an appetite for hauling him into court, at his age and in his condition." I gave an ironic chuckle. "In fact, I understand that he's planning to make restitution. Putting money into trust for Caitlin, I mean. It won't make up for the loss of her father, but it'll make her comfortable for life."

This had not been entirely Ted's idea, of course. Yesterday, I had told his attorney—the durable Christopher Brandon—that, as Miles' executor, I was planning to file a wrongful death suit for something on the order of four million dollars. Brandon considered this for about ten seconds and offered to settle for two. I chuckled, stood, and went to the door. Brandon offered two and a half. I put my hand on the knob and opened the door.

"Three." Brandon breathed a heavy sigh. His legislative career hung in the balance on this one, and both of us knew it. When Stone lost the suit (he would, no question), Brandon's uncle, once a political powerhouse, would no longer be an asset. And Brandon's contribution to Miles' murder would no doubt come to light, with embarrassing consequences. It was a large barrel to be over.

"Four," I said. "Hell, Chris, there's no telling what a jury might do. O.J. got socked with thirty-three and a half, remember? You want to put your uncle into that kind of jeopardy?"

"Damn," he said disgustedly. "Bloody damn."

"See you in court, counselor," I replied, in a sprightly tone. "There's nothing I like better than a good wrongful death suit, especially since you've already pled your client."

He put up his hand. "Hey!" he said hurriedly. "I didn't say no, did I? Did you hear me say no?"

I put on my sweetest smile. "What I want to hear is *yes*, Christopher. Yes, we'll settle for four. Four million, that is. Dollars."

He lifted his shoulders, let them fall. "Oh, all right," he muttered. "Yes."

"Yes to four, please."

A big sigh. "Yes to four," he said in a grudging tone. He put on a stern look, as if he were the one who was dictating the terms. "And no disclosure. I don't want a word of this in the press."

"That'll work for us," I agreed. "No disclosure." It would not make Caitlin's and Marcia's lives any easier for the media to broadcast the girl's net worth to the wide world. A settlement like this would make it possible for Marcia to be a stay-at-home mom, and give her and Caitlin the time and anonymity they needed to work out their lives together. Perhaps they would even decide to go somewhere else to live, where there weren't so many sad memories— not too far, I hoped. I didn't want to lose touch with Caitlin, whom I was coming to love.

"Done," Brandon said firmly. "I'll get the paperwork together."

It was the easiest four-million-dollar settlement I'd ever

managed. Or maybe not, when you stopped to think about the bullet that had whizzed past my head at Stonebridge Ranch.

Cass—a splash of sunshine in her bright yellow bathing suit, cleverly draped to minimize size—hoisted herself out of the water and sat on the edge. "And the guy who shot at you? The Engineer?" She picked up a towel and wiped her sweaty face. "Sounds like your classic big-time bad guy. Like something out of a Jack Nicholson thriller flick."

"He is." I shivered in spite of the warmth of the water. "He's not talking, of course." Sonny Bryce was out of the hospital and in jail, although it would be a while before he completely recovered from McQuaid's below-the-knees shotgun blast. "But evidence speaks louder than words. The chrome ring and glass that the cops swept up in the parking garage match the headlight on Stone's ranch truck, and the paint flecks in Miles' clothing are a match for the truck's paint. Bryce has no alibi for the night of Miles' murder, and his are the only fingerprints in that truck. There's enough for a conviction on that charge, at least—and on attempted murder."

"That's right," Amy said, glancing over to where her partner, Kate, was diapering Grace. "There were eyewitnesses to that one." She looked back at me, her eyes wide. "He tried to kill you, China!"

I frowned. "I really don't think he was gunning for me, Amy. Ted was the one who knew where the bodies were buried. Once he was safely out of the picture, Bryce probably figured he could bluff his way through the rest of it."

"More likely," Sheila said darkly, "he figured to drop Stone with the first shot and you with the second."

Cass whistled. "It's a good thing McQuaid got him first." She kicked some water in my face. "The world just wouldn't be the same without our China!"

"Thanks," I muttered, wiping the water out of my eyes. Everybody else laughed. "But it would've been a better thing if either McQuaid or Ramos had dropped him before he got a shot off. If he'd killed Ted, those cold cases would never have been closed."

"But Ted Stone wasn't the mastermind behind those killings," Ruby put in. "That was his brother, wasn't it? The guy who owned the engineering company?"

"Right," I said. "G. W. Stone, of Stone Engineering. The whole string of murders began when the company's vice-president, Keith Madison, decided to turn state's evidence in a bribery and bid-rigging case. He knew enough to bring the entire company—subsidiaries, too—down with him, so G.W. directed Bryce to arrange for a convenient 'suicide' and bribed the cops to overlook a few small problems with that theory. When Vine and Spurgin got too close to the Madison story, they were next. And then my father."

Ruby made a sympathetic noise. "How awful," she murmured.

I nodded sadly. "Madison's murder was the tipping point for him. The two of them had been college friends—fraternity brothers, actually. On the tape, Laura Danforth says that Madison discussed his intentions with my father. When he turned up dead, Dad decided that was it. He was going to the Feds with what he knew. So Bryce engineered the car wreck."

"A handy guy to have around," Amy said wryly. "If you don't like what's going down, turn it over to the Engineer. He'll take care of it."

"I suppose that would have been the end of it," Cass remarked, "if it hadn't been for Laura Danforth. Sounds like she just couldn't let it go."

"A good thing, too," Ruby said, gracefully drawing her arms through the water as if she were in a water ballet. "But I still don't understand why Laura dropped her investigation. After all, it was her son's father who was killed in that car wreck. You wouldn't think she'd drop it so easily." She ducked her head under and came up again, water streaming down her face. "I wouldn't, if it had been me."

"We know, Ruby," Sheila said with a comfortable laugh. "You and Kinsey Millhone—you never give up on a case."

I shifted, feeling the warm water bubbling up against my back, easing the pain and stiffness. It felt good. It felt good, too, to see that Ruby and Sheila had settled their differences. Whatever Ruby did or didn't know about Sheila's relationship to Colin, it no longer seemed to matter, to either of them.

"Laura dropped her investigation because G.W. threatened to kill Miles if she didn't," I said.

"But then G.W. died, didn't he?" Ruby persisted. "He was no longer a threat. So why didn't she pick it up again?"

"By the time G.W. checked out, Laura herself was in no condition to carry on," I said. "It was left to Miles to pick up where his mother had left off." Which he had done, although he hadn't quite come clean with McQuaid or me about what he knew or when he had learned it. McQuaid and I had decided that I was right about Miles wanting to control the investigation by holding back the most important information—the location of the car, for instance, and the contents of his mother's safe deposit box, which had yielded more bits and pieces of her investigation. McQuaid had turned it all over to Jim Hawk, who thought it would be useful in wrapping up the cold cases.

Cass got to her feet and padded over to a low table, where a melon-and-fruit tray—cantaloupe, watermelon, honeydew, along with kiwi, pineapple, strawberries and red grapes—was laid out, with a bowl of honey-ginger dressing and a pitcher of hibiscus tea.

"But if G.W. was dead," she said, filling a plastic plate with fruit, "why would the Engineer kill your brother? Good heavens, China—that was eons ago!"

"Because while G.W. planned Dad's murder," I replied, "Bryce was the one who tossed that Molotov cocktail into the car. And there's no statute of limitations on murder."

Cass looked at me, her head tilted to one side. "There isn't?"

"Nope. Bryce couldn't be sure that Miles wouldn't find out what had happened." I splashed water into my face. It was time to cool off a little. "Hey, pour me a glass of that iced tea, would you, Cass?"

"And you might just put that tray of fruit over here where we can reach it without getting out," Sheila said lazily.

"Yes, ma'am," Cass said, and giggled.

"Especially since Miles had located that old wreck," Ruby went on, shaking her head. She waded to the steps and climbed out, water streaming off her sleek silver and blue and green swimsuit. She looked like a red-headed mermaid with legs. Very long legs. "The Engineer must have been blown away when he found out where the car was hidden. All that time, in a barn just down the road." She began toweling herself.

"Speaking of the barn," Amy said, "how is that lady? The one who owns the barn and grows those crazy tomatoes. Is she recovering?"

"Tomatillos," I said. "And yes, she's going to be just fine. She's another of Bryce's victims, of course, and she's ready to testify against him. If I were his attorney, I'd be looking for the best deal I could get for my client." It wouldn't be a good one. The only leverage he'd have would be the chance to clear up those cold cases.

"Another of McQuaid's saves, too," Ruby said. "If he hadn't got there, that poor woman probably would have bled to death. I'm glad she's going to be okay." She went over to Kate. "Come to your *grandmere*, precious," she cooed, holding out her arms. "It's Kate's turn to get in the water." With a chortle, Grace went to her, and Ruby sat down and held her close.

Cass handed me a frosty glass of hibiscus tea, decorated with a slice of lime, and put the fruit tray on the side of the pool where we could reach it. She looked at me. "I'm curious, China. Do you feel differently about your father, now that you know more about what made him tick?"

I had been thinking about this, remembering all the pain, the pinching sadness, the wild anger I had felt over the years. Was it gone? No, of course not. When you feel something that deeply, that long, the feelings don't disappear. But they had changed, a little, at least.

"Yes, I think I do," I said honestly. "None of this explains why Dad was never there for Leatha and me, or why he chose to lead a separate life with another woman. I'll never know the answers. But maybe he didn't know himself. Maybe he did what he did because . . . because he had to." And that was as close as I could come.

"He died doing something he believed in," Kate said softly. She put her hands on Amy's shoulders and began to massage.

"Yes," I said. "That helps."

Ruby brought the baby to the side of the pool and sat down with her on her lap. "I guess it's a good thing Ted Stone had that stroke, or he'd be on trial, too."

"He's been on trial ever since my father died," I said quietly. "In his own mind, anyway. He closed the firm, and from what I learned in reading Laura Danforth's notes and listening to her tapes, he pretty much broke off with his brother. Of course, that doesn't exonerate him—he and G.W. were in cahoots for years. But Dad's death brought Ted's career to an end. His wife died, he retired and moved out to the ranch, and now that I look back on it, I can see that he tried to make amends to me and to Leatha." I smiled. "In fact, I think his reason for wanting to marry her was so that he could somehow make it up to her."

"As if it could." Ruby rubbed her cheek against the top

of Grace's head. "Nothing can make up for losing somebody you love."

"True," I agreed in a practical tone, "although how much my mother actually loved my father by that time in their lives is open to question. How can you love somebody who gives you nothing but grief for two decades?"

"China," Ruby said patiently, "people love whomever they love, grief or no grief. Why do you always have to question everything?"

I narrowed my eyes at her. "Speaking of questions, what have you done about you-know-what?"

"You-know-what what?" Sheila asked curiously.

"You know," I said, in a meaningful tone.

Sheila's eyebrows went up. "Oh, that," she said. "Yes, Ruby, what have you done?"

Cass got back in the pool. "I suppose you guys know what you're talking about," she grumped. "I don't."

"I don't either," Kate said. "What is it?"

"They are talking," Ruby said with dignity, "about Colin's legacy. And yes, China, you nosy snoop, I have done something about it."

Amy looked curiously at her mother. "Colin's legacy? Did Colin leave you some money, Mom?"

"He sure did," I said with satisfaction. "Ruby, can I tell how much?"

Ruby patted Grace's hands together, doing patty-cake. "You can if you like," she said, a small smile playing around her mouth.

I leaned forward and said, in a whisper loud enough for everyone to hear, "He left her a quarter mil."

"A quarter million!" Cass squealed, and clapped both hands over her mouth. "You're kidding!"

"Nope," I said, shaking my head. "Ruby's rich."

"*I'm* not rich," Ruby protested. "It's for Grace, so she can go to Harvard."

"I hope you've kept a little out for yourself," Sheila said quietly. "Colin would have wanted that, you know."

Ruby shrugged. "Well, yes, a little," she said. She giggled. "I'm buying myself a new car."

"Glory be," I said, casting my eyes to the heavens. "Now you won't get stranded on the interstate, and I won't have to go and pick you up."

"And I've signed up for both the Essential Rosemary Skin Conditioning and the Eucalyptus Body Polish," Ruby went on, "and I'm not going to let myself think about how much they cost. And tomorrow, when we leave here, I'm going to buy a new outfit. Something really glamorous." She smiled. "And the next man who asks me out, I might even say yes. If I like him, that is."

"Ooh-la-la," Cass said. "Look out, guys, here comes Ruby. She's empowered."

"If you've got it, flaunt it," Ruby said modestly. She patted Grace's hands together again. "Right, cupcake? Right, my precious little petunia? We'll knock 'em dead, won't we, sweetheart?"

Grace chortled, Amy laughed, and Cass giggled. Sheila winked at me, and I knew what she was thinking. Ruby was herself again. Yes, she would probably always love Colin, somewhere down deep in her heart. But the way was forward, and Ruby is not the kind of woman who keeps looking back over her shoulder.

It's a lesson I need to learn, too.

# Nightshades: Nice—and Nasty

Over the centuries, the nightshade family (a large group that includes more than two thousand species of annuals, perennials, vines, shrubs, and even small trees) has gotten a very bad rap—which is a pity, because it ranks high on the list of plant families that people have found extremely useful. It's hard to imagine our menus without potatoes, tomatoes, chile peppers, and eggplant, or picture our gardens without the showy petunias that splash color all over the landscape. Surgeons of antiquity, who relied on plant narcotics for anesthesia, found both the mandrake and deadly nightshade indispensable when they needed to put people to sleep—although they no doubt lost a few patients in the process.

On the other hand, the nightshade family also includes the notoriously addictive tobacco, that great cash crop that has made some people hugely rich and millions of people desperately sick, and three narcotic plants that have long been associated with soothsaying, black magic, and witchcraft. It's this side of the Solanaceae—the dark side—that has given these herbs such an evil reputation.

## NIGHTSHADES ON YOUR TABLE

Chances are, you'll enjoy at least one nightshade today—tomato juice and hash browns for breakfast, perhaps; a chile-pepper and tomatillo salsa on your lunchtime taco or burger; a vodka-and-tonic or bloody Mary at happy hour; eggplant Parmesan for dinner.

In its native Peru, the potato was a staple food and medicine for nearly eight thousand years, used to treat everything from arthritis and frostbite to infertility. But when the Spaniards brought it to Europe in the 1570s, it was a different story. A botanist assigned the potato to the Solanaceae family and nobody would touch it for fear of being poisoned—or of being thought too poor to afford anything else: *Only the wretched eat this root,* it was said. It was another two centuries before the potato climbed the social ladder and Europeans accepted it as a delicious, nutritious vegetable. It was Thomas Jefferson who introduced the potato to polite American society, when he served a platter of elegant, tasteful French fries at a presidential dinner at the White House.

The tomato, valued as a food and medicine by American Indians, suffered a similar rejection when it first traveled eastward to Europe in the sixteenth century. It was said to be unwholesome at best and poisonous at worst, although a few herbalists thought it might be good for the treatment of eye ailments and scabies. The Italians took to the tomato more readily than other peoples, and their sixteenth-century practice of drying the fruit in the sun has come back into favor today. Scientists now tell us that the tomato is not only nutritious, but helps to prevent certain cancers and strengthens the cardiovascular system.

The eggplant (*Solanum melongena*) traveled the opposite way, from east to west. The Moors took it from southeast Asia to Spain, and the Spaniards took it to America. In Asia, it was both food and medicine, used as an expectorant and a diuretic and as a treatment for throat and stomach ailments. In Europe, it was called *Solanum insanum* (popularly dubbed the "mad apple") but began appearing in cookbooks in the nineteenth century, reflecting its growing use as a vegetable. Americans call it eggplant because some eighteenth-century European cultivars bore yellow or white fruits the size of goose or hen's eggs.

The tomatillo (*Physalis philadelphica*), also known as the husk tomato, is widely used as a condiment in south-of-the-border cookery.

## NIGHTSHADES IN YOUR FLOWER GARDEN

Ornamental nightshades, especially the petunia, are a staple in modern gardens. Brought to Europe from South America in the early part of the nineteenth century, they immediately captured the attention of hybridists. Now, through the magic of plant breeding, we can obtain fringed, doubled, and ruffled petunias in an amazing range of colors and markings, for garden beds or hanging baskets.

Other ornamental nightshades, *Datura* and *Brugmansia* (Angel's Trumpet), have a more ambiguous reputation. While they delight and amaze us with their stunning flower trumpets, these plants contain significant levels of the tropane alkaloids atropine and scopolamine and have a long history of use as medicines, ritual hallucinogens in sacred ceremonies, and poisons. They are highly toxic if ingested. If you grow these beautiful plants, do so responsibly, guarding against their misuse.

## DEADLY NIGHTSHADES

Of all the plants in human use, few are regarded with as much fear as the Solanacae trio: deadly nightshade (*Atropa belladonna*), mandrake (*Mandragora officinarum*), and henbane (*Hyoscyamus niger*). In antiquity, their high levels of tropane alkaloids made them the weapons of choice when it came to murder. In the Middle Ages, they were used to induce the hallucinations associated with the practice of witchcraft and sorcery. Numerous superstitions surround all three plants, and their poisonous properties are legendary. However, deadly nightshade remains the chief source of scopolamine (in some countries, mixed with morphine for use as an anesthetic in childbirth) and atropine, used by ophthalmologists to dilate the pupil of the eye and in the treatment of heart attacks. Atropine is stockpiled by the U.S. military and some hospitals as an antidote for biological and chemical poisons.

## THE DEADLIEST NIGHTSHADE

From a broad cultural point of view, the deadliest night-shade of all is tobacco (*Nicotiana tabacum*), which contains the tropane alkaloid nicotine. According to the National Center for Chronic Disease, cigarette smoke is responsible for some 438,000 premature deaths each year in the United States alone, while smoking-related health care and lost productivity are estimated to cost the nation over 167 billion dollars per year. Globally, it is predicted that by 2020, the use of tobacco will account for some 16 million new cases of cancer each year and 10 million cancer deaths. Tobacco, regarded by its original American Indian users as a sacred plant with magical powers and by sixteenth-century Europeans as a medicinal panacea, is now understood to be a dangerously addictive carcinogenic herb.

# Books to Read

*The Fascinating World of the Nightshades,* by Charles B. Heiser, Jr. Dover Publications, 1987.

*Murder, Magic, and Medicine,* by John Mann. Oxford University Press, 1992.

*The Natural History of Medicinal Plants*, by Judith Sumner and Mark Plotkin. Timber Press, 2000.

*The Potato: How the Humble Spud Rescued the Western World*, by Larry Zuckerman. North Point Press, 1998.

*Tobacco: A Cultural History of How an Exotic Plant Seduced Civilization,* by Iain Gately. Grove Press, 2003.

# Recipes

### China's Creole Aubergine
## (CHAPTER ONE)

**1 eggplant**
**salt**
**2 tablespoons vegetable oil**
**2 tablespoons onions, chopped**
**3 tablespoons green bell peppers, chopped**
**3 cloves garlic, minced**
**¼ cup mushrooms, sliced**
**2 cups canned diced tomatoes**
**4-ounce can tomato paste**
**¼ cup fresh basil, shredded**
**1½ teaspoons ground bay leaves**
**1 teaspoon dried oregano**
**½ teaspoon thyme**
**¼ teaspoon ground cayenne pepper**
**Freshly ground black pepper**
**½ cup yellow cheese, grated**
**½ cup seasoned bread crumbs**
**1 tablespoon margarine**

Slice or cube the eggplant, sprinkle with salt and set it aside while you make the sauce. (This "sweating" will remove some of the natural bitterness.) Heat the oil in a skillet and sauté onions and bell peppers for 2–3 minutes, stirring. Add garlic and sauté for another 2–3 minutes, then mushrooms. Cook for another minute or two, then add tomatoes and tomato paste. Simmer for about 15 minutes, then add herbs and seasonings and simmer until thick, about another 15 minutes. Rinse eggplant well and drop into boiling water; parboil 7–8 minutes, or until tender. Arrange a layer of eggplant in the bottom of a casserole dish. Cover with sauce. Continue layering, finishing with the sauce. Sprinkle on the cheese, top with seasoned bread crumbs, dot with margarine and bake at 350 F. for 30 minutes, or until bubbling. Serves 4–6.

### *Cass' Tomato-Basil Soup*
## (CHAPTER FIVE)

4 cups canned crushed tomatoes
2 cups tomato juice
2 cups chicken or vegetable stock
1 teaspoon dried thyme
2 dried bay leaves
2 cloves garlic, minced fine
⅓ cup fresh basil leaves, chopped
1 cup half-and-half
¼ cup unsalted butter, softened
Salt and pepper to taste
Garnish:
Sour cream
4 tablespoons fresh basil, chopped
4 tablespoons fresh parsley, chopped

Over medium heat, combine tomatoes, juice, stock, thyme, bay leaves, and garlic in a large saucepan and simmer for 15 minutes. Remove bay leaves. In a food processor, combine tomato mixture and chopped basil in several small batches and process until smooth. Return blended mixture to saucepan over low heat. Stir in half-and-half and butter, season with salt and pepper. Continue stirring over low heat until soup is heated through. Ladle into 8 bowls. Add a dollop of sour cream and 1 tablespoon basil-parsley garnish to each bowl and serve.

### Ellie Hanson's Tomatillo Salsa Verde
## (CHAPTER SEVEN)

1 pound tomatillos
2 small serrano chile peppers
2 cloves garlic, minced
¼ cup green onions, chopped
1 cup fresh cilantro leaves, chopped
2 tablespoons lime juice
1 teaspoon sugar
Salt
Hot sauce to taste

Remove the husks from the tomatillos and cut each one into quarters. Coarsely puree uncooked tomatillos, chiles, garlic, green onions, cilantro, lime juice, and sugar in blender. Add salt and hot sauce to taste. Serve with soft tacos or burritos and as a dip for corn chips. Makes about two cups.

### Slow-Cooked Beef and Chipotle Burritos
## (CHAPTER TWELVE)

These delicious burritos are made with four members of the nightshade family: tomatoes, chile peppers, potatoes, and tomatillos.

1½ pounds boneless beef round steak, ¾-inch thick
14½-ounce can diced tomatoes
1 medium onion, chopped
1–2 canned chipotle peppers in adobo sauce, chopped
1 teaspoon dried oregano, crushed
1 teaspoon ground cumin
2 cloves garlic, minced
1 cup potatoes, cooked and diced
6 large flour tortillas, warmed
1 cup shredded sharp cheddar cheese
2 cups Ellie Hanson's Salsa Verde

Trim fat from meat and cut meat into quarters. Place meat, undrained tomatoes, onion, peppers, oregano, cumin, and garlic into a slow cooker. Cover; cook for 8–10 hours on low setting or 4–5 hours on high. Remove meat from cooker and shred, using 2 forks. Return to cooker, add diced potatoes, and stir to mix. Spoon one-sixth of this mixture onto each warm tortilla just below the center. Top with cheese and roll. Serve hot with salsa verde. May be chilled or frozen for later serving.


### Ellie's Chicken-Tomatillo Soup
## (CHAPTER TWENTY)


1 boned chicken breast, pounded about ½-inch thick
3 tablespoons olive oil
1 onion, chopped
3 garlic cloves, minced
1 pound fresh tomatillos, husks removed, chopped
   (or 2 cups canned tomatillos, drained and chopped)
2 stalks celery, chopped
½ cup yellow bell pepper, chopped
½ cup red bell pepper, chopped

2 jalapeño peppers, seeded and chopped
1 teaspoon dried oregano
1 teaspoon dried thyme
1 teaspoon dried sage
1 tablespoon ground cumin
5 cups chicken stock
¼ cup fresh lime juice
2 tablespoons cilantro, minced
Garnish:
Sour cream
Cilantro leaves

Pound the chicken breast lightly, then sauté over high heat in a large saucepan or Dutch oven in the oil until both sides are browned, about 2 minutes a side. Remove the chicken, shred to bite size, and reserve. Add the onions and garlic to the pan and sauté until golden. Add the tomatillos, celery, bell peppers, jalapeños, herbs, and stock. Bring to a boil, then reduce heat, cover, and simmer for about 15 minutes. Puree the solids in the blender and taste for seasoning. Return to pot, add lime juice, and reheat. Add the chicken to the soup. When ready to serve, stir in the minced cilantro and ladle into bowls. Drop a spoonful of sour cream on top and garnish with a whole cilantro leaf.

# WORMWOOD

## Susan Wittig Albert

China's friends and family are urging her to get some rest—and a Kentucky Shaker village seems the ideal place for it. China plans to assist with some herbal workshops and absorb the Shakers' peaceful ways. But when a shocking death occurs during her stay, China begins digging up clues in an investigation of sabotage, sins of the past, and a modern-day murder.

penguin.com

M372T1108